The Dominant

Michelle Medhat

MINDBLOWING
BOOKS LTD

THANK YOU FROM MICHELLE MEDHAT

I would like to thank you for reading this book.

If you've picked this up, and you haven't read the earlier books, please check out The Trusted (part one). A direct link to The Trusted can be found at the end of this book. There is also a link book to book three - The Resonance

Also, at the end of this book you can find details on how to get the free eBook **Operation Snowdrop**. This book is only through sign up to my newsletter *'Fearless Spies, Amazing Realms and Ice-Cold Villains'*. It's not available anywhere else. Operation Snowdrop is the mission that is cited throughout *The Trusted Thriller Series*. Together with this free eBook you'll get early bird discounts, the latest news on this series and access to incredible free thrillers bundles to keep you entertained.

But for now….

Dive in, hold on tight and enjoy!

Chapter 1

March 23, 2017

Ellie Noor lifted her head groggily. The bag covering her head had robbed her sight completely. She focused hard to look through the bag, but the tightly packed weave made it impossible. She realized uncomfortably that most of her clothes had been removed. But, thankfully, her underwear still remained. Cold inspired by fear shuddered through her. Instinctively, she tried to move, to cover herself and preserve her modesty, but as she tried to pull her hand, it was as though a knife carved through her arm, and she whimpered.

Why was she in pain?

Ellie moved her hips, as if to turn, and that slicing feeling caught her again. She swung back and forth, and waves of agony washed through her.

The cutting sensation didn't appear when she didn't move. Only when she tried to use her limbs did the hurt surface. She reasoned that it had to be something they'd given her. Maybe it was something affecting her muscles, forcing agony to prevent her movement.

Amongst the pain, Ellie felt metal around her wrists and ankles. Someone was set on her being as inanimate as possible.

Hooded, nearly naked and chained to a chair, overwhelming panic swept through her. Why had she been taken? Who had taken her? Would she ever see Sam again?

Ellie swallowed hard, and despite her intractable situation, she forced herself to be calm. She breathed slowly and fell into the rhythm.

She was a managing director of a top EmTech business. She'd handled presentations and negotiations with many multi-billion-dollar companies.

She'd never panicked once. She'd just got on and done what was needed.

What did she rely on then?

Logic.

Common sense.

Understanding the environment and making her play.

Her thought processes had started to quell her panic.

She couldn't see, but she could hear. Without sight, her listening naturally became more acute and Ellie attempted to define her surroundings according to what she could hear. She listened but couldn't hear anything, just the sound of her own breathing.

Then, suddenly, footsteps approached. The footsteps were light. If the owner was a man, he wasn't large, or else he'd been trained to push the weight off his tread like in stealth combat. The owner may even be a woman. Ellie sniffed the air for any scent, but apart from the sterile, chemical smell ingrained in the hood, she smelled nothing.

Her analytical mind took over, lessening her fear as she began to 'see' through her other senses.

Ellie sensed that it was a man. She couldn't figure why she thought this. Maybe the way in which the person walked. Although light, the step still sounded manly.

She forgot she couldn't move and made to turn to face her captor, but that sharp cutting feeling once again shot through her body. She inhaled sharply.

The footsteps stopped.

Arrival.

Ellie breathed out.

She tried again to focus, but her mind was cloudy and heavy like a great weight was upon it. She couldn't remember anything. She couldn't even remember her clothes being removed. That fact disturbed her. How could she not remember that?

Ellie was terrified. She was more terrified than she ever believed she was capable of feeling. In fact, the feeling of being terrified, so often spoken about by people who had been kidnapped, was a totally physical manifestation. Ellie's brain frazzled with stimuli and backstory. What had already happened to her? What was going to happen to her? It was all conjecture. But such was its power, it could easily have sent Ellie into an internal frenzy, a hysterical madness, as she waited for her captors to commence whatever they intended to do.

She didn't have to wait long for her captors to get to work.

Sharp pain shot up her arm. A needle had been inserted. Ellie tried to turn her head but couldn't. Again, she concentrated but whatever they'd given her was too quick and too powerful.

Within the hood, she had the sensation she was spinning and sliding. It was like she was very drunk. The dark seemed to accentuate the effect of what they'd given her and Ellie felt instantly nauseous. She wanted to vomit but couldn't move.

"We know you're activated, but not in the same way as the nano-bomb. I wouldn't be standing here if you were loaded."

Someone gripped her hood and pulled it away.

A light came on, shattering her vision. Brilliant white everywhere, burning like a laser in her eyes. She desperately wanted to shut out the painful whiteness, but she couldn't lift her arm. It was chained to the chair.

"Sam Noor's your target, isn't he?"

The words came from behind her. They sounded like the perpetrator was under water. Ellie couldn't believe what she was hearing. Her husband was her target? What the hell was he talking about?

Ellie tried to turn, but sharp pain caught her. Whatever they'd given her was working at full strength. Any movement Ellie tried to make instantly caused her severe agony.

"I said, Sam Noor's your target. We know all about it. No point in denying it."

Ellie didn't say anything. The idea that Sam was her target, it was insane.

The person whose footsteps Ellie had heard eventually came into her eye line.

Tall and gaunt with blond hair and dark grey eyes of steel, he walked softly. He had a slightly effeminate element about him, which somehow made him more sinister. He tipped his head to the side and stared at Ellie, eyeing her body slowly. He reached in and placed a finger to her cheek. Ellie trembled.

"Hello, sweetie. Let's see what you're about."

The interrogator walked around the chair to which Ellie was chained. Ellie tried to follow him, but a sharp, jagged, burning sensation cut like a lathe through her body. Ellie caught her breath. Her body ached. She breathed in and out in long gasps and struggled bravely to cope with the violent torment.

"Oh, now I wouldn't move if I were you," the interrogator sneered, as he watched Ellie. "It could get very painful if you do. Just stay still, listen to me, and answer my questions."

Ellie looked in front of her and not at the interrogator. This stance annoyed him and he pulled at her shoulder, forcing Ellie to face him. Ellie cried out as the quick twist brought a wave of agony within her muscles, and she held her breath as the deep, cutting hurt surged through her.

"That's better. Now keep your face on me. I don't want to hurt you."

Ellie stared at him. His smirking, sly mouth and steel ice eyes did not reflect his words.

Defiance stormed within her.

She wasn't going to give him the satisfaction of seeing her fear. She wasn't going to give him the satisfaction of getting anything from her.

Somehow, the drug they'd given her had brought clarity. A fog lifted in her mind. Fear had been her enemy. But she wasn't filled with fear now.

She was filled with hate.

Ellie glared at her interrogator and did not utter a word.

"We saw you talking in your kitchen yesterday morning. But no one was there. Who were you talking to?"

Ellie remained silent. Her eyes glazed over, and she ignored her interrogator.

"Did you know that Sam Noor was MI6 before yesterday?" he asked. "Are you with Al Nadir?" the interviewer continued. "We saw you scream. We know that was the initiation, wasn't it?" The bland emotionless voice persisted. "The Sleeping Assassin technology, we know all about it."

Ellie, ignoring all questions, pulled frantically at her clamps. Pain cut through her mercilessly and her beautiful face mutated into a horrible grimace.

"Who is Sam Noor? Who are you with? Why did you scream? Who were you talking to in your kitchen?"

The interrogator spoke pointedly. He wanted answers.

He stood in front of Ellie, and then dropped down. He grasped her legs and moved up, stroking her thighs. Ellie swallowed but forced herself to stay strong. He nudged up so close Ellie could feel his hot breath on her stomach. She recoiled.

"Listen, darling, Guantanamo Bay is heartbeat away, and we all know how they'll treat a pretty thing like you."

Ellie flinched at the words, understanding the inference, but retained her silence.

The interrogator scowled, rose to his feet, and looked straight down at Ellie with impatience.

"I will continue to ask you questions all day and all night. I'll be replaced with another person just like me. But we're gonna keep you in that chair until you speak. No toilet breaks. No food. No water. No sleep. You will speak to me. Sooner or later, you'll have to. So let's avoid all this unnecessary stress. Tell me what I want to know."

The interrogator walked around and then came in close to Ellie, sneering.

"Your friend, Rikard, 'fessed up just before he blew in Oslo. He told us everything. Keeping silent isn't going to help you."

Ellie stared ahead and said nothing.

Infuriated by Ellie's silence, the interrogator continued with the same drill over and over. Ellie knew he wanted to break her, but his monosyllabic interrogation technique was having no effect on her at all. She sat silently, every so often pulling her bonds or trying to rise from the chair, only to be dissuaded by the painful cutting sensation that ravaged her body every time she moved.

Ellie was aware of time passing but she could not be sure how many hours she'd spent in the white room. Closing her eyes, she tried to block out the interrogator's persistent, penetrating mantra. But his voice broke through, invading her place of solace.

"Oh, no you don't! You're not going to sleep," said the interrogator sharply, and he shook Ellie awake. As he shook her, vibrations of pain cut into her body. Her head was splitting with a new headache and nausea had returned full blast.

"Are you with-" The interrogator didn't had chance to finish his incessant questioning.

Ellie interrupted, screaming, "Oh! Go fuck yourself!"

Ellie's somewhat ill-advised words of courage ejected from her shaking lips. She'd had enough of his boring bloody voice. She felt like shit. Her head was splitting and if she heard another word from the fucker's lips, she'd puke.

Yes, it was a reckless thing to say. But sometimes Ellie spoke first and thought later. The droning, debilitating voice had pushed Ellie beyond caring. With her customary impulsiveness on overdrive, at that moment, caution was not in her vocabulary.

Hearing her words, and the only words she'd said in the entire interrogation session, the interrogator yanked her arm to the side. As he pulled, the chains dug deep into her wrist.

Ellie felt a sudden stabbing.

Yet another needle was driven with naked brutality into her skin.

Ellie winced and tried to look around, her neck shaking in pain by the simple movement, but she withstood it long enough to see, in her peripheral vision, the hands of the interrogator taking a blood sample.

Ellie broke into a sweat. Who the hell were these people? Why did they need her blood? Somehow, she had to get out, but her body from the head down was completely immobile. The drugs that had caused her such agony now delivered total paralysis.

Imprisoned in her own body, she could do nothing.

The interrogator smiled at Ellie in a way that made her stomach flip, and the vicious whiteness of the room extinguished as it was absorbed again into the dark.

Chapter 2

In the room adjacent to the interrogation cell, Quentin Ludlow, UK Foreign Secretary, watched Ellie's interrogation with dispassionate aloofness through a two-way mirror. Sir Justin Maide, Head of MI6 British Intelligence, had just left. He had given explicit orders to Quentin to get to the bottom of who Ellie Noor really was and if she was a national security threat to MI6 and Sam Noor.

Most of all, Maide wanted to understand why Ellie had screamed.

He demanded for Quentin to find answers to those critical questions. Spencer was the interrogator Maide had personally selected. He was not only highly effective in his job, but he was also a ruthless individual whose psych profile bordered on sociopathic. His specialty was wearing a person down with his grinding, bone-crushingly boring voice on continuous play.

Ellie didn't know she was in the presence of a star interrogator. But, according to Quentin observing from behind the glass, her reaction to Spencer's interrogation hadn't been commensurate with his previous track record.

After first administering the paralyzing agent to prevent movement, Spencer then gave Ellie sodium pentothal to get her to reveal her secrets.

But Ellie remained silent.

She struggled bravely to cope with the violent pain flooding through her body. But she didn't reveal anything. The truth drug had no affect at all. Both Spencer and Quentin were amazed to see Ellie ignore a direct question after being given a heavy dose of the truth serum.

Quentin couldn't understand what he was watching. She was just an ordinary woman, but she was acting like she'd been preconditioned to withstand interrogation. Without training, very few agents could take the drugs cocktail Ellie had been given in such a short time and not talk. Ellie, so far, had not been influenced to say a word.

He peered through the two-way mirror at Ellie. She pulled at her chains and rotated on her hips as Spencer kept expertly in her blind spot. Quentin could see her pain from the paralyzing agent was getting worse. Ellie's beautiful face was turning into a contorted mask of misery.

Pain tore mercilessly at her, but she withstood it all.

Hours progressed and Ellie didn't say anything. But she was getting tired and irritable.

Her outburst, given what she'd been subjected to, wasn't unexpected. But Quentin was amazed at her bravery in such an untenable situation.

Quentin knew Ellie's reaction would hack off Spencer and he'd adopt more drastic means to get to the truth. And he did. Quentin watched him take a blood sample from Ellie, and then leave to synthesize the NMS drug.

Quentin shook his head. Maide would have to know about this. If she wasn't Al Nadir, she had to be someone's asset. They had to break her to find out the truth.

One thing was obvious: Ellie was not the woman Sam thought she was.

Chapter 3

The elliptical, cavernous hall was dark on one side and light on the other, with walls of onyx and opal that transmuted into an elaborate circle of thrones.

The hall, dissected by a line of gold inlaid into the crystal floor, had a sense of Yin and Yang about it, an overpowering ambience embodying a need for perfect balance. The atmosphere on the onyx side seemed to be heavier, as if the molecules in the air were laden with dense elements. The opal side had a sense of hope, of future, whereas the darker side impressed a conclusion that the search for hope was a failure of the weak.

This mysterious place was Kudamun. This place wasn't on Earth, nor was it to be found in the entire universe. Kudamun was a place outside of the universal plane, and was hidden from inhabitants of the universe by the Reality Gap.

The great hall in Kudamun gradually filled with urbane, aristocratic figures who entered from both the light and dark sides of the hall. Wearing sumptuous, silken robes, they positioned themselves in front of ornate thrones, draped their flowing robes and sat in unison. Like the great hall, their robes of ebony and ivory reflected the stark polarity of dark and light.

From the light side of the hall, an extremely tall figure entered and walked over to a raised throne situated on the center of the gold line. His throne was more ornate than the others with intricate carvings in swirling patterns resembling galaxy formations from afar. The tall figure smiled; his black eyes shone. The flowing ivory and gold robes hid his incredibly muscular body. His face was oval, his skin tanned, and he looked middle-aged. His jet-black hair, styled in ringlets, was pulled with a gold clasp and fixed to the back of his head. A dark, silk-like beard fell in unusual corrugations and framed the lower half of his face. He moved with an inherent graciousness. He looked first to the left, then to the right, and then lowered his head slowly and sat.

Now that Aby-od, the Leader of Kudamun had arrived, the High Council could finally begin their session.

Chapter 4

One day earlier

Dr. Ross Whyte, Director of the secret government weapons program, Project David, heard gunshots.

He heard them on the phone screen and then very close by. But his reaction time was slow, absorbed completely in the moments he'd just witnessed.

"You'll all be together real soon."

Words of confirmation from molasses-voiced man. Then he'd placed the live stream in front of Ross, forcing him to watch the horror of his own family being shot.

Seconds before, Ross had believed his family would be released.

Naïve and trusting, with no real comprehension as to what Al Nadir would do, Ross had seen his beloved ones drop to the floor one by one. Shock overwhelmed him and Ross hadn't really registered his own fate. Too caught up in his family's demise, he hadn't sensed the other man at the window. Tears were falling from Ross' shocked eyes when he felt something skewer into the side of his head.

A pounding vibration erupted inside his brain, and he was aware of molasses-voiced man getting out of the car. Ross had wanted to stop him. But he couldn't move.

The car door slammed and Ross was alone.

Behind him, a powerful engine kicked in and a dark SUV drove off in front. Ross wanted to chase after the car. He wanted to alert someone.

His strength was ebbing rapidly. Ross pushed himself forward and grabbed the steering wheel. He looked out. He was behind the diner still. He needed to drive. To get away. To tell someone. Ross' head lolloped forward. He stared at his hands, trying to remember how to use them. Vibrations in his skull were pounding harder. The color of everything was falling away and his eyesight became fuzzy. He saw the car key in the middle compartment. *Start car*, his mind screamed. But the instruction was lost to the thumping tremors inside his brain. All he could see was Patsy, Zoe and Pete. Blood spurting out of their bodies as they fell. Tears of pain dropped heavy.

Ignition. The word seemed to tumble into Ross' mind through the agony of loss and throbbing vibrations.

His fingers dragged down the dashboard. Fumbling and feeling for a button. *It makes car go.* He found it and pressed it. The engine fired up.

Within him, Ross' mind tried to instruct further but control was breaking down. The vision of his family's massacre wouldn't leave him.

His tears flowed.

Ross tried to turn the steering, but not being in gear, the car remained stationary.

Oh, Patsy, I'm so sorry, darling.

Ross' mind had fixed on his wife. The car's function had gone again. The vibrations in his head grew louder, battering down his concentration. Ross struggled. He had to get away.

His hand dropped, as he recalled somewhere within the pounding vibrations that it was something he needed to do. He touched the gear shift. Contact with the leather covered knob of the shift stick brought back one word.

Drive.

Ross slotted the stick forward into drive mode and pulled his hand back onto the wheel. The pounding had intensified, and Ross, dizzy with sorrow, fought hard to see through his misted eyes. Things were losing definition and a shadow outlined his sight.

Concentrate, he said to himself, and air burst out of him as he struggled to turn the steering wheel.

The car moved. Its movement brought a new impetus for Ross, and he gripped hold of the steering wheel. He looked out of the windscreen. Everything was too blurry again. His car carried on, but it was like he was in a snow storm, and the pounding in his skull carried on relentlessly.

Squinting against the white static snow in front of his eyes, Ross edged around the side behind the trash bin area. That was when he saw it.

The dark SUV. It had stopped.

Ross breathed deeply, and as if in parallel, the shattering agony in his head built up. The vibrations were shaking his body.

His trembling hand pressed in the ignition and the engine cut out.

The car door of the dark SUV opened, and Patsy, Zoe and Pete emerged.

Ross pushed his body forward to see through the snow. *But they are dead,* yelled his mind.

The agonizing vibrations took over. The snow became heavier. Ross tried to hold his vision, but everything descended into an incoherent mass of faint outlines against the overpowering snow.

He thought he heard his car door open, but the pounding in his head was stealing his senses.

"Daddy."

"Ross, darling."

The heavy thump of a bullet flying out of a barrel.

Three times.

Their screams reverberated within Ross' mind, mingling with the vibrations that pulverized his brain.

The pressure in Ross' head increased.

His sight drenched in red. Tiny vibrating bombs exploded concurrently within his brain.

He felt himself falling down.

Perfume was all around him. Patsy's scent. Her gentle, loving hand was soft on his brow.

Pain ceased.

"Welcome home, Ross."

Chapter 5

March 23, 2017

Ellie waited for his return.

Thoughts of evil burrowed like maggots in her mind. The people who held her were evil. It wasn't a difficult deduction. No challenge was made to her cerebrum. Their behavior defined their evil. No one with the shallowest glimmer of goodness could engage in such acts.

Her life had been relatively free of what one might term evil. She had faced bad luck, injustice and even downright revenge, maybe, but never, no-holds-barred, all-bets-are-off evil.

Until now.

What purpose did evil serve? If only to deliver pain, suffering and anguish, why did evil exist at all? Ellie corrected herself. Evil didn't exist. Evil was inanimate, intangible and unseen. Like good, it breathed life, took shape and grew from the measures of mankind.

Two days earlier, such thoughts would seldom have found a home in her mind. But now, they descended, enveloping her in shadow, sparking her synapses, churning her mind over, and forcing her to imagine the depths of evil. What lengths would these people go?

Chained to a chair, half naked, Ellie knew her chances of survival were slimmer than a single sheet of paper.

Alone, in a darkness so absorbing, so deep she could visualize her own soul being swallowed, Ellie sought out reason and waited.

And waited…

Ellie sensed her interrogator had been gone for hours. Why had she been kidnapped? It had to be because of Sam.

She wasn't made for this. She felt so naked and vulnerable.

Her mind started imagining. They were going to torture her, do terrible things. Her body would give up and give in. She would die. This, she knew with the certainty of her own existence.

Her bladder felt full. She needed to go. Vivid thoughts of her forthcoming demise and the coldness of the chair brought on the feeling. She couldn't hold back. Hot liquid dripped down her legs. A faint smell of ammonia hung in the air. Tears rolled down her face filled with shame and fear.

The footsteps returned.

Here it comes, thought Ellie, and she braced herself. Her arm was pulled back and sharp pain shot through her.

Oh, Sam, I wish you were here. I wish you could save me.

Chapter 6

Unbeknownst to Ellie, she'd been injected with an intelligent DNA-based hallucinogenic drug that military intelligence had developed to secure answers from terrorists in their capture. The drug, Neural Magnified Stimuli, nicknamed 'NightMareScene' or NMS, was an alternative form of torture and had proved successful. Given the purpose of its use, NMS never went through clinical trials. But it was certainly trialed heavily by the intelligence agencies around the world. Through its use, the agencies discovered NMS carried a very useful side-effect; it wiped the captive's mind clean of any memory of the interrogation.

Ellie was in control of her voice and her hearing but nothing else. All that she sensed, all that she saw, and all that she felt would be a trompe l'oeil, an illusion generated by the powerful drug.

"Are you with Al Nadir? Is Sam Noor your target? Who did you speak to? What is too far gone? Why did you scream?" repeated the interrogator all at once, much faster than before.

Ellie's head fell back. Her eyes rolled and she perspired. The interrogator watched as Ellie began to scream.

Her nightmare scene had begun.

"Tell me what I need to know and the pain will stop. You'll be safe. Are you Al Nadir? Is Sam Noor your target? Who did you speak to? Why did you scream? What is too far gone? Tell me what I need to know and I'll make it all go away. You'll feel no pain."

The interrogator was careful to speak in generics. He didn't know what Ellie's fear was, only that the drug was manifesting it and that he was giving her the backdoor to freedom. If she spoke, if she answered his questions, the trigger to the outside would be released through the intelligent drug's framework. Then Ellie would be free of the pain she was so clearly enduring.

But Ellie didn't respond.

She only screamed. The interrogator didn't flinch at the sound of Ellie's howling cries.

"Who did you speak to you in your kitchen?" the interviewer said, his tone icy and controlled.

Ellie shook her head. "No." Abject pain was traced out in Ellie's response.

"What is too far gone?"

Ellie writhed and screamed with bloodshot eyes streaming. She breathed fast.

"Tell me what I need to know and I'll stop the pain."

"No," Ellie screamed defiantly.

"I know you're in pain. It doesn't have to be this way. Just tell me what I want to know. I'll take the pain away."

"Go…fuck…your…self," Ellie breathed contemptuously, and her eyes flared with utter hatred.

The interrogator stared at Quentin, puzzled, and shrugged. She was strong. Very, very strong.

She screamed for Sam to help her.

Then she just screamed. No words. Just a terrifying scream of someone dying.

Her lids dropped. Her body began to slump. The interrogator knew unconsciousness beckoned.

Ellie's screams grew weaker.

She was losing the battle with NMS.

Death raced upon her fast.

The interrogator looked around at Quentin.

"It's not working."

Chapter 7

Salim loved power.

He was in love with the idea of holding the entire world to ransom. The men hand-picked by Sabena had delivered exactly what had been required. The quantum compound bomb, previously in the claws of President Treeborne now resided with him. Sabena had taken his idea to abduct Dr. Ross Whyte's family and blackmail the top government scientist into stealing President Treeborne's quantum compound bomb, and carried it out to his exact expectations.

Sabena's team had cleaned house, as per Al Nadir's MO, and massacred the entire family, including the eminent scientist.

The team then flew directly from Blacksburg to Dubai, where Salim had taken possession of the bomb, before heading out to Al Nadir's advanced quantum tech labs in the Zagros Mountains on the Iraq/Iran border.

He'd left Sabena to check on their new base just outside Cambridge, and to ensure all was ready for the quantum bomb hit on the UN Peace Summit taking place in London's QEII Conference Center.

Things now, however, weren't going quite to plan.

"Salim, it seems there is an issue. Our comms have picked up different wavelengths talking about a change strategy on the Peace Summit. It might not be London, but somewhere else. The amount of chatter those bastards have put out, I just don't know what to believe. Our assets are hitting brick walls too. It's a fucking mess."

Sabena's frustrated face erupted onto the satcom screen.

Salim just stared, unblinking, as Sabena displayed her ineptitude. Salim was the master of the emotional hold. It led those before him to believe he didn't appreciate the situation or else he was being understanding of their predicament.

In truth, neither of those scenarios was true.

Salim just liked to play people. Even those closest to him.

He could flip his emotions on the turn of a card. He could shoot someone and not even flinch. He could cut their throat, with blood spurting across his face from their carotid artery, and look as calm as a Sunday morning.

Salim could lie face on and not show a tell. The CIA had never seen his true purpose. He'd led all the intel agencies on a merry dance and they never realized what he'd been capable of.

Not until Al Nadir had gone live, exploding multiple bombs in thirty cities around the globe simultaneously back in 2011.

"I don't want to hear that, Sabena," said Salim, almost softly. He knitted his fingers and held them underneath his chin. He stared into the camera. Although his voice was unruffled, his eyes bore into Sabena with dark intensity.

Sabena swallowed. "I know you don't, Salim. I'm sorry."

"I also don't want your apologies. Just get me the summit's location. London, Hong Kong, wherever. And I don't care how you do it. Just do it."

Salim watched Sabena. She pushed back her long dark hair over her shoulder and averted his eyes.

Salim could see she was nervous. He smirked. He enjoyed keeping her on edge. Then, she thrust forward, assertive and commanding. The low cut Dolce and Gabbana number she wore just skimmed her pert breasts, and Salim felt a flood of heat within him.

He recalled their last encounter, entwined on a sun lounger on the roof top of his mansion in Dubai, overlooking the beach. They'd just stolen the quantum compound bomb. In celebration, he had taken her with a ferocious passion. Her screams, he could still hear.

"I will, Salim. You know that."

"I know *you* know what will happen if you don't. That's enough."

"I'm telling you. I won't let you down. I'll find the summit's location if I have to wring it out of fucking Ashton himself."

Salim smiled, savoring the image. "Good girl. Don't take too long. I want you back here splitting this bomb. We're on the clock."

Salim had been confident of Sabena's success in securing the intel on the UN Peace Summit's location.

They were on a roll and soon the world would be paying.

Salim just didn't count on Sam Noor.

He'd just arrived in his Zagros Mountains base when a trusted asset within the CIA called to alert him of the capture.

"Dr. Al Douri, they've all been detained. Stein-Muller, Lupez and…" The voice on the other end descended into a mumble.

"And? Oh. Not Rasheed," completed Salim, suppressing the fury inside of him.

"I'm sorry, sir. Yes. Your cousin as well."

"That is bad. How did this happen?" asked Salim, forcing a deadpan tone.

The caller's timbre had dropped to a mere whisper. "Dr. Sam Noor of British Intelligence arrived today to interrogate. I'm not sure but I think he's the reason for their incarceration."

Salim hit his keyboard, typing fast as he held the phone. Information flashed up on his screen. Various photos came up. Salim scrolled through them rapidly. He stopped on a photo of a dark-haired, handsome man in a gun-metal gray boiler suit and strange, purple-lensed glasses running and shooting with another hulk of a man with blond hair in a cragged back ponytail. More photos showed them tearing away like crazy, shooting and climbing the wall in his lab facility just outside Dubai.

Salim zoomed in on the dark-haired guy's face.

"Thank you for your service to Al Nadir," responded Salim with absolute politeness.

He cut the line and threw this mobile against the wall. Someone behind him jumped as the device shattered into pieces. But Salim didn't react. His eyes stared at the wall that had just been pelted with the phone. Others came over to check on Salim, but it appeared he didn't know they were there.

He just fixed on the wall and stared.

No one spoke. They hardly breathed.

Then, from being totally inert, Salim's personality carved in two, and he roared.

"Fuck!"

He spun around in his chair, leapt up, and strode over to a massive satcom screen at the far end of the room.

Sabena popped up. As he accused her of her incompetence, he noticed she looked genuinely surprised. That angered him more. She was his second in command. The one who should have his back. But her pride and need for revenge against Matthew Kinley, the MI6 double agent who had infiltrated Al Nadir by screwing, literally and metaphorically, with Sabena, had been so great, she'd taken an unwarranted risk on the new nano-bomb. Although it wasn't properly tested, she'd deployed it to wipe out Kinley and his family. In doing so, she'd left an unmasked frequency trail for the agencies to find.

Perhaps it was just bad luck that MI6 operative Dr. Sam Noor happened to be a nanotechnologist. Of course, it didn't help that Sam had been in Dubai five weeks earlier when Sabena had been testing with Russo. Sam had seen everything. It had been a case of right place and right time for MI6. But now, the reverse would be true for Sam.

Salim watched Sabena wriggle around, clearly annoyed with herself and her stupidity. He glared at her, and then shut his eyes, put his hands together as if in prayer, and raised his head to the heavens in search of some divine inspiration.

Salim was aware of utter silence around him.

He could discern labored breathing, as if all in the room, and Sabena on screen, were engrossed, waiting on his next reply.

Salim opened his mouth and a pure scream of incensed, pent up rage came out.

"I want Sam Noor dead!"

Sabena nodded.

"Thirty million dollars to the first person who confirms the kill. I don't care who it is. Put this out across our networks. Include back channels to all the agencies. Loyalty to their flag is one thing. Loyalty to Sam Noor is very much another. Cash speaks. Get it done!"

Chapter 8

Quentin was absolutely gob-smacked. He had never seen an agent, let alone a civilian, who had not broken during NMS. Ellie had not even given up her own name.

Instead, she had castigated the interviewer with focused expletives.

Incredible. Quentin wanted her in MI6 special operations. If she could resist to that level, her talent couldn't be wasted on running a business. Whoever she was an asset for, they'd find a way to flip her. She'd make a fantastic agent. She was bright. They'd train her to be the best. After she'd been returned to her home, and this whole thing of who she was really working for was over, he'd make a play to get her. He'd talk to Sam. He'd be agreeable. Quite frankly, mused Quentin, he didn't have a choice.

A scream interrupted his selfish thoughts. He looked up. The scream sounded from the interrogation room. Ellie pitched forward. Quentin dived into the room. He pulled the interviewer to one side.

"What have you done?" yelled Quentin.

The interviewer shook his head. "She didn't say anything. Not even her name. She only swore at me. Then she opened her mouth. I was in front of her. She looked straight at me. But I know her eyes couldn't see me. I really thought she was going to come through. I really thought she was going to talk. Then she screamed and fell forward. I think she's dead. There's no pulse."

Quentin froze. Interrogation was one thing; murder was very much another. Sam would mete out justice for this reprehensible act. Quentin felt for a pulse.

Nothing.

He pulled Ellie's head back. Her eyeballs rolled back in their sockets, showing only ghostly white.

"Oh, fuck!"

Quentin's anxiety rose as he realized the cost of his persistence.

He took out his phone and called the base's chief medical officer.

"Davison, come to room D08. There's been an incident. One of our subjects has had a heart attack."

Almost immediately Quentin hit another contact on his phone. Maide answered. Quentin told him the news.

Maide simply stated, "Deal with it." Then he slammed down the phone.

Quentin knew he was on his own. He bent down and undid the clamps on Ellie's ankles and wrists.

"For Christ's sake, help me," Quentin screamed at the interviewer, who was standing by the side of the wall in a state of shock.

At that moment, Davison ran into the room. He stared at the sight: a beautiful, almost naked woman secured to a chair, her head lolloping to the left side.

"Jesus. That's Sam Noor's wife."

He recognized Ellie from the picture Sam had on his desk back at River House.

"Hurry up. Do something," Quentin screamed hysterically.

But he could *do* nothing. Davison could see that Ellie was already long gone. He bent over and sounded her chest with his stethoscope. Not a beat. Not a flutter. Her lips had started to turn pale blue around the edges. He tried to move her head to an upright position, but it fell to the other side. With no internal force, it was at the mercy of gravity. He felt her skin. She was getting cooler by the second. Rigor would soon be setting in.

"Quentin, I'm sorry. She's gone."

"Oh, God," Quentin whispered.

"Don't leave her like this," Davison said, indicating Ellie's state of undress.

Quentin collected her clothes from the locker they'd been stuffed into earlier. In his haste, he didn't notice Ellie's *Longines* watch that sat at the back of locker.

Between him and Davison, they dressed her. But they didn't need to. She was dead.

Their gross disrespect of Ellie's body couldn't harm her anymore, but their shame demanded that she be properly attired.

Davison took her legs and Quentin took her shoulders. In silence, they carried Ellie out to a medical trolley. Quentin turned away from her and shook with uncontrollable fear. He realized the future of his own mortality would now be in question. He sadly resigned himself to the fact that his fatal mistake had signed his own death warrant.

Sam would kill him.

Chapter 9

One Day Earlier

In his private office in the White House, US President Jonathan D Treeborne scowled at his laptop screen. The image of British Prime Minister Richard Ashton flashed up.

"You okay, Rich? Not too late for ya?"

Treeborne didn't give a damn whether it was late or not, he had things to say to Ashton, and their time difference was immaterial to him.

"No, no, I'm still up," said Ashton, riffling his fingers through his dark blond hair, flicking a glance at his watch: 2:10 a.m. He stared into the camera. "Got things to sort out with the Peace Summit coming up."

"Yeah, Rich, that's what I wanna talk to you about. That Summit is critical to my next move on Al Nadir."

"Your next move?" said Ashton, and Treeborne detected that the British PM had taken exception by his words. The president sneered.

"Yeah, Rich. Mine. I gotta get that Resolution 8091 through quickly. No backlash from bleeding heart liberals and other fools in the UN who think we can still negotiate with Al Douri. You know what I'm saying, Rich. Just need to speed up all the talking. 8091 will grant us and all allied forces the right to use extreme unreserved force against Al Nadir."

Treeborne glared at Ashton, preempting any political recalcitrance from the seemingly super-diplomatic Brit. Treeborne always considered Ashton a touch too vulnerable. He had a slightly delicate air that screamed of public school that never sat too well with Treeborne. He liked a man to be a man, not some kind of namby-pamby imitation.

"Extreme unreserved force. What are you planning on deploying, Jonathan?" asked Ashton, his face concerned.

Treeborne smirked. "Richie, baby." Ashton stiffened, not liking the endearment, but Treeborne repeated, reveling in Ashton's discomfort. "Richie, I got me a weapon that'll turn Al Nadir into a downtown DC whore. They're gonna get fucked every which way!"

Ashton raised an eyebrow.

"Care to elaborate further?"

Treeborne smiled broadly, pushing his bulky body forward with enthusiasm.

"I'd love to, buddy. It's a quantum bomb. An itty-bitty amount can knock out a twenty-mile radius. And when I say itty-bitty, I'm talking half a millimeter worth."

Treeborne rested back in his chair to watch Ashton's reaction.

"Where did you get it?" asked Ashton. His face remained impassive, much to Treeborne's annoyance.

"I've been developing it for a while. Those guys in DARPA in Blacksburg. They sure got some brains down there. The team finally got it to work. Al Nadir ain't got long, Rich. So you make sure, with the summit on your soil, nothing happens. I don't wanna hear about some fucking terrorist attack preventing 8091 from going ahead. Just lock down everything with your boys. Make sure MI5 do their job. Right?"

Treeborne sneered again, loving his power play, as he noticed Ashton bristling at Treeborne's insinuation his intelligence guys couldn't keep things safe at home.

"I assure you, Jonathan, Al Nadir will be no threat to proceedings. We already have a crack team working on total elimination of their latest cell."

Treeborne fell forward, a dark storm rising, taking up the whole screen. "What d'ya mean latest cell?"

"Don't worry, Jonathan. We've got it sorted," said Ashton, dismissing Treeborne's sudden anger.

"Hell, Richie, I do worry. If you fuck this for me-"

"Jonathan, for God's sake. We're not amateurs over here. Don't treat us as such!"

"Yeah, yeah, Richie. I didn't mean to insinuate you were. Anyway, your guys and mine need to coordinate their thing. Very soon, we'll be kicking Al Douri's motherfuckin' ass for good."

At that announcement, Ashton smiled, and in his hazel eyes, Treeborne saw a flicker of deep aggression. Treeborne was surprised. The PM's reaction didn't chime with his usual suave and politically sensitive personality.

Perhaps, I got you wrong, thought Treeborne, as he said goodbye to the British PM.

Chapter 10

March 23, 2017

Ellie felt the flames building faster. Her end was coming at a velocity she could never have anticipated. She closed her eyes, prayed a silent prayer and sent her love to Sam forever. The flames engulfed her. Intolerable pain raged through her body.

The end.

She wasn't afraid.

With her eyes shut, she felt a sudden coldness. She tried to open her eyes but could see only darkness.

"Step forward."

A voice reverberated within the dark. Peaceful, calm and kind. Ellie recognized it from somewhere. She'd heard it before. But where?

Instinct told her to trust it. Blindly, she stepped forward as she was told. Then she was falling through the darkness.

Endlessly falling.

"Do not be afraid, Ellie."

The kind, soothing voice returned.

Her descent stopped but still her eyes couldn't see. Darkness remained.

Ellie wanted to ask something but didn't know how. She felt she didn't have a mouth.

A chill swept across where she thought her face should be, but Ellie realized her body wasn't there.

Nothingness.

She didn't exist.

Ellie had no past, present or future. She had no memory. She had neither a corporeal nor spiritual body. She had no form at all on any plane.

Then something happened.

A blinding white light assaulted her, a lethal contrast against the darkness that enshrouded her.

Colors, sounds, images, voices. So much streamed into her. She would have closed her eyes if she had eyes to close.

A force propelled Ellie forward and she began to hurtle downward.

"Return."

Within the nothingness, she heard the calm voice. It reverberated around and inside her. An immense force powered her descent.

She felt like a torpedo that had been shot through a long, narrow conduit held perpendicularly to the ground. She could almost sense the wind blowing against her as her velocity sped up.

Ellie sensed a destination was close. She plummeted onwards.

Chapter 11

Kudamun was not situated within the known universe. It was on a horizontal plane hidden by a fluctuating, powerful quantum field known as the Reality Gap. This positioning had a purpose. The people of Kudamun, known as Kudamaz, had one responsibility: to guard the planets in their care.

Out of time, out of space, and not part of the universe they guarded, the Kudamaz were assigned their role by the Ancient Ones, the almighty force that oversaw everything since a time before time began.

Inhabitants of the planets guarded by the Kudamaz were unaware of their intervention. But occasionally, some being, somewhere, would sense something, would feel out of synch with their surroundings and suddenly possess heightened senses detecting the equilibrium of life. Just occasionally, during such moments, the movements of the Kudamaz could potentially be revealed. Of course, these times were very rare. And even then, these moments would be seen as just coincidence or fate.

The simple reality was that beings across the universe, whatever their level of development and intelligence, remained nescient to the Kudamaz and their responsibility to nurture, manage, and maintain the equilibrium of good and evil.

And that was exactly how things had to be.

The Kudamaz were the most integral part of the laws of the universe and revelation of their existence would bring a systemic downfall threatening life itself.

Cracking the eleventh dimensional transportation equation was the only way to enter the Kudamun dimension. As that ability was designed out of every being, irrespective of their level of intelligence, the Kudamaz remained forever hidden.

The Kudamaz's High Council was the governing body of Kudamun. Two houses made up the High Council. The ruling House of Giznu was also known as the House of Light. The opposing House of Etima was referred to as the House of Dark.

Allegiance to a house was not a political preference; it was decided by heritage. Loyalty to either house was passed from generation to generation. A seat on the High Council was the highest accolade a Kudamaz could achieve.

Although High Council seats could be passed down in a family, a Kudamaz had to prove himself or herself worthy. Under the tutelage of a senior elder, they would be set assignments. The result of these assignments determined their acceptance as an elder.

Such was the complexity of these assignments that few Kudamaz ascended to the position of elder. The majority of the people of Kudamun were content to play a minor role and thus provided the monitoring and support framework needed to keep a watchful eye over the planets. They left the real problem of solving of a planet's fate to the elders.

The High Council only convened at times when a planet in their care was in a state of unrest. Their current gathering was at the bequest of the tall figure: the Great Ensi, Lord Aby-od, ruler of Kudamun and lead elder of the House of Giznu.

Softly but firmly, Aby-od delivered his opening address.

"Honorable members of the High Council, please accept my gratitude to you for convening here with such swiftness. Events taking place on Ki are concomitant to the hurried summoning of this congress. Preparations are already underway to initiate the Protector. The balance shift on Ki is significant. However, I believe the Protector will still be able to redress the Balance Shift and restore equilibrium."

Aby-od's address caused considerable consternation amongst the elders. Aby-od scanned the circle of assembled dignitaries. His words were being met with increasing discomfort. They jostled, moved and wriggled as if they were all seated on one giant anthill. Instead of the obligatory quiet calm the High Council usually displayed when a senior elder was delivering an address, the members turned to one another, murmuring annoyance and displeasure.

A sea of disquiet rippled in front of Aby-od's eyes. He expected their reaction. They had no conviction in his crusade. They couldn't see the uniqueness, the beauty, the love of which the people of Ki were capable.

The elders couldn't see beyond the crimes the people of Ki had committed, the wanton destruction of their planet with war, famine, and greed. The inhabitants of Ki had been served warnings over the millennia but had chosen not to heed the signs. In the beginning, they had been believers. They had been penitent. But now, the people of Ki no longer believed or cared. With an utter disregard for life, they had progressively broken every ancient antediluvian law written.

The Kudamun elders had run out of patience, and Ki, it seemed, had run out of time.

Aby-od was unsure of his ability to save Ki from the fate the High Council would soon demand. While he considered his options, heads turned as another senior elder rose to his feet. Seeing the elder rise, Aby-od knew that his own time had also run out.

Chapter 12

Quentin stared down at Ellie's dead body lying on the medical bed in D08 interrogation room in MI6's black site in Berkshire.

And he traveled on a journey of private guilt in his mind. Alone, he allowed himself a solitary cry. But his tears were connected to the fear of his own inevitable demise at Sam's hands rather than Ellie's recent one. He could not understand what had gone so terribly wrong. Why hadn't Ellie succumbed to the drugs like any normal person? Why hadn't she responded? Nothing had affected her. She had been impervious to the truth drug and NMS hadn't broken her.

She had been so very strong. She'd held everything back. It was like Ellie had been programmed or conditioned before. She held no value for self-preservation. Otherwise, she would have talked to avoid the pain.

He played out the interrogation scene in his mind and Quentin's obfuscation of the disastrous incident grew. No matter how he viewed it, he always reached the same conclusion. Ellie had surrendered to the terrible illusion that NMS had manifested and had suffered a massive coronary heart attack as a result.

Ellie's heart had literally stopped out of the fear that they had induced her to live through, immobile and paralyzed.

He closed his eyes. On the edge of his imagination, just before the darkness shrouded his thoughts, Quentin could just about visualize the horrors that Ellie must have gone through.

The drug's nickname, NightMareScene, was not adopted to sound cool. It was a highly accurate description of an extremely cruel and effective drug that military intelligence had created to get the truth out of hostiles in record time. In partnership with the scientists in cutting-edge genetic manipulation,

NMS had been devised to focus on two areas of the brain: the amygdala, responsible for fear, and the hippocampus that handles memory. The NMS drug, synthesized from a hostile's blood sample, was then aimed directly into the brain through a nanocarrier-based protein delivery system with a hallucinogenic base.

When NMS was administered, it recreated and played out a hostile's darkest fear with absolute clarity. Forced to experience what they had previously banished to the deepest recesses of their mind, the hostile virtually always talked.

Inside the NMS makeup was a 'back door', a psychological trip-switch, amounting to a single word that the interrogator would say once the hostile had broken and revealed their intel. The hostile would then be pulled instantly out of their nightmare.

When faced with their darkest fear, hostiles had, given the opportunity to talk, hemorrhaged information gladly. The majority had talked to save themselves from the pain and terror of NMS. Unless they'd been loaded with a nanobomb, Quentin had, so far, not seen anyone die to protect the information they held when their greatest fear was generated.

Except Ellie.

Maide stood next to Quentin.

"Good God, man. What the hell was she hiding? She was only supposed to be a bloody housewife!" said Maide.

What should have been a straightforward interrogation had descended into murder. Now parties were gearing up, ready to commence the blame game.

"Quentin, she must not remain here. It must be seen to be an accident. Take her car. Crash it. Burn it. No evidence. Got it?"

Maide snapped his words with icy efficiency and left the room. Quentin swallowed hard. Orders had been given. He had no option but to follow them. He picked up the phone and proceeded to put Maide's plan into motion.

Chapter 13

Deep, tens of meters below the poplars and green fields of Langley Fork Park, Sam strode away from a cell housing Rasheed, the cousin of Salim Al Douri, and one of three hostiles that Sam had been instrumental, with the CIA, in capturing.

Within him stirred a barely controlled rage.

He'd just started working on Rasheed, but even after a strong blast of enhanced interrogation, the terrorist hadn't batted an eye. Sam decided he needed more time in 'the cage', a torturous, metal lattice cube containing a space of no more than twenty-seven cubic feet. The strips making up the lattice structure were five centimeters in width, and had been left intentionally razor sharp on their edges to exacerbate maximum pain to those being incarcerated.

On leaving, Rasheed had directed an insolent eye at Sam and wheezed, "We knew about him. We played him. We played your intelligence agency. We fed him shit and, like the dog he was, he ate it greedily."

Rasheed's words stung Sam's ears. The 'him' Rasheed referred to had been Sam's close friend and fellow agent, Matthew Kinley, a true patriot up to his final moments.

It had been Kinley's mission, Operation Snowdrop, to infiltrate Al Nadir at the highest level, making them believe he'd flipped sides, hated MI6, the UK government, and the establishment. Operation Snowdrop had been architected by Kinley and himself, and was known to only two other people: the British PM Richard Ashton and Head of MI6 Sir Justin Maide.

It had been touted by the quartet as the operation to bring down Salim Al Douri and, with him, Al Nadir.

All had proceeded to mission objectives. Kinley had convinced Sabena, Salim's second in command that he'd flipped sides, but Salim, himself had wanted more proof. Kinley had been given details of a horrific bomb attack on central London. He'd told Maide who received strict instructions to 'take no action'. With Maide and Ashton, the three of them had wrestled with their conscience, deciding what to do. If they'd checked on the bombs, Snowdrop and Kinley would have been blown. If they did nothing, lives would be lost. Ashton coldly took the decision. Sam recalled that moment as he'd stood up directly against the British PM.

"We can't let this go."

"We can't let this *not* go," responded Ashton, his voice edged in granite.

"Kinley gave us this heads-up for a reason. We have to protect the British public," said Sam, staring down Ashton. He didn't give a shit if Ashton was the PM, he wasn't going to sign up to state-sanctioned murder.

"What's wrong with you, Sam?" snapped Ashton. "You and Kinley always knew it would come down to this. God, we even spoke about it in this very room a few months ago."

"If we take action and send sniffer dogs and bomb detection systems into Piccadilly Circus underground, Al Nadir will know Kinley hasn't really turned. Snowdrop and Kinley will be burned, and we'll have lost the best chance we've ever had to break Al Douri," said Maide, in his usual, calculating tone.

So, in that room, which Kinley used to call somewhat aptly, the Obsidian Cave, the three of them decided to do nothing.

On June 28, 2013, Maide and Sam had watched as over five thousand lives were taken by their decision.

Kinley's silence won him immediate acceptance and acceleration within Al Nadir's ranks. Over the four years Kinley had been in Al Nadir, he'd still remained loyal to MI6 and to the UK. He'd operated as an Al Nadir terrorist with the help of a nanomask and a new moniker, Stuart Kingswood, and had eventually become the fourth most powerful person in the terrorist collective.

Salim and Sabena believed throughout that time that he'd been lying to MI6, and he was true to Al Nadir's goal of world domination. Now, Rasheed's allusion that Al Nadir knew about Kinley and had played him hurt Sam badly.

Sacrifice had been the sub-heading for Operation Snowdrop.

He couldn't believe they'd known all along. The missions and bombings that had been foiled on Kinley's intelligence and the subsequent lives that had been saved, that had happened because Kinley had been trusted. The loss of part of Al Nadir's war chest to the tune of a hundred billion dollars, after one of Salim's global tech companies folded, had been engineered by Kinley. At the time, it had been made to look like another rival tech company had been in play. Such a risky assignment wouldn't have gone through so smoothly if Salim or Sabena had been in any doubt about Kinley's true intentions.

As Sam walked down the fluorescent-lit corridor to the next cell, he felt sure that Al Nadir hadn't known for very long about Kinley.

He would make sure his next target for enhanced interrogation treatment would tell him the truth.

Chapter 14

A massive electrifying jolt surged through Ellie. Pain seared in every organ of her body. Her nerves awoke, shocked and tingling. Her synapses fired up to transmit the massive sensory stimuli that raged through her body. Her heart pounded, registering the new chance that it had been given.

Ellie breathed in deeply, taking a full gulp of air. Oxygen circulated through her grateful respiratory system. She wheezed slightly and coughed. Her eyes sprang open. Her vision was blocked by something over her head. Ellie looked down. A sheet was covering her body from head to toe. Why was a sheet over her body? You only do that when someone is dead. A chill ran through her. Where was she?

With a sudden rush of adrenaline, she lifted her hand up and tore the sheet down from her body. The second it fell, Ellie was acutely aware she was in an alien and cold environment. She pushed herself into a sitting position and swung her legs over the side. Ellie noticed that she was on a medical trolley, the type used as a temporary bed when hospitals are overcrowded. Ellie looked around her, taking in the details of the place. It looked a little like a medical room. It was certainly sterile and clinical. Banks of stainless-steel lockers faced her. She thought, at first, that they looked out of place. They looked vaguely familiar.

Ellie dropped down slowly to the floor and walked over to take a closer look at the lockers. Her footsteps echoed faintly each time her short stiletto sling-backs hit the grey flagstones. Hearing the noise, Ellie stared nervously around the room. No one came to investigate. Ellie continued slowly in her approach to the lockers. On arriving, her hand reached out and grabbed the handle. It felt like ice. Ellie shivered and the hair on the back of her head raised like it had the power of premonition.

She pulled open the locker door. It swung outwards easily on its hinge. Ellie swallowed on witnessing the contents. She realized why the lockers had looked so familiar. Countless police detective programs on TV had introduced her to these lockers. Except they weren't lockers. The place was a morgue. And she was staring at a dead body.

Shaking, Ellie closed the door and shut out the gruesome sight.

She stepped backwards. Cold sweat dripped down her neck. Her stomach twisted into a tight knot. Why was she in a morgue? Why did she have a sheet pulled over her head? Ellie started to panic. What had happened to her? Where the hell was she? She tried to think coherently but fear overpowered her. Why couldn't she remember anything? She looked around, trying to see something that would trigger her memory. She forced her mind back. What day was it? Sunday. How could she tell whether she was right? She looked down at her wrist. Her watch wasn't there. Where was it? Did she have it on when…?

Ellie tried to recall her last memory.

She remembered, through a cloudy haze, working on her laptop at the apartment. But something told her that wasn't her last memory. She concentrated hard. White. All she could see was brilliant white. She could hear distant voices, but their words were distorted and unintelligible. When she thought back, a wave of nausea hit her. Her head thumped viciously. She swayed and put her hand out against a cupboard to steady herself.

I must be ill, thought Ellie, wiping the sweat from her forehead. But the sensation was more akin to the feeling she had when she was extremely drunk. Maybe I'm in a hospital? Ellie's mind was a maelstrom of confusion and shame. I've got to speak to someone and find out what the hell's going on.

Ellie walked through the morgue doorway into a very long, poorly lit corridor. It was olive green and smelled faintly musty like it was unused and needed a good clean. Ellie paused. Holding onto the door frame, she looked up and down. From her position, she could see that the morgue was halfway down the corridor. Doors were placed equidistantly on both sides, branching off to other rooms. The oppressive lighting gave the place a surreal quality. It reminded Ellie of a labyrinth. She imagined a kind of Alice in Wonderland scenario, in which one door lead to another door and another and another. Ellie couldn't decide whether to go left or right. She flicked her head back and forth, peering up and down the corridor.

"Hello? Is anyone there?" she called out cautiously.

Ellie found herself smiling despite the macabre surroundings. The line sounded so corny, she could hardly believe it was coming out of her mouth. Ellie waited for a second. She could feel her heart beating. No one came. There was absolutely no one. That's so odd, thought Ellie, taking the right-hand side of the corridor. Hospitals were usually places bustling with activity.

She walked gently past each closed door. From a few meters away, the doors looked like wood but, up close, Ellie could see they were made of metal. Ellie put her hand out to touch one. The metal reminded her of Waterloo Bridge. It had the same cold but strong texture. The bridge was steel and so was the door. It had been painted a dark hue of green to complement the walls. She noticed that some doors had a CCD camera above them. The red light signaled the camera's operational status. Ellie looked up into one of the cameras as she walked past. It whirred around and followed her movement.

"Hello?" Ellie called out tentatively.

She tried the handle to one of the steel doors. She expected it to be locked. It wasn't.

Gently, she turned the rounded handle. Ellie heard a faint click as the mechanism inside the lock pulled back. The door swung open. Ellie moved softly forward, her burning curiosity overpowering her cautious sensibilities. Curiosity was part of Ellie's nature. She couldn't pretend to be disinterested. Even if it was dangerous, she had to find out.

Edging through the door, Ellie didn't know what to expect. But she didn't expect to be looking at three single beds with restraints attached. Her intrigue growing, Ellie walked fully into the room. She stared at the small, black, metal boxes by each of the beds. At first, Ellie thought they were testing the flow of an electrical current. Then she examined them closely and noticed a thick cable rolling out the back and along the skirting. Ellie tracked the thick cable to a cupboard. One glance at the sign of a stick man zapped by lightning confirmed to Ellie it was an electrical supply junction box.

Slowly, she backed away, horrified, and swung a look back at the restraints tagged against the beds. Ellie shuddered as her body flushed with cold, and she tried to stop her mind from imagining the obvious horrors the room had seen.

Fear instantly shot through her. Ellie vacated the room hastily and ran back into the corridor. The torture chamber she'd wandered into declared that this 'hospital' wasn't being run by the NHS.

Where in God's name was she? And why couldn't she remember anything?

She stared at the green doors and green walls. She'd seen that color before. Her mind flashed back. Speeding down the M3. On the other side of the road, a convoy of army trucks. Their color had been the same shade of green. Combat green. It hit her. She was in a military facility.

The random thoughts that had been circling furiously in her mind clicked into gear. Was this connected to Sam? Wasn't MI short for Military Intelligence? Yes. All this had to be because of Sam. Maybe this was MI6. Or maybe it wasn't. Ellie was unsure. Should she carry on searching for someone? Or should she just try and find an exit? An escape route.

Ellie continued warily, constantly searching for signs that could validate one of her assumptions. Was she in the arms of the friend or the enemy? Her forehead wrinkled and she bit her lip, unsure of what to do next.

Her consternation over the dilemma was captured by the camera that followed Ellie as she walked gingerly past the next door.

Chapter 15

Across the Al Nadir workforce network of spies, in-government operatives, rogue agents, assassins and freeloaders, a message popped up on their secure phones: $30M target and an image of Sam Noor's face. The sender was seen by all. It was their great founder and leader, Dr. Salim Al Douri himself.

In Langley, in the restroom, inside a cubicle, the senior-level analyst who spilled the beans on the CIA's capture of Stein-Muller, Lupez and Rasheed to Salim stared at his alternative phone. It was a phone whose operation wasn't even on the CIA's radar due to its advanced comms running over a cloaked satphone network.

The analyst recognized Sam's face immediately.

He swallowed as he looked at the $30M flashing brightly like an online casino ad enticing him to spin the wheel. Did he have it in him to kill another person?

The analyst pocketed his burner phone and stepped out of the cubicle. He caught his reflection in the mirror in front of the pristine white wash basins. Short, tubby, approaching the bad side of fifty. He recalled Sam. Tall, muscular, imposing. The kind of guy who you'd avoid at all costs in a bar brawl.

Then the analyst thought about what he could do with $30M.

A completely new life.

He could leave his loveless marriage; Avril and her constant jibes of 'you're just not good enough' could soon be an evaporating memory.

He could leave his ungrateful kids; their constant view that he was a bank and that life owed them a living, all the while obsessed with brain-dead celebrities and getting likes on Instagram, or whatever the hell next platform of mindless engagement, had long since confirmed they had no place in his life.

He could leave his job; he'd been passed on promotions so many times he'd lost count, all because he didn't carry the right look, have the right balls-out attitude, and shit on people instead of helping them.

He could reinvent his life.

Everything would be a breeze with $30M.

He flicked a glance back at the mirror.

If he could only find the strength to kill Sam Noor.

Chapter 16

Several layers beneath where the senior analyst pondered in the restroom, Sam stepped through the threshold of a cell. His heart quickened and he could feel the heat of rage surging up.

A largely built man with grey-blond hair in an orange jumpsuit and chains on his wrists and ankles sat on a bench. He turned his head away the moment Sam entered. The man's reaction spiked at Sam's shield of control. He gripped both hands into tight balls, his nails digging into his flesh, and advanced.

"Stein-Muller, you and I have some talking to do." Sam tried to keep his words stable and measured.

The man didn't revolve to face him.

Sam sighed and breathed deeply. The rage inside was increasing. He had to control it. He had to try not to remember Kinley, not recall his sweet wife Angie, and their angel of a daughter, little Lotte. Sam had to forget, lest he descend into the hell that beckoned within his rage, and rip Stein-Muller apart.

"You have been busy, haven't you? The next-gen nanobomb. Creating it from smart dust. Quite something. I bet Al Nadir gave you a medal for that. Or another twenty million dollars in your black account in the Caymans."

Stein-Muller's mouth slipped into a slight grin as he faced the wall, but he still said nothing.

"Pity the frequencies weren't masked properly," mocked Sam. "But I guess, as you're sitting here, you already realized that mistake."

Sam walked forward until he stood directly over the rogue scientist.

"Sabena killing the Kinleys with your new bomb, now that really was the wrong move. I'm sure Sabena's ass is smarting from the punishment Salim will have administered for such a fuck up."

Sam detected a quiver of a smirk at the side of Stein-Muller's face.

"Especially as it led to his precious Rasheed being taken."

Sam moved to sit down next to Stein-Muller but didn't touch him. As Sam's weight hit the bench, Stein-Muller shuffled a little to the side and kept turned to the wall.

"Kinley's an interesting case, isn't he? I mean, he was loyal to Al Nadir for more than four years. Took you guys to new heights. So why did Sabena decide to kill him? What changed?"

Stein-Muller remained silent.

Sam raised his eyebrows, breathed rhythmically, and rubbed his hands on his thighs.

"Into pain, are you, Stein-Muller?"

Stein-Muller flinched at Sam's inference.

"I suggest you talk."

Stein-Muller slid further to the left-hand side of the bench, away from Sam. Sam shoved up closer to the scientist.

"Tell me, why was it necessary to take out the whole family? Why didn't Sabena just shoot Kinley when they were on an op together?"

Sam swallowed, holding down his wrath. He wanted to give Stein-Muller a chance to speak. He knew he wasn't a true terrorist like Rasheed. He was only a man who had used his scientific talent in a very evil way.

"Really, Stein-Muller, I think you should speak to me now. Or at least look at me!"

Sam knocked against Stein-Muller's arm, attempting to get his attention. But the man pulled back and hunched up into the far corner of the bench beside the wall.

"Look at me for God's sake!"

Sam felt his voice deepening with emotion. The words were being dragged from him and his breathing was labored. Time slowed. He was aware of what was rising within him: all the hurt of the last few hours since he'd heard of Kinleys family's demise. He did his best to wrestle the feeling.

"Why kill his wife? She knew nothing. She was innocent to everything."

Sam allowed his feelings to wheedle into him. Little by little. The coldness that had flushed through his body now iced over his humanity.

Sam glared at Stein-Muller as visions poured into his mind. His and the Kinleys' last meal in the lounge, all together. Sam in a comfy chair, and Kinley, Angie and their four-year old daughter, Lotte, curled up on the sofa watching 'Frozen'.

Just like when he'd heard the news of their deaths, the vision blew apart, And suddenly, that rage Sam had been trying to control burst out with a force unstoppable.

"Why Lotte?" he screamed.

Sam's black eyes, like coals of hatred, burned into Stein-Muller. Before the scientist could process what was happening, Sam grabbed him off the bench and threw him against the wall. Without a second to spare, Sam drove his balled, rock-hard fist into the man's face. As it connected with his nose, he heard a crack and blood flowed down Stein-Muller's face. Sam slammed his fists into his prisoner, hitting his body, punching him relentlessly until the man dropped to the floor. Sam didn't stop. He pulled him back up to a standing position and pummeled his body again. Stein-Muller, although a hideous individual, wasn't an operative. He wasn't trained in tactics of hand to hand combat. He had no way to defend himself from Sam's unyielding onslaught.

He only yelped in pain as Sam's fists flew.

Stein-Muller slipped down to the floor, broken by the persistent pounding of Sam's iron fists. Sam didn't bother to haul him back up again. He could see Stein-Muller could hardly stand. Instead, Sam switched to kicking. He rammed his foot into Stein-Muller, striking him in the face, ribs, stomach, genitals, thighs. Everywhere down his body. Stein-Muller tried to draw himself up into an embryonic ball, but Sam dragged the man's hands away from his face, forcing him to straighten.

"They didn't need to fucking die!" yelled Sam, as he launched into a further bout of unrestrained violence, hammering into Stein-Muller's trembling body with feet and fists.

Stein-Muller didn't move.

Finally, Sam's blistering hot rage abated.

On the floor, Sam saw Stein-Muller eyes closing. He tugged up his bloody and bruised body, and sat it back on the bench. Stein-Muller heaved up, vomited, and slumped sideways.

"Stein-Muller, you stupid fucker. You listen to me. Al Nadir made it personal when they took out the Kinleys with your new nanobomb. You made it personal when you ignored me just now. I came in here, and despite what your bomb did to the Kinleys, I didn't intend to hurt you. All I wanted was the truth. But you chose not to comply with my simple request to talk. You have only yourself to blame."

Sam turned away from Stein-Muller and made to leave the interrogation cell.

"You're no different to us," wheezed Stein-Muller slowly.

Sam whipped around on his heel. His eyes bore into the scientist.

"What do you mean?"

"You dress it all up, you speak of national security, the greater good, but in the end you're as vicious and cruel as we are."

Sam now faced Stein-Muller.

"Is that what you think?" said Sam skeptically, raising his eyebrows and he tilted his head. The rogue scientist shivered under Sam's defiant glare. "Well, the last time I looked, British Intelligence didn't kill an innocent wife and their little daughter."

As he spoke, Sam's mind flashed back to the wreckage of Piccadilly Circus and the body parts strewn across the burning pavement. He breathed in. He couldn't let the past haunt him.

"No," said Stein-Muller. "But they let that animal Kinley run rogue, killing, torturing, and doing whatever the hell he needed to get on. I saw what he did. He was no innocent. I doubt by the end he even knew what side he was really on."

Sam twitched. He would never believe Kinley had turned.

"You saw what you needed to see," said Sam. "But having Kinley there saved lives. All you've done is take them. You may think we're the same as you, but we're a million miles away."

"Believe what you want. That is your prerogative. But you were the one who wanted the truth."

Sam shook his head, refusing to listen. Deep within him, it was the truth he didn't want to acknowledge.

Chapter 17

Three military police officers watched the bank of monitors in front of them. Every few seconds, the images changed. Level D images popped up on their screens. They had the schedule for everything that was happening on the base. Level D had no activity at all that day. They gave the images a cursory glance and one of the MPs reached over to flick the channel back to Level A.

"Hold on, Joe. I just saw something." The second MP officer placed his hand over his colleague's, stopping him from changing the surveillance channel.

"You must be joking. It's dead as a dodo down there today." He shook his colleague's hand away.

"No. I saw something near the door. Back it up and run it. I'll carry on monitoring from this one."

"Okay. But I think you're seeing ghosts!"

He backed up the visual a few frames and ran it. An empty corridor showed.

"See. I told you. You're imagining things."

"Wait." The second MP watched the screen. He was sure he'd seen something. He pushed the visual forward frame by frame. Then she appeared. "Look!"

All three MPs stared at the little monitor. A woman with stunning features came into view. They wolf whistled when she looked straight into the camera. Now there was a woman they would *really* love to interrogate.

"Bring her up on the big screen. I want to take a closer look at her."

"Wouldn't we all," muttered his colleagues in unison.

"This is serious. M needs to be told of this." The first MP picked up the phone and dialed Maide's extension on Level A. "Sorry to bother you, sir, but we've got a security breach on Level D. A woman's been seen walking around the interrogation rooms. We have her on visual. We're tracking her now. She seems to be lost and frightened."

"What does she look like?" asked Maide, tension rising in his voice.

"She's Caucasian, tall, blonde and she's wearing a denim skirt and woolen jacket."

"Patch the op-link into me. Now," said Maide sharply.

The guard heard his boss breathe heavy, and then appear not to breathe at all.

"Sir?" the guard asked, perplexed by his boss' unexpected silence.

"Please detain her and keep her secure in room D03 until I arrive. Do not, I repeat, do not tell her where she is. But tell her that she is safe. She may be abusive. Keep your temper. She is a special…"

The guard didn't press his boss to quickly finish his sentence, as that would have been insubordinate. He just left Maide hanging on the line, mentally considering the right word to use.

Eventually, Maide found it. "She's a special friend."

"Yes, sir. Copy that." The guard radioed into one of his patrols. "All personnel on Level D, unauthorized woman seen near D4I. Detain and keep secure in D03 until M arrives."

The guard stared back at the screen and enjoyed another glance at the gorgeous woman, who had somehow found her way onto their interrogation level.

Chapter 18

Maide breathed hard and thought quickly. She couldn't possibly be alive. Could she?

It sounded like her. But how?

He had to see the intruder for himself.

The screen in front of him lurched into life showing the frozen frame of the woman caught by the CCD cameras. Maide glared at the woman, amazed and incredulous.

It *was* Ellie.

How in God's name?

Maide's throat was dry, his mind racing. They had no time for how, where or why. Only time for damage limitation. Maide breathed in, collecting himself, to stop his voice from cracking, as he gave his order to the waiting MP.

Maide replaced the phone then dialed it again. Quentin answered.

"You and Davison in my office now. We have a situation."

"Pardon!" Quentin said indignantly.

"Ellie Noor is alive. Get here now."

"What? How do you know?" asked Quentin.

"Camera caught her. I've got MPs holding her. I'll explain when you get here."

Maide slammed down the phone on Quentin before he could ask any more questions. Jesus Christ. What was happening? How could she be alive? What did she know? Had NMS wiped her memory of their interrogation?

Maide stood up and stared at her still on his screen.

"What are you, Ellie Noor?" he asked the silent image.

Quentin put down the phone and rubbed his ear. Maide slamming the phone down hard on him caused his ears to ring. The feeling accompanied the whirling sensation in his brain that he felt since he'd heard that Ellie was alive.

He couldn't believe what Maide had said. Quentin had seen her die. He had witnessed Davison undertake all the appropriate tests to conclusively confirm that she was dead. Short of doing a post-mortem, they had proved that Ellie Noor had definitely died during their interrogation. She had been dead for at least two hours. There was no record of anyone 'dying' for that period of time and then 'returning'. A couple of minutes, maybe, but not a couple of hours. What Maide was telling him was not humanly possible.

Until he saw it for himself, he couldn't accept it. Quentin picked up the phone and asked security to patch through the feed showing the woman on Level D. The image came direct to his PC. The slight bluish glow on his flat screen made the image look ethereal, like he was looking at a ghost. He stared at the screen. No question about it; the woman was Ellie. He shuddered, remembering how he'd dived into the interrogation room and found her dead. Her beautiful eyes had rolled back in her head and showed only ghostly white. He remembered checking her pulse and finding nothing. He remembered Davison coming in and sounding Ellie's chest with his stethoscope.

The doctor had shaken his head and stated, "Quentin, I'm sorry. She's gone."

He remembered her dying. How could she be alive?

Quentin turned away from his flat screen and dialed Davison.

"Ellie Noor is alive." Quentin didn't procrastinate on explanation. "We have to see Maide immediately."

He could hear the doctor spluttering with amazement.

Quentin ignored him. "She's being held in D03."

"How?" Davison said when he'd regained his ability to talk coherently.

"I don't know."

"But she can't be. I tested her. There was no brain activity. Her heart had stopped. Quentin, she was dead before she left the interrogation room. You know. You remember! I couldn't even use the paddles. Christ! I can't believe this."

"Neither can I. Not until I see her in the flesh." Quentin turned back to stare at the image. "Just get here. Now!"

Quentin slammed down the phone on Davison in the same way Maide had done to him. It was easier than entering into a convoluted explanation. They would all know the truth soon enough.

Chapter 19

The elder who had risen was similar in size to Aby-od, with the same stunning features: long, jet-black hair fixed with a clasp at the back of his head, a full beard that fell in silky corrugations, and a tall, muscular frame. But it was his eyes that were different. His black eyes lacked the compassion that shone from Aby-od's. This elder's eyes were illuminated with an ancient, cold wisdom and an utter disdain for everyone else. He had no time for primitives, especially those who made mistakes.

The elder was Lord Aswa-da, leader of the opposition from the House of Etima.

"Why should we wait for the Protector? It is obvious from our observations and current reports that the planet Ki has experienced a significant balance shift. They are already in the Zone of Great Risk. I do not believe the Protector will be able to redeem the position. I vote that we dispatch Ki."

Aswa-da stared ruthlessly at Aby-od. His posture exemplified his abject defiance of everything that Aby-od believed in.

The other elders clapped their hands together in support of Aswa-da's decision. Aswa-da watched as Aby-od looked around the hall. He could see the approval that showed in the faces of his peers. Even the elders from his own house were in agreement with Aswa-da.

Aby-od was backed against a wall.

His only play, Adwa-da knew, was to flip the disposition of the elders before they agreed on a decision to dispatch Ki.

"Lord Aby-od, what is your vote, Great Ensi?" Aswa-da's voice dripped with sarcasm and his eyes flashed with impertinence.

All heads turned to view Aby-od's reaction.

Aby-od tried to show he was impervious to Aswa-da's power play and theatrical orchestrations. Great Ensi was a term of respect for the ruler of Kudamun, but Aswa-da deliberately delivered the line with a caustic inflection portraying a total lack of respect.

Aswa-da had placed Aby-od in a moral corner with devastating political implications.

A vote for dispatch would sound the death knell for Ki. However, a vote against could potentially be perceived as weak leadership.

Abstinence was not an alternative.

Aswa-da had a line on the politics. Aby-od voting against the High Council's unanimous decision to dispatch Ki would leave him estranged. He would be isolated and vulnerable. In no way could he allow that position to manifest. But voting for dispatch would cast Aby-od's precious little planet into oblivion.

Aswa-da regarded Aby-od, who now stood before him, unmoving. Waiting.

It seemed the Leader of Kudamun had more patience than Aswa-da gave him credit for. Perhaps his belief in his favorite planet's Protector was also far stronger than Aswa-da could discern.

Patience, however, was not a virtue of the High Council.

Having grown tired of Ki's flagrant abuse of antediluvian laws, they did not consider the planet to be worthy of saving. They were eager to dispatch and move on. Aswa-da held down a smirk of satisfaction.

One thing he could always count on with the High Council was their cold, logical decisions, and their persistent dispassionate stance regarding the lives of those they watched over.

In the same emotionally detached manner a human may snuff out the life of an insect under foot, so the Kudamaz High Council issued their orders of dispatch, effectively snuffing out the life of entire planets under their own lethally charged cosmic foot.

Aswa-da, with the rest of the High Council, stared with growing impatient at their leader.

Aby-od was not surprised. In the past, he had faced similar examples of the High Council's obdurate position to planetary survival. And just like now, Aby-od had been saddened by their indifference.

Aby-od had always taken a different position. At times, almost at odds with the High Council, he'd worked directly with designated Protectors, assisting them in returning their planet's balance shift back to equilibrium. In the process, he had saved millions of species throughout the universe from dispatch.

Aby-od's hands-on approach was regarded as 'vulgar' and 'archaic' by the other elders in the council. But even they could not deny his unique methods had secured success for the Ruling House of Giznu.

Before that day, Aby-od had reflected on his past successes with a certain intrinsic pride, but he knew all his victories would descend into the mêlée of darkness if Ki was dispatched.

Ki's survival was essential, more essential than any other planet in the universe, for Ki had been given something by Aby-od's own forefathers.

Neither the High Council nor Aswa-da was privy to this knowledge.

Only Aby-od had been blessed with the information so sacrosanct that, not even on pain of death, would he reveal the identity of that which was trapped on Ki.

Chapter 20

Two MPs walked down the corridor, approaching a corner.

"Subject on the other side of the corner," said the MP in the control room into the earpieces of his two colleagues.

"Copy that," said the first MP, and he took his gun out of its holder.

They rounded the corner, facing the intruder. The woman looked afraid. They were cautious, recalling the explicit instructions from their chief. She was a 'special friend'.

Ellie stood in front of the MPs. She eyed them up and down and looked confused and in pain. She held her head and pulled an agonized face as she swallowed.

The MPs could see she was very agitated and in obvious discomfort.

"Oh, God! At last. Someone is in this place. Where the hell am I? Is this a hospital? Am I ill? How did I get here? Come on. Talk to me. Where the hell am I?"

Ellie machine-gunned the MPs with her questions. They looked at each other. Neither expected her to be forthright. She looked so timid in the images.

"Miss-"

"I'm a Mrs. Okay?" retorted Ellie angrily.

"Mrs. Right." The MP raised his eyebrows to the ceiling. Why did he *always* get the difficult ones? He started again. "Well, you're safe. There's no reason to worry. Come with us. Someone wants to meet you."

He took Ellie gently, but she pulled away, lifting her arm up and out of his grasp. Ellie stared with fixed intent at the MPs, and again, examined them from head to foot. The MPs shuffled awkwardly. They didn't like such blatant inspection by a woman.

"Who wants to meet me?" Ellie snapped. She stood firm, not moving or allowing herself to be moved.

"Our boss," stated one of the MPs cautiously.

"I'm not going anywhere," proclaimed Ellie, folding her arms and sitting down on the floor. On her face was a scowl of utter defiance to authority. "Not until you tell me exactly where I am."

The MP shook his head and bent down a little to grab Ellie's arm and pull her up, but she yanked him downward. The MP, taken unawares, momentarily lost his balance. He was only stopped from falling against the wall by his colleague, who steered him back.

Ellie smirked. Her expression was disdainful.

The MP noticed she was looking at the color on the walls. Then she asked, "Is this a military base? Are you MI6?"

In her eyes, the MPs could see she wasn't scared. Instead, she was fearless and determined. The MPs were worried. M had explicitly stated that she was not to be told where she was. But somehow, she had already figured it out for herself. They weren't sure how to proceed. One of the MPs moved away from Ellie, out of earshot, and spoke into his cuff microphone.

"Sir, she's sitting on the floor. She's refusing to move. She won't go anywhere until we tell her where she is. Sir, she asked if this was a military base, if we were MI6. What do I tell her?"

Like before, the line went silent for a moment. The MP waited for the chief to decide on the next course of action. It was beyond the pay grade of the MPs to even consider what to do.

"Keep her there. I'm coming down," Maide said wearily.

"M is coming down," stated the first MP to his colleague, who nodded and stared at Ellie.

Ellie pulled her jacket tight around her and glared. The MPs could see her anger building. They tensed on their guns.

"You know what you are?" Ellie shouted impulsively from the floor.

The MPs looked confusedly at the woman who appeared so gentle and sweet, but now almost glowed with hatred.

"You're all a bunch of perverts."

"Excuse me?" said the MP, bewildered by Ellie's outburst.

"And sickos," Ellie continued. "I saw those *machines*. God. How do you live with yourselves?"

The woman in front of the MPs was now screaming. She held her head and her eyes were sweeping back and forth between each of the men. She had flickers of fear but her raging attitude suppressed it.

The MPs looked bemusedly at each other. What *was* she on about?

"Sorry, madam, we don't know what you're referring to."

"No, of course you don't, Mr. Innocence 'doing-it-for-Britain' MI6 spy person. But I *know* what goes on here. The same as I *know* how you spied on us. God. My husband is one of your lot. He's a top agent and you still fucking spied on us, you bastards."

"What do you mean, your husband's a top agent? Who *is* your husband?"

Chapter 21

Sabena had only joked about wringing the truth out of Ashton. But now, as Godley, her trusted Cabinet ally, seemed to be taking an inordinate amount of time to provide a final reassurance about the exact location of the Peace Summit, Sabena knew she'd have to take drastic measures of her own.

Judy Katzenberger, the well-known and respected political journalist with a nifty line in short designer suits and fluttering eyelashes, was just about the only journalist who appeared to have unfettered access to the PM. From the intel gleaned by Sabena's summit team, who'd hacked the woman's phone, tablet and laptop, Katzenberger was due to be at Number 10 for lunch that day. Sabena brought intel up on Katzenberger. Swish apartment just down from Millbank Tower. Lived and breathed politics 24/7. Had a taste for French food and wine. Enjoyed the odd puff of grass and had been seen snorting coke at West London dinner parties. Appeared not to have anyone special in her life. And, from the photos in her encrypted folder, she flip-flopped between male and female partners.

Sabena smiled. Quite a lot to work on.

Katzenberger's diary had her working from home. Sabena requested a hack stream on her tablet from her summit team, and within minutes, Katzenberger's face popped up on Sabena's tablet.

Well hello, Judy!

Katzenberger had an elfin, soft face, with disarming deep brown eyes, full, luscious lips, and dark brunette hair similar to her own. Sabena captured her face and imported it into Stein-Muller's nanomask software program. The software quickly deconstructed the topology of the face, picking up various vector points and skin tone. Sabena's phone buzzed. In the smiley face app that denoted Stein-Muller's nanomask software, Katzenberger's face came up in her list.

Sabena took out the nanocream from her bag. Anyone not knowing its power would just think it was expensive face cream in a squarish, squashed glass jar with a gold screw top. Sabena grinned as she dipped a slender finger inside the slightly greyish cream and smoothed it into her skin. She could feel a light tingle across its surface and knew it was the electro-magnetic residue within the nanocytes within the cream. They were ready to connect and start re-sculpting her face to Katzenberger's specifications. Sabena always felt a thrill of excitement as she put on the cream.

Becoming someone else was such a turn on for her. Somewhere inside, Sabena knew that must 'mean' something, but as she wasn't into all that psychobabble claptrap, any inner meaning could go take a hike!

Sabena checked Katzenberger's address. Just a short drive, maybe ten minutes at the most from where she was in her Al Nadir owned hotel in Victoria. She touched on the smiley face app to invoke the nanomask program and glanced at the approximate transform time: fifteen minutes. She could stay in the car until the process had finalized.

She took out the tablet and brought up the feed into Katzenberger's apartment. The woman's elfin face jumped onto the screen again. Katzenberger was staring hard at the screen in deep concentration, and Sabena could hear the reverberating tap-tap of the keyboard through the tablet's speaker.

Sabena picked up the hotel phone and dialed Katzenberger's mobile. Two rings. Sabena watched as she picked up her phone and scrunched up her face, trying to recall the number. Three rings.

Come on, Judy. Pick it up. There's a good girl.

Fourth ring.

Katzenberger flipped her head to the side, trying to figure out who was calling, then she frowned, looking annoyed. Sabena thought she was about to decline, but-

"Yes? Who is this?"

Katzenberger's brittle bite came through clearly on the phone. So much for your sweet elfin face, eh sweetheart.

"Is that Judy Katzenberger?" Sabena put on an American accent, cultured New England, of a gentle persuasion.

"If you've got this fucking number, you know who I am, but who the hell are you?"

Sabena watched Katzenberger on her tablet. Fiery little miss, aren't you? Fancy we could play a nice game together if I had the time.

"I'm Ellen Chancer. I'm on President Treeborne's summit team, and I've got something you may be interested in. And perhaps Prime Minister Ashton may be interested too."

Sabena listened and watched as Katzenberger typed furiously, checking who Ellen Chancer was. Katzenberger moved her head forward, her eyes scanning the info on screen. What she was reading, Sabena knew, was Ellen Chancer's background. Chancer, a Harvard graduate in International Politics, had been a White House intern, and later was brought in to be part of the advisory team for Foreign Secretary Dick Cowl. She had recently been seconded onto the president's summit team where Secretary Cowl was deputy chair.

Katzenberger's eyes grew wide with amazement.

"Miss Chancer, you're here already. Is Secretary Cowl with you?"

Sabena knew she had to be careful. Katzenberger would definitely check her authenticity. Sabena had verified Cowl's whereabouts earlier with her DC ground team. Cowl hadn't left, but was in preparation to do so. Chancer had already left ahead of her team to be in London. She was staying in an apartment block owned by the US government in Belgravia. Al Nadir had eyeballs on her, and they confirmed she hadn't left since arriving on the red eye flight that morning.

"No. He's back in DC. I have friends I wanted to catch up with before it all happens." Sabena's tone was conversational and a touch reserved.

"Right. So why are you calling me?" snapped Katzenberger, and Sabena watched her sneer at the phone.

"As I say, I have something that may be of use to you. And to Prime Minister Ashton. I know you and him get on pretty well."

On Sabena's tablet, Katzenberger's eyes glinted and she smiled broadly. Her tongue flicked out swiftly licking her lips at Ashton's name. "You're well informed, Miss Chancer. When do you want to meet? Tonight? I can't do lunch, I…erm…have to be somewhere else."

"Could we meet in half an hour?"

Sabena watched Katzenberger look down at her watch, and then pouted, appearing torn between whatever she was writing and meeting with Chancer, who may have the potential to become a White House source. Katzenberger rubbed her eyes, and moved her hands down her face. Sabena thought she seemed suddenly tired.

"I'm on a deadline."

"Look, that's okay. Forget it if you're too busy. I'll find one of your colleagues."

Katzenberger's competitive streak fired. "No. Look, fuck it. Let's do this. Thirty minutes. You're on. Beansprout Café on the Embankment. You know it?"

"I'll find it."

"But this had better be good."

"It's Pulitzer Prize winning good, Miss Katzenberger!" said Sabena, living it up in the role. Katzenberger's reaction on the tablet was exactly what Sabena expected. She beamed at the enticement.

"Call me Judy."

"See you soon, and please call me Ellen. I have a feeling we're going to become close friends."

Katzenberger nodded on Sabena's screen. "Me too."

Chapter 22

Aby-od knew if the sacred silence was broken, it would endanger every planet in their care. But in remaining quiet, Ki was at risk of being destroyed by Kudamun's High Council for its grave misdemeanors.

But Aby-od also knew that destroying Ki would change the universal equilibrium and eradicate the finely tuned balance that presently existed.

"Are you going to vote, Great Ensi?"

Aswa-da's voice brought Aby-od out of his ponderous thoughts and back to his present focus. The dark lord's repetition served only to undermine Aby-od and underline his weakness. Aswa-da had the dominant position. Aby-od had no alternative but to speak.

"Honorable members of the High Council, hear this. We awaken the Protector if our own measures do not restore the balance shift to equilibrium. Only in extreme cases, when the Protector cannot align the equilibrium, do we have the ancient authority to dispatch a planet. Remember it is a requirement under ancient law to show that a planet awaiting dispatch is a planet that presents a serious threat to other planets in the universe. In short, honorable members, we have to show evidence that a planet is on an irreversible path of self-destruction. Only then do we have the right to dispatch. If any of our honorable members wish to circumvent the protocol and breach our antediluvian laws, then they must expect to be charged and tried on the grounds of grand treason under the order of Kudamun. Are there any members wishing to dispatch Ki?"

Silence fell across the hall. Aby-od continued his show of strength.

"Can I, therefore, take it that no members here today wish to pursue dispatch of the planet Ki before the Protector has been given due time to align the equilibrium? In the light of this clear show of confidence, I vote that we all follow protocol and awaken the Protector. Or live with the consequences of our hurried actions."

With the threat of death for grand treason, the elders were submissive.

"It is agreed then that we will awaken the Protector."

The members of the High Council from both houses stood up and clapped.

Aswa-da clapped slowly and bowed his head, respectfully indicating that, for now, Aby-od had won.

Chapter 23

Maide heard the voice of the MP coming through on his speaker phone. Maide's eyes hadn't moved from the screen. It was like he was entranced by Ellie's image. Captured on screen, she was something beautiful to behold. Captured in real life, she was a pain in the ass.

Why couldn't she have stayed dead? God knows what was going to happen now.

Maide left his office and headed down to the basement. In his earpiece, he listened with growing worry to the conversation between his MPs and Ellie. He turned the corner and caught the moment before Ellie had time to answer and tell them the name of her husband.

"I'll take it from here. That'll be all." Maide looked fiercely at the MPs. They didn't need telling twice.

"Yes, sir," said the first MP.

The two MPs clicked their heels quickly, saluted and departed.

Maide waited until they had fully disappeared around the corner then he turned to Ellie, now red-faced, her temper erupting like Vesuvius.

"My dear, you've awoken. Thank God."

Maide turned on the charm. It wasn't difficult. She was gorgeous. Sam was a lucky man. He smiled and took her arm, careful to take her left and not her right.

"Where the fuck am I?" Ellie screamed.

"Now, now, there's no need to be rude."

"Yes. There is. I've got a headache. No one's told me anything. This is all because of Sam, isn't it?"

"Sam?"

"Yeah. Sam Noor. My husband. I'm in this hell hole because he told me he worked for you."

Maide feigned astonishment. She was so bloody quick. Even after all she'd been through, she saw through everything so damn easily. He had to be extremely careful.

"I'm not sure I know what you're talking about."

"Yes. You do. Don't lie. You know *exactly* what I'm talking about."

"I assure you, Mrs. Noor. I do not."

"What did you mean by awoken?"

"Excuse me?"

"When you saw me just now, you said, 'My dear, you've awoken. Thank God'. What did you mean?"

Maide's reactions were well below par. Maybe the shock of seeing Ellie alive had jumbled his reflexes. He couldn't justify any reason for saying that line. He certainly didn't mean it. If it had been up to him, she'd be six feet under. But say the line, he had, unthinking and bordering on stupid, and now he had to live with the consequences.

"What did you mean? What have I 'awoken' from? And why was I in a bloody morgue?"

"Erm…"

"For Christ's sake. Answer me. Why am I here? Was I in a coma? Did you think I was dead? Why wasn't Sam informed? You must know. You seemed pleased I had awoken. Tell me."

Ellie's persistence shot straight to Maide's cerebral cortex. His nervous system frazzled as he realized that this situation would never get any better.

"Why don't you come this way and we can talk about it over a cup of tea?"

Maide pulled her gently but she remained still. Ellie Noor was more than a handful. Maide desperately controlled his impulse to slap her face. Sam's wife or not, he couldn't abide insolence from a woman. In a different time, in a different place, he would have enjoyed showing her some of his unique form of discipline.

"I'm not moving until you tell me what I need to know."

Ellie was infuriatingly, unbendingly obstinate.

Maide stared at her stubborn eyes. His only way out was to trick her. Slowly he nodded, giving Ellie the impression he had caved in to her questions.

"You have been asleep. You've been ill. I promise you, I'll explain everything," said Maide with a resigned sigh.

"Why wasn't Sam told?" Ellie started, glaring with rage at Maide.

"He has, and he is returning from the US. Please walk with me. You have a right to know the truth."

Maide took the stance of a doctor informing his patient of her terminal disease, professional but compassionate. In his pocket, his fingers grasped the smooth body of the hypodermic.

Ellie was still immobile and still staring angrily. But her dirty mouth had stopped shouting.

"Please, come this way," said Maide. "I promise you, Mrs. Noor, you will know everything."

Maide's soft enticement worked. Beckoning chivalrously for Ellie to follow in front of him, Maide smiled. Ellie continued her vitriolic glaring but accepted the gesture and joined Maide. The moment after Ellie had passed him, Maide was in her blind spot. Using it as cover, according to the tactics taught by stealth combat, Maide whipped out the hypo and drove it hard into her neck.

The choral hydrate worked instantly. Ellie dropped to the floor like a used tea towel in a sagging heap.

Maide breathed deeply, crouched down and picked her up. Her fragile look belied her weight. Ellie had been a gym freak, and although recently she hadn't attended as much, earlier months of body building had made her body firm and surprisingly muscular. Maide positioned Ellie in his arms and straightened up. An unexpected puff escaped through his lips, but not because he was out of shape. No, he was in good shape. But he had expected Ellie to be lighter and hadn't had chance to compensate.

Desk bound, Maide's field service had finished a long time ago but that didn't stop him training in his own private gym every morning.

Looking into the mirror, Maide didn't see himself getting older, just more experienced. He considered himself more than capable of doing field work, even now, and he chastised agents if they appeared to hesitate or falter in making a decision. That was why he admired and feared Sam.

Sam never vacillated. Right or wrong, he got the job done. Nothing stood in his way. Maide glanced down at Ellie. If Sam could see him now. He shuddered, knowing full well what Sam would do, and could do, given the chance.

That was what scared him, knowing that his ghoulish thoughts weren't the product of an over-active imagination. Maide had read a very real operations report that detailed how Sam, in a moment of extreme rage, had 'dug his fingers into the shoulder of the assailant and tore his arm out of its socket'. The comparison, condemned as sick at the time, described the action as 'tearing a chicken leg off of a Sunday roast'.

The assailant had died through a combination of shock and excessive bleeding, and Sam's fellow agent ended up in therapy.

If he was to avoid Sam's wrath, and God knows, Maide wanted to avoid Sam's wrath, he knew he had to get Ellie off the base immediately. No time could be wasted. Sam was safe at Langley, but he would call her sooner or later. He was a doting husband. If he got her voicemail too many times, he would know something was wrong.

She had no meetings to attend, no business to engage in. Ellie would be waiting on his every call, and Sam would know that. Sam would start to investigate and piece things together. The truth would unravel, and everyone involved would be held under suspicion. Maide couldn't risk Sam ever knowing.

Actions had to be swift and precise. In his current confused state, he couldn't think clearly. He couldn't make any more slip ups like the one he made in front of her. He had to use others as a sounding board.

Maide continued down the corridor to D03, deep in thought.

Ellie lay heavily in his arms, reflecting the heavy fear in Maide's heart for his own survival.

Chapter 24

After ringing off from Katzenberger, Sabena touched her earpiece.

"Get the car now. I'm ready."

Inside the black Audi SUV, Sabena pressed on the app and selected Katzenberger's face. The command <ACTIVATE> came up on screen. Sabena tapped on it and almost instantly felt her face tingling like an electrical current was bouncing across her epidermis. She noticed her skin was warming up as the nanocytes activity intensified, creating Katzenberger's facial topology over her own. Her face rounded and her chin became pointy. Sabena's high cheek bones had a little extra weight to them, and her lips filled out into more of a heart shape rather than the wide snarl of vermillion she always carried on her natural face.

Within fifteen minutes, the nanomask was complete.

Leaning over, Sabena popped open a drawer housing transdermal RFIDs, phials in different colours, and strange looking cellophane packs with tiny dots in them. Sabena reached in and selected a phial containing a light-yellow liquid. She held it up in her slender, strong fingers and made a face. She always preferred to create a new personality rather than impersonate an existing one. The face was easy to disguise, but a person's voice was an immediate give away.

Sabena knew that much of the brain's recognition processing was created by visual stimuli; you see someone with the same face and accept that person to be the real one, even if their voice doesn't sound quite the same. The visual stimuli can be overpowering; thus any slight vocal change and the brain tends to compensate and accept it ahead of other senses. However, Sabena was aware that even for such compensation, enough of the verbal recognition needs to be activated to enable acceptance by the brain.

Sabena ran the recording of Katzenberger's voice captured on her tablet and hit an in-software app, another smiley face, but this time in blue.

'Analyzing' came up on screen.

Sabena swallowed heavily. What I do for you, Salim, she thought. Then she snapped off the fixture at the top of the phial.

'Complete. Ready for voice box assimilation'.

She opened her mouth, tipped the full contents of the phial into her throat, and simultaneously hit on the command that appeared on screen, 'Transmit'.

Sabena dropped the phial as a surge of electricity flowed through her, and her hands dug into the leather seat, shaking. Inside her throat, she knew, the nanobots had swarmed onto her voice box. Inside her larynx, the signal from the app had been transmitted to the nanobots, which now had the vital configuration to recreate the top journalist's voice. The signal gave the nanobots the vibratory frequency of the vocal folds together with the degree of separation of Sabena's vocal cords. The nanobots had taken control of her vocal cords to produce the correct amount of adduction (coming together) and abduction (separating) of the folds thereby creating an exact imitation of Katzenberger's voice. Such control couldn't be given over, for an extended time, as the nanobots had the potential to damage the carrier's vocal cords irreparably. Stein-Muller had always given her the two-hour max warning, and she never went past his sage instructions. Sabena hated the constant acidic chemical taste and the sharp electrical pricks like needles in her throat. But she knew, with security tighter than anything she could penetrate normally around Ashton, this full impersonation of Katzenberger was the only way she was going to get close to the British PM.

The tingling electrical charges had subsided. Her tablet flashed, 'Transmission complete. Awaiting activation.'

"Right, sweetheart, let's see about your eyes," said Sabena.

On the next shelf were a range of color and SmartLens contacts. She looked at the picture on her phone, then down at the selection, and picked up a dark brown pair of contacts that had the feel of Katzenberger's. Sabena popped them into her eyes, snapped open the mirror in the front headrest, and examined the transformation.

Sabena doubted Katzenberger's mother would be able to tell the difference.

On her tablet, she tapped on the tracker. Her summit team had uploaded an ID onto the journalist's phone when they'd hacked it earlier, enabling Sabena to quickly locate Katzenberger. She'd chosen to walk rather than take a cab for the meeting.

Sabena pulled out another drawer in her well-equipped SUV and chose an appropriate shade of lipstick, a dusky red. Through her darkened windows, Sabena watched Katzenberger striding forward with power in her step.

Zipping up her navy sweater, Sabena flung the hood over her head, slipped on her Gucci sunglasses, and made to alight the car as it pulled against the curb. With eyes on Katzenberger ahead of her, Sabena stepped out and continued to walk behind her target. Her sporty, leisure wear was so dramatically different to Katzenberger, those around her didn't give Sabena a second glance. No one clocked that the famous journalist's doppelganger was just a few steps behind.

Sabena could see Beansprout Café ahead of them, but before that, there was an alley. Sabena picked up her phone, pressed a button to alias the call, and dialed Katzenberger. Ahead of her, Sabena saw Katzenberger dive into her bag, retrieving her ringing phone.

"Yeah? What?"

"Judy, it's Ellen. Sorry, I can't meet at the café. I've just seen. It's way too open. Is there anywhere nearby?"

Sabena observed as Katzenberger looked to the right of her and down the alley. Then, as if instinct told her to, she marched down it.

"There's a tiny alley before you get to the café. Turn right and I'll meet you there."

"I'll be there shortly," confirmed Sabena, speeding up her walk.

Sabena turned into the alley swiftly, just a few steps behind Katzenberger. Without a second for Katzenberger to breathe, Sabena leapt on top of her and pushed her to the wall. Her lips encased those heart-shaped ones of Katzenberger with violent determination.

Katzenberger stared in total horror and confusion at Sabena, who now carried Katzenberger's face.

Sabena took out her phone and clicked on the flashing <ACTIVATE>.

A chilling look of satisfaction sneaked across her face. She touched her earpiece.

"Clean up now, on my location."

Sabena grinned as she heard Katzenberger's voice coming out of her mouth.

Katzenberger heard Sabena speak. Her eyes filled with sadness as she started to slip down the wall. The tetrodotoxin paralyzed her body, hitting her heart and respiratory system. Astonishment pronounced in the soundless.

"Why?" she tried to say.

Movement at the top of the alley caused Sabena to look up. Her three-man clean up team had arrived as paramedics. She could see the nose of their estate car poking into the alley.

Sabena whipped a tissue out from her pocket and carefully wiped away the poison from her lips. Then she stuffed it inside Katzenberger's open mouth.

Smiling, she said coldly, "Time to put a gag order on the press."

Chapter 25

Davison and Quentin arrived a few minutes after Maide laid Ellie on a trolley bed. The three men slipped into a side office in an attempt to keep the conversation private. Quentin looked back at the trolley and shook his head.

"You've knocked her out again?" began Quentin, his tone accusative.

"What choice did I have? She knew that she was in MI6. She knew her being here was connected to Sam. She wouldn't stop asking questions," said Maide, pressing down his building exasperation.

"What are we going to do?" asked Quentin, staring hard at Maide.

"We've got to get her out of here. We've got to find a way to cover up this bloody mess!"

"Have you tried talking to her?" suggested Davison.

"Talking to her?" Maide was close to incredulity. "What do you want me to say?" said Maide, glaring back at Davison.

"Well, you could have told her the truth."

"Are you completely insane?"

"I agree with Davison. What harm would it do?" said Quentin.

"Have you forgotten *who* her husband is?"

Maide was aware he was trembling. Davison ran a professional eye over him. Maide realized he was being scrutinized and straightened up.

"You do know what Sam would do to us if he ever found out about Ellie's incarceration. I don't know about you, but I intend to enjoy my retirement."

"I think you are being over-dramatic, Maide."

"Am I, Quentin? What do you think, Davison? You've read the field reports. You know how Sam handles situations. You think I'm being over-dramatic? Or risk averse?"

"Sir, I agree that Sam has a unique ability to-"

"He's fucking killing machine," said Maide. "I should bloody well know. I signed off all the damn requisitions for his advanced training."

"But, sir, that doesn't mean to say he would kill us. He's on our side."

"He won't be. Not if he knows we tortured and killed his wife."

"I still think you're dramatizing this. Sam isn't a problem. He knows about the Masters case. He knows the capabilities and reach of Al Nadir. He'll be sensible about this, and so will his wife."

"So you think I ought to tell her the truth about the interrogation?" said Maide. "How we took her against her will, used horrific drugs on her and killed her? Is that what you want me to tell her?"

Quentin and Davison were embarrassed. The idea of disclosure, put like that, did sound insane.

"Gentleman, we have a situation here that needs to be handled carefully," Maide continued. "God forbid it ever gets to the ears of the PM. If it does, we can all kiss goodbye to our golden handshakes. He's liberal in matters of interrogation and turns a blind eye to torture of real terrorist suspects. But this is different. Heads will roll. Literally."

"Why did we do it?" blurted Quentin suddenly. "I told you there would be consequences. I bloody warned you. But, as usual, you wouldn't listen."

"Spilt milk," replied Maide. "No good crying over it. We need to move on."

"We wouldn't need to move anywhere if you hadn't extracted her."

"Well, I did. I believed she could be a threat. I don't regret making that decision."

"I do," said Quentin, squaring up to Maide.

Maide stared hard back at him. Eye to eye. Both didn't blink.

"Well, that's too bad," said Maide, coldly cutting through Quentin's acrimony. "Now, as I said, we need to move on. Let's have your suggestions."

"A terrorist attack," suggested Davison, looking at Maide then Quentin for validation.

"Where and how?" said Maide, not giving anything away.

"At her apartment block. A hit by Al Nadir," Davison said, thinking fast.

"Why would they hit her block?"

"Hasn't Charles Godley got a place in Silent Waters?" Quentin chimed in.

"The defense secretary?" Maide said, his voice strained.

"Yes. Al Nadir could have been targeting him and got Ellie instead. What do you think?" said Davison, biting his bottom lip nervously.

Maide thought, then muttered, "I think it sounds lame."

"Godley's in the US at the moment," said Quentin, realizing that their idea wasn't as smooth as he'd hoped.

"Would Al Nadir know that?" Davison asked, looking at Maide.

"Of course they bloody would!" Maide said. "They monitor us as much as we monitor them. No. Godley as a target won't work. But I like the idea of having a target and Ellie getting in the way. Who else lives in Silent Waters?"

Maide walked over to the laptop terminal in the office, typed in his access codes and ran a query to select all residents in Silent Waters. The list flashed up on the screen.

"A few celebrities. Three footballers, a couple of soap stars, five pop stars. The place is obviously popular," said Maide, reading down the list. But he couldn't see anyone who could potentially be a political target for Al Nadir. There were ministers but they were all B-list, no-hopers.

"Couldn't we just say Ellie was the target?"

Quentin had a new idea gestating. He hadn't intended to speak until the idea had matured into a full-blown plan, but his excitement got the better of him. Now, looking at Maide's red face, full of fury, he wished he'd kept quiet.

"Go on," Maide said. His expression was near boiling point.

"Matthew Kinley was MI6. He was taken out yesterday. Al Nadir are getting personal, hitting our agents and their families. It's not inconceivable that they wouldn't think of hitting Sam's wife."

"Sounds plausible. Especially, as Sam was instrumental in the capture of three of their top global lieutenants today," muttered Maide, rubbing his chin, still in thought. "But we're going to have to have to intercept a transmission describing the attack through our surveillance channels at River House. It's going to have to be totally believable to everyone, including Sam."

"Oh, Jesus. He'll never buy it," Quentin said.

"He will if one of our operatives intercept the transmission. We'll keep Ellie sedated a little while longer until the transmission's been manufactured. Although Sam's caught up with Kinley's death, and those interrogations, he'll go crazy when he hears. Of course, he'll leave Langley immediately, which means we have…"

Maide looked at his watch. It was 2.55 pm. If they were to do this, they had to be quick. He raised his head to his waiting colleagues.

"Until midnight to get our story straight. Before Sam returns."

Chapter 26

The room was empty. Aswa-da slipped softly inside. Translucent smooth walls encased him. Every now and then, a misty light flickered beneath the surface like a firefly through greaseproof paper. Aswa-da's attention focused on the far side wall. Etched out in gold against the translucent wall was a seven-pointed star. A small circle was at its center. Raising his hand up, he brushed it over the circle. Melting away, the wall revealed an inner compartment. Aswa-da peered inside. Palm-sized crystals arranged in chocolate box configurations throbbed and pulsed with Technicolor rhythm.

One of them was important to him: a seven-sided crystal that glowed bright, pulsing a spectrum of color. Snatching the crystal, an inauspicious smile snaked across Aswa-da's noble features.

In his hand, the crystal continued to throb, but deep inside, its inner heart started to darken. Forced to change by sudden capture, the crystal grew darker every second Aswa-da's touch lingered upon its surface. Still smiling, Aswa-da brushed over the open compartment and the translucent wall took shape again. Atoms seemingly joined together in the wake of Aswa-da's sweeping hand.

Now fully formed, the wall did not look like it had ever been touched.

Aswa-da rolled the crystal, now a black diamond devoid of its former displays of color, in his hand. It had succumbed to the overpowering darkness completely. Secreting it amongst his silken ebony robes, his task complete, Aswa-da vacated the room silently and entered the barren corridor. The first phase had been activated.

Chapter 27

Inside a small, darkly lit office, with Ellie's body directly outside on a trolley, in the bowels of a black MI6 site in Berkshire, Quentin stood with Maide and Davison and began to hatch a plan that might keep them from being Sam's next target. Whether it would keep them all out of jail was something he had a significant question mark over.

Quentin was aware of his lower lip quavering. Maide stared at him as he gripped the side of a filing cabinet. Bile flooded within him, and he held the side tighter to prevent him from collapsing. How did they get into this mess?

Maide sighed and snapped, "What is it, Ludlow?"

Quentin's wide worried eyes connected with Maide's.

"You know we're committing a crime. We could all get locked up for this. Or at the very least, lose our jobs. Sam's Stateside isn't he. What if he takes matters into his own hands and gets someone at the CIA to contact one of our officers to qualify the intel?"

Maide stood up from the desk and walked toward Quentin, taking a dominating stance.

"Qualify the intel? I don't think so. It'll be coming from me, for God's sake. And do you really think, given the number of Al Nadir attacks, that someone's going to question a piece of intel about an attack that follows Al Nadir's current strategy of attacking high profile targets, like Kinley for instance?"

Put like that, Quentin didn't see how they could fail. He shook his head. But a persistent, nagging doubt surfaced, casting a shadow on his belief that they could execute their plan flawlessly.

"What about the two guys we used to bring Ellie in?" Quentin said. "And the interrogator who saw her die? How do we handle them?"

Quentin started to tremble again. It was all getting more complex. The two men who captured Ellie were Maide's people. They were safe. The interrogator, however, was more difficult. He had originally been told that the woman was a suspected Al Nadir spy and that her target was Sam Noor.

"What do you suggest?" Maide looked at Quentin for answers. "You were there with him. Does he know she's Sam's wife or not?"

The interrogator had not known Ellie's true identity. He'd been given a set of questions with the usual minimal information about the suspect. It wasn't until Davison had burst in, blurting out, 'Jesus. That's Sam Noor's wife' that the truth had been revealed.

Quentin remembered how the interrogator had been mortified. Guilt had shifted over his anxious face when he realized the duplicitous actions that he'd been party to. He had silently vacated the interrogation room amidst fervent attempts from Davison to revive Ellie. He hadn't been seen or spoken to since. That had been a negligent oversight.

"He screamed out," said Quentin, accusing Davison.

"I was in shock. I didn't expect…" muttered Davison in defense.

Maide waved his hand to halt his explanation. "Well, we only have one course of action. Tell him the truth. Everyone here knows the Sarah Masters story. Use that to vindicate your actions. Don't go into too many details and let him know that Davison saved her life."

Quentin nodded. But he was aware that inconsistencies to their plan still plagued their chance of success.

Maide detected his reticence. "Something wrong?" he asked sharply.

"How is all this going to work?" Quentin said. He'd heard how they going to fabricate the lie. But how were they going to stage Ellie's rescue?

"I've just explained it," replied Maide.

"No. You've explained how we're going to cook up the evidence that Ellie was hit by Al Nadir. But as soon as that transmission goes out, we're going to have to get a real rescue squad out to Ellie."

"Yes. So?"

"But she's here. And there's no Al Nadir attack! How are we going to make that real?"

"We smuggle her out of this facility, stage a false flag attack, give it the hallmark of Al Nadir, and rescue her. Is that real enough for you?"

"Smuggle her out? What if someone sees? And what kind of attack are you planning? God, Maide. I don't like the sounds of this. What if it all goes wrong? What then?"

"Quentin, will you stop worrying? You're starting to sound like a whimpering girl. God, man, haven't you the balls for this anymore?"

Quentin's eyes sparked with fury. He could be just as cold and hard as Maide, but he liked plans to be watertight. The plan they were placing into motion still had far too many leaks for his liking.

"I don't like this at all. I don't like the smuggling bit. I don't like the attacking bit. And I don't like the fact that the interrogator knows the truth. He's a stray end."

"Then kill him." Maide's words came out of sheer frustration. It wasn't an intended solution. But his words scythed through Quentin's bickering.

"Haven't we done enough killing for one day?" Quentin's tone was openly confrontational. He'd had his fill of Maide. The man was turning in to a loose cannon, and he would bring everyone down with him when it all went wrong, as it inevitably would. If Maide expected Sam to believe it, he must be out of his mind.

Maide and Quentin glowered at each other.

"Then I'll leave the decision of the interrogator up to you, Quentin. You know your own business best." Maide was good at effortlessly shifting responsibility.

"Fine!" Quentin said, riled that Maide had off-loaded on to him, yet again. He whipped his head around, looking for someone to accuse for the debacle. He glared at Davison. "This is all your fault, Davison," Quentin quipped madly. "Why the hell did you have to open your bloody mouth?"

"I told you. I was in shock. I didn't expect to see Mrs. Noor sitting there, you know, exposed. And dead!" Davison shouted back.

"Oh, for Christ's sake," said Maide.

The three men glared at each other.

"We've got nothing to feel guilty about. Nobody died." Maide took a beat. "We acted correctly. It was all above board and in accordance with national security protocol."

Nobody spoke. Quentin was numb, and he could see Davison was still traumatized. Too much had happened. They just wanted to finish the plan and get on with their lives.

Quentin watched as Maide clearly mistook the silence for submission.

"Right. Okay. Good," Maide said, clapping his hands together, as if to finish off the discussion.

Quentin looked back through the door at Ellie. Her skin still had a faint blue tinge. She looked deathly peaceful. A shiver ran through him.

"Do you think we'll ever find out how?" Quentin asked.

"What? How she awoke? I don't know. What do you think, Davison? You're the so-called expert here." Maide's voice was tetchy. His sarcasm was obvious. Quentin recognized it always surfaced when Maide was faced with something he couldn't explain.

Davison took umbrage at the 'so called' reference. He stiffened his back and walked outside; the others followed. The three of them stared down at Ellie.

Davison turned his head and spoke back at Quentin. Medically speaking, he knew the doctor was on fragile ground.

"I can't explain how she came back to life. Maybe, and this is purely conjecture, but maybe, some effect caused by the drugs we gave her reacted with some other unknown agent that was already in her system and delivered the reaction that we construed as her death."

Maide held up his hand to stop Davison. Fear rose in his face. A fear generated by Ellie.

"So she could have had something inside her that appeared to kill her during our interrogation?"

"I don't know, to be quite honest. I've never in all my life encountered a situation like the one that occurred today."

"So what you're saying is that she could have been loaded, but with a different type of bomb. One that put her into say, a coma, then triggered a release that woke her hours later. Does that sound plausible?"

Quentin watched Maide. He rubbed his hands together. His mind was in racing mode. He rattled off his words, almost falling over his enthusiasm.

"I knew it. I bloody knew it. I'm right. She *is* Al Nadir. And we've got her."

Davison's expression curtailed Maide's exuberant position.

He shrugged. "It's plausible. But I don't think she was loaded," said Davison. "She was given NMS, right?"

Maide nodded, his face slowly falling out of its excitement. Quentin closed his eyes, recalling her painful screams.

"When they ran the gene sequencing from the DNA in her blood to build the NMS, the process would have detected and identified any agent in her blood that was alien," explained Davison. "It's been designed like that."

"Shit!" said Maide. "So maybe she's not Al Nadir. Maybe she's just a freak of nature."

"I'm going to do a full medical test on her. I'll get to the bottom of it," Davison said confidently.

"See that you do."

Quentin had been thinking. His face was pensive. "What if she remembers?"

"She won't. NMS has that effect," Davison confirmed.

But Maide was shaking his head. "On normal subjects, yes, I agree. It has that effect. But with Ellie, with what we've already seen, we can't be sure of anything."

"So how can we get around it?" asked Quentin.

"I think it would be safer for all of us if she had her short-term memory wiped permanently." Maide delivered his remedy and Quentin noticed without a shred of remorse.

"She could end up brain damaged. You know that process has errors." Davison was horrified by Maide's suggestion. He turned to Quentin for backup, who looked extremely uncomfortable.

"So, that's the price we pay," Maide said coldly.

"We don't pay any price. It'll be her that pays the price. We're getting ready to ruin her life," Quentin shouted furiously. Maide's cold efficiency had pricked his dormant conscience back to life. "God. Haven't we done enough to that poor girl? We killed her. We tortured her to death. You know that. You know we killed her in that room. I don't know how she's alive now. But I'm confident that NMS will deliver its amnesiac effect. Please. Don't touch her memory. She'll be a shell for the rest of her life if you do."

Quentin was shaking. He'd never considered that he had the inner power to expurgate such words. All his life, he'd been a yes man. He'd taken decisions, made choices and ruined lives systematically. His dual role with MI6 enabled him to rise quickly to one of the highest ministerial offices in the Cabinet. His goal was Number 10. But he was subservient to the grey individuals, people like Maide who commanded the real power.

"Now look, it's not a question of humanity," Maide began. "Of course, I don't want to ruin her life. But this is national security. We have to protect our country."

Quentin was sickened by Maide's sanctimonious demeanor. His position had always been unimpeachable, but distaste was now in the air. Quentin knew he could no longer contain his fury.

"National security? National security! She's a fucking wife. Not a spy. Not a terrorist. She's not Al Nadir. She's not a threat to our country. She's just Sam's wife, a man who has put his life on the line for us many times. All this started because we didn't trust Sam. We thought he was going off the rails.

Okay, he blabbed. He told his wife what he really did for a living. Big fucking deal. She's intelligent. She's no fool. She knew to keep tight-lipped about the information Sam told her. Why didn't we just trust Sam and monitor Ellie using our usual surveillance methods? All this interrogation was unnecessary. We made Ellie suffer for no reason. Please, Maide, don't let her suffer any more. You saw her. She doesn't know how she got here. Her memory has already been wiped by NMS. Please. Let's leave it at that."

Quentin finished his invective and looked back at Maide. He was totally exhausted.

Maide straightened and coughed. "You're wrong saying all this started with Sam. It started because Ellie screamed for no reason, spoke to an empty kitchen, and all that. We thought she was talking to her handler, that she was an assassin or a spy like Sarah Masters. But, okay, I understand your anxiety. We don't want her to suffer any more," Maide awkwardly conceded. "But I want those tests to conclusively prove there is nothing in her system before she leaves here."

Quentin's rampage had forcibly put Maide in his place and had won Maide's respect for the first time in their fifteen-year relationship.

"You know what you have to do, Davison," continued Maide. "Complete the tests and prep Ellie for transfer. I'll handle the intercept transmission and plan the attack. Quentin, you need to be on point following the hit. Gentlemen, let's turn this thing around."

Maide's voice was strained. Quentin knew he hated being spoken to the way he had spoken to him. But Quentin realized he'd given a clear rationale. Wiping Ellie's short-term memory could have resulted in even more problems. It was a damage limitation exercise; they already had more than enough damage to handle.

"Are we all clear?" Maide spoke abruptly. On his face, it showed he wanted this day over. He'd had enough.

Silent nods registered acceptance.

Chapter 28

Salim fingered the quantum compound in his hand. He pulled at it, fascinated by its auto-shaping properties. The strange twinkling compound popped back into shape, forming a rectangle again. Salim was intrigued by its physical behavior. He'd read up about the compound and how to use it from the files Sabena had downloaded from Treeborne's laptop. He smirked thinking about what Sabena had gone through to get that access. The vetting at the political fund-raiser had been reliably poor, despite the president being a guest of honor. Provide a sizable donation in millions, and Salim knew doors would open. Using Stein-Muller nanomask cream, Sabena had become a stunning Spanish heiress, and easily infiltrated into the dinner as a wealthy donor and staunch advocate of the party.

The rest had been up to Sabena and her ability to handle the rough stuff. Knowing Sabena's penchant for such activities, Salim didn't think the mission would have stretched her capabilities too much.

He picked up the sleek pen and brought it close to the sparkling compound. Within the strange iridescent material, Salim could see a bright light glowing. Although the pen hadn't been activated, its energy resonance close to the compound tapped latent energies from within the block at a higher quantum state.

Salim sat down the pen in the box, picked up his tablet, and tapped on HoloTab mode. The air in front of him lit up, bouncing with quantum equations, schematics, and energy flow patterns. Salim used his index finger to flick through the pages suspended in midair. He stared intently at the diagrams, absorbing all the pages contained. Sabena was the quantum queen, but it didn't hurt to bone up on that knowledge too. As he looked through the information, he shook his head. How *on earth* did Treeborne come up with something like this?

The presentment of the quantum information, its simple complexity, Salim could never believe had come out of that fat-assed idiot. He even doubted the US DoD had come up with it.

No, Treeborne had been given this by someone with an extraordinary mind. An almost superhuman one.

That thought concerned Salim.

Did the president really have someone like that behind him?

As if to acknowledge Salim's brooding thoughts, the president's face rolled up on the massive screen in the boardroom adjacent to the quantum lab he was in. Someone had left Fox News running. Salim placed the quantum compound back into the box and stood up with his fingers curled around it. He wandered into the boardroom to hear what Treeborne had to say.

"We are no longer going to bow down to Al Nadir and their sadistic leader, Al Douri. The tables are turning. That's all I'm going to say on this, folks. But hear this. I have God on my side and no one can stop me with that kind of firepower."

Treeborne shot a glare of dominance into the camera for broadcasting effect, and then turned away from the podium in the White House press room, amid calls of, "What do you have, Mr. President? How are you going to shift the balance, sir?"

Behind Salim, Maria, one of his faithful global lieutenants came up to watch. Maria was a pretty woman in her mid-twenties who'd joined Al Nadir when a recruiter had clocked her abilities in Harvard law school, and presented her with a financial compensation package she couldn't refuse. She sidled up to Salim, who slipped an arm around her trim waist, pulling her close. Salim could feel her pointy hips digging into him, and her rounded breasts pushing against his chest.

"Look at him," said Maria with disdain, indicating towards the television. "He doesn't even know we have his precious bomb. He's an absolute buffoon."

"He's a buffoon who has $100 billion of my money and I'm going to get it back."

"Your money? But I thought you said it was that tech CEO Kolchak who was behind Seeker going into market freefall?"

"Yeah, at first that's what Kinley lead us to believe. But it was all a pack of lies. I had my doubts, but you know, the guy was good, really good, at convincing me otherwise. I've since been able to dig into the facts. That nose dive was instigated by Kinley. It was a coordinated attack to break me financially."

Maria's eyes opened wide at this revelation. "What are you going to do?"

"I'm going to teach the world that if they screw with me, they're gonna get fucked hard."

"Well," murmured Maria, moving in on Salim's neck, "let's hope they have protection."

Chapter 29

With his colleagues gone, Davison was left alone with Ellie.

He shuffled about her bedside uncomfortably. He felt weird watching her chest raise and lower. She was breathing.

Shaking his head, Davison tried to focus.

In his mind, he could still see himself saying to Quentin, 'She's gone'. He recalled typing the med-ops report just half an hour ago, pronouncing her dead.

Davison lifted up the needle and moved towards Ellie. Then he stalled. Her jacket, it was in the way. He replaced the hypo on the little bedside table and leaned over Ellie. He could feel her warm, soft breath on his skin. It should have felt sensual. But to him, it felt downright creepy. He remembered the vampire movies he used to watch when he was younger, the ones in which the unsuspecting, innocent guy always gets it from the ravishing lady vamp. Ellie fitted the bill. Half expecting her to sit up, with fangs where her teeth should be, and lunge at him, he wasted little time in front of her.

His actions were rough and hurried. With a tourniquet wrapped around her arm to increase the pressure, he grabbed a hypo and slid the needle into her bulging vein. The needle sucked up, extracting her blood. Ellie didn't move. Davison would have expected an involuntary twinge at the subconscious level. But there was nothing at all.

More strangeness, he thought, looking at Ellie. A woman who had defied the laws of nature.

He stuck a plaster over the top of the needle's incision. He needn't have bothered. Ellie's right arm was beleaguered with angry, red puncture marks and dried blood like someone had used her as a dart board. The middle of her arm, towards the shoulder, was extremely swollen. Jaffa orange and pansy purple bruises had erupted across her skin. It was the only evidence NMS ever left behind. The bruising would be gone in a few hours.

Davison, with his back to Ellie, was deep in thought over what they had done when he heard a faint moan. Turning round, Ellie stirred, slowly moving her head to one side on the pillow. Her face was trapped in painful frown. But she did not open her eyes. He swallowed gently. He could not let her wake up. They weren't ready.

Coldly, Davison snatched up the phial of chloral hydrate, positioned the syringe and drew in the drug. He flicked the needle as he had done a million times before and watched the chloral hydrate shoot into the air.

Grabbing her arm, Ellie let out a deep sigh. Her eye lids moved but didn't open. Davison swallowed. In his hands, she didn't feel human.

She was more like an abomination of nature. A freak. A monster.

Like an animal handled by a vivisectionist, Davison was impervious to feeling any emotion for Ellie. With stark cruelness, he stuck the hypo severely into her arm. The drug entered Ellie's system and she slumped heavier in the bed.

Chapter 30

Sabena snatched Katzenberger's Anya Hindmarch tote bag, complete with her press ID, and headed for Downing Street in a taxi rather than her SUV. It was how Katzenberger arrived at Number 10, and Sabena couldn't change what her intel informed her to do.

In the back of the cab, she looked in her compact and removed every single trace of lipstick she could see, and then picked up a similar shade *sans* deadly toxin, and applied it. She then sat back and admired the view of inadequate people going about their meaningless lives.

She played out the events in her head. Maybe she should have grabbed Katzenberger from the curbside. She'd run the risk of many variables with that alley. But one thing she knew; there wasn't any CCTV in that vicinity, unlike the stretch of road from Vauxhall to Embankment, which was awash with surveillance cameras on every building and street corner. With River House and Thames House just a stone's throw away, it was unsurprising. She pushed down an urge to giggle. Both intelligence agency HQs just in spitting distance of her recent murder and they'd seen and heard nothing.

Al Nadir really were the dominant ones in this war, thought Sabena smugly.

Just at that moment, the cabbie clocked Sabena's face in his rear-view mirror and called out, "Oh my God. You're Judy Katzen-something on the BBC, aren't you?"

Sabena smiled at the imbecilic specimen who couldn't even properly recall Katzenberger's full name.

"It's Katzenberger, and yes, that's me."

"'Ave you got a meeting then? A press thingy?"

"Yes. I have a press thingy. Now, if you'll excuse me, I have some calls to make," said Sabena softly. But the cabbie detected a Sabatier sharp edge, for he backed off from further discourse and stared at the road.

Sabena smiled into the window and played back the moment she took Katzenberger's life. The astonishment in her eyes as Sabena's lips met hers. For a flicker of a second, she registered a dark want, and then acceptance, before the poison soaked through transdermally into Katzenberger's lips and then into her blood, making its way at speed to her heart and lungs.

Maybe she should have just knocked her out, considered Sabena, recalling how friendly Katzenberger had become on the phone. But she was too aware of Al Nadir's strict and unflinching code of 'leave no witnesses'. If she broke that code, there would be reprisals from Al Nadir's senior management team. She didn't want to consider what their actions would be in such a situation.

"We're here, madam," said the cabbie, keeping a considerably more formal footing than before.

Sabena grabbed Katzenberger's tote, dived into her wallet, pulled some cash out, and handed it to the driver.

The security at the gate of Number 10 turned immediately as Sabena emerged from the black cab. At first, they placed a hand out, attempting to stop her from advancing further, and then one of the armed police officers recognized Katzenberger from the television and the many times she'd been there before.

"It's ok, fellas. It's Miss Katzenberger."

Sabena heard the policeman's exclamation at the same moment she flashed her press ID, and gave a wide grin to all the policemen.

"I'm seeing the prime minister today. I should be on the list."

One of the policemen called in her visit and waited to gain clearance for Sabena to enter. The wait didn't take long. Sabena strode through the security blockade into Downing Street. By the time she reached the door, another policeman had instructed his security pal behind the door to open it.

Wow, this Katzenberger must really have a serious thing going on with Ashton to get this kind of service, thought Sabena, marching over the threshold into the home of the British prime minister.

Ushered quickly into the prime minister's morning lounge, Sabena looked around her. The home of British PMs for centuries, Number 10 was actually smaller than she'd thought it would be. Certainly, it wasn't a patch on all her palatial residences around the globe. But, of course, that wasn't the point. It wasn't about the décor, nor the splendor. It was all about the fact that whoever had residency had command and control of an entire country.

Ashton wasn't like other prime ministers. They'd all been a kind of tiptoe type leader, afraid to make a move in case they'd annoy the US, Europe, China, you name it. Keeping in line had been their parliamentary doctrine.

Until Ashton.

He appeared to the British public as someone who held the sensitivities of the nation close to him, that he was still a little vulnerable where it counted, in matters of his family, for instance. But Sabena had always read him as someone who was capable of hard-hearted decision making. She'd always sensed a coldness within those hazel eyes. With their meeting imminent, she wondered whether she'd see more in his eyes than just the stare of a puppet politician.

The door opened and an assistant beckoned Sabena forward.

"Prime Minister, Miss Judith Katzenberger to see you, sir."

Ashton was seated on the sofa in his morning lounge. He leapt up, smiling broadly on Katzenberger's name being announced.

"Judy, darling, lovely to see you."

Ashton's arms outstretched to Sabena's and encased her body in a tight hug. Sabena noticed he kept one eye on the door closing, and when it did, he locked it swiftly then brought her closer.

"Been working out, darling? I felt a bit more muscle than usual," said Ashton, moving to stare at Sabena deeply.

Sabena shuddered under his stare. Oh God, he was analyzing her. She had to flip the situation quickly.

"Yes. I needed to lose a few pounds. Too many of these press junket lunches. No good for the figure," Sabena purred, raising her eyes up to Ashton and blasting him with open seduction. "I thought you'd be pleased."

Ashton's arms tightened. His grip was stronger than Sabena expected. His slightly effeminate look belied the strength she could feel in his body.

"I am," growled Ashton, and his lips dropped onto Sabena's. He pushed his tongue violently into her as he pushed her jacket off her shoulders.

Suddenly, Sabena knew he was most definitely more than a friend to Katzenberger. Their intel hadn't been able to identify an actual relationship. She'd had suspicions. But now she knew the truth. Getting naked was absolutely not happening. Katzenberger could have a birthmark, an identification that Ashton knew about. He'd know instantly that it wasn't her.

Sabena pulled away from Ashton, stepping backward towards his desk full of files and papers.

"On the desk, darling. Come on," responded Sabena, keeping the wording on balance with her psych analysis. Instinct told her Katzenberger had liked it rough, and Ashton was into a bit of domination.

Ashton moved forward, a dark lust in his eyes. He unclasped his belt, slid it out of his trousers and cracked it on the floor like a whip. Sabena watched and licked her lips, getting turned on. This definitely wasn't the Ashton she'd seen on Prime Minister's Question Time in parliament.

This Ashton was dangerous.

Then he pounced on her, pushing himself into her, pinning her to the desk with a surging, almost destructive passion she'd only felt with Salim and Kinley.

My God, thought Sabena, unable for a moment to form a coherent thought. What the hell was happening?

Sabena was well versed in honey traps and using her body to get the results she needed. She prided herself on keeping everything compartmentalized. Emotion on the surface. Ice cold inside.

But this time…

The summit. She was there to ask him about the summit. The thought wrenched from a place inside her mind. Concentrate, she instructed herself.

And then she shook, forgetting everything, as a mind-blowing orgasm ripped through her. As she threw her head back to scream, Ashton clamped a heavy hand over her mouth. His eyes glared. He held his hand across her mouth so tight she had to breathe through her nose. Above her, he shivered, coming fast.

Ashton lay upon her for a short time. Then, he withdrew, grabbed some tissues to clean himself, and pulled up his trousers. Sabena still couldn't move. Ashton had pushed her skirt up and now it bunched underneath her ass with the papers and pens that were on the desk.

"Katzy, that was the best one yet, darling. That workout's certainly helped you build up your muscles in all the right places," Ashton sneered, staring between her legs.

Sabena slipped off the desk and pulled down her skirt. She smiled but didn't respond to his salacious remark. Sabena knew the more time she stayed with Ashton risked her being found out. His eyes scanned her constantly, reading her every move.

"Darling, I want to spend longer, but I'm on a deadline."

"But I thought we had at least another hour. I was going to take you to the penthouse. Give you another real workout!" said Ashton, glaring at her, annoyed.

"I know, but things change. You know that." Sabena arranged herself, and sat down on the sofa. Ashton joined her on the other side.

"Shall I call Bob? Give you a bit of extra time?" offered Ashton.

Sabena recalled Bob Fitzpatrick was the head of news at the BBC. "No, it's ok. I'm already into extra time. Don't want to piss him off any more than I already have."

Ashton got up, his face sullen. His appointment with his Katzy was clearly a high point in his day, thought Sabena. He moved to the drinks cabinet and poured two drinks. He obviously knew Katzy's liquor of choice.

Taking the glass that Ashton handed, Sabena held it in her hand but didn't drink.

"Any more? What have you done?" asked Ashton, sitting back down on the sofa, his eyes fixed on Sabena.

"Oh, you know what I'm like." Sabena grinned, and tilted her head towards Ashton. "It's ok. Anyway, you probably haven't got much time to spend either, what with the summit and everything," said Sabena in a matter-of-fact way.

"Now, Katzy, you know I can't talk to you about that. I don't want you to get charged under UN Resolution 458. It's an act of treason. I'd never see you again." Ashton's eyes caught Sabena's and concern flashed in them.

UN Resolution 458, that ole bug bear, thought Sabena bitterly. It was a resolution that prevented the world press from covering or even talking about an event that impacted international security. The outright ban meant that, despite the chatter and obvious indications of enhanced security around the QE II Conference Center, no one could tell the press that the summit was definitively taking place. Many times since the resolution had been passed had countries created decoy venues complete with full security, put out misinformation and disinformation, and generally tried their best to hide events of international security. As such, events rarely happened these days due to the risk of Al Nadir.

And when they did, massive amounts of resources were used to hide them.

"Sorry, darling. I won't speak of it again." Sabena sniggered into her drink. "But make sure you put old Treetrunk in his place. It's your playground. You're ruling the roost here, not that jumped-up geologist's son!"

Sabena's subtle affirmation of Ashton's position in the political brinkmanship would also enable Ashton to assert his position in the summit's preparations and, in doing so, confirm the location of the venue. Or so Sabena hoped.

"Yeah. Tell me. I've had him at all hours trying to tell me what I can and can't do. He's paranoid about Al Nadir fucking up his grand plans."

"Grand plans?" said Sabena slowly.

"Yes. A new resolution. But, Katzy, remember 458. I can't say anymore." Ashton stared, his mouth downturned, and his face hardened.

"Oh, I know. I won't say anything. What we do here is confidential. You know that, darling." Sabena fluttered her eyelashes.

Ashton moved to sit next to her. She placed her untouched glass on the coffee table and twisted her body as the weight of his pushed down the cushion.

He put a hand out and touched Sabena's face.

"Katzy, darling, I care about you. You're ambitious. You're gorgeous. But someone could get hold of you. They could hurt you to get such information from you. I couldn't live with that." Ashton moved closer.

But Sabena backed away. "Darling, I can take care of myself. I'm a tough girl at heart."

Ashton smirked, and Sabena could see he was in recall about some assignation in days past. "Don't I know it!"

"Darling, I care about you too. If the summit is here, you have to be careful." Sabena lilted her voice and soaked it in compassion.

"Every precaution has been taken. The venue is the safest place on earth," said Ashton, not giving anything away verbally.

"The QEII?" pressed Sabena, determined but softly.

"The *venue*," repeated Ashton, but his eyebrow rose, and his head went forward, indicating to Sabena that London was still the location.

"I'm close by," Sabena said. "So once it's over, I want the exclusive on this new resolution."

"Of course. Wherever the venue is, you know you'll get the exclusive on what is ratified after the summit is over."

Ashton was infuriatingly closed about confirming the exact location of the venue. Sabena knew she couldn't press any more. The fact he'd given non-verbal indications, and the higher pitched assurance in his voice, suggested to Sabena that the summit was going to be at QEII. There was also a slight latency in his voice when he'd said 'wherever the venue is', which indicated that Ashton was lying about it being somewhere else.

Tiny tells that spoke volumes.

Sabena swept a look down at her watch.

"Darling, I'm sorry. I really want to stay for round two…or three." Sabena smiled and flicked out her tongue. "But I've got to get back."

Ashton moved forward, grabbed behind her head and kissed her. He stared into Sabena's eyes.

"You know I want to be with you, don't you?"

Sabena nodded, now wanting to leave.

"But it's Natasha and the kids, and the look of the thing. I'm seen as the caring father, the loving husband. It'd shatter my image."

"I know," ventured Sabena, struggling to slide back off the sofa. "I'll take whatever I can get."

"Thank you, Katzy, for finally being so reasonable. I know you want me to leave her. But I really can't."

"Darling, I've got to go. This is difficult. I've got to keep my head straight if I'm to finish my work." Sabena pushed a level of emotion she considered appropriate from what Ashton had just said. Katzy had probably begged Ashton to leave his wife and given him grief over it.

"Ok," said Ashton, moving back, looking miserable.

Sabena took the moment, to snatch her bag and get up.

"I'll call you," said Ashton, holding onto her arm.

"Ok."

Ashton pulled her back and planted his lips upon Sabena's.

"You know I may be falling in love with you."

Sabena stared at Ashton through her long lashes. Her lips trembled. "I know. But we can't."

Sabena watched Ashton recognize the position. He released Sabena and stepped back. He nodded. Sadness flared up in his face and glints of tears at the sides of his eyes glistened.

"You're right."

He straightened up, smeared the tears back from his eyes, ushered Sabena towards the door, and unlocked it.

"Thank you, Judy. I hope that the position is now clear," said Ashton, making a statement for those beyond the door.

Very clear, thought Sabena, realizing that, inadvertently, she'd done something of good.

She may just have saved Ashton's marriage.

Chapter 31

Whyte had no way of knowing, but his decision to move the car pushed back his body being found by at least one more day. His white Toyota SUV nestled cozily behind the wooden panel of the shed area that housed the restaurant's large, green, plastic trash bins. The last surge of energy to follow the dark SUV had caused Whyte's body to collapse, falling across the passenger seat and, in turn, concealing his body from anyone outside. If one looked hard, blood on the headrest may be discerned. But a person would *really* have to be looking for such a mark.

The fact was both Whyte and his car couldn't have been more hidden, even if he'd made a conscious decision to do so.

It was a perfect piece of serendipity in an ironic universe.

Bill, Taco Express' proprietor hadn't even noticed it when he'd put the trash out later that day on Saturday evening, and Sunday was his day of rest. His punters could search for their meals elsewhere. His clientele, realizing this, ensured Taco Express was devoid of their attention on that day.

However, Saturday was Bill's busiest. All through the day and late into the evening, a steady stream of cars parked in front of the restaurant. Families rowed, couples necked, and kids misbehaved, completely blind to the fact that less than a hundred yards away was the body of one of the world's most eminent scientists.

And a man whose final moments of desperation to get back his doomed family would soon deliver to an unsuspecting and totally oblivious world a horror of biblical proportions.

Chapter 32

"Believe what you want to."

Stein-Muller's words rang inside Sam's mind. Maybe that was what he'd been doing for so long: believing that everything was right with Ellie, with Maide, with Kinley.

Had he really tried to look beyond a preconditioned belief and see the truth?

That Ellie had secrets, Maide didn't trust him, and Kinley really had turned completely to be Al Nadir.

For the first time in over a decade since he'd been in the Secret Intelligence Service did Sam feel he didn't know what was really happening. Control was ebbing from him and he couldn't preempt his next play.

He looked up the corridor, sandwiched between the rows of interrogation cells on either side. Apart from the chatting of agents at the top of the corridor, no other sounds could be heard. All the cells were heavily soundproofed and as Sam moved further from agents' conversation, the corridor became eerily quiet.

No sound bore witness to the activities taking place within the cells.

Sam had been up and down the corridor hundreds of times during his career, but he'd never considered that silence before. He'd always been too focused on getting to the hostile and wringing the truth out of them. By any means.

He thought about what he'd done in those cells, what he'd just done to Stein-Muller. Had it got him the result he wanted? Or just a spew of words of any form to stop the pain?

He arrived at the cell harboring Sacha Lupez. From the file, he recalled Lupez was an old lieutenant from Carlo Penla's drug cartel in Columbia. That was until Al Nadir took over the cartel from Penla three years before. Al Douri took a shine to Lupez, accelerating his ranking in the terrorist collective.

Sam unlocked the door with his retina scan and entered.

A Latino guy with dark, silky hair, a sharp, striking face, fierce, olive eyes and a body that moved like a predatory panther greeted Sam as he padded in chains across his cell. Sam could see at once why Al Douri had promoted him so quickly. The man oozed lethal dominance. One look and any adversary would capitulate, lest he fall into Lupez's terrifying hands.

Of course, such a look was lost on Sam.

He stood in front of Lupez and smirked. "You and I are going to have a little chat."

"Fuck off!"

"Yeah, I thought you might say that," said Sam, punching Lupez hard in the gut. Lupez doubled under the force of the blow, but quickly brought himself up, and tried to bang his forehead against Sam, who knew the move. He dodged out of the way and kicked Lupez's legs from under him, knocking him to the rock-hard floor. Within a second, Sam was on top of Lupez, his hands around his neck, pressing his thumbs upward underneath his chin and whacking his head against the concrete.

"Now I'm going to ask again and you're going to behave nicely. Otherwise, I'm going to slam your head through this floor and the next person you'll be telling to fuck off will be Satan himself."

Sam fixed Lupez with a dark glare of conviction. He wasn't bluffing. Lupez grunted in acceptance to the terms.

"Ok. Now I'm going to pull you up."

Sam grabbed Lupez by his orange jump suit lapels, yanked him up, and flung him onto the bench, where he landed hard on his ass. Lupez snarled but didn't retaliate.

"Right. That's better. You help me and I'll help you."

"You're never going to help me," said Lupez, spitting blood from his mouth.

Sam tilted his head to the side, looking quizzically at Lupez. "That's not entirely true. You tell me what I need, and I'll help you get what you need. Deal?"

Lupez stared coldly at Sam, but the agent knew he was considering the offer.

"Ok," muttered Lupez.

"Good. So what do you need?" asked Sam, going on the charm offensive first.

"To get out of here!" said Lupez with a wry sneer.

"Yeah. That can be arranged. But first, you tell me what I need."

Lupez nodded hesitantly and looked at the floor, as if embarrassed by his acquiesce.

"Where is Salim Al Douri?"

Lupez shook his head. "No idea. Could be anywhere."

"That answer is going to get you a short walk to a long and very painful death. And I'm sure that's not something you need."

Lupez shrugged his shoulders as if accepting the inevitable. Sam didn't want that response. He moved a little closer to Lupez who eyed him with a feral glint. Sam shot back the stare of a cold-blooded killer. It said, 'Try anything and you're dead'.

Sam's signal was quickly picked up, and Lupez relaxed, slouching his body against the back wall. He looked, confused, at Sam

"Why are you after Al Douri? You know the way things work. The Agreement. You can't touch him."

Sam heard the words. *The Agreement.* It was an unofficial arrangement of sorts between the agencies of Al Nadir and the global intelligence world. The moment Salim or Sabena were touched, all hell would reign down on the country that broke the code. Not that they didn't already stir up all kinds of damnation for the world. But, as Sam understood it, Al Nadir kept a muzzle on their true capability.

It could be a giant bluff, thought Sam. But the politicians of the world couldn't spin the dice with people's lives. Not every political leader was as cold-hearted as Richard Ashton, a man who didn't blink over sending more than five thousand people to their death for Operation Snowdrop to work.

So anyone else in Al Nadir was free game. But the elite couple would remain forever out of season.

"Come on, Lupez. You know where Al Douri is. You're fifth in the whole organization. You tell me, and once it's been validated, I'll get the DG of the CIA to sign your release."

Sam knew DG Downer would never agree to that, but it didn't matter. Lupez wasn't going to be around long enough to realize he'd been duped.

"You can't do anything to him. So why do you want to know where he is?"

"Call it curiosity," said Sam, issuing a sly smirk.

"Your own people will take you down if you touch him."

"That gives you a vested interest in telling me. Signs my death warrant."

Lupez smiled at the thought Sam had purposely suggested. You'd like that, you little shit. You smile again and I'll punch that smile through to the back of the wall.

"I want the signed release papers and then I'll tell you."

"No deal," growled Sam, and he spun on his heel away from Lupez and headed for the door. In a barter, always walk away. Same in negotiation. A retreat speaks volumes to a desperate prisoner.

"Zagros."

Sam's head turned. "At the Iraq/Iran border? The mountain region?" he asked slowly, measuring Lupez's response.

With his back turned to Lupez, Sam hadn't been able to observe him and check for micro-expression tells. But he'd heard a slight inflection in his voice that sounded like a reluctant confirmation of truth.

Lupez's eyes were straight, looking forward. His hands were on his knees and he'd stopped slouching. He didn't scratch his face or hair.

"Yeah. Around there," said Lupez. "Now do I get outta here?"

Sam grinned, opening the door, and looked over his shoulder.

"Outta here? You must be *fucking* joking!"

Chapter 33

Maide had a headset on. His face was in deep concentration. He hadn't done this kind of work in a long time. It was usually the remit of his tech officers. But he couldn't risk asking for their assistance. He couldn't risk exposure.

Although he was the boss, Maide wasn't an ivory tower man. He was thoroughly up to date with the techniques and technologies used by MI6. And at that moment, he was pleased he'd read all those tech-briefings, otherwise what he was planning wouldn't have been possible.

Maide accessed Al Nadir transmission intercept logs and pulled some of the more recent files into his system. First, he deconstructed the sentences at the granular level using sophisticated voice analyzing technology, and then reconstructed a new sentence.

"Payload dispatched. Silent Waters target neutralized."

He played it back and listened. The owners of the voices were Arabic, but because he'd assembled the words to make the sentence from different transmissions, different Arabic dialect inflections could clearly be heard, although they were talking in English. Maide had to standardize on one dialect. The voice recognition program told him the dominant dialect was Syrian. He overlaid the entire sentence with a Syrian dialect and ran the sound file again. He was getting closer, but it still had a lot of conflicting ambient noise. He needed to clean it up. So he homed in on the ambient noise around the sound 'p' at the start of the pronunciation of the word 'payload'.

A faint hum could be heard in the background. He tuned down the sound of the 'p' and tuned up the ambient noise. It sounded like an aircraft. He ran the analyzer and waited for the program's hypothesis.

It came up with 97% probability that the sound was a CFM56-3C aircraft engine from a modified Boeing 737-300.

Maide was content with that. Most of the time, Al Nadir operatives were transmitting from the skies. It was to be expected, which made it even more believable.

Maide overlaid the sound of the aircraft engine across the entire sentence. He adjusted for split second sound wave variations due to the plane's altitude and other nominal background sounds. Then he ran the file again and listened. He smiled. His top techies would never know the difference. Most of the time, the transmissions they intercepted were of appalling quality and had to be touched up to make any sense of the transmission. If it was too good, too clear, it would be detected as a fake. He ran the file again and listened. It had just the right amount of noise for it to be accepted as genuine.

He saved the file to a tiny flash memory device that looked like a sweet and wiped his system clean of the fake sound file. He knew that several backups had been created at remote secure servers around the world for safety. Maide accessed each one with his clearance codes. His position as head of MI6 gave him carte blanche to access everything.

Maide deleted each file in turn, including those stored in the cache. Now the fake sound file only existed on his key ring.

The fabrication was almost complete. All he needed to do to make it totally convincing was to transmit the file using one of Al Nadir's own satellite broadcasting frequencies. He recalled Al Nadir used different frequencies when they were stationary to when they were on the move in the air. It had to tie in seamlessly. Maide pulled up the intel for the transmission intercept logs. He made a note of one of the frequencies Al Nadir previously used, and then closed all the files.

Going into the central server, he overwrote the files that he had accessed. If anyone ever suspected anything, it would show he hadn't accessed any sound files, nor had he used the voice analyzing and recognition programs. Maide was confident that his tracks had been truly covered.

The broadcast would be delivered from an analogue satellite phone. He had just the right old analogue sat-phone at his home in Godalming just 20 miles away. Of course, he had to be back at Central in River House in the comms room when the broadcast was picked up.

He wanted to be standing right behind the guy who would turn around and say to him, 'Sir, you should hear this'.

Maide thought for a second. Timer software would do it, and with a digital to analogue converter programme with standard AV I/O line from the laptop to the analogue sat phone, he could ensure the incriminating evidence was broadcast at the exact moment he was in the comms room.

Maide nodded subconsciously at his plan, switched off his computer, and left for his home.

Chapter 34

In her SUV heading back to the Cambridge base, Sabena took a deep breath and pressed on the vidcall button on her tablet.

Salim's sculptured, sardonic face loomed up on the screen.

"Tell me. Is it still London?" snapped Salim, hardly waiting for Sabena to say hello.

"I couldn't get an absolute definitive yes from Ashton, but-"

Sabena didn't have chance to finish.

"You didn't get a definitive answer!"

"Hold on, Salim," thundered back Sabena. "I'm trying to tell you that I got Ashton to talk, and he gave enough away to suggest that it will be the QEII and that it's definitively London."

"He told you it was London?" Salim glared.

"Yes. In so many ways."

"No, Sabena. Not in so many fucking ways. One way. Venue is London. Yes or no?"

"Salim, he's not an easy one. He's not like a politician at all. If I didn't know better, I'd say the guy is ex-intelligence. He's so damn closed. And he's constantly reading you, like he's looking inside you. I was scared he'd make me. He knew his Katzy very well indeed. She wanted to be the next Mrs. Ashton."

"I'm not concerned about his fucking domestic situation," screamed back Salim, eyes widening. "Are we okay to hit the QEII or not?"

Sabena knew Salim was approaching one of his insane rages. Normally, she could counter him with her persuasive body, but with thousands of miles between them, she couldn't use that tactic.

She made a decision.

"Yes. It is definitely London and the QEII Conference Centre."

"Good." Salim appeared to calm a fraction. Then he sneered, "But if it isn't, I'm going to ram a piece of that quantum bomb inside you and explode it!"

Sabena laughed, pretending to enjoy Salim's sick joke. But inside her was genuine terror. What if she'd read Ashton wrong?

Should she question Godley again?

Was Ashton's implied word *really* enough to gamble her life on?

Chapter 35

Maide looked at the clock again. He wondered how his men, David and Gary, were progressing. Maide used them, and others like them, for all his 'little duties' that carried sovereign authority but were left undisclosed to the intelligence and security committee and never audited.

Conspiracy theorists named these duties as black operations. If the rumors were to be believed, black ops were responsible for most of the criminal acts the security agencies were trying to prevent.

Sam had been seconded to black ops for a while.

Maide recalled Sam's brief but breath-taking secondment, how he'd been exacting and remorseless in the achievement of his assigned duties. Assignments that would have turned the stomach of most agents, Sam carried out to the letter. For the greater cause. He was totally loyal. Totally dedicated. An idealist who believed in the higher reason. He really was the best agent they'd had in the past decade.

And now they had his wife. In the name of national security, they were preparing to attack her as Al Nadir. This was surely the lowest point to which Maide had ever traveled. The rapid meeting he'd convened with his boys, David and Gary, earlier flashed into his mind. They'd entered within minutes of his call and sat with cold expressions on the swivel chairs in front of his desk. Maide remained standing. He walked over and closed the door. He revolved to face them. His boys glared at him expectantly.

"We need an ME9," said Maide calmly.

The men nodded and looked sharply back at Maide. Both knew what ME9 stood for: masquerade as a hostile and deliver an attack to ensure that blame was placed on the hostile. Latterly, such intelligence codespeak had translated itself into the populace as false flags.

"What's the MO?" David said, moving forward.

"Return Sam Noor's wife to Silent Waters and then attack her," said Maide.

He watched them for a flicker of resistance. The target was, after all, the wife of a fellow agent.

Gary was in his mid-twenties. He'd been snapped up by Maide's top recruiter directly from his training ground as a Royal Marine commando. He had the combination they searched for: intelligence, strength and stamina. Now Maide looked at him. Gary's shoulders were pulled back, sharp and square, like he was restraining himself. His palms were on his thighs, hiding the rewards of countless assault courses and eye watering hours in the gym. Muscles like giant walnuts rippled underneath his low-cut, black jeans. His bright eyes were alert, assimilating everything. He could feel the adrenaline rising in his blood. His stance was primed like he was ready to leap. His jaw hardened as he listened to the details of the mission. Gary clearly wanted to get on with it.

Maide turned to take in David. He was ten years Gary's senior. His posture was more relaxed. But his strength was no less formidable. He was focused and waiting. The excitement that Gary had of receiving a new mission had long since left his worn, lackluster features. His eyes were ones that had witnessed horror, mostly by his own hand. The ravens of life had pecked out all the emotion, leaving behind impassive orbs. They flickered, empty and soulless. He was detached. It was a requirement of being an assassin, amongst other things. Maide had seen in David's file that he stated, in his own words 'he prided himself on his supreme detachment'. No one ever got close to him. That was his achievement in life, keeping kindness and love at bay. His arctic coldness was a sought-after value. Maide noticed a whisper of a smirk on his face. Was he up to it? Could he hold it together? Twelve years in black ops could screw anyone's head. Doubt crept into Maide's mind as to David's ability to execute the job in hand.

Suddenly, like a blackboard eraser removing unwanted words, David's words removed his doubt completely.

"What kind of attack are you after? Physical, sexual, or both?"

His face showed he was willing and capable to deliver any option. Gary shifted in his seat. His eyes shone with determination to get the job done, whatever the job was.

Maide's eyes widened. Jesus. These boys were raw. Starving Rottweilers without a muzzle.

"God, no! David, not that kind of attack," Maide caught himself, realizing he sounded a little weak and emotive. "It should be a terrorist attack that has the mark of Al Nadir. That's why you're here. I need your suggestions. How are you going to do it?"

David jumped straight in asking questions on security. Maide replied and watched as David's plan unraveled from mind to mouth. Finishing, David and Gary rose simultaneously from their seats. David turned around to Maide, his face somber.

"Good luck, sir," he said.

Maide looked back. He could read in David's face a flicker of darkness. They both knew that if anything went wrong, each was out on their own. No alibis. No joint complicity. They would all be alone to take the consequences.

"Good luck. God speed," Maide replied coldly, and watched David's back disappear through the door.

Chapter 36

The midnight blue BMW 745 slid past the checkpoint guards. They saluted Maide as he drove past. Maide nodded his head and proceeded calmly through the gates. It was a procedure he'd done for many years. But on this occasion, the drive out held more than just a departure. His hallowed existence as head of MI6 and all that that conveyed could soon be in question.

Maide was aware his blood pressure was up. The whooshing sound in his ears, like he was permanently under water, was incessant and debilitating. He was unbalanced and his reactions were sluggish.

He dove into the glove compartment, amongst papers and the car manual to find his beta-blockers. After a couple of attempts with one hand, he pulled off the obdurate top. He shoved three tablets into his mouth, swallowed and pulled a face. The bitter chemical taste trapped at the back of his throat, making him retch. He dug into the central compartment to find his soft mints, pushed at the top of the silvery paper, and tipped the packet. But instead of one mint, all the remaining mints dropped out and scattered across his lap and onto his shoes. He grabbed the ones in his lap and popped them into his mouth, but the hideous taste of the tablets was still there.

"Oh, sod it!" muttered Maide, as he slipped down in the driver's seat to collect the last few mints resting on his shoe. With his right hand still on the wheel, Maide dropped his head for just a mere second.

Immediately, the car veered to the left. Maide pushed the mints into his mouth and turned the steering wheel quickly. But he was a moment too slow. The lane had curved at a sharp angle and he couldn't prevent the car scraping deep into a hedge, causing several tree sparrows to chirp in unified fright and flee like an exodus from the hedgerow. They flew straight across the bonnet of Maide's car. He could see their scared pinprick black eyes, rushing for sanctuary to a place of freedom. He'd had a lifetime of those looks. Not on sparrows, of course, on people caught in the crossfire of political unrest, the accepted casualties of their missions. Ignorant to such matters as international foreign policy, they had known only that their world had been disrupted. Like the sparrows, they had to flee to find a new place, a place where they could continue to live out their humble existence in peace.

Memories overwhelmed him. Maide blinked hard. He had to concentrate, not think of the past but look to securing his future. Abruptly, he brought the steering wheel back and lined up with the road. His head was heavy. The pills weren't working fast enough. He turned the plan over in his mind. His synapses sizzled with a fireball of what-ifs.

Maide knew if it didn't work, it was all over. Sam possessed the power to bring them all down. One word in the public domain about Operation Snowdrop, any suggestion that Piccadilly was a known target before the explosion, and there would be outright anarchy. Everything would change. There would be no going back. Maide shuddered as he imagined the headlines. The plan had to work. There was no other alternative, bar killing Sam. Maide paused for a moment, considering this remedy. Then sanity struck and he knew it was unthinkable.

Sam was the product of their making. He was millions of pounds invested over a decade, just like all their other defenses. You didn't just destroy a weapon because it misfires a few times.

Chapter 37

Davison sat back in his seat. The tests confirmed everything. And nothing. Ellie was a normal human being. There was nothing extraordinary about her. He could not begin to understand how she had cheated death. It would remain a mystery, just one of a few unexplained miracles.

The sedative he'd given her would wear off soon. She had to be sedated while they smuggled her outside, and throughout the journey. Davison quickly took the hypo and injected her with another dose of the sedative. He packaged the sedative's anti-agent for Maide's men to use to awaken Ellie later. He was scheduled to arrive at the scene soon after 5:35 p.m.

"Sir Justin told us to come here. We're taking her."

Davison looked up. He'd been heavily lost in thought and hadn't heard Maide's men approach. He straightened up, smoothing his palms down on his white coat, and pointed to Ellie.

"It's a covert op, so-" Davison began, but the burly men arrogantly pushed past him.

The larger of the two grunted, "We know. Sir Justin has briefed us."

"Has he?"

"Have you completed the tests?"

"Yes, but-"

"Have you got the cocktail?"

Davison nodded shamefully. Maide had called him to request him to synthesize the drug cocktail. He'd combined mescaline, LSD, and PCP. The intensity of the combination removed the usual half-an-hour delay for the trip to kick in. Ellie would start to trip the second the mixture entered her bloodstream. The high milligram dosage and the fact the drugs were mixed would guarantee a bad trip. Amplified by Ellie's already emotional, highly unstable condition, Davison sadly knew that Ellie was in for one scary ride.

He handed the hypodermic loaded with the cocktail to the thug.

"Remember, only inject up to this point," Davison said, pointing to an indicator line on the hypo. "There's enough in there to kill her," he added nervously.

The thug took the hypo and placed it in his pocket, ignoring Davison's instructions.

"Is she sedated enough for the journey?" asked the other thug, pulling a sheet from one of the nearby beds and draping it over Ellie.

"Yes. I've given her-" began Davison.

But the thug talked over his feeble voice. "Good. We need to move her now."

"Now?"

"When did you think?"

"Erm, well, I thought we'd have more time."

"We haven't. Get out the way. You follow when Sir Maide receives the intercept at Central. Any problems, you can contact us. We're tagged. Track us on Sat 5, GPS code 87964. Got that?"

Davison looked underneath the papers on his desk, trying to find a pen to write down the numbers. He wasn't agent stock. Numbers weren't something he could remember easily.

"8796?" asked Davison, once he'd found a pen.

The thug stared at him with pure ignominy. Then he repeated slowly with patronizing scorn, "8…7…9…6…4. Have you got that now?"

Davison flushed red, embarrassed that the gorilla had treated him with such disdain.

"Got that?" repeated the thug, glaring at Davison.

Davison thought that the thug's patience was on a fine thread and someone had cut into the middle.

Davison nodded.

The first thug pushed Davison away from the trolley bed, mumbling 'moron' under his breath. He released the brake and, with his fellow thug, maneuvered the trolley out of the door.

Davison looked on, fuming. His power had been usurped by a bloody gorilla.

Damn you, Maide!

Chapter 38

Maide turned off the little lane onto the A322 and picked up speed. The road was devoid of traffic. Maide pushed down on the accelerator. The speedo zoomed past eighty-two. The road, however, was only a single carriageway, and he was taking a monumental risk in driving so fast. A set of traffic lights were approaching fast. He tried to break but the lights flashed from amber to red in a blink. Nothing left to do but shoot through the light and pray no one clocked his plates. The road wasn't the best to be travelling so fast, but he had training in high speed, tactical maneuvers. The training served him well, but the junctions and roundabouts were still slowing him down. He cursed himself for not living near a motorway, and he cursed MI6 for having their interrogation base in the sticks.

A learner driver, not looking, pulled out at the T-junction and ambled in front of him, forcing Maide to break to the statutory 30 mph.

"Oh, for fuck's sake!" he screamed, hitting the steering wheel and glowering at the terrified learner.

The young girl could see in her rear mirror the sight of Maide's huge BMW steaming up towards her, a raging midnight blue bull, its bright eyes flashing with menace. It looked to her like he wasn't going to stop. She shook, terrified, and instinctively took her foot off the accelerator. Her speed fell. The instructor stared nervously over his shoulder, pleading with his eyes for Maide to have some patience and compassion. Maide had neither.

Seeing he would be stuck for the rest of his journey behind the learner, Maide whipped the steering wheel to the right in an attempt to overtake and narrowly missed an oncoming recovery truck approaching in the opposite direction. He swerved back, sweating slightly, and fell in line behind the painfully slow learner who was trundling along at just over twenty-two mph.

Maide groaned and shot a wrath-filled glare at the learner.

Why did this have to happen today? He glanced at the clock on the dash. It was 4:23 p.m. He didn't have time to be held up like this. He had to be back in the comms room at River House by 5:30 p.m. at the latest. His target had been 5:15 p.m. But that was proving increasingly optimistic. It would take him a good thirty minutes to drive from his home back to River House, provided there were no delays on the A3. And, of course, traffic around Vauxhall, even on a Sunday afternoon, could be a nightmare. He had no choice if he was to meet the deadlines imposed; he had to get away from Miss Learner Driver. He edged out to the right again and peered out of the window. There was a Peugeot 306 coming down quickly but Maide judged it was sufficiently far enough away to risk it.

He swung out into the oncoming lane and pressed hard down on the accelerator. But the car he had espied suddenly came hurtling down the road far faster than he'd anticipated. The driver, his lips moving rapidly, his mouth growing wide in response to an unheard joke, was preoccupied. His elbow was jammed tight up against the window, and his manicured hand sat at an angle against his ear. A tell-tale slip of silver at the side confirmed a mobile was present.

Maide's BMW bore down on the 306. The driver, horribly visualizing the impact that was about to happen, dropped his phone instantly, and swung his car to the left, mounting the pavement. Maide locked his wheel hard to the left and skimmed in front of the learner driver, who had suddenly sped up.

Maide pushed his foot with force down on the accelerator, escaping the scene. Seeing the road was clear, he sped away, leaving behind a traumatized learner and an extremely irate management consultant.

Chapter 39

The sleek Gulf Stream jet shot through the clouds like an arrow through candy floss. Inside, Sabena luxuriated in her king-sized bed, wrapped between black satin sheets. Beside her lay Russo, her second in command in Al Nadir. Just eight weeks before, Kinley had been in his place.

Sabena thought back. Everything he'd done. All the damage Kinley had been responsible for. Part of her still couldn't believe, despite the damning evidence they'd found in steganographic encrypted website Forever Flowers, that Kinley was really working for the other side.

He'd been so obsessed to do anything for Al Nadir. Sabena shivered remembering his glorious sadism. He'd enjoyed all the killing, all the torture. And all the *other* stuff. Sabena felt a tingle inside her. Kinley had made her revel in her own darkness. She'd pushed the bar, but he'd gone further.

Much further.

Sabena had never been wrong about a person. She'd been able to read anyone with just a glance. It had been an ability she'd acquired during her formative years, when her parents had lugged her around the globe, learning new languages, living in new cultures. Her father, a world-famous linguist had expected her to learn languages rapidly. From a young age, her linguistic ability transcended into a greater awareness of people, cultures, and social norms, what were acceptable behaviors and what weren't. That awareness morphed into a deeper ability to immediately 'know a person'. To read someone with absolute certainty.

This ability served her well throughout her life and especially in her latest career as a super-terrorist. Salim had used her on many occasions as a human lie detector. She had rooted out spies who'd insinuated themselves into Al Nadir from the alphabet soup of global intelligence agencies. No one slipped through.

Only Kinley.

How did he fool her?

Sabena couldn't really figure out how he'd done it. Was it really her infatuation that blinded her to the truth?

With his boy-next-door charm, blond hair, startling crystal blue eyes, and a body Adonis would kill for, Kinley had been the perfect balance to Salim's dark, sultry, and dangerous sculptured looks. Sabena had basked in the powerful sexual energy of having both men.

They were like dark and white chocolate. The dessert she just couldn't get enough of.

Her obsession had shielded her.

He had been the trusted one.

Sabena swallowed hard and looked down at Russo. She prodded him with a talon-sharp fingernail.

"Yeah? What?" muttered Russo, waking at Sabena's touch.

Russo stared at Sabena with dark eyes. Sabena took in his immutable, rock-hard face.

"I did you wrong in so many ways, Pedro."

Russo pulled himself up onto his elbows. On his face was an unanswered question. Sabena read it. Why her conciliatory tone?

"What do you mean?" said Russo, rubbing Sabena's naked back.

"You knew what Kinley was right from the start. You never trusted him. Even after Piccadilly, you never thought he'd given himself over to us. Salim did. I did. You didn't. And I hated you for that. I cut you out. I blocked your role. Intentionally, I sidelined you completely. I made you look a fool in front of Salim. He was on the verge of kicking you down to fourth place and bumping Kinley up to third. He thought you'd lost your way, and I didn't tell him any different."

Russo glared at Sabena. His eyes iced over, and his sensual lips slid into a thin line.

"Kicking me down, eh?"

"I'm sorry," whispered Sabena, and she moved in, running her fingers up his thigh. "I should have been more aware of what was happening. I let myself be fooled."

Russo shook his head seeing, probably for the first time, Sabena actually admitting a mistake to anyone other than Salim.

"I've really fucked up, haven't I?"

Russo shrugged, unsure of what to conclude.

Sabena noticed his reticence to agree. She knew he was wary of her power. Sabena didn't press.

"First I allowed Kinley to get too close, and then I used the next gen nanobomb on him and his family without ensuring the frequencies were properly masked. Salim's going to fucking kill me, isn't he?"

Sabena looked through hooded eyes and fluttered her eyelashes with girlish allure. Russo held her close. She shivered under his hold and he brought her closer.

"Darling, I won't let him. You've done so much. Without you, Salim wouldn't have achieved the heights he has. He knows that."

Sabena stared. She pushed a hesitant, trembling expression, and bit down on her lip as worry flooded her face.

"You think?"

"Absolutely. But if he doesn't, he'll have to get through me first."

Russo lent in and kissed behind Sabena's ear and then down her neck. She purred softly, and arched her back in response to Russo's kisses.

"I knew I could rely on you," said Sabena.

Rely on you to take the bait, that is, thought Sabena, sneering inside. A woman has to survive. And although her and Salim were two faces of the same coin, she was critically aware that she had to employ 'safety mechanisms', just in case Salim's anger overflowed too much in her direction if, for any reason, London turned out not to be the summit's location.

A little 'exposing of one's soul' in front of Russo was just an insurance policy. Or rather, a survival policy.

And Russo had lapped it up, behaving like the protective lover he always wanted to be.

"Thank you, Pedro. I think I've got some making up to do," murmured Sabena, sliding across Russo's body. She straddled his muscular frame.

Russo smiled beneath her.

"Shouldn't we be looking through Project David papers to get an idea on splitting the quantum bomb?"

Sabena moved forward and snatched her tablet. She tapped on the screen with one hand, whilst the other slipped beneath the sheets to trace Russo's taut torso. On her action, a stream of complex mathematics popped up with schematics on where and how to position the quantum bomb pen against the bomb compound to slice it.

Sabena swept through the pages, her eyes scanning with avid intensity, and then she smirked, reached over, and dropped the tablet on to the bedside table.

"Got it!" proclaimed Sabena. "Now, where were we?"

Russo stared in amazement and disbelief. "You've got it? Sabena, you barely looked at them!"

"Don't need to. Scan read with instant capture and recall helps, darling. I was born with it. Means I can spend my time doing something that fulfils me. Like you!"

Sabena grinned and raised herself up then sank down onto Russo, who sighed with pleasure, and gripped her sharp hips.

"There's at least another three hours before we land in Zagros. Let's see what I can do to make up for all the injustice I've served you over the years."

Russo held Sabena tightly, cupping a pert breast.

"I think you're going the right way to getting my complete forgiveness," he said, pulling up to encase her wanton lips.

Chapter 40

Aby-od often came into the Observation Room to check on various Protectors on planets across the universe. He found a sense of solace in knowing those hybrid creatures – one-part planetary native and one-part Kudamaz – were in situ, ready if their planets needed them.

His thoughts had been fixed on Ki for a while. The High Council's ministrations for the planet had been mostly negative in their construct, and he'd had to fight to prevent the council from taking actions to dispatch the planet.

He recalled seeing the Protector of Ki on screen before. Soon he would bring the Protector back to Ki. He had the urge to observe them again. Aby-od instructed the sentient crystals within the Observation Room, but they'd already picked up on his resonance wave that reflected his need.

Up on screen, the Protector of Ki across the ages appeared. Aby-od smiled as he watched. They were truly a wonderful being. Compassionate, strong and fearless.

He moved the viewing on to present day Ki, and observed the Protector in its current form. Still magnificent, with a strength undeniable in every way. And that was why he would see it would be kept.

Nothing could harm the Protector.

Far behind Aby-od, not quite locked in Kudamun's reality plane, shimmered Aswa-da. He stared at the screen and realized that, with the Protector's present incarnation, new opportunities were presenting themselves in abundance.

He smiled, and then, like starburst from a firework, the smile vanished.

Chapter 41

Maide mopped the perspiration from his brow with his silk handkerchief. Despite what he thought, he really couldn't do this field agent stuff anymore. He'd been desk-bound far too long. Too pampered. He didn't have the mindset for it. When he'd been younger, an episode like the one he'd just faced wouldn't have fazed him in the slightest. But he looked at his hands on the wheel. They were shaking. Maide suddenly felt old.

Maybe it was time to retire. But if it was, he would leave of his own accord. He didn't want to be pushed out. He wanted to go out on a glorious high note. Nothing must tarnish the outstanding reputation he had spent his entire life building. He'd dedicated his life to MI6. He didn't want one slight misdemeanor to cloud an otherwise illustrious career. Maide thought on his past exploits. In his long and colorful life with the MI6, he'd engaged in many heinous acts, but what he'd just been party to had been a first. Even by his standards. But if everything had gone to plan, the mad dash he was making wouldn't have been necessary. None of this plan would have been necessary.

Sam would never have known and would have continued in his job, ignorant to the truth. They would all have been safe. The whole episode would have closed.

Only now the chapter was still wide open. Ellie Noor was an unknown variable. She disturbed him. So many questions surrounded her. Maide permitted himself a second to warmly remember her performance from the surveillance stream, although his highly disciplined control kept his feelings in check.

He recalled her weird behavior. Who was she talking to in an empty kitchen? And that scream. Ellie's face contorted. A wicked mask of horror stretched over her beautiful features. His experts had spent hours pouring over every pixel on the images. They had zoomed in, zoomed out, extrapolated the image, viewed the image with UV and IR overlays, reverted the image to a wire frame to analyze dimensions, modelled, and made a composite of the image with other images taken of the lounge, hallway, dining room and study to provide a 360-surround view. But nothing had been found. They had found no reason for the scream. As far as his experts were concerned, Ellie had screamed for no visibly apparent or discernible reason.

He'd run checks on her. She had no instances of mental illness or breakdowns of any kind. Her family history, if a little eccentric, could not be classed as mad. Her mother, Athena, had Ellie when she was fifteen. She never disclosed to Ellie the identity of the father, but it had been presumed, at the time, to be one of the rock stars from psychedelic set that her mother mixed with. She had been the original wild child of the early 1970s. MI6, in doing their background security checks before Sam joined discovered Ellie's biological father had been a guy called Stardust Traveler, who'd been born with a less exciting moniker of Tim Jones.

From her early teens, Athena had trailed around with rock bands in a love-struck LSD haze. In the summer of '74, soon after Ellie was born, she'd headed off to a commune in New Mexico, leaving Ellie to be brought up by her Great Aunt in Fulham. From the reports, it showed that mother and daughter were still estranged. Ellie had had no contact with her mother since the moment she had been born. Her mother married a senator from Texas and now had three children. She was an upright, respectable pillar of society. Ellie was obviously a part of her life she wanted to forget.

Ellie had been an average child. 'Always attention-seeking but highly likable', said the school reports Maide had read. She was a natural actress and played the lead role in many school productions.

In her early teens she had started a band called SOL, Sex on Legs, with a couple of her schoolmates. They didn't amount to anything. It was just a teenage phase, a rite of passage for Ellie. She had teenage angst, creativity and rebellion, and her band was the perfect channel to release these emotions. Although deemed just another mediocre teenage band, an entertainment reporter for a local rag covering one of their pub gigs claimed that, 'Ellie Vale had star quality and could expect greater things'.

Ellie had left school when she was sixteen and drifted in and out of various administrative jobs. She was bright and a fast learner, but her beauty overpowered people and she was treated like a dumb blonde.

Maide recalled the reports of her as a model. She had been very successful but had suddenly dropped out to take an entry-level secretarial job at IBM. That was the place where Ellie first met Sam.

Maide thought about Ellie abruptly cutting short her modelling career. Why would any girl want to do that? She was heading for stardom. Why turn it all down and walk away? The more he thought of Ellie, the more he realized everything about her was a conundrum. She was a puzzle he was trying to put together with a blindfold on.

Maide had encountered strange and terrifying people and been exposed to incredibly unreal situations. But something about Ellie disturbed him more than anyone he'd ever met. Everything on the surface appeared normal. She was a walking example of normality. But instinct told him her scream was the key. Find the reason behind it and everything else would fall into place.

Chapter 42

"Is she okay?" asked David into his mic. He was following close behind the van in Ellie's Porsche.

"That stuff Davison gave her would have knocked out a rhino," replied Gary. "What do you think?"

"Check her. You know her background. Don't take anything by chance."

"Okay."

Gary flicked his head around to check on their load. The driver's cabin wasn't completely enclosed. A little square arch enabled Gary to see clearly through to the back. A pale pink mattress lay on the floor of the van and on top of it lay Ellie. She was still in the same position they'd placed her in back at base. She hadn't moved. Her body was straight and stiff like uncooked spaghetti. She barely looked like she was alive at all. Gary turned back to the road. A slight shiver ran through him.

He'd heard about her 'dying' and 'resurrecting' hours later. M had called her a freak of nature. He agreed. No one cheats death. Suddenly, Gary began to recite the Lord's Prayer in his head. He felt comfort in the words. They acted as defence to the gruesome visions of zombies and ghouls that filled his mind.

"Well? Is she okay?" The impatient, gruff voice was David bellowing in his earpiece.

The sound of his voice brought Gary back to his senses. "Yes. She's out cold. No movement at all," he replied sternly, masking the fright he'd felt a moment earlier.

"Good," answered David, a smile in his voice as he detected a whisper of fear in Gary's voice. "Hey, Gary?"

"What?"

"You let me know if she starts eating your brain," David said, then laughed, unable to control himself.

"Fuck off," Gary shouted.

"We're gonna be switching soon. You'll feel better then," David said, his voice deliberately soothing, like a mother talking to her baby. The tone made Gary even more irate.

"I'm okay. Right! So leave it."

Gary was not laughing. He was serious. He took the whole interplay seriously. He was a trained commando. He'd fought terrorists hand to hand but talk of the supernatural really made him uneasy.

"Oh, Gary, for fuck's sake. Have a laugh. I was only joking."

Gary was aware David had touched a raw nerve in him. Unexpectedly exposing a fear that Gary wanted to keep hidden. In black ops, thought Gary, you're not allowed to have fears of any kind.

"Wanna talk about it?" David asked.

"Talk about what?" answered Gary.

"Your fear."

"I haven't got any fear."

"Right. If you haven't got any fear, why the hell are you so worried about pretty miss in there attacking you?"

Gary was dumbstruck. David had pinpointed his fear exactly. How? David couldn't even see his face.

"She's human, Gary," continued David. "She's not a zombie. You don't need to worry."

"Yeah. I know that. But I can't get out of my head the fact she's been dead for…what was it?"

"Just over two hours."

"Yeah. Over two hours. And there's nothing wrong with her. Shit! She should be a vegetable. But I saw the security data back at base. She was feisty when questioning those MPs. She didn't look like she'd just come back from the brink of death. I don't scare easily, Dave. You know that. But sitting here with her in the back, knowing what I know, I'm fucking freaked, man."

A shudder ran through Gary. His mother had told him that a shudder was the response of someone in the future walking on his grave. If this were true, there must be one hell of a party on top of his grave, for his body was shuddering quite a lot on that journey.

"Yeah. I know what you mean."

The joke had ended. They both slipped into uncomfortable silence. It wasn't an irrational fear. Ellie was an unknown. Fear of the unknown was more powerful and terrifying than the most brutal, sadistic terrorist. With a terrorist, you knew what you were dealing with. You could take the offensive or defensive depending upon the situation. But with the unknown, the rules of the game were different. There were no rules.

Ahead of Gary stretched the end of the M3. Then they'd go onto the A316 and to a desolate back street for the transfer.

Gary read the details on his satnav screen and decided on their next course of action.

"There's a slip road up ahead. It leads to side street. Looks like an industrial estate is at the end."

"Perfect place. I'll see you there," David stated. His voice was clipped and efficient. He didn't engage in any more derogatory comments about Gary's fears.

"Okay," Gary replied, turning off onto the slip road and down into the side street.

David followed behind. The road led into a deserted industrial estate. Gary continued to drive down the road, flanked on either side by oblong concrete and rusty corrugated iron units.

The place was dilapidated but not despondent. Echoes of better times were still visible. Bright, weather-worn signs hung down like brassy earrings on an old tart, trying to attract attention but knowing that their currency on the open market had long since passed. Further down, a new generation was turning tricks. Walls of smooth dove-grey and doors of shiny, leaf-green abounded. Clear and pronounced fascias regaled the names of the businesses within. It was a brave new world. But even that area, for all its inviting newness, was deserted on a Sunday afternoon.

Gary was vigilant. Although it was free of people, the location was still too open for the switch. They needed somewhere secluded. Gary continued his drive further into the estate and, in answer to his request, he saw an archway with an old, abandoned viaduct above it. Gary turned into the arch and waited for David to arrive.

David parked the Porsche at an angle, almost horizontally to the back of the van, enabling the easy transfer of Ellie straight from the van to his passenger seat.

"Good spot," David said, getting out and looking around. "Let's get her." He opened the doors and climbed in while Gary kept watch outside.

David bent down and picked Ellie up in his arms. She was rigid and very cold. Gary was right. She did look dead. Then he shook his head. Mustn't go there.

He grabbed her handbag, stepped down out of the van, lay Ellie in the seat, adjusted her seat belt and placed her handbag by her side.

Gary's hawk eyes constantly scanned but no one was around. He looked at his watch. 5:03 p.m. on a Sunday. Quiet was to be expected. Most people would be in their homes, sleeping off their Sunday lunches and, thankfully, not hanging around industrial estates.

"Synchronize at 17:04. ETA 17:20. Hit 17.30. Right?" David said, adjusting his watch.

Gary did the same.

"Let's go."

Chapter 43

The senior analyst watched Sam emerge from one of the interrogation cells. His skin was pulled taut across his face as if he was concentrating with an almost painful determination on something.

He took in Sam's huge muscular body beneath his leather jacket and trendy chinos, and his sharp, dark eyes that seemed to drill rather than look. He'd heard Sam was a scientist as well as a killer agent. Brains and brawn. Some guys have all the luck, thought the analyst bitterly.

He could feel the smooth barrel of the hypodermic in his hand.

He'd have to choose his moment. He was, after all, in the middle of the CIA headquarters in Langley. He had to think about his escape options if things didn't go well. And even if they did, they'd shut the place down. He had to find a way to leave without being noticed.

Once the thirty mil was in his account, his life, as he knew it, would be over.

He didn't care. Only Al Nadir recognized his talent. They saw his potential. They were the only ones to which he held any loyalty.

The analyst followed Sam as he marched down the corridor and headed for the gents restroom. He caught up with Sam and watched him barge into the toilet, a surly snarl on his face. Seeing Sam's angry expression, at first, the analyst backed away and headed for the cubicle. And then he turned.

He'd been running away from everything his whole life.

No more.

Today he would make a stand.

Today would be day one of his new life.

With that singular thought, he pushed himself forward behind Sam.

Chapter 44

David closed the van doors. He slipped into the driver's seat, turned a rapid circle and sped away. Gary lumbered in the van far behind. David looked at Ellie beside him. She was so still and hardly breathing. David felt the hairs on the back of his head rise and his skin flushed with sweat. There was something about Ellie, something weird. It was tangible, like it was in the air. He now knew why she had spooked Gary. David wrenched his eyes from her and fixed them on the road. He was stronger.

"You okay?" Gary asked suddenly.

"Yeah. Why shouldn't I be?" David replied.

"Nothing. You don't feel weird with her, do you?"

"No."

"Are you sure?"

"Yes!"

"Really sure?"

"Gary, what the fuck are you on?"

"Nothing. Must just be me then."

"Must be. See you at the target."

David pulled the Porsche away quickly and headed back to the A316. Gary kept a distance behind in the van. Looking into the mirror, David could see sweat bubbles like warts rise up on his forehead. He never sweated on missions. Any mission. What was wrong with him? He cast a sideways glance at Ellie. She was out, her head drooping to the left, resting against the window.

She looked so normal. Just an extremely pretty, normal woman. What was he worried about?

He must be neurotic, paranoid, or simply plain mad to believe that she could harm him. As his machismo feelings increased, he started to relax. He reached over and switched on the music system. Bryan Adams' Summer of '69 burst loudly out of the speakers. The deafening sound made David physically jump. He didn't expect to be greeted with music set at such an ear-splitting volume. It was nightclub loud. Then he remembered. The music brought it all back. When they'd extracted her, Ellie had been playing that song. She'd had it blaring out when they opened the door and sedated her. At the time, he'd hit the off button but obviously not reduced the volume. He shook his head, looking casually at Ellie again.

What he saw made him double take and lose concentration on the road.

Brake lights flickered in his peripheral vision. He looked up to see the car in front had almost stopped. Lights were on red. David slammed on the brake. It was only his split-second reflex that averted an accident that would certainly have written off the Porsche and the Lexus in front of him.

David returned to look at Ellie, eyes wide with amazement and denial like a little boy told that Santa Claus doesn't exist. He watched Ellie's sleek index finger move against her thigh, tapping out the beat to the music. Subconsciously, she kept perfectly in rhythm with 'It was the summer, the summer, the summer of '69'.

David could see that she was still heavily sedated. No reaction showed in her face. Her eyes were shut. But at some level, inside her, she could *feel* the music. David leant over and turned the volume down.

Ellie's finger stopped beating out the rhythm. Then he raised the volume high again and her finger resumed its dancing. He'd heard of coma patients being broadcast music to wake them. Something to do with the alpha level in the brain responding to sound stimuli. But Ellie wasn't in a coma. She was heavily knocked out. Nothing should be moving. And she should not be aware of external stimuli, least of all keeping in time with a rhythm.

He reduced the volume and spoke into his microphone. "Gary, did you play music when she was with you?"

Gary jerked slightly, not expecting David to contact him until they had reached Silent Waters. "Sorry, what?" Gary said distractedly.

"I said, did you play music when she was with you?" David repeated in his testy tone usually delivered to those who met his chagrin.

"No, of course I didn't. Why?"

"I did and she moved."

Gary couldn't understand why David had been so careless. They'd have to stop somewhere and inject her again. His voice was deliberately scathing. "Oh, shit! You've woken her up."

"No. Of course I haven't, you idiot!" David was exasperated with Gary. "She's still out cold. But her index finger has been moving in time with the music."

"It couldn't be. She's knocked out. The drugs Davison gave her shield any sensory stimuli."

"I know what Davison gave her. But Gary, she did move, and she moved in acknowledgement of her surroundings. She knew I was playing one of her songs. That shows she is experiencing stimuli at the subliminal level."

"So what?" asked Gary, confused.

"So what? Think about it. Maybe everything we're doing now, she's aware of and maybe even storing up in her mind. Say Sam uses regression therapy on her, he'll find out the truth. We'll all be fucked!"

"Oh God, David. I knew this mission was jinxed. What are we going to do?"

Gary sounded desperate. But David knew exactly what to do. "We've got the cocktail. Davison said one shot. I'm going to give her the whole fucking lot." David's voice was granite.

"That could kill her," said Gary.

"So? We're fucking terrorists. Let's do the job right."

Angrily, he pushed in the button, halting the music, and pulled out his earpiece, severing the connection with Gary.

"David, we need to talk about this. Please, David. Respond!" shouted Gary, infuriated.

In the Porsche, shooting far ahead away from Gary in the van, David stared coldly at Ellie's virtually lifeless body, and said under his breath, "You're not going to bury me!"

Chapter 45

Maide looked at the clock again. He wondered how it was all progressing. Realizing what was being committed, Maide knew he was, indeed, at the lowest point of his career.

Aware of his wandering thoughts, Maide jarred himself back to reality. He looked around and realized his private road was near. He broke quickly, glancing at the clock. It was 4:39 p.m. He hardly had any time. Twenty minutes max. He had to leave the house at 5:00 p.m. He couldn't delay. Maide turned in and sped up the gravel track of the private road, his wheels kicking up dust like wild horses in the sand. Imposing carved wooden gates appeared at the end of the road. He pressed a button on his dashboard. The gates silently swayed open. Like a feather running over a rock, no sound could be heard. It was a testament to Maide's fastidious attention to detail.

Cameras affixed on high poles and buried in the trees turned to eye Maide's progression up his sweeping driveway. A palatial Andalusian-styled residence slipped into his vision and stretched graciously out in front of him. He parked his BMW right in front of the house, leapt like a young gazelle out of the door, grabbing his tiny flash drive, and quickly opened his front door. The countdown on the alarm sounded immediately. He punched in the seven-digit combination to silence the din and ran quickly to his office. The drapes were constantly drawn. He switched on the light and moved over to the fitted shelving and cupboards that took up the back wall.

It held an Everest of books, files and documents. He tried the cupboards and eventually, after a few misfired attempts, found the satellite phone in one of the lower cupboards. He took it out and placed it on the desk. His fingers were still trembling. Keep it together, he told himself sternly, reaching for his laptop. He copied the *.wav* file from the flash drive to the laptop, clicked on the sound file and listened. The enunciation was perfect. It was absolutely Al Nadir. Basking in a moment of hubris, Maide forgot about the tiny sweet-lookalike flash memory device.

Maide ran the digital to analogue converter and connected the AV I/O line so that the *.wav* file was sent directly to the analogue satellite phone. Maide had set the satellite phone to transmit the message over a well-known Al Nadir frequency. He invoked the timer software and linked the wav file broadcast event for 17:30. He synchronized his watch to correspond exactly to the LED readout on the screen. The time was 16:57. He had to go.

He switched off the light and looked around at the timer on the screen. Something about the scene perturbed him. The red LED on the laptop flickered, counting down the seconds. Its stark red glowing hue illuminated the dark room. It had a demonic presence as though Maide's actions were being overseen by the devil. Maide tried to shake such illogical feelings and closed the door to shut out the image. He ran over to the front door and punched in the seven digits to fix the alarm. The alarm screamed its setting sound as he slid back into his car, slipped the key in the ignition and sped back down the drive, through the gates onto the private road.

Back to River House. To get his career back on track.

Chapter 46

Sam bent down, cupped the water in his hands, and threw it over his face. God, what a morning. Stein-Muller pushing his buttons and Lupez probably talking shit. He was ready to give Rasheed the once over and make sure the bastard talked this time.

He moved over to the dryer and noticed a tubby guy behind him. Sam smiled as amiably as he could muster in the mirror. Tubby guy nodded and smiled back.

"Heavy morning. Needed a moment alone," said Sam, making casual conversation. He checked the guy's badge, reading the reverse image swiftly. Simon Walters, Senior Analyst, FinTech. He wondered why the guy was down in the interrogation cells.

"A long way from home, aren't you?" said Sam, turning around to face Walters.

"Erm, sorry? What…what do you mean?" stuttered Walters, trying to move around the other side of Sam to the basin.

Sam didn't move and he blocked access to the basin.

"FinTech, that's quite a few floors up from where we are. Have you got someone down here you're assisting?"

The hackles on Sam's neck had risen. That thing he felt, like a vibe, that something wasn't right…

He felt it now.

Sam took in Walters, eyeing him top to toe, and noticed his right hand was curled around an object.

He moved to the side a little, as if moving away from Walters and heading for the door, but then he spun around, and swept his leg under the analyst. As Walter started to lose balance, Sam stamped on his tibia, forcing him to the floor. Walters screamed in agony, and his hands went out to grab the basin to stop his fall. As his right hand opened, the syringe dropped out. Sam snatched it up.

He rounded on Walters, who now cowered on the floor.

Fury flared in Sam's eyes. He shoved the hypo in front of the analyst's face.

"What the fuck is this?"

Walters said nothing.

"Is it your vitamin shot then, Simon Walters? Just about to shoot up? Well, I won't stop you."

Sam stretched out the syringe in his palm and handed it to Walters.

"Well, go on then. Shoot up!"

Walters backed away, shivering.

"Shall I do it for you?" snarled Sam, taking the hypo and, in parallel, seizing Walters' arm.

"No. No!" screamed Walters.

He tried to pull his arm away but Sam's grip was too strong.

"Right," said Sam, holding the hypo over Walters' artery. "Now you had better tell me who you're working for right now otherwise this needle goes in. Understand?"

Walters nodded.

"So who is it? Al Nadir?"

Walters didn't move. His eyes gave it away. Sam pressed the hypo into Walters' skin as he moved forward to check his jacket pockets.

"Try anything and this goes in," said Sam, pulling out a CIA-standard Blackberry Passport, which he threw down beside him, and another phone, not government issue.

"What's this? Switch it on," said Sam, handing the other phone to Walters.

Walters took it. Sam noticed his hand shaking. He switched it on and handed it back to Sam without a word.

One hand on the hypo, the other holding the phone, Sam stared at the screen. A message application flashed. Sam clicked on it.

His throat tightened as he read the message, and a growl grew within him. He pocketed the phone, and then tugged at Walters lapels, dragging him up with one hand. His other hand still gripped Walters' wrist, holding the barrel of the hypo close against his skin.

Sam pushed Walters against the basin, but the man slipped as his busted leg wouldn't hold his weight. He fell against Sam, who thrusted him back against the marble sink. But a moment passed where Walters' right hand vanished from Sam's eye line.

Sam glared at him. "Like winning the fucking lottery eh?" He spat the words at Walters, who couldn't meet the agent's eye. "Where you're going, there will be a ThunderBall for you every night!"

Sam took the syringe away and threw it behind Walters on the marble surround, out of his reach. He hauled the man forward and wrenched his left arm back, pushing it fast and hard upward, almost out of its socket. Walters screamed. His other arm swept in and suddenly, Sam felt heat and piercing pain. He looked down and saw a pen sticking out of his side. Sam gritted his teeth, still wrenching Walters' arm back. He pulled out the pen, now covered in blood, and threw it to the floor.

"That was a fucking stupid move!"

Sam rammed Walters into the mirror adjacent to the basin, smashing him hard, and then yanked him back and hurled him against the door to one of the cubicles. Walters sank into a lump, and then tipped onto his side. He made an effort to crawl on all fours away from the raging agent, but Sam lifted him upward from behind and flung him against the mirror, shattering it. Walters, with his back to the wall, shrank back as Sam gripped hold of his lapels and squeezed them tighter around his neck.

Sam snarled, his face close to Walters' stubby nose and flabby jowls.

Walters saw the moment. His hand sneaked out toward the hypo that, in the fracas, had rolled towards the edge of the marble sink surround. Sam noticed and yanked him away. But Walters had the hypo in his hand. As he brought his arm around to stab the agent, Sam moved lightning-fast, gripping Walters' arm and forcing the trajectory of the needle to land on Walters' shoulder. With a hefty thrust, Sam pushed hard, pressing down the syringe and releasing whatever was in it directly into Walters' blood stream.

Walters' face contorted in a mix of surprise and release.

Sam let him go and he started to slip down the wall. His eyes rolled and his mouth dripped saliva as the toxin took over his body.

Sam stepped back and took out Walters' other phone again. He looked at the message. $30M for his head. He hit delete.

No one in the Agency, or in any agency, would know he was a marked man. That would ruin his chances at getting to Al Douri.

And for what he did to Kinley and his family, Sam was determined to get to Al Douri.

The door opened and Sam heard footsteps approaching.

"What the hell?" said the owner of the footsteps, staring at Sam's bloody side, then at the man with a CIA badge slumped, looking dead on the floor.

"Want to tell me what's happened?"

"Not really," said Sam calmly. "Just had to do a bit of rat-catching. They're coming up through the sewers now, don't you know."

Chapter 47

David reached Silent Waters. The building was steel with pale green reflective glass. The top three floors had balconies. The penthouse floor had roof terraces. The front two overlooked the Thames and the back two gazed over the immaculate landscaped gardens, which were an acre and a half in size. David operated the buzzer in the car and drove through the gates. Looking around him at the luxurious environment, he snorted with jealously at how the other half live.

He followed the path down to the garage basement. The sensors at the garage were alerted as David approached and the massive thickened steel door began to rise. David descended into the basement car park. He had the sun visor down as he drove past the CC camera. If Harold was watching, he would see Ellie asleep in her car with a man driving it. Harold, having the brainpower of a goldfish, would naturally assume that the man was Sam.

The car park was reasonably full of cars. David looked for the registration number Maide had given him of Sam's C63 Merc AMG. David found it close to the lifts. He parked the Porsche beside the Merc AMG. From the floor of the car, he snatched his tool bag. Gently, he opened the car door and stepped out, making sure to keep out of the eye line of the cameras. Skirting around the wall, like a lizard searching for food, David reached the first camera by the entrance. He dove into his bag and retrieved a device that looked like a small digital camera. It was an image jammer. Swiftly, he positioned the device beneath the camera and switched it on.

Immediately, a wireless frequency was shot from the jammer straight into the transmission box on the CC camera. An amber light on the device came on and the flick-out, tiny LCD screen showed the image that Harold was now seeing on his bank of monitors in the foyer. David inched in front of the camera, all the time watching on the tiny screen for a flicker of change. The image of the empty basement car park remained. David was totally invisible to the camera's eye. Reassured that the tech actually worked, David jammed the images on remaining cameras beside the lifts.

With the basement's internal surveillance blocked, David was free to move. He focused on the lifts. He was very lucky. Both were in the basement. He got to work immediately, unscrewing the control panel. Inside the panel were wires and switches. David delved into his bag and removed a small device with wires protruding out of the top. On the other end of the wires were crocodile clips. He clipped them onto two open wires inside the control panel. David slid a button at the side of the device and a holographic keyboard appeared, hovering in front of him. Almost simultaneously, the device's screen lit up showing an incoherent stream of computer code.

David typed quickly, breaking into the code, and uploaded the sub-routine that had been developed for hacking into the lift's operating system. The machine code stopped running. His screen went pale blue showing the schematics of the two lifts. The schematics had clickable areas. David clicked on the left-hand lift to select it. The screen zoomed in, making the left lift large and emphasized a series of functions. David could see that for both security and maintenance each lift was on a separate power circuit. He selected maintenance status and shut off the power to the left-hand lift. By selecting maintenance status, the lift's system didn't cut in with the backup generator. David flicked back to the right-hand lift and selected floor control. He omitted from the lift's operation all the floors except for basement and seventh. Everything from lower ground to sixth floor levels on the schematic turned red, showing that they were out of operation. David removed the crocodile clip, switched off the device and returned the panel back as it was. He knew there were three other families on the seventh floor, so he had to be quick.

He didn't want to strike anyone until he carried the mask of Al Nadir.

"The truth has been blinded," said David into his mouth piece.

It was the signal to Gary to let him know that all was on track and proceeding to plan.

Gary was pleased to hear David at last. He was parked on double yellows in a side street just off Silent Waters, and hadn't spoken to his colleague since their discussion over Ellie moving. He awaited David's second signal.

David returned to the car, grabbed Ellie, swung her over his shoulder, and held her legs with his right hand. He snatched her bag and locked the car.

Stepping into the right hand lift he hit the seventh-floor button. With all the other floors temporarily removed, the lift whooshed upwards in seconds, meeting its target with a familiar ping. David laid Ellie on the floor of the lift and fumbled for a wrench to prop open the lift door, just in case someone in the basement called for it. Cautiously, he poked his head out, looking from left to right. The cameras were pointing the other way. David raced over and shot the left one with the blocking signal from the jammer. Then he repeated the action on the right-hand camera. In the back of his mind, he prayed no one would come out of their doors. He wasn't in the mindset to be a terrorist yet.

Hauling Ellie back on his shoulder, he placed both his bag and her handbag back in the crook of his arm. Her door keys were in his left hand. He stepped over the lift's threshold, removed the wrench, and stuffed it in his bag. Moving fluidly with expert precision to the door, David quickly opened it. He slipped inside and closed it softly.

Inside the apartment, David moved with the rapidity of a quark in a particle accelerator. He placed Ellie on the sofa and bunched up some cushions behind her head. Scanning the lounge, David looked for the right place to locate her bag. He could see her briefcase by the side of the two-seater sofa. He dropped it next to the briefcase. Given her businesswoman profile, it seemed the right place. The scene he intended to portray was that she was relaxing on a Sunday afternoon, watching a film and having a glass of orange juice. He ran over to Ellie's DVD collection. It was an eclectic mix of romance, sci-fi, comedy, drama and documentaries.

He selected *Bridget Jones Diary*. Always a good choice for females, he thought chauvinistically, and slipped the DVD inside the player. He jumped to a scene towards the end of the movie and started to run it. The sound was low. He increased it, turning to stare at Ellie for any reaction similar to her movement in the car. But she didn't respond in any way. Placing the DVD cover on the table, he realized the final element in their elaborate invention was missing. The drink.

David shot into the kitchen, opening eye-level cupboards in search of a glass. He found one stocked full of cut crystal. Placing his hand forward to grab the glass, he paused, contemplating. She wouldn't use cut crystal for a quiet afternoon drink. There must be other glasses for everyday use. He opened two more cupboards and found one with coffee mugs, high ball and tall glasses. Then David opened the fridge, took out a carton and poured the juice into the glass.

Returning to the lounge, he placed it in her hand, lodging it beside the side cushion so it wouldn't fall. David reached into his pocket and pulled out the hypo containing the antidote to the choral hydrate. The hypo had a cover over the needle. He removed it and walked over to Ellie. He would have less than a minute to get out before the antidote took effect. He smoothed her neck, lent in, and inexplicably had the urge to smell her. Vanilla ice cream. She looked so innocent, so sweet. So defenseless. He reached out to touch her cheek. He was captivated. His lips moved towards her, trance-like. Then he caught himself.

Jesus. What was he doing?

He had to stick her, and then get the fuck out. Abruptly, he plunged the hypo into her neck but withdrew it too sharply. Blood trickled out onto the cushion.

"Shit," said David.

Looking at the blood, he realized he'd been too hasty. He grabbed his bag and sped towards the door, but turned around to look at Ellie. She had mesmerized him for a second. Her hand was twitching. Her head moved a little. She was waking.

David opened the door silently and closed it behind him. He ran towards the lift and pressed the call up button. With nowhere but the basement to go, the lift had remained on the seventh floor, just as David hoped it would. He slipped inside and hit the basement button.

Exiting the lift, he said into his mic, "The bird's back in its nest. Time to ruffle the feathers."

Chapter 48

Ellie woke from a heavy sleep. The chenille cushions were soft and comforting against her face. She felt absorbed in their lush softness. Reluctantly, she lifted her head up. The TV was on. She rubbed her eyes and stared at the clock on the TV. The LED showed it was the afternoon. When had she *ever* slept in the afternoon? Ellie moved to get up, and the glass in between her hand and the cushion tumbled sideways. Ellie felt the cool orange juice trickle through her fingers. She looked down in time to stop the drink from falling. Encasing her fingers around the glass, she had to tell her hand to hold it firm. She leant forward to place the glass on the table. But disorientation flowed through her body.

She sat back down, still holding the glass. Ellie stared at it. Did she drink it? She couldn't remember. Ellie licked her lips, expecting to taste orange. But her lips were dry and tasteless. She forced a swallow and registered a slightly metallic taste in her mouth like she'd sucked on a coin. She couldn't detect any orange juice at all. Ellie looked around the lounge, trying to balance her mind to take in her surroundings.

It felt like she'd been travelling. Inside of her, there was a sense of displacement. She felt strange. Something had happened, something against her control, something bad. But maybe something good. Her feelings were ambivalent.

She stared back at the TV program and noticed the play arrow on the DVD player was illuminated. It wasn't a TV program. It was a DVD. She couldn't remember putting in a DVD. She looked quizzically at the screen. Renée Zellweger was running in the snow in her underwear. Must be *Bridget Jones' Diary,* thought Ellie. It was one of her favorite films, and it was almost finished.

I must've played it, started watching and fell asleep, thought Ellie. She stared at the DVD box on the table, trying hard to recollect placing it there. Why the hell would I play a DVD and not run one of my on-demand channels like Netflix or Prime, thought Ellie, confused. She tried hard to remember why she was playing a DVD on Sunday afternoon and not working. But her memory was lost. Her sleep had been too heavy. It was a sleep with dreams. She couldn't understand it. REM sleep during the day. So strange!

Her dreams had been disturbing. Ellie shivered. It had all felt so real. But drifting back into consciousness, aware of the world around her, Ellie's recall was less lucid. Fuzzy fragments of sensations and feelings were leftover. Brilliant light, searing heat, biting cold. A stainless-steel wall. Dank, dark places. Utter fear, indignation, anger. And white everywhere.

Ellie thought she could remember people in her dream. But the mist in her mind obscured their faces. Old, young, short, tall; they all melded into one confusing contortion.

She lifted the glass to her lips and drank voraciously, draining it in seconds. Why was she so thirsty? She needed more. She pushed down on the sofa. Her gaze landed on the ivory cushion. A thin crimson line stood out like graffiti on a white picket fence. Ellie stared at the line. Her hand moved across to touch it. It was faintly damp. She ran her finger along the line like a blind woman reading braille. Bringing her finger up close, she smelled the deposit her finger picked up. A warm, sticky, faintly metallic smell. Blood.

She looked at the position of the line, and realized it corresponded to where her neck had been resting. Gently, Ellie touched her neck. Immediately, she could feel the slight wetness. Anxiously, Ellie stood up and headed for the mirror.

Chapter 49

Gary received the message. "The bird's in the nest." All was on schedule. Now it was time to turn up the heat. He switched on the ignition and headed towards Silent Waters. The residence was gated with a keypad. David had the pin code already from M

"ETA?" asked David quietly into his mic.

"Thirty seconds," replied Gary, turning into Silent Waters.

David walked out of the garage from the side entrance. The van drew up beside him. David got in beside Gary.

"Ready?" he asked, staring hard at Gary.

"Ready."

David reached behind the seat and pulled out the balaclavas. He handed one to Gary, who quickly put it on. David pulled the other over his head. The coarse wool rubbed against his face. The sensation was too familiar. He closed his eyes as memories took over him. Cold, damp concrete against his face, smelly mud in his nostrils, bullets whizzing past his ear, and cheeks burning in the sweltering heat. The abrasive fabric unlocked a multitude of past experiences.

He turned back again and hunted behind the seat. He withdrew the other ops bag containing Ruger MK4's, CS gas canisters and a hypodermic. Gary took his gun out of David's hand with uncontained excitement.

David held his arm tight. "This is for real. Are you ready?"

"Ready as I'll ever be." Gary's gung-ho attitude reflected his immaturity.

David was having none of it. "No accidents. Be precise. We want to be out of there quickly. Time check. 17:30 hours. Let's go!"

"Hang on, David. Are you okay?" asked Gary, remembering their earlier argument.

"Yeah, yeah. I'm ok. Don't worry. I'm not going to kill her. I'm not that crazy!"

David knew he'd been rash at even making such a suggestion. Maide had told them he wanted Ellie 'roughed up pretty bad, but don't for God's sake kill her'. He didn't want to go against an explicit order. But he still hoped she hadn't been aware of her surroundings. He really didn't want to face the consequences of Sam Noor on his tail.

"That's…that's good," said Gary, relieved.

Gary hurtled the van up the driveway towards the closed gates. He lent out and punched in the code then waited for the huge gates to open.

From his position, Harold the security man at reception could see the white van speeding up the driveway. He thought that it was contractors late for a job. But looking closer, he noticed the windows were darkened. Maybe the paparazzi were trying to catch a glimpse of the footballers and pop stars residing in Silent Waters. Harold got out of his chair and walked slowly, holding onto the ledge around the pinewood desk. His piles had given him gyp that morning. He could hardly walk. With the speed of a pregnant sloth, he lumbered towards the door. Bloody gutter press, he thought. He'd show them. Harold's hand dropped to the gun holstered on his thigh.

David could see Harold movements behind the glass.

"Now!" he screamed, looking at Gary, and they leapt out of the van in parallel, running towards the entrance, firing in rapid succession at locks on the double doors. One stray bullet sailed through the glass and hit Harold in the top of his shoulder. Blood bubbled out of the hole the bullet had made. Harold watched the blood flow out. Dizzy with nausea and traumatized by shock and pain, he fell to the floor.

David led the way in, still firing. Crunching shards of broken glass beneath his boots, he ran in through the lobby over to Harold. Gary came up behind, pointing his gun and signaling his fierce intentions, while David tied and gagged the terrified security man. Harold stared at him. David pirouetted on his one knee and smashed the side of Harold's face with the butt of his gun. Harold dropped back unconscious.

David made sure Harold was out, and then ran with Gary to the lift. They remained silent, waiting for the ping to register the seventh floor. When it came, it seemed louder than before, echoing through an empty corridor. The doors opened. David and Gary looked at each other grimly and ran to finish their assignment in apartment 702.

Chapter 50

Ellie stood with the intention to inspect the blood on her neck, but on standing, she heard the ping of the lift and footsteps in the hallway. She knew it wasn't Sam. He was still in the States. And she knew it wasn't her neighbors. They were away on holiday. Deep inside, she felt that footsteps equaled danger. Suddenly, her senses sprang into life. The footsteps approached her door. Someone was coming.

Where was the gun Sam had given her? She cursed, remembering her bag was in the bedroom. Turning, she heard shots and a tremendous thud behind her.

Ellie ran like a champion-bred stallion towards the back of the apartment.

One of the men sped after her, lunging out to grab her arm, but she turned and landed a high kick at his jaw. Astonishment registered in his eyes.

Yes, you fucker, I'm a kickboxer!

On the next kick, the element of surprise had gone. The man snatched hold of her foot and flipped Ellie. She lashed out, her nails digging into his face, but she lost her balance and fell to the floor. Her head smashed against the marble with a bone-shattering crunch. Her vision clouded for a second and she forced herself to focus and regain her sight. But her timing was a fraction too slow. Heavy hands were upon her. Grabbing her shoulders, they turned her around.

Through the balaclavas, the men's eyes looked rabid and insane. She noticed they were both very tall, but one was slightly taller than the other. The taller one raised his hand and slapped her face with such ferociousness Ellie expected her cheek to burst open. He hit her face again. Ellie tried to fight back, but the other man pummeled her like she was a punching bag. His fists smashed into her, hard and fast. Ellie crumpled.

Taller man hauled her onto the sofa and the smaller man held her. Taller man took out a hypodermic. He moved it in front of Ellie. Her terrified eyes followed the needle.

"For the glory of Al Nadir," said the taller man, and he plunged the needle into Ellie's neck.

Then the men released her.

The room spun wildly. The gleaming white walls lost their paintings and morphed into honeycomb structures. Ellie walked towards the structural transmutations. She peered inside the dark comb caves. Something moved. Fast. She stepped back as long tentacles stretched out from deep inside the labyrinth. Emerging into the light, the tentacles opened their bulbous ends to reveal red eyes glaring angrily at Ellie. She heard a rasping noise. Turning her head around, she watched as green amorphous blobs with razor sharp teeth oozed out of one of the honeycomb caves behind her. Ellie screamed, terrified, and backed down into the sofa, her arms over her head, trying to protect herself. Then she realized the sofa was pulling her inside it, trying to eat her. Leaping up, Ellie saw the creases in the cotton fabric had turned into a wicked smile. She tried to run away from the honeycombed walls, horrific blobs and her lethal sofa, but her movements were bumbling, and she slammed into her table. It growled, ejecting a carved leg and kicked her in the stomach. Winded, Ellie fell to the floor.

In reality, Ellie had run into David who punched her hard in the stomach, sending her into Gary's arms. Gary threw her to the floor.

Ellie climbed to her feet, shivering. Her eyes were glassy and wide. Nothing made sense. What was happening? Where was her home? She had to get out of this madness. She knew there was a door. She could see a door. But she couldn't get to it.

In her altered state, the floor was the major obstacle. It was full of holes, deep, dark bottomless holes. *I mustn't fall into the holes. I'll die. All holes lead to hell,* thought Ellie, breathing heavily. She jumped over the deep black chasms.

Ellie leapt with determination around the room. She felt the taller man's eyes on her. He was amused. Smiling cruelly, she saw as he motioned to the smaller man to look at her.

Sweating, Ellie landed on the floor between the holes. But with each jump she made, the holes increased. The black holes engulfed each other, gradually taking over the entire floor until only a tiny piece of floor remained. Ellie couldn't move. Staring down into the endless blackness, she froze manically to the spot.

Mustn't move. Can't move. Must remain here. Forever.

Ellie forced herself to be still. She kept her feet close together like she was standing on a small stepping-stone across a river filled with crocodiles.

Taller man reached inside a bag and took out two canisters. Heading away he pulled the canisters open and threw them directly at her. The canisters exploded in her face, releasing some kind of gas. Ellie screamed and her hands flew up to her face to shield her eyes from the gas.

From the moment she'd been injected, David had wondered what she'd been seeing. Her weird behavior confirmed her trip was immediate, as Davison had promised. When he'd injected her, he'd been careful to give her the dosage the doctor had advised and no more.

David heard her coughing and wheezing. The gas was taking effect. David looked at his watch. It was 17:35 p.m. Time to go.

Together, David and Gary headed for the stairway. But then, David stopped, reached into his bag and took out a wrench. He wiped it for prints and rammed it between the lift edge and the frame. There he left the lift, trapped on the seventh floor, another problem for the rescue squad to face. He figured that any Al Nadir operative worth his salt would have done the same.

Chapter 51

Calm. Keep calm, Maide told himself.

His journey back via the A3 to Central had been quick and uneventful. No learner drivers, no unexpected collisions, just a straight drive at a modest speed. Maide entered the building, passed through the usual security checks, took the lift, and then walked briskly onto the surveillance floor.

Calm. Keep calm. It was like a mantra to Maide. He kept saying it in his mind.

He looked down at his watch. Two minutes to go. A sudden panic swept through him. What if the timer didn't work? What if he'd somehow connected it wrong? What would happen?

Calm. Keep calm.

Maide breathed in, stepped through the security cubicle and onto the surveillance floor. Banks of monitors suspended from the ceiling greeted him. The room gleamed with the latest surveillance technology. It was the jewel in MI6's crown. Personnel with earphones and intent looks stared at screens and punched on keypads. Here, in this room, comms streams came in from GCHQ, having already been monitored and verified for hostile activity. The voice, email and other assorted data that descended upon the teams of scanning eyes and intently listening ears needed further analysis as to whether a hostile source was involved.

With step-change developments in technology, information streamed in from the physical as well as the electronic world. Nano-mote receivers, created from a molecular base upwards to resemble insects, transmitted conversations holding keywords that could be a risk to national security. Although most of the time Al Nadir blocked surveillance opportunities, occasionally the nano-motes got through and picked up on vital words, and even whole conversations. Their usage became a key tactic in the war. At the point of transmission from the nano-motes, split-second correlations were made with data held on Echelon and appropriate intel immediately delivered to in-field MI6 operatives.

Maide walked towards a group of operatives scanning satellite communication transmissions. He glanced at his watch. It was 5:30 p.m. He started to sweat. Why hadn't anyone picked up on anything?

"Sir? Excuse me, sir. I think you need to listen to a transmission we have just intercepted. It's on an old Al Nadir frequency. It sounds serious. It refers to a Silent Waters target being neutralized."

Maide breathed in again.

Calm. Keep calm. This is it.

"Put it on the speaker. Let me hear it," Maide replied quickly.

His hands were tight behind his back. It looked regimental. He was the commanding officer and he was in charge. Had anyone inspected closer, they would have seen Maide was holding his hands so tightly to stop them from shaking.

"Payload dispatched. Silent Waters target neutralized."

The transmission was patchy. A faint hum could be heard in the background. The comms operative ran the analyzer and waited for the program's hypothesis. It came with ninety-seven percent probability that the sound was a CFM56-3C aircraft engine from a modified Boeing 737-300.

"Airborne broadcast, sir".

The voice was male and unmistakably Arab. Maide was enthralled by how real his work sounded. Caught for a second in a moment of personal conceit, he failed to respond appropriately. Realizing his miscalculation, Maide compelled himself to react.

"Query on Silent Waters? What is it?"

"Excuse me, sir." A round-faced girl stood up and looked sheepishly at Maide.

Maide swallowed, remaining calm and stern. "Yes?"

"Erm, sir, Silent Waters, that's an apartment block in Chelsea."

"Are you sure?"

"Yes, sir. One of Xcite lives there. I've, erm, been there and tried to take his picture. The place is definitely Silent Waters."

"Excuse me, sir," the comms officer interrupted, having run the query.

"Yes. Speak. Come on." Maide appeared irritable, but inside, he was loving it. The smooth execution of his plan was like good sex, wonderfully satisfying.

"Silent Waters is a key residence for the undersecretary for defense. And Dr. Sam Noor. A complete list of tenants is here."

Maide snatched the paper, his eyes dilating in shock as the officer relayed the information.

"When did this transmission come in?"

"Just now, sir. We intercepted at 17:30. Obviously, there were other parts of the communication we didn't pick up. This is serious, isn't it, sir?" The comms officer stared at his boss' terror-struck reaction.

"Yes," Maide replied, picking up the phone. "This is serious".

Dr. Davison, MI6 Chief Medical Officer, answered. It was a call he was waiting for. "Hello?"

"We need a medical squad ready to go in five minutes. We have a suspected Al Nadir attack at Silent Waters, Chelsea."

"Yes. Okay," Davison muttered, replacing the receiver.

Maide called the special operations division. "Cartwright, we need a counter terrorism squad to Silent Waters, Chelsea. There's been an Al Nadir attack. I'll meet you in five in the basement."

Maide listened, affirmed the action and replaced the receiver.

"Sir, there's some really important people living there. I hope no one's been hurt," muttered the round-faced technician.

"Yes. So do I," Maide replied.

Chapter 52

Sirens shattered the smug afternoon quiet. The artery of pathways in Silent Waters clogged with vehicles and people. Its lush landscaped gardens overflowed with activity.

Maide looked out at the scene from the backseat of his Jag. Quentin sat opposite. Nathan Cartwright, Head of Special Operations, was in front next to the driver. He turned around to ensure he was part of the conversation.

Cartwright had risen through the ranks in MI6 far quicker than Maide. He was fifty-one, very smart and very fit. Naturally good looking, without being overtly so, the combination of his tall frame, auburn hair and hazel eyes still managed to turn heads. Knowing Maide was close to retirement, he made no effort to conceal the fact he was openly gunning for the number one position. His working manner was abrupt, just skirting downright rude. His earpiece squeaked. He touched the button behind his ear. News from the frontline.

"Cartwright." He listened and relayed the information to Quentin and Maide. "Security guard's shot. Seventh floor's hit."

"Jesus Christ! Oh no. Oh my God! Not another Al Nadir attack. The UK just can't take another one."

Cartwright watched Quentin bleating and shook his head. The bloody minister couldn't hold it together. They didn't even know who'd been hit and he was more worried about the government's popularity poll.

Maide pressed the button on the satcomm panel in front of him.

Back at Central, a communications officer came on the line. On seeing Maide calling, he immediately straightened his back and looked more alert. Maide didn't engage in any pleasantries. His tone was cold and hard. Cartwright could hear the sheer determination in his voice.

"Patch me through to Langley. Now."

The comms officer's counterpart at Langley came on the line. He recognized Maide instantly.

"Yes, sir?" he clipped, toning down his Bronx accent.

"Get me Sam Noor now!" Maide shouted.

"Yes, sir." The comms officer flicked a few buttons.

The screen went dark. Maide swallowed heavily. Cartwright watched him. Maide raised his eyes to meet Cartwright's scrutiny, but he didn't say a word.

The screen flickered back to life. Sam's angry face filled it.

"Yeah, what is it?" Sam glared into the screen, waiting intolerantly for his boss' reply.

"Sam, we're at Silent Waters. There's been an attack. The seventh floor has been hit. It's Al Na-"

Maide stopped as Cartwright waved his hand as more intel streamed into his ear.

"Entered flat 702. Woman, Caucasian, conscious. Medical team assisting."

Cartwright knew that flat 702 was Sam's home. And he knew Sam was married.

Chapter 53

Sam heard Cartwright's words. His body temperature plummeted like liquid nitrogen had just been pumped into his veins. He froze. He felt alone. Sam was aware of silence around him. All he could hear was his own breathing. Comforted by the rhythm, he fell into its pace, breathing gently but forcefully. But something was burrowing up from deep inside him.

From the other side of the satcomm, Maide stared. Sam tried to find words, but he could only spout silent gasps.

Sam listened, numb and shaking, as Maide filled in the words he couldn't say.

"702. Oh God, Sam. I'm so sorry. It's Ellie. She was the target."

The something inside Sam forced its way up, vibrating his body like an earthquake. Pain immersed him. He tried again to open his mouth but still no sound came. He'd gone beyond expression to a place of sheer darkness. Death was in his eyes.

Maide paled in front of Sam as he watched his reaction.

"Sam-" Maide started gently.

But Sam's incensed response, as he suddenly found his tongue again, overpowered Maide completely. "Oh my God. Ellie! Fuck!"

Gone was compartmentalization, or any tiny tinge of it. Sam's words tumbled out in a free-flow of raw, unfettered emotion. An unseen force had stuck its hand into his stomach and ripped his guts out. He was bleeding inside. Ellie was hurt. Maybe dead. The love of his life. The one thing that made the difference to his life could be dead. And where was he? Stuck in fucking Washington interviewing a bunch of bastards, while his baby, his love, had been targeted by fucking Al Nadir. He thundered back at the screen.

"How is she? Is she alive? Go there. Tell me exactly what happened."

Sam was shaking with fury. His face had become a starless night.

"Sam, I'm sorry." Maide attempted to deliver his consolations. But Sam wasn't hearing anything.

"Just go, sir. Go and see her. Then tell me what the fuck has happened to her." Sam was spitting the words. His pronounced mouth had thinned to a line. His eyes were solid, holding back the tears.

"Sam, what can I-" Maide started.

"Just go!" Sam screamed insanely, standing up and moving his hand forward like he was going to hit the screen. "Just fucking go. You tell me she's okay." Sam eyes flashed, exposing raw fury. "I'll be waiting."

Chapter 54

Without looking at anyone inside the car, Maide opened the door and stepped out. An MI6 officer placed his hand in front of Maide, stating it wasn't safe. Maide bristled.

"I know what's safe. Let me pass if you value your job!"

The officer stepped to the side without a further word. Maide brushed past him and entered the building. He moved quickly, filtering through his ops people milling around the foyer and heading over to the stairway. After an attack, lifts were never used until the place was deemed safe and free of devices.

The stairway was full of people, mostly residents who had been affected by the CS gas. His fears of the gas getting into the AC ducts had been realized. People were screaming. He stared at them on the stairway. Officers were leading them outside, trying to calm them down. They were crying, their eyes bloodshot, and they were shaking. They were confused and afraid. He pushed past the stream of people coming down the stairs. It was never-ending. Maide was amazed by the effectiveness of the hit. It looked like the gas had impacted the whole building. He reached the seventh floor and held onto the doorframe to brace himself for what he would see. So far, he'd seen only terror and panic.

He turned the corner. A trolley stretcher was parked in the hallway. A body was on it. Maide moved in to examine the owner. It was Ellie. She looked in a state.

Maide looked up as Davison approached.

"What happened?" Maide asked.

"Mrs. Noor has been subjected to a horrific attack. As far as we can tell, she's been physically assaulted and injected with some kind of hallucinogenic drug. The attackers even dropped CS gas. Very nasty, sir. If we hadn't intercepted that transmission, she would have been dead. An unconventional attack. But nevertheless, highly effective."

"How is she?" Maide asked.

"We've administered a countering agent to what we believe is in her system. We've given her oxygen. She came around screaming, I had to sedate her to give the countering agent chance to work. She'll be okay. But it was very close, sir. Very close, indeed. She was in a mess when we arrived, in abject shock, nearing respiratory failure. Any later and we'd have lost her."

"She's going to be okay though?" Maide asked nonchalantly, like he was making a passing comment about the weather.

Maide didn't make eye contact with Davison. Uttering an uncomfortable cough, he bent down to inspect Ellie.

What greeted his eyes made him feel that, once again, he'd gone too far.

Chapter 55

It was alright for him to look at her now, thought Davison, but Maide hadn't been the one to see her first. He hadn't been the one to witness the horrific mess those gorillas had left her in.

But Davison had.

Moments after the transmission, everything had been frantic. Everyone was running. The air was charged with responsibility. People were running for the sake of running, compelled to be busy, to look busy, even if they weren't.

Davison arrived at the scene with his medical squad.

Bounding up the stairs, through the throng of terrified, screaming residents, he sent two prayers: that Ellie would still be alive and that she wouldn't be too hurt. One prayer got through. The other shot off, missing its target.

Ellie stood stock-still, feet clasped tight together, arms sandwiched up to her face. She was shaking and coughing violently. Davison had moved forward, but his team ran past him into the apartment, hurriedly opening the windows and doors to the balconies to let in the fresh air.

Ellie turned her head. Davison knew she could hear their footsteps, but her eyes would be seeing nothing but nightmares. Davison had to be extremely careful. Anything that he or his medics did could harm Ellie more in her super drugged-up state.

Davison made an attempt to pull her into his arms, but she screamed wildly and pulled herself back to the small piece of floor she'd previously stood upon. He let go of Ellie. He couldn't move her as she would go into shock.

What in God's name was she seeing? He gently attempted to pull her arms away from her face. Ellie stubbornly held their position. Davison upped the force and pulled her arms down. He stared at her face. The whites in her pretty eyes were bulging red, heavily lined with blood vessels. Her pupils had contracted in an effort to shut out the gas. Tears streamed down her bruised face. Her breathing was fast and irregular. She was hyperventilating. It seemed, a form of temporary insanity had gripped her.

Davison released her arms and they sprung back to her face to form a pathetic shield. Davison turned away, softly instructing his team not to touch her. He opened his medical box, and as he looked for an appropriate countering agent to the hallucinogenic cocktail he'd created earlier, he heard a chilling scream.

His head snapped back to Ellie. One of his team, who hadn't heard his instructions, or thought he knew better, had picked Ellie up in his arms and was walking towards the door.

Ellie screamed and turned around. She pushed hard against the medic's arms. As he carried her, Ellie's screams began to subside. Panic had taken her over and she gasped for air.

Davison saw immediately that Ellie couldn't breathe. She was losing color and turning blue.

"Put her down. Get her oxygen!" Davison hollered.

The medic set Ellie down on the floor. She arched upward, her eyes frenzied, her arms and legs fighting against something in her mind.

Davison shoved the mask over Ellie's face.

"Breathe," he yelled. "Breathe!"

Ellie's mouth let out a painful, wheezy moan.

"Fucking breathe, Ellie! I'm not going to lose you!" Davison shouted, catching the word 'again' before it passed his lips.

Maybe it was hearing the expletive, but something registered in Ellie. Her lungs inhaled the oxygen. She coughed and retched, and rolled onto her side.

"That's it. Good girl. You're going to be okay."

Davison held onto Ellie, bringing her close to him. Her wild eyes darted around the room. Davison was sure she still couldn't see him. He took out the hypo and injected a countering agent. She slumped in his arms. He lifted her onto the trolley. After only a few minutes, Ellie came around, screaming.

"Don't kill me!"

Davison dug into his box and withdrew a sedative. Ellie saw the hypo and backed away, terrified.

"Please, don't hurt me anymore," whimpered Ellie, her bloodshot eyes pleading with Davison.

"I'm not going to hurt you," he replied. "I'm here to help you. But you need to sleep to get better." His soft compassion came naturally. He injected Ellie with the sedative. Her lids flickered and closed over terrified eyes.

"But she's going to be okay?" persisted Maide, bringing Davison back to the present.

"Yes," answered Davison, his eyes full of disdain. "She's going to be okay."

Chapter 56

Sam stared at the blank satcomm screen, the harbinger of doom, numbed and motionless. He had no patience and no time to wait. After the fight with Walters, his adrenaline was pumping. He'd squared what had happened with Greene, and told him Walters was an Al Nadir spy and the contents on Walters' phone vindicated Sam's position. Greene was just going through the final details when Maide had rung. Angrily, Sam got up and paced, wringing his hands more thoroughly than a diligent washerwoman tending the linen. He willed Maide to come back on the line with good news.

His ability to compartmentalize emotion had broken down. Tension coursed through him and he turned away from the screen, staring at some first aid posters on the wall. His gaze went beyond the expert diagrams showing CPR. Sam faced the wall, his hands running through his hair, thinking a million horrific thoughts, when he heard the door of his temporary office open.

Sam detected a slight moan, deep and resonant. It was not a moan of pain, but confirmation. Sam knew of only one person who made that sound before asking a question: Morgan Greene.

Sam blinked back the tears that had started to form in his dark eyes. He couldn't show any emotion. He had to be on his guard. Greene was a devious devil. If he sniffed a problem, Sam would be pulled from the interrogation. Hearing your wife's just been hit by Al Nadir does not make for an impartial, clear-headed interrogator. And God, did he want to get his hands upon Rasheed.

"Everything okay now? I heard Maide called. Did you tell him about that thing with Walters?"

Sam could almost feel Greene eyeing him attentively, waiting on his response. Sam had his back to Greene, so he couldn't see his face. Sam straightened, keeping his usual stiff and tense stance to throw Greene off any scent.

Sam turned.

"Yeah, yeah I did. Maide wanted to know how things are progressing with the interrogations. The broadcast frequencies we got from Allan have changed. Reconnaissance of possible sites has shown nothing. They still can't ID the new cell thought to be in Cambridgeshire. Maide wants me to question Rasheed about it."

Sam realized he'd just told a pack of lies. But as far as he was concerned, it was a feasible lie. And lying was his job, after all. Greene nodded, buying it.

"Okay. Good that we've got him in custody. You guys would've had to go back to the drawing board if we hadn't."

Sam wasn't going to take the smug shot Greene had fired.

"Remember who located the DIY store in the first place."

"Noted." Envy flared in Greene's face again. "But hey, Sam, it was a combined effort."

"I think you'll find it's called a team effort," Sam snapped, in no mood for political backstabbing.

Greene half-grinned. Sam's quick repartee always got to Greene.

"Right, well, yeah." He started to head out, but then turned, "And, Sam, get back to this meeting quick. Still got some details about Walters we need to go through. I'm fucking pissed that bastard was recruited from within!"

Sam nodded. He knew Greene would exit quickly. With a spy in their ranks and the screw up they'd initially made of the Kinley investigation, it was clear Greene didn't wish to prolong further embarrassment. Greene harrumphed again and slipped through the door.

Sam breathed freely.

In the corner of his eye, the red light flashed on the satcomm. Sam flicked a button on the remote to open the secure channel.

"Well?" Sam shouted, hardly waiting for the screen to fully engage.

Maide's face appeared. It spoke the horror that Sam feared.

"She's dead, isn't she?"

Sam blurted out his deepest fear, before he could hold back. Acknowledgement of the spoken word chilled him. Sam's world was breaking apart. He doubted he could carry on living without Ellie.

"No, Sam. She's not dead."

Sam breathed out, hearing, quite possibly, the most wonderful words ever spoken. An unexpected smile graced his face for a millisecond. His world rushed back, coming together as a whole from the dark places it had, for a second, inhabited. She was alive. Thank God.

"How is she?"

"The hit was bad. She was assaulted," Maide explained in his usual matter-of-fact manner.

"Assaulted? What do you mean?" Sam's mind twisted as he imagined every husband's worse nightmare.

"Oh, Sam, no. I…Oh, God. No. I meant she's been beaten up. A heavy dose of GBH. But nothing else. They didn't touch her in any other way."

"Let me see her."

Hearing information from a third party wasn't satisfactory. Sam had to see for himself what Al Nadir had done to his baby.

In Maide's face, Sam witnessed sheer horror. Whether it was because of the attack, or something else, Sam didn't know. But he sensed that Maide definitely did not want him seeing Ellie right now.

And Sam couldn't understand why.

Chapter 57

Maide wavered in responding, and then somewhat inarticulately mumbled, "How?"

Sam stared, astonished. "Use your phone. Launch the secure system and the pre-set protocols automatically kick in when the camera's turned on. Sir, you should know this."

Maide did know it, but he was playing for time. If he could fumble enough, pressing wrong buttons and icons, maybe he could keep Sam waiting, by which time the medical team would have whisked Ellie away. By the time Sam got to see her, she'd be in hospital looking better than the horror-movie victim she looked right now.

"Hurry up. What's wrong with you, sir?"

Maide's initial reticence had been read by Sam. Maide saw rage burning in his face.

"Show me her. Now!"

Maide couldn't hold out any longer. Sam's suspicions were building, and he would soon be sniffing around more rapaciously than a police dog at a rave. Maide had to keep him on his side.

"Almost there," Maide muttered, booting up the system. A bar on screen flashed up and scanned for current networks. It recognized the satcomm frequency Maide was broadcasting on. A tiny green LED lit up on the phone. Two boxes emerged on screen. One showed Maide looking into the camera. The other showed Sam. Maide tapped his picture and it went small, enabling Sam to take up most of the screen.

"Ready?"

Maide stepped out of the car and ran up the path into the foyer. He didn't need to ascend the stairs. Two medics with Davison were wheeling Ellie out on a trolley stretcher.

She had come around, but was still sedated. Her eyes flicked from side to side as if she was trying to register her surroundings.

"Just a second." Maide stood in front of the trolley. "I've got Sam Noor on the line. He wants to see Mrs. Noor."

Maide's unruffled, bland posture, like he was serving afternoon tea, wasn't lost on Davison, who appeared to grit his teeth as he pulled the trolley around to give a better angle.

"Sam, can you see okay? I'm going to turn the camera onto Ellie now."

Maide revolved the phone.

Sam's face was not visible, but Sam's voice resounded in his earpiece. At first, Maide heard his breathing, shallow and fast. It sped up as adrenaline coursed through Sam's body. Then his vocal cords engaged, and Sam let forth his tirade.

"Oh my God. What have those fuckers done to my…my darling? I'm going to fucking kill them. I'm going to rip their fucking heads off. They can't get away with this."

"I'm sorry, Sam. We're tracking the bastards down. But you know what Al Nadir is like. It could take a while."

"I'll shortcut the process."

Sam's voice dipped to absolute zero. He pulled away from the screen and flicked off the transmission.

"Sam? Sam, where are you going?"

An uncomfortable twinge centered in Maide's stomach. He knew something was going to happen, and there was no way he could stop it.

Chapter 58

After snapping off the transmission, Sam stood up. His face was expressionless, a mere victim of mind control in receipt of an ultra-sonic trigger that delivered a subliminal command. He pulled his hunter's knife from his bag, stuck it in his back pocket, hidden from view under his jacket, and walked out.

On the walk to the interrogation room, he passed officers and agents. But all he could see, in front, behind, and all around him, encasing him in a suffocating, suffusion of pain were Ellie's eyes. Beautiful, smoky blue overwritten by bloodshot and bruised. Instant iridescent overlaid by instant fear. Windows shattered by demon children. Triangular shards at obscure angles, reflecting and revealing the interior, their razor points inverted, plying torture to an already broken soul.

Sam entered the interrogation room. Rasheed was still in the cage. Sam dropped to the floor. His face remained expressionless. Slowly, he unlocked the cage, pulled Rasheed out and pressed him against the whitewashed wall. As he touched Rasheed, a change sparked. Sam was aware of his calling. A blood-red rage of retribution, an intensity of emotion, unlike anything before, swept over him.

Like an insane robot from the future sent back to kill the savior of mankind, Sam raised Rasheed off the ground. His steel right hand of power wrapped around Rasheed's muscular neck. Bringing up his left to gain better purchase, Sam pressed into Rasheed's clammy skin, pulping his Adam's apple and crushing his esophagus.

Rasheed kicked out. But his aim was off target. Sam tightened his death grip.

"Tell me about the attack on my wife. Who organized it?" Sam snarled.

A beast had been unleashed.

"What?"

Rasheed heaved, genuinely confused, breathing through his nose, his windpipe albeit crushed. Sam's hold had forced his face to experience a kaleidoscope of color. Pale red flushed when Sam grabbed him and morphed into deeper red as his grip strengthened, then diffused into purple as the pressure built in his head. His veins popped, ears rushed and eyes stalked. He was a playtime balloon squeezed to bursting point.

Rasheed had to wonder whether his head would really explode under the pressure Sam applied. The vision of this actually happening tore into Rasheed with graphic lucidity, and delivered what no torture had thus far achieved. Rasheed was scared.

"Don't give me that shit. Tell me who organized it. Who the fuck was behind it? Was it Salim? Sabena? Pedro? Which one? Fucking tell me. Otherwise I'll kill you!"

"You can't kill me. The CIA won't allow it," Rasheed gasped.

"Fuck the CIA. This has nothing to do with them and everything to do with me. Al Nadir attacked my wife today. And I want answers. Now, Rasheed, do you want to live or die? Because I've had it with you. Salim's cousin or not, I'll kill you if you don't give me a fucking answer."

Sam's hands, if it were possible, tightened even harder around Rasheed's throat to prove he wasn't bluffing. A greyness washed over Rasheed's dark eyes. Oxygen wasn't getting to his brain and unconsciousness would soon cover him.

Sam watched as Rasheed centered his strength, stared out through black eyes and spat back at Sam, "Then, you're going to have to kill me because I don't know about any attack on your wife."

"You know about the attack. Don't fucking play me. Tell me who was behind it. It's revenge because I got you guys. Isn't it?"

"I am telling you," wheezed Rasheed, his broken English breaking further under the strain. "I don't know anything about the attack. But…"

Sam noticed his eyes drooping. Rasheed forced a painful upturn at the side of his mouth and a thin smile sneaked painfully across his face.

"My compliments to those who did it!"

Sam exploded. He had no control. All his training, everything, it just went to hell. He remembered his wife's beaten face and crumpled body. How they'd used her like a punching bag.

He didn't think. He just snatched the knife from his backside pocket and in a sweep perfected through a decade of experience and training, he stuck it straight through Rasheed's neck, sticking him to the wall as efficiently as the drawing pin affixed the first aid poster in his office. Rasheed's body dangled, pinioned, at least a foot off the floor. The knife penetrated right through him and buried itself into the concrete wall of the interrogation cell.

Rasheed spluttered, spitting blood. It trickled like strawberry sauce from an ice cream sundae down his chin. Gravity pulled at Rasheed's bulk, opening the wound at the back of his neck and splaying out his blood on to the white wall behind.

Someone shuffled outside and the door opened. Morgan Greene entered with two agents and a medic.

"Sam, that's enough. That's enough!"

Greene had learned about the Silent Waters attack via the security feed and second-guessed Sam's next move. The two agents pulled Sam back, attempting to restrain him, while the medics treated Rasheed.

"That fucker's gonna tell me the truth!" screamed Sam, pushing hard at the agents holding him.

"That fucker," replied the medic adopting Sam's vernacular, "is going to tell nothing to nobody. His vocal cords have been severed. He won't be speaking anytime soon."

"Thank you, Sam," fumed Greene, "for completely fucking up the best chance we've ever had of nailing Salim Al Douri."

Sam's enraged eyes stared at Greene, but he remained silent.

"Get him out of here. Get him on a plane back to the UK, back to his wife. He's useless here."

Compassion was not Greene's forte. Sam recognized that he had only one concern. His chances at promotion had been screwed by Sam's revenge.

The agents pushed Sam outside. He looked back at Rasheed over their shoulders. A savage intensity radiated from Sam.

"We're quits."

Chapter 59

President Jonathan D Treeborne picked up the phone. Within seconds, the caller, Ted Downer, Director General (DG) of the CIA, gave news that Treeborne hadn't expected or wanted to ever hear. He'd been so delighted about the CIA's capture of the three high level Al Nadir operatives. His delight had turned to ecstasy when one of those operatives turned out to be the much sought-after Rasheed, Salim Al Douri's elusive first cousin and one of the most connected individuals to Salim, outside of his first line command of Sabena Sanantoni and Pedro Russo.

"How the fuck has this happened?" snarled Treeborne, his face blossoming into a balloon of red, and he gripped the receiver tighter.

DG Downer breathed deeply on the other end, taking Treeborne's targeted vitriol. "Mr. President, sir, it wasn't the CIA's fault. The Brit that helped with the capture, apparently his wife was hit by Al Nadir earlier today in London."

"So?" spat Treeborne. "He's a fucking professional. He should have kept it together. Who is this fucking Brit anyway?"

"He's Dr. Sam Noor," said Downer. "A few hours before, he'd uncovered an Al Nadir spy deep in the CIA. The spy almost killed him. He's a star agent."

"He hasn't won any stars with me today, slicing my golden goose like that. Rasheed could have spilled it all. Clear intel. What I needed for my strike back. This guy is a fucking idiot!" Treeborne demonstrated no compassion at all. He listened to Downer swallow down his discomfort at having to say his next line.

"Mr. President, I appreciate your position. But Dr. Noor had just received news his wife had been attacked. There is perhaps some vindication in his-"

"Vindication!" screamed Treeborne, his ire boiling over. "There's no fucking vindication for him touching my prisoners. What the hell was he doing in there anyway? Didn't fucking Greene know about the attack? Why did he allow that Noor guy anywhere near Rasheed? I thought you're supposed to be intelligent? There's more fucking intelligence in my kid's pet goldfish. I want that fucking Noor gone. Out of my country. He's a fucking liability. And don't let the Brits over here taking control again. They're too fucking unstable. I got no place for them. You got it? You guys run the show. Tell them what to fucking do. That's what Brits are good for, taking orders, making queues, having afternoon fucking tea. Not interrogating terrorists."

"Yes, Mr. President, sir. I understand. Yes, sir. I'm sorry, sir. I'll tell them. I'll make sure Sam Noor is on the next plane out of Langley. We'll handle everything from hereon. Six will be advised of this position," fawned Downer.

"Damn right you'll advise them. At least we still have Lupez and that nanotech guru."

"Stein-Muller, you mean?" said Downer.

"Yeah, yeah, that guy. Better start wringing him and Lupez both out hard."

"Rendition them out," suggested Downer.

"Whatever you need to do, Ted. I'm not the one to be telling you how to do your job. Just get it all out of them. Okay!"

"Yes, Mr. President, sir. You can count on the Agency to deliver." Downer's voice forced confidence and assurance into the president's ear. Unfortunately, his stance didn't hold well.

Treeborne growled as he realized that, once again, he'd been prevented from getting that bit closer to taking down his nemesis, Salim Al Douri. Treeborne felt a slow fire building inside him. He'd had Rasheed, for God's sake. So damn close.

As that thought grew, a wash of anger came over Treeborne and incensed with the injustice of what had happened. He exploded, almost blasting Downer's eardrum to pieces with his next retort.

"I sure as hell hope so! There doesn't seem to be anyone else! If I hear of another clusterfuck like the one that's just happened, you're out, Ted. No place in my team for a loser. Hear what I'm saying? D'ya get me?"

Downer's tremor in his voice was audible to Treeborne. "Mr. President, sir, of course I get you."

"Good! See British Intelligence gets me too. Have Greene talk to that pompous ass, Maide. He's got to keep his men in better order."

"Yes, Mr. President. It will be done," clipped Downer, and as he spoke, Treeborne noticed a drop in tempo. It was obvious he wanted to get off the phone. Not so fast, sonny, thought Treeborne.

"Yeah and, Ted, one last thing," said Treeborne, adopting a slightly calmer tone. "The wife of that Six guy, Noor, is she alive or dead?"

"Alive, as I understand it. Why?"

"Well, huh…" started Treeborne hesitantly. "Y'know, if she'd been dead, I'd have sent flowers or some other condolences shit. Never know when we might need Noor on our side. Gotta keep our cousins sweet, especially with the summit coming up. Don't want no bad karma. Anyway, she's alive. So it doesn't matter. Kick Greene's ass good and let me know when you've opened up Lupez and Stein-fucker."

"Muller," corrected Downer.

"Yeah, him," snapped Treeborne, not giving a shit what his name was.

"Yes, Mr. President. You'll be the first to know the moment we have actionable intelligence."

"I expect it," said Treeborne, and without any parting pleasantries, he slammed the phone down.

He sat and stared into space for a few seconds after the call. His anger wasn't diminishing. He lurched out of his chair towards the liquor cabinet and poured himself a large bourbon. His hand shook with continued rage. Treeborne poured a small trough full, drank it in, making a reservoir inside his wide mouth, and gulped it down in one hit. He frowned as the slightly bitter taste of the bourbon touched his throat. Then the smooth kickback heated him and seemed to quell his wrath.

His weasel eyes narrowed. He pondered, his hand moving to his chin, and he stared at his laptop. Treeborne placed the glass down and typed in his top-level security access code to enter into the CIA files. He ran a check on Dr. Sam Noor, MI6. Then, as the results started to emerge, Treeborne clicked on the HoloTab app on the side of the screen. Sam's cold, hard face and bordering on savage eyes floated some thirty centimeters above his desk.

Treeborne lent back in his chair, grabbed his glass and slugged back another enormous measure of bourbon. He flicked at Sam's hovering image with his thumb and index finger like he was ejecting a piece of dirt from his nail. He sneered, full of resentment.

"You and I got some unfinished business, Dr. Noor."

Chapter 60

Ellie awoke. An IV drip loaded with vitamins and a light sedative stuck out of her hand. A heart rate indicator covered her index finger. Her bruises had been treated and were already diminishing. Davison knew the real damage was psychological. Hampered by horrific flashbacks, Ellie's next few hours would be a rocky ride.

Hearing the door open, Ellie turned her head in Davison's direction. Her eyes, still big and glassy, were no longer bloodshot.

"Hello, Mrs. Noor. How do you feel?" Davison smiled, approaching her bed.

Ellie looked startled. Although the sedative controlled her fear, she still swallowed nervously.

"Can I see?" said Davison. He bent in to check her throat with a tongue depressor. It was still hot and raw. "Mrs. Noor, does your throat still hurt?" he asked gently.

Ellie nodded. "Feels like it's been scoured out with sandpaper. Oh, call me Ellie, please," she rasped, and tried to swallow.

"I'll get you a drink. What would you like?"

"Water."

Davison walked over to the water cooler, pulled off a plastic cup and filled it. He handed the cup to Ellie. She lifted it to her lips. The cool water, although soothing, brought out the heat in her throat. She drained the cup and put her hand out to Davison.

"Another," Ellie wheezed.

Davison took the cup, filled it and returned it to Ellie. On the fifth cup, Ellie licked her formerly chapped lips, pleased they were now smooth.

"Feeling better?" Davison asked.

"Yes."

"Do you feel ready to know what happened? Or do you need more time?" Davison could see from Ellie's questioning expression that she was desperate to know.

"I think I can piece it together."

He heard her confidence and his heart thundered. "Go on then." Davison kept his voice balanced to shield his unease.

"I was attacked by Al Nadir. They hit me, injected me with a drug and exploded poisonous gas in my face. I know they wanted to kill me but they didn't succeed. Can I have some more water, please?"

Ellie's eyes were cold and hard. They were full of defiance and inner vengeance. He'd seen that same look in Sam's eyes earlier. They were certainly a well-matched couple.

"Ellie, your account of events is most accurate." Davison turned back to the water cooler to get another cup.

"This place is MI6, isn't it?"

Ellie's exclamation came from nowhere. Shocked, Davison almost dropped the cup.

How the hell did she know that?

He breathed in. "MI6?"

"Yeah," slurred Ellie, pointing to the wall, "That's khaki green. Same as on the army trucks I've seen on the motorway. This is a military facility."

Ellie was glaring intently at him. Her recovery was swift. Davison was both pleased and perturbed. Alert to her surroundings, Ellie would, once again become the 'great deal to handle' that Maide had spoken of.

Eyes of cold, determined grey-blue caught his in a deep stare, unblinking and unnaturally focused, given what she'd already endured. Davison could feel Ellie's eyes searching his soul. That was, if he still had one to search.

He coughed nervously and answered, "Ellie, you are quite accurate again. This medical facility is run by British Intelligence."

He had no reason to lie.

"Is Sam here?"

Satisfied with the clarity of Davison's response, Ellie looked across to the door. Expectancy glistened in her recovering eyes.

"No. Not yet. But he's on his way. We've been in touch with him."

"Can I speak to him?"

Davison couldn't see any harm in her request. "I'll see what I can do."

"What's your name?"

"Dr. Davison."

"Dr. Davison, I'm worried."

"What about?"

"My memory. Bits of it are gone. I can remember working on my laptop, waking up at the end of Bridget Jones and the attack. But nothing else. Why can't I remember the rest of the day?"

Ellie's face was stricken and confused. Tears formed in her eyes.

"You're suffering from selective amnesia. It's a side effect of the treatments we had to administer. It'll soon pass."

A raft of questions then flowed from Ellie.

What was the gas? What was the drug? Had they caught the terrorists?

Davison smiled and handled the stream of questions with charming aplomb.

"Dr. Davison, I was targeted because of Sam, wasn't I?"

"We're not sure. But it does look that way."

"Is he in danger?"

"Oh, good heavens, no. Sam can take care of himself. Don't you worry about that."

"But I do worry. Please, Doctor, get him on the line. I want to speak to him."

Davison left Ellie and ran down the corridor to his office to get his laptop. A joyful little tune vibrated from his pocket.

"Davison," he said, and lent forward to unplug and snatch his laptop from his desk.

"How is she?"

A clipped, sharp tongue of authority crashed through his mechanical fumbling. Coldness, like someone had dunked him in vat of ice cubes, caressed his body. His visceral thought was to switch off the phone. He had no wish to speak to the bastard. But the bastard was his boss. And as he didn't have a *penchant* for the dole, he had no route other than a compliancy.

"She's well. Much better now than when I first saw her."

"And?" encouraged Maide.

"And what?" His concentration on Maide was distracted by the need to get the laptop back to Ellie.

"And," Maide repeated anxiously, "does she remember anything?"

"No. She's a clean slate. Only the attack and working on her laptop this morning. The rest of the day has vanished forever."

"Good. Good," Maide mumbled.

Davison chewed hard on his trembling lip in a pathetic bid to stem his urge to say something that would definitely result in his premature eviction from The Firm.

"And does she know she's in MI6?"

"She worked that out almost immediately."

Davison took certain pride in telling Maide. Whatever Ellie was, she had rammed herself underneath Maide's skin like an itch that just couldn't be scratched. Davison thought of Maide squirming and took perverse pleasure from it.

"Did she? Well, it's a good thing we did what we did then, isn't it? Otherwise we'd all be up the proverbial creek." Davison heard Maide breathe deeply and knew he was waiting for him to agree that they'd acted right in their duplicity.

"Well, maybe," Davison responded, his tone non-committal.

"Yes, well, what's the next step? How long is she going to remain at CD1?"

"She wants to go home."

"Isn't it too early for that? It's only seventeen twenty hours."

"Well, from her recovery, the fact that her faculties have returned full blast, I'd say that in an hour or so she'll be ready to go home. Quite frankly, sir, she'll be better at home."

"Why?"

"She's extremely smart. She'll constantly plague us with questions about her lost memory. The color of walls, a sound, anything, could trigger a flashback. But if she's returned quickly to her home, she'll have familiarity comforting her. Sam will soon be back. Before she knows it, today, what little she remembers of it, will be a distant memory."

"You really believe she'll be less of a risk outside than inside?"

"Absolutely, sir."

"And you don't think she'll start tripping again?"

"No, sir. She's clean of the drugs."

"Well, if that's your final medical opinion, you have my authority to release her. But if you're wrong about this Davison…"

Maide didn't complete his sentence. He left it hanging in the air. Its sinister inflection rang with disturbing finality in Davison's ears.

"Yes, sir. I understand."

Davison was shaking. He doubted Maide meant firing in any employment sense. More like in the literal sense. He didn't want a visit from Maide's psychopathic primates.

Switching off the phone, he grabbed the laptop, snapped down the lid and hurried back to Ellie. Inside the room, he was surprised to see her sitting with the pillow puffed up behind her back. He could have been mistaken, but Ellie's face looked much clearer. Her swelling had virtually vanished and even the bruising was diminishing fast. He pulled a trolley table across the bed and placed the laptop on the Formica. He opened the screen, clicked on the video sat link, and requested one of Six's comms officers to put a call through to Dr. Sam Noor. He gave Sam's ID number to confirm the call was genuine. The comms officer nodded.

The screen blanked out and then returned showing Sam on a plane.

"Darling, how are you, sweetness?" said Sam softly.

As Davison watched, the agent that he'd read about, who had done the most ruthless things, turned gradually to marshmallow in front of him.

Ellie smiled. "I'm so much better seeing you. Baby, I have so much to tell you."

Listening to Ellie, Davison's stomach flipped.

"Dr. Davison," clipped Sam abruptly, "a little privacy, if you please."

Davison nodded. He slipped out of view, and then out of the room.

"Now, sweetness, tell me everything," said Sam, his hard edge suddenly appearing. "And don't leave anything out."

Chapter 61

Downer's mind was still spinning like he'd had a session in a centrifuge, and his ear smarted from the blasting reprimand he'd just received from President Treeborne. Although he appreciated why the president was so angry, he really couldn't comprehend his total lack of compassion.

Downer wanted to ask the president how he'd have felt if it had been his wife, and not Noor's, that was attacked. But he was of the impression that breaking Rasheed would somehow have been more important than even the president's wife.

Treeborne was of a singular mind: use whatever is necessary to bring Al Nadir to its knees.

Downer shook his head, running his hand through his thinning salt and pepper hair. A president needed compassion. Okay, he suggested flowers if the agent's wife had died, but that was just for show. Treeborne really didn't give a damn. His obsession was unhealthy. Almost fanatical. It wasn't good for the US. That way led to illogical, passion-driven decisions that ended up with people dying.

Having been a Navy SEAL before joining the Agency, Downer was a patriot and wasn't averse to killing for his country. But there had to be a reason. A really good reason. Not just a crazy fixation borne out of a need to show personal domination.

God knows, Downer hated Al Nadir for what they'd done to his people over the years. Downer shuddered recalling all the hideous photographic evidence. He wanted them annihilated and Al Douri destroyed. He wasn't different to the president in wanting to see the end of Al Nadir, but that was where the similarity ended.

Irrespective of what happened in the course of events, during take down, capture and enhanced interrogation, Downer, despite what kind of road of rage he traveled down, he'd still hold a place of empathy with his agents.

If he didn't get his people psychologically, how could he possibly hope to lead them?

Sam Noor heard his wife had been attacked by Al Nadir. Downer knew any agent hearing such news would have flipped and gone into revenge mode. He couldn't agree it was right. However, he understood Sam's motivation.

Treeborne's words stung in his ears. "There's no vindication for attacking one of my prisoners."

The president made everything so personal.

Rasheed wasn't the president's prisoner alone; he was an enemy of the state.

Downer played back Treeborne's threat to everything he'd worked so hard for. "You're out Ted." The president had said it without hesitation, nor consideration of what that really meant for him. Hire and fire politics. He despised it.

Downer stood up and looked out of his office. The edge of the trees in Langley Fork Park could be seen. Times like these, he just wanted to make a mad dash into those trees and disappear.

He turned back to his desk. The knifing of Rasheed had been vicious, and a big inconvenience to proceedings. But he wasn't dead. Rasheed was still in the CIA's custody, and given a little more time, they could unlock his secrets.

Did he need to rock the boat with Morgan Greene, his deputy at the CIA, and, in turn, MI6? Just when he was getting some terrific buy-in from his British cousins. He'd worked at this stance. His administration had been about conciliation and cooperation, not incitement and hindrance.

That was all about to come crashing down.

He couldn't pontificate any longer. The president would be expecting a call back to confirm the ass-kicking he'd been ordered to give.

Downer breathed deeply. His massive, muscular chest heaved in and out, straining against the buttons of his shirt.

He couldn't screw up his future, nor his pension.

Resigned to treading the political line, Downer snatched up the phone and hit a number. He waited for Greene to answer.

"This Sam Noor business has made the Agency look like a bunch of fucking amateurs in front of the president. The Brits are to blame, Greene. So you had better tell Maide to sort his boys out before they come back on our soil."

Downer forced a show of anger, which didn't take long when he thought about the MI6 agent being the reason he could lose his hallowed position at the top of the intelligence tree.

"I understand, sir," rumbled Greene. "Leave this to me."

"Don't hold back. If I hear that Maide doesn't appreciate the gravity of his agent's actions, your days with the Agency are numbered. No place for losers on my team. Got it!"

He listened to Greene's usual growl descend into a murmur of crawling.

Downer disconnected, acutely aware that he'd just used the president's line on his own subordinate.

Effective and simple.

And so much better than having to find more words within his addled brain, thought Downer sadly.

Chapter 62

The beige foolscap folder appeared on his desk. 'Eyes Only Confidential' was stamped across it in green ink. Richard Ashton, British Prime Minister, picked up the folder and leafed through the papers inside. It was about a minor traffic offence, hardly needing such a high level of security. Ashton peered at the plate registration. Then he understood the need for secrecy.

He picked up the phone meaning to make a call but faltered on pressing the speed dial. He would handle this situation another way. He raised the receiver and dialed a different mobile number.

"Godley, my friend, how are you?" Ashton asked with little sincerity.

Charles Godley was the British Secretary of State for Defense. He'd been on a visit to the Washington DC meeting state officials in a bid to gain financial backing from the US for their continued fight against the ever-increasing terrorism in their midst.

In a plane, 10,000 feet above the Irish Sea, Godley replied jovially.

"Superb, Prime Minister. The meeting went well. Contributions to the kitty will be forthcoming, so to speak. I'll be at Heathrow in about an hour. Fancy a drink at the House?"

Godley wasn't often in good spirits. But after his meeting with his US counterpart, US Defense Secretary Frank Weitz, who confirmed the US would back the UK financially in their united fight against Al Nadir, he was in a party mood. Fair enough, he'd had to agree to buying weapons from American arms manufacturers, but the terms had been very favorable. Almost interest free. And they had years to pay them back. By that time, perhaps the opposition would be in, poor buggers, and they'd be left to sort out the mess. Either way, it was the chancellor's problem. Not his.

Despite the on-the-go, 24-hour roundtrip, jetlag hadn't set in. Godley didn't plan on it doing so either. He'd knock that risk away with a few stiff whiskeys. No chance of jetlag if you're blotto.

But the PM's voice crushed instantly his party spirit. "I'm sorry, Godley. I'll have to refuse that drink." The PM was grave and determined. "I need to see you in private. I have a matter of some delicacy I need to discuss with you."

"Right, well, I quite understand, Prime Minister. Does it have national security implications?" asked Godley, all at once sullen, his pitch-black, rat-like eyes narrowing with sudden concern.

"Indeed, it does. Come to Number 10 at nine tonight."

Ashton closed the line, looking back at the information in the folder.

"What the hell were you doing there?" he muttered to himself, leaning back in his chair.

Chapter 63

Call it intuition, but Maide could have detailed to the letter what Sam was going to do when he broke that transmission. Carnivorous rage flashed in his eyes like a lion protecting his lioness from encircling hunters. Distance denied Sam from directing his vengeful violence at the actual perpetrators. He sought out the next best alternative. An Al Nadir top man. A possible link to Salim himself. And to hell with the consequences. Only this time, MI6 were up to their necks in consequences. And Maide had no one to blame but his own paranoid, inquisitive and relentlessly determined self.

Sunday was dragging on like a stubborn child refusing to go to bed. Had it only been that morning when…? He didn't want to think about it. He didn't want to remember the line he'd crossed. Maide tipped a treble shot of malt into his glass and swigged it back, barely bothering to complete the swallow before he poured another huge measure. He had to stop drinking so much. It clouded his thoughts and made judgement difficult. But the drink was comforting. Like a liquid splint holding him up against the turbulence of life, it caressed him with the full softness of the bosoms belonging to the nubile 'friends' he frequently visited. He needed it badly.

His pride blistered from the acidic grilling he'd received earlier from Morgan Greene. But what hurt him even more was that the grilling had come from DG Ted Downer's deputy and not the man himself.

"What kind of show are you running, Maide?"

Greene's ragged, grave face exploded from his consciousness as the whiskey started to take effect. Rasheed had been their golden goose with the prospect of giving golden eggs of information. Now that he'd been sliced open, like the goose, his ability to deliver his gold had been taken away.

"Excuse me. Have you an issue that you wish to discuss?"

Maide's clipped, pompous delivery had driven home his breeding. It also drove home his superiority. Maide had played it before. The tone he used always incensed Greene. He used it to put Greene in his place. It was a verbal slap in the face, a cultural dissection that opened to reveal an absence of history or heritage. It ground into Greene's skin, ground into his bones, his molecules, his very being, delivering vilipend to victory and scorn to success.

Most of all, it lit Greene's emotional touch paper.

"Damn right I have an issue. Your boy Sam just stuck a literal dagger into our chances of getting close to Salim Al Douri. He knifed Rasheed in the throat. Slashed his vocal chords. Medics doubt they'll be able to repair him. He's lucky to escape with his life. Interrogations will now be conducted via keyboard. Imagine what fun that'll be!"

Greene's face was a red cabbage of concern, a crimson-purple pulsating mass of tension and angst. His loud seething complemented Maide's quiet calm in a bizarre stage double act.

"Yes. Quite. Well, there's a reason that I believe vindicates Sam's behavior. His wife had just suffered a terrorist attack by Al Nadir. She almost died, I believe."

Maide's informative, instructive delivery, steeped in self-righteous sanctimony, issued, once again, the suggestion of Greene's inadequacy and his lack of knowing the full facts. Maide's natural adoption of authority gave his timbre of a teacher, the one who knew everything.

"So?" Greene replied coldly. "I couldn't give a shit what's happened to his wife. And it certainly doesn't vindicate his attack on *my* prisoner."

Maide's astonishment at Greene's take on Sam's revenge was obvious. He was aware his own mouth was open, fish-like, catching air, saying nothing. Greene looked on and appeared delighted by Maide's sudden erosion of oratory capability. Snapping his mouth silently shut, Maide stared at Greene. A slippery smile appeared on his face, sweeter than Greene's mother's pecan pie.

Trying for the compassionate, feeling approach, Maide said, "My friend, I really do think you're being hard on Sam. What would you do if your wife-"

"I'm divorced," snapped Greene tersely.

It was clear that no amount of persuasion from Maide was going to affect Greene. He was determined he wasn't going to be sucked into Maide's emotive vortex of vindication, a whirlwind of reasonableness warranting the actions that Sam had conducted.

Greene was firm on the ground in his convictions. And he wasn't a fool.

But Maide's clement persuasions persisted.

"Well, if you had a wife and Al Nadir had attacked her, and you saw what they had done, you would have reacted the same way as Sam."

"Show me what they did to her. Email me now."

Maide emailed Greene, attaching the digital images of Ellie taken at the scene of the crime. Greene flicked up the email, opening the files. He looked. His expression remained cold with no flicker of compassion and no indication of understanding the reason for Sam's outburst.

Greene's eyes told the story. Maide knew he'd see Ellie's injuries as tame. A lifetime of seeing images of such graphic horror no human should expect to witness had left Greene immune to the more docile depictions of mankind's cruelty.

"Looks like she's been done over a bit. That doesn't mean Sam had to lose it and stick Rasheed."

"Done over? Oh, good heavens, Morgan. She was almost killed. Are you looking at the right photos?"

"Yeah. I am. And what you're telling me suggests that if Rasheed had been in your custody instead of ours, it would be okay for Sam to stick him, even at the expense of losing the chance to get your hands on the world's most wanted terrorist."

Greene glared, his lucid logic defying Maide's opportunity for defense. He was like a courtroom lawyer delivering his final line to secure his defendants acquittal. It didn't sound right. Maide listened. What Greene said just didn't sound right. As much as he hated to say it, Greene was correct. Sam had done wrong. If he continued to excuse Sam, Greene could, and from his almost rabid expression, would, make life hell for Maide.

Treading carefully along the political path, Maide did a spectacular U-turn.

"No. That's not what I'm saying. What Sam did was unethical and completely out of keeping with protocol. I merely wanted to present the mitigating circumstances of his wife's attack. He will be suitably disciplined on his return. Where is Sam now?"

"I wanted him out of here. We've got no place for an unhinged liability. He's on his way back to you. I don't want to see him here again until he's sorted himself out. And he's certainly not going to get access to *our* prisoners until he observes that over here, we go by the book."

"Quite. I understand."

"I don't think you do understand, Maide. Your boy has caused a huge mess here. My ass is in a sling and the president himself is looking to take a good kick. This is going to set me back years."

Maide did understand, only too well. This wasn't about Sam attacking a prisoner. Sam had killed prisoners before whilst extracting information from them, and neither the CIA nor MI6 had batted an eyelid. On the contrary, he'd received commendations on his performance. This was about Greene, his promotion, his pension and his security.

Not national security.

If he could have identified and captured Salim Al Douri, the president would have made a special place for him, perhaps even made him director general of the CIA. The present director general, Ted Downer, was waiting for his retirement, looking forward to escaping to his ranch in Texas. Greene would have had the world at his feet. As if he'd unlocked a genie in a bottle and been granted three wishes, he could have asked for and gotten absolutely anything. But only if he delivered Al Douri's head on a silver platter to President Treeborne.

That chance, for the moment, had been postponed.

Greene was right. Interrogating through a keyboard was going to be laborious and lengthy. Given the knife's angle of trajectory and the murderous force applied, a voice box would be a hit and miss affair.

Medical teams would naturally employ their latest techniques, but weeks would be lost in operations and recuperation. They would be vital weeks where 'appropriate' interrogation could have revealed remarkable results.

Maide was aware that, as his CO, he had to reprimand Sam. But Maide was reticent. An aftershock of conscience moved him, creating a tremor of uncertainty and apprehension beneath his skin and in his mind. The abduction had been the catalyst, the acorn that grew a hulking oak of disaster, a gaseous spew that chain-reacted to create a universe of unfortunate incidents.

Maide remembered Quentin's portentous words. 'Maide, sir, you can't do that. Sam's our best agent. You don't know what the repercussions could be'.

At that moment, he didn't know what the repercussions could be. He couldn't know. He wasn't psychic. He had no way of knowing, within the universe of tomorrow, the intricacies of infinite probabilities whipped up within the layers of time and space. He could never have predicted that Sam's revenge would deliver profound confrontation, affecting and reversing the fortune of the world's most powerful security agency. But now he knew. And he hoped that this incident would be the only consequence of his actions. But somehow, Maide wasn't so sure.

Chapter 64

Sam's world had been shattered and reassembled in matter of seconds. When he'd learnt about the attack on Ellie, he'd subconsciously gravitated toward a dark conclusion. If Ellie was dead, Sam fully intended to kill Rasheed, Stein-Muller and Lupez, and use everything at his disposal in Langley to search for the whereabouts of Salim, Sabena and Russo. Then he would have left to kill Al Nadir's three-line top command, to hell with the consequences to the UK, US and any of the allied forces caught up in the war against Al Nadir.

Of course, such action would have been suicidal. Even if he'd managed to take out Al Nadir's terrorist royalty, Six would have assigned a cleaner on him, not to mention the retaliatory strike back from Al Nadir's armies in waiting.

A marked man, Sam knew he'd have eventually been taken down fighting. But he'd have been reassured in his final breath to know he'd avenged Ellie and would soon be meeting his love again.

But that scenario hadn't been necessary to take forward.

Sam stared at the sat screen as Ellie popped up.

Alive.

Thank God.

Sam savored her wide, warm smile of happiness and her grey-blue eyes glittering with renewed love and affection.

Whatever she showed on the surface, Sam recognized her ordeal had been brutal. Beneath the sheets, hidden from view, were the results of the attack that Dr. Davison, in Six's medical unit, CD1, had tried to treat.

Nevertheless, however harrowing the experience had been for Ellie, she still remained with him. An apple-sized lump jammed in his throat. He knew how very close they'd both come to getting a very different fate.

At Sam's stern behest, Dr. Davison had vacated the medical room.

Ellie nodded when Sam asked her to recount everything from the beginning.

Sam watched Ellie screw up her face; confusion seemed to grip her.

"It's so weird, sweetness," began Ellie.

Sam scrutinized every twitch of Ellie's body and nuance in her voice.

"Weird? Tell me why," said Sam with a determined, powerful edge.

Ellie shuffled, and perplexity rippled across her beautiful features. "Well, where terrorists are concerned, I'm no expert. Not like you." Ellie stared hard at Sam. Deep hurt shone in her eyes, making him look down, ashamed by what his wife implied. It was obvious she was still very raw about the cascade of lies he'd told over the years.

"Yes, Ellie," said Sam softly. "Tell me."

"Well, as I say, darling, I don't know much about these things, but something didn't feel right."

Sam moved closer to the satcom screen, intently reading his wife's expression.

"What do you mean?"

"Well, erm, they didn't *feel* like terrorists. Don't get me wrong, sweetness, they were terrifying. I really thought I was about to be killed. But that's the weird bit. If they'd been real terrorists, I'm sure I'd be dead. Everything I've read and seen about Al Nadir says they never leave anyone alive. If they'd wanted to attack and kill me, they'd have shot me, blown me up, poisoned or stabbed me. Any number of methods to kill me completely. But they didn't, Sam. They felt more like awful thugs being paid to rough me up. Maybe Al Nadir was sending a warning to you. Perhaps they wanted me alive. I don't know. It's all confusing. It was like a nightmare, but I knew I was awake. I had no control. I couldn't see anything, only strange creatures. They drugged me with something potent and I couldn't breathe. They gassed me as well. The gas seared my eyeballs and burned my throat. I thought I was going to end up blind. For a short while, darling, I know I went insane. I couldn't move from the spot I was on as the floor had turned into chasms leading to hell. I knew this with absolute certainty. I didn't doubt my understanding. I couldn't run away from the gas otherwise I would have dropped to hell."

Ellie shook her head and tried to play down her embarrassment by grinning. But Sam could see there was no amusement in her eyes.

"It sounds crazy, me telling you this now. But when I was in the zone, stuck in that nightmare, I believed with all my being that the flat had turned into the equivalent of the Grand Canyon with deep drops into the abyss. And the door had vanished. I couldn't recall who I was, why I was there, anything that made any rational sense. Only that I had been there forever and would remain that way, for fear that any movement would cast me to the very bowels of hell itself."

Tears started to well up in Ellie's eyes. Sam just wanted to comfort her.

"I wish I couldn't remember it. But it's there with vivid clarity. It was truly a horrendous experience."

Ellie breathed deeply to control her emotions. Sam could see that the turmoil of what had happened plagued his wife. He didn't want her to recall any more, but he knew, for the sake of his investigations, he had to.

"You remember it all with vivid clarity?" repeated Sam, moving forward.

Ellie nodded.

"Tell me what you remembered about the attackers. Did they have accents? Were they British? Were they big and tall? Did you smell anything? Did they have anything that stood out on their body? Did they have guns? What color was their skin? What was their deportment like? Aggressive, demanding, commanding, sadistic, calculated?"

"For fuck's sake, Sam. Ease up! I'm not one of your subjects being interrogated!"

Ellie backed away from the screen, pushing up against her pillow, and scowled at Sam, who swallowed down his enthusiasm and looked sheepish.

"I'm sorry, darling," said Sam coldly. "It's just that if I'm going to catch these bastards, I've got to have immediate on-the-ground intelligence. You're the link to them. You saw them. The nuggets that will lead to me finding these fuckers is in your head. That's why I lambasted into you. I'm only doing it because I care so much about you. I love you, Ellie. You know that I'd do anything for you. My top priority is uncovering these bastards and teaching them a lesson never to mess with my family again."

"You're going to kill them, aren't you?" asked Ellie, and the calm look on her face shocked Sam. Was she finally accepting the way things had to be? Was she accepting him as a killer?

"Yes," responded Sam.

There was no point in lying anymore. When he caught up with the perpetrators, they would be ripped apart.

Ellie pushed down on the bed clothes and turned her face away, biting her bottom lip. Then she returned to face Sam. He noticed a sense of closure, that a decision had been made.

"Then if you're going to find them, you need to know what I know. The guys that attacked me were not Al Nadir. I would say they were very bad thugs paid to make me suffer, but not kill me. There were two of them. One a bit taller than the other. They wore dark clothes and balaclavas over their faces. They used the lift. They broke or blasted in the front door. I'm sorry, I don't know which."

Ellie hesitated, trying to recall exact features of the attackers and any other salient points Sam may need in his investigations.

"I remember their eyes were rabid, crazy like sadistic animals wanting to create fear before the final strike. That's what scared me. Their eyes. They looked like they were capable of anything. It was like they were barely human."

Sam listened. He knew his wife was describing a highly-trained black ops fighter that had humanity burned out of him by the horrific acts he'd committed. Al Nadir used black ops people all the time. Ellie's words only confirmed that they were terrorists.

Sam was just about to finalize his assumption that Ellie was wrong in her conjecture when she stated something extremely strange.

"I barely had time to process what was happening when they stormed in. I'd got up from being sound asleep and felt a wetness. That was why I was up and at the big mirror at the side of the lounge to check myself over."

"What wetness?" said Sam. "Where?"

"On my neck. I had bled a little onto the cushion. I couldn't figure out where I'd cut myself. Maybe a mozzie took a good old chunk out of me."

Sam scrunched up his handsome face. His brow furrowed.

"Ellie, do something for me. Lift up the laptop and position it really close to your neck where that puncture mark was. I just need to see if it's still there."

Ellie made a face, not convinced that what he'd asked would help. But Sam urged her to comply. Ellie couldn't see what she was doing. Sam tried to direct her.

"Just a bit closer, darling. I think I can see it now."

"What are you looking for?"

"That little mark you mentioned earlier."

Sam snapped a still of the screen image using his capture software and brought up the still on his laptop. He zoomed in on Ellie's neck. Whilst he kept talking to his wife, he concentrated on the small puncture mark, now large on the TV inset in the plane's lounge area.

"Wouldn't it have gone?" said Ellie, touching her neck.

Sam shook his head and murmured, "Maybe not."

The more he looked at the faint mark, the more his anxious thoughts started to take hold. He pushed down any worry in front of Ellie. She'd already been through enough.

But Sam was worried.

If Ellie bled before Al Nadir attacked her, what had caused her to bleed?

He stared at the large, high-definition image on the TV screen. The skin was raised like a small crater. It was the same formation as one made by an injection.

Sam shivered, suddenly feeling ice cold.

But just who the hell had injected Ellie that day?

Chapter 65

Maide wondered if Sam would detect anything during the reprimand. What had Rasheed told him before the knife descended? And would Sam believe him?

Maide had no answers, just half-formed estimations, guesses generated by thirty-eight years of investigation, analysis and deception.

When he thought of the reprimand he was going to have to deliver to Sam, his fear surfaced like a dead body dislodged by the ebb and flow of a river. It would be a reprimand for actions borne out of his own selfish behavior.

Maide picked up the phone and instructed one of the comms officers to patch him through to Sam Noor en route. In seconds, a light above the screen flashed to signify his requested channel was open. Maide's hand lingered over the remote control for the satcomm. The on switch had taken on monstrous proportions. Huge and filling his sight, it glared at him, a single dull red eye, taunting him to touch it.

Succumbing to the challenge, Maide depressed the button. A face appeared on the screen. Orbs of darkness, blacker than the coals that fired the very flames of hell, locked with his own eyes. Their pain transcended the distance, through the satellite waves, to infest his soul with grief more encompassing than if he'd learned that the world would end in his next blink.

Maide swallowed, terrified and saddened. He didn't know how to begin.

Sam did.

"I expect you've heard."

Sam's voice was thickened with anguish and tragedy. If black had a sound, it would reverberate within the tone Maide was now hearing.

Crushing his heart as thoroughly as a pestle crushes cloves, the tone brought pinprick sensations to Maide's eyes. It pulled at his optic nerves, sending a signal of sorrow and regret, but simultaneously, a signal of dread. He felt a cold, sweaty instinct that told him something terrible was going to happen.

Maide forced the omen back into the aniline abyss of his mind, but it was a dead weight, an extra sandbag caught in the rigging. He wanted to be rid of it. He wanted to let his balloon of optimism soar, high and free. But it was weighed down and he plummeted down to a hell of his own fabrication. It was a hell where Sam would physically tear him apart, as he had to others before. He would face a live dismemberment by a loving husband for the acts of injustice wrought on his wife. Maide's terror was metaphysical, an altered reality inspired by the knowledge of Sam's capabilities.

Maide's heart jammed in his throat. Although Sam was on a plane, thousands of miles away, he could sense him applying his characteristic iron grip around his own arm. Maide could feel Sam's hands press, vice-like, inwards, squeezing until the circulation cut off and his arm numbed. With a snarl, Sam's hands morphed into massive tiger paws. Claws unfurled, they tore into his flesh, through his jacket and shirt, pulling with inhuman violence downwards, with gravity as the accessory to the murderous assault.

"Sir, I said I expect you've heard about Rasheed."

Sam's black voice brought Maide back from the brink of his guilt-induced illusion. It just caught him before he emitted a scream of no return, echoing the pain of a living hell, a constant conflagration caused by the confluence of tiger-man hands and severed limbs. Mentally shaking free from the ghastly apparitions, Maide stared at Sam, cloaking his emotions.

He spoke as if he hadn't heard Sam's previous words at all, which, in fact, he hadn't.

"Sam, are you alright?" The cold, clipped efficiency melted back into his voice.

"Yeah. Fine."

Maide saw Sam's quizzical expression. He knew his agent was confused by his boss' behavior. Maide had to somehow keep it together. Gain the upper hand. Deliver the ripping Sam deserved for screwing relations with the CIA, not to mention his own personal standing with them. Maide had to show Sam he couldn't just pin Rasheed like a filthy rag to the wall and expect no comeback. However justified he felt the action to be.

He had to show to Sam there was a penalty to pay for the line he'd just crossed.

And he hoped he wouldn't be suffering for leaping across his own line earlier that day.

Maide heard the word 'fine' from Sam's lips. It was, surely, the most inaccurate and inappropriate use of that word ever to be said by any human being. Fine: used to express good health and feeling well. The antithesis of all that Sam was at that moment. Or maybe not, Maide thought, suddenly capturing on the meaning of the word.

Not knowing why, perhaps to protract the inevitable confrontation, Maide recalled other descriptions. Fine: of a point, sharp. That was more like Sam now. A sharp point. A human knife ready to gut someone if they looked at him the wrong way.

Maide recognized his concentration was wandering as Sam's quizzical look drifted into uncomfortable concern. The reprimand Maide envisaged giving was taking forever.

The silence of Maide's presumed contemplations threw a curve ball into proceedings. On the other side of the camera, it was obvious from Sam's face, he didn't know whether to jump, squat, run or remain where he was to catch it. Maide, despite his ability to read people, was blind to the consternation his silent musings had placed on Sam. Slowly, he continued with the staccato-paced admonishment.

"Greene has informed me of the situation."

"I bet he has."

Maide could virtually hear the bile in Sam's throat.

"Why did you do it, Sam?"

Maide adopted a tone of a father asking his son why he'd let down the tires on the next-door neighbor's car. Firm and direct but trying to understand.

"You saw her, sir. You *saw* her."

Sam turned away, exasperated choking on his words.

"Did you learn anything before you…"

Maide didn't need to finish the sentence. Sam's head shook rapidly from side to side. Raging fire flared in his voice.

"He claimed to know nothing."

"Of course he would. That's standard practice."

"But this time, sir, I think Rasheed spoke the truth."

Sam's eyes, piercing and ruthlessly hard, targeted and locked on Maide's. Like a heat-seeking missile, his fiery stare burned up the miles between them. Maide tried to ignore their destructive quality, but his fear, previously quelled, started again like a reawakening bacterium with terminal results for the host. It began to burrow insidiously inside his intestines, gnawing at him, digesting him, and devouring him from the inside.

Chapter 66

Maide listened to Sam. The nape of his neck tingled. Hairs pinged to attention like sailors as if the command 'captain on the bridge' had been given across the deck of his skin.

The very last thing that Maide had believed possible was for Sam to consider the possibility that Rasheed might be telling the truth about it not being an Al Nadir attack. If doubt trespassed into Sam's mind, it would open the gates to the abandoned mansion house for squatters of suspicion to loiter, take hold and take root. Maide couldn't let that happen. He had to serve an eviction order quickly.

"Sam, he's a terrorist. He lied. They all lie. That's what they do. You know that. Don't you, Sam? You do know that."

Maide's voice was clipped and strong. It probed at the uncertainty and confusion Maide saw in Sam.

"I know they all lie. But this time…Something about this was different."

"Different?"

Maide's anxiety in his face was all at once transparent. He took a beat, camouflaging his concern, and looked back to Sam, praying he hadn't noticed.

"What do you mean, Sam?"

"Look at it, sir. Rasheed had no reason to lie. As a prisoner in a CIA cell, he wasn't going anywhere. If he'd known or had any knowledge of the attack, he'd have been only too pleased to rub my face in it. He's Salim's nearest and dearest. He would have known. But, sir, he didn't know. I realized that when he gave me the look."

Sam said it with the intonation suggesting that Maide should know about this mysterious look. But Maide arched his eyebrows in bewilderment.

"Oh, you know, sir," Sam continued. "The look on his face, on any captive's face, that shows absolutely, complete ignorance."

"Really, Sam? Is that what you thought? Then, unfortunately, he was playing you. He was acting ignorant."

"He wasn't *playing* ignorant. He *was* ignorant. He was blind, devoid of knowledge. Use whatever metaphor you like, but he didn't know anything about the hit."

Maide was desperate. His adrenal gland pumped epinephrine into his network of crimson tunnels, making his heart race faster than a prize-winning greyhound. This was bad. This whole line was really, really bad. He had to detract Sam's focus, pull him away, bifurcate his mental pathway, and give him another route.

"He may not have known anything," said Maide. "We know that, for security, Al Nadir isolate one cell activity from another. He may look ignorant simply because he hadn't been told anything."

"He's Salim's first cousin. He'd have been briefed on every major hit. If he said he didn't know, he really didn't know."

"So, Sam, where's all this leading?" Maide fought against the cold dread growing in his stomach. "What are you saying? It wasn't Al Nadir that hit Ellie?"

'Jesus, what the hell are you doing Maide, you stupid little prick?' the voice in his mind scolded.

"The MO's all wrong. Al Nadir is more about explosions and assassinations. GBH, yeah, that's on the button. But hallucinogenic drugs? And CS gas? I don't know, sir. Something just doesn't feel right."

"But they tried to kill her. They would have, if we hadn't gotten there. Remember the transmission. Our men confirmed it to be an Al Nadir frequency. The ammo used on the security guard was the same as one used by Al Nadir in the past."

Maide watched as Sam considered the broadcast and the ammo.

"That's true. They did all say Al Nadir. Maybe I'm wrong."

Fear slipped from Maide on hearing Sam's summation. But unfortunately, fear wasn't going to slip very far.

"But Ellie had the feeling they weren't terrorists at all," continued Sam. "She felt they were more like thugs wanting to frighten her. She said, and I'll quote her, verbatim, 'if they'd been real terrorists, I'm sure I'd be dead. Everything I've read and seen about Al Nadir says they never leave anyone alive.' I really hold onto that. If it had been Al Nadir, Ellie would be in the morgue now."

Maide's heart bounded into a frightened sprint. It was a fox sensing the hunter's horn, prescient of a danger unfolding in the minutes following the hollow sound. The mention of Ellie's name turned Maide upside down, caving in his world of command and order.

She who had no order.

She was a woman who, even in her absence, beleaguered him like no other enemy before. Maide found his voice. He found the courage to speak through the fear that was embalming him in slumbering misery.

"When, erm, when did you speak to Ellie?"

"Half an hour ago. She's much better. Davison's done a great job. She's going home after Davison's finished with the tests. But I guess you already knew that."

"Yes. Yes, erm, we all thought, given her speed of recovery, it was better for her to be at home."

"Good call. I can't wait to see her. Maybe she'll remember more about the attack after resting."

Maide tried to engage but fear silenced him.

Chapter 67

Sam watched Maide speaking. Maybe it was the transmission delay, but he appeared much more tense than usual. His voice was tired, confused and as much as he tried to disguise it, afraid.

Sam picked up on it. He didn't work in intelligence just because he could do the *Times* crossword in under twenty minutes. He was naturally perceptive to the point of premonition. A little waiver in the voice or a smile angled the wrong way spoke a multitude to Sam. It could mean the difference between life and death. His senses were always primed, acute and ready. He was always listening, looking, interpreting and analyzing.

Ten years spent in special operations had taught him to abide by the golden rule: what you think you know, you don't. In the field, facts change in a second. He'd been double-crossed before. He'd been lied to before. He knew the signs. He could decode the cipher. As he looked at Maide's momentary twitch on screen, revelation struck him.

Maide was hiding something.

But hiding what?

"So what's your take on all of this, sir?" Sam forced his response, but Maide looked still shaken by something.

"I believe it was Al Nadir." His boss' forthrightness stood steadfast.

Sam shook his head. "I totally disagree, sir. I think we need to look somewhere else. I don't think Al Nadir was connected to this attack at all."

Sam stared at Maide. Surprise crossed his dark features. Maide looked almost paralytic with fear. Leaping to the conclusion that Maide was a victim, that somehow Al Nadir, or another party, had a hold over him; Sam trod carefully and subtly.

"Are you alright, sir?"

"Yes. I'm fine."

"Isn't that where we came in?" Sam adopted a lighter tone, his demeanor moving away from the absolute black that had immersed him.

"Yes. I believe so."

The two looked at each other in an emotional impasse.

'Boys, for every action there is a reaction.' Mr. Granville, Sam's chemistry teacher had drilled those words into him like a chant. Suddenly, Sam couldn't get it out of his mind. For every action, there was a reaction. What action had caused Maide's reaction? What action had caused Maide's flicker of fear? Sam decided to a little provocation was called for.

"Sir, when you contacted me, I thought you were going to discipline me for what I did to Rasheed. But so far, you've tiptoed around the subject. If I was you, I'd lay into me like there was no tomorrow."

"You're right, Sam. But let's talk when you get back. Given all that's happened today, it's better for us all to sleep on our actions."

'Sleep on our actions'. Sam homed in on Maide's turn of phrase. Sam knew what he'd done and the actions he'd been part of. But what actions had Maide done for him to need to sleep on them?

Sam reflected. He replayed the words again in his mind, making sure he wasn't mistaken.

'Given all that's happened today, it's better for us all to sleep on our actions'.

The sentence, when analyzed, spoke instantly the truth.

Maide wasn't just referring to Ellie's attack, or to Sam's assault on Rasheed. He was referring to something personal. Something that affected *him*. Something that happened to him that very day. Sam started to think, his mind churning, gradually faster, eventually spinning. As if at light speed, he recalled that Maide's fear had heightened when he'd discovered Sam had spoken to Ellie.

Why should Ellie instill such fear? Why had he tried to stall him from seeing her? And why did his wife bleed *before* the Al Nadir attack?

Then, as the pieces slowly slotted together, a hideous hypothesis he barely wanted to consider materialized like a finished jigsaw in his mind. Sam ran cold.

This was *all* about Ellie.

She was the reason Maide had to 'sleep on his actions'. Beyond the Al Nadir attack, something else had happened to her.

What did Maide know? What wasn't he telling? And why?

Chapter 68

Maide realized what he'd said seconds after the words had passed his tired lips. Inwardly, he cursed his foolhardiness. Something inside of him was forcing the truth out. And he couldn't stop it.

Sam smiled at Maide. But Maide could see this was no smile of delight. It had an anguine quality, a boa constrictor's smile before it squeezed its victim into the next life.

Interpreting the meaning, Maide broke Sam's eye line and reached for his malt, instinctively pouring a huge shot. The slightly warm liquid gave him Dutch courage. His fear temporarily tapered off. He returned to the screen.

Maide sensed Sam's eyes on him. Engrossed. Analyzing.

An agonizing pain seeped through Maide's body. Fear grew a physical form. Erupting upwards and touching the back of his throat, it made him close to gagging. But swallowed the sensation with the bile back down.

Did Sam know? Did he suspect?

Maide felt he'd traveled a circle of despair.

"Whatever you say. You're the one with all the moves. Aren't you, sir?"

It was a throwaway line. Both knew it. It served only to lead into Sam's final address.

"But know this, sir," Sam continued. "I'm not going to stop looking until I've found the truth. And then, when I find the fuckers behind Ellie's attack, I'll make them pay."

Sam paused, his chocolate eyes darkening to ebony. His once-tanned face now turned grey and cold like granite. His smile fixed like some insane axe-wielding maniac before the final strike. Sam drove his fist hard down on the table. The sound of cracking made his flight attendant turn around, astonished.

"And I know that you know what I mean by pay. The same as Rasheed and every other fucker who got in my way knows."

Sam fixed ice eyes on Maide, who nodded, desperate to get off the line. The fear in him was tangible. Retribution, he thought, was a very ugly concept. His hands broke out into a sweat and hovered over the cut-off switch. He knew Sam was coming. He knew he was coming back to deliver his message of revenge.

"Are we in agreement?" asked Sam coldly.

Maide nodded, hardly daring to speak.

"Good. I'll see you, sir, very soon. Then we'll get to the truth. Won't we, sir?"

Maide nodded numbly.

Without further address, Sam snapped off the satcomm screen. On the other side of the Atlantic at River House, Maide trembled.

His worst fear was being realized. It was just a matter of time.

The whiskey was comforting, but Maide couldn't just drink himself into oblivion. He had to take appropriate measures. He picked up the phone.

"That situation we feared. It's happening."

Maide heard Quentin swallow heavily. "Oh shit!"

"Meet me at 10 p.m. tonight."

"Where?" trembled Quentin.

"Whitehall. Usual room. Tell Davison he also needs to attend."

"Until ten…then," stumbled out Quentin.

"Yes. Quite. Until ten."

Maide replaced the receiver.

Punch drunk, as if he'd done ten rounds with a prize-winning heavy weight, Maide stood up and swayed. He lifted the glass and downed the remnants of the golden liquid. On the battlefield or in the city, it was all the same.

The goal was the same.

Survival.

Chapter 69

Godley's plane touched down and the waiting car swept him to the PM at speed. He'd been in a cold sweat throughout the journey. Was it possible the PM knew about his connection with Al Nadir? Was he going to be arrested? Was Ashton going to kill him? Could he even risk saying anything about the Peace Summit anymore?

He'd never put a foot wrong before, but now he was unsure of his footing. With trepidation, he entered Number 10 and was escorted to the PM's office. Ashton was seated at his desk, a folder in front of him, his face a story of deep anger.

Sitting down, Godley stared at the folder and asked with as much strength as he could, "Well, Prime Minister?"

Ashton didn't answer. He thrust the foolscap folder in front of Godley, his face still like thunder.

Godley opened the folder and read the contents. Hiding his relief, he said, "What do you plan to do?"

"I can't be seen to be involved. I want you to handle this."

Godley nodded. "What is our degree of exposure?"

"Depends upon what he has already done."

The PM leaned back in his chair. "That reckless driving report had him on the A322 at 4:25 p.m. He was also at the interrogation base earlier. The report was filed as a possible terrorist suspect. But eventually the interviewer confessed it was Sam Noor's wife who was being held."

"Jesus Christ! What the hell did he think he was doing?"

"His job. He must have had his reasons. The interviewer broke down when he was confronted. He stated he didn't have any background information on the suspect, only that she was very dangerous, and potentially Al Nadir. He didn't know who she was, until…"

Ashton paled slightly and poured a cognac for Godley and himself.

Godley took the drink and waited for Ashton to continue. But he didn't. He shook his head, swigged back the alcohol and poured another.

"Well, Richard, are you going to tell me? Or are we going to continue until this is finished? Either way, I don't mind. I wanted a drink tonight."

"She died."

"She what?" Godley almost dropped his glass. "Who died?"

"Ellie Noor."

"Ellie Noor! She's dead? Oh, Christ. That ups the exposure. Who knows besides the interviewer? Does Sam know? Oh, for fuck's sake. What the hell was Maide doing? Where's the body? Does MI6 have it?"

"Enough of the questions, Charles. There is no body. She's still alive."

"But I thought you told me she was dead." Godley was confused.

"According to the interviewer, Davison was called, and he confirmed a massive coronary. But two hours later, in the morgue, no less, she awoke."

"So, Davison got it wrong?" Godley sipped his drink

"Seems that way." The PM raised an eyebrow. "I mean, she couldn't rise from the dead."

"So what has all this Ellie Noor stuff got to do with Maide's turn as boy-racer?" asked Godley, looking back at the file.

The PM looked pensive, and then he picked up the glass and swigged down the contents.

"You know what happened at Silent Waters this afternoon?"

"Yes. Of course. The Al Nadir attack."

"We know the target was Ellie Noor. Reports stated she was almost killed."

"You think they were trying to eliminate one of their own?"

The PM didn't answer Godley. He stared with icy calculation in front of him, and then turned back to his defense secretary.

"Why do you think Maide authorized Ellie Noor's extraction?"

"I don't know. Maybe he thought she was a security threat. An Al Nadir spy out to hurt Sam. Like that business with Sarah Masters."

"And why was Maide on the A322, taking a huge risk and driving like a maniac?"

"Late home for supper, perhaps," suggested Godley.

"Don't be facetious. I'm in no mood for it," snapped the PM haughtily.

"No. Sorry, sir. Well, maybe he had a reason to hurry."

"And what would cause a man of Maide's stature to run the lights and drive recklessly?"

"A bloody good reason to hurry," answered Godley, tempering his sardonic attitude.

"He had to be somewhere quickly. He had a target ETA."

"It sounds, sir, as if you already have a theory."

"I have," said Ashton. "Would you like to hear it? You may not like what I'm going to say."

"I understand, Prime Minister. Go ahead."

"I don't think there *was* any Al Nadir attack. I think Maide was behind it."

Godley couldn't believe what the PM was saying.

"Good God! Why? What possible reason would he have to stage a false flag?"

"To cover up for the interrogation he'd engaged in earlier."

Godley didn't at first understand. The PM could see he was confused. He enlightened him.

"It wasn't routine. She was tortured. They used NMS on her."

Godley stood up, looked from side to side, and sat back down again. He felt like he needed to move. To get out. He really didn't want to hear any more. This wasn't a slight exposure. This was a whole bloody centerfold.

"How can you be sure?"

"The interviewer confessed all. He couldn't stop. He believed he'd killed her."

"What do you want to do?"

"I told you. I can't be *seen* to do anything. But I want this matter cleared up, quickly and quietly. You have full reign. Do whatever is necessary to ensure exposure is non-existent."

"Yes, sir. I understand."

"I can't tolerate mistakes. If the press gets hold of this, the brown stuff will really hit the fan. God knows where it could lead."

"Who else knows?" asked Godley

"The interrogator confirmed that Quentin was at the base," said Ashton, reviewing the intel.

"That was to be expected. Who else?"

"Obviously Davison, the interrogator, who we already have, and potentially, at least two others from Maide's black ops team."

"How do you know just two?" said Godley, narrowing his eyes.

"Oh, that security guard at Silent Waters. You know him."

"Harold?" Godley did know him, ever since he'd moved into his luxury apartment in Silent Waters a year ago.

"Yes. Harold confirmed that only two people were responsible for the attack. If there were others, he didn't see them. Ellie Noor corroborated his account. I think it is safe to assume that Maide employed only two of his most loyal agents."

"He must be out of his mind. Why did they follow his orders?"

"Blind obedience. Totally conditioned. Believed it was for the greater good. I've seen it happen before."

Godley looked at Ashton. The PM's tired, enigmatic voice brought back his speculations. Would Godley ever really know Ashton's background? What the media and the public were told was a smokescreen. He doubted he'd ever find out. But little indications, and a turn of phrase, such as the one Ashton had just used, served to fuel his inner theories.

"What are we going to do about them? They're a liability and a threat."

"You need to neutralize that threat," the PM stated coldly.

Godley swallowed and nodded, his mind going down the list of available operators for the job.

"I have your assurances you'll handle this?" asked Ashton.

"Yes, sir. Nothing will get out. Where's Maide?"

"He's at River House under surveillance. He's spoken to Quentin and Davison, and he's contacted Sam Noor, who knows nothing of what's happened with Maide. Sam believed it was Al Nadir. He's flying back from Langley after an unprovoked, revenge attack on an Al Nadir suspect. The president is furious about the attack. The suspect was Salim Al Douri's first cousin. He could have led us to Al Douri, but now he's in intensive care. Maide's planning to meet Sam at Northolt to reprimand him personally."

"That's ironic."

"Maide's also arranged a meeting with Davison and Quentin in an hour's time at Whitehall. You're now up to speed with developments. I need you to take things from here."

"I understand, sir."

"Remember, Godley, zero exposure, utter discretion. These are our watchwords. I don't want to hear from you until you have handled this situation."

Godley nodded, knowing exactly what he had to do.

Chapter 70

"Ellie, we just have to run a few more tests, just to make sure you're clear. Then you can go home."

"Yeah. Okay. Do whatever you need to. I just want to go home."

Ellie, weary with exhaustion, didn't argue. She dangled her legs over the edge of the bed and accepted the next barrage of prods and pokes.

Davison rolled up her sleeve and positioned the needle. Ellie turned her head away. She hated needles. She couldn't stand anything being inserted into her skin. Angry puncture marks forced a secret wince from Davison as he administered the injection. Feeling the point penetrate through her skin, Ellie's face flinched.

"Sorry. It's a little tender around there," he said.

Ellie bit into her bottom lip and turned away. The veins on her neck were taut and blue as she strained to look away from the hypo.

Ellie was silent throughout the doctor's examinations. She didn't want to watch what Davison was doing. It would have made her more nervous. But closing one's eyes was an admission of weakness, something Ellie could never subscribe to. Instead, her glassy eyes, hardly daring to blink, fixed on the middle of the wall, intently staring at a small imperfection as if her life depended on her close inspection of the dent.

"All done. Time to get you home," he said softly. "Let's sort out a car. Come with me."

Still very dazed, Ellie followed Dr. Davison instinctively. Walking, she had a sense of repetition. Had she followed someone else that day? Her memory was so hazy. So many images. Nothing well defined.

Trance-like, Ellie asked, "My memory, will it come back?"

"Of course it will!" Davison stated with absolute confidence that reassured her.

Ellie didn't realize Davison was watching her as she walked.

Ellie was an innocent, unaware of the evil assault on her psyche, unaware of the shame that haunted the doctor and unaware of the way in which her life was about to change in ways she could never conceivably imagine, even in the wildest of her wild dreams.

Chapter 71

After his meeting with Ashton, Godley slipped into the gents and applied Stein-Muller's nanocream. He rubbed it in like face cream, and it dissolved quickly. He departed Downing Street on foot and grabbed a cab once he was outside of the security blockade. Inside the cab, he headed for the Double Tree Hotel, just minutes away from Downing Street. The second he was seated, he retrieved his phone and clicked on a strange app that just had a smiling face. It opened Stein-Muller nano-face selector that linked to the nanocytes in cream he'd just applied. He chose one of his identities that only required a few minutes to achieve. Godley clicked on the face of Steven Tayler, and then on <ACTIVATE>. Quickly, the nanocytes began to add a little more weight to his nose and made his lips look fuller. It wasn't a complete change. If someone looked very closely, they could potentially discern Godley. But few people looked at each other these days.

A little change to his face was all he needed to be disguised in a world where people wanted to be seen and be liked online but, in reality, hardly regarded their neighbour.

A world of insular obsession.

At reception, Godley kept his head down, refraining from eye contact, and took a room. He was just another man on a business trip. The foreign receptionist barely glanced at him. She just gave a perfunctory smile as she swiped his card. Of course, he'd handed over a card attached to his alias, ensuring his true identity remained hidden.

Inside the room, he took out his burner phone, texted a single number, and waited.

Within ten minutes, a small wage-packet envelope was thrust underneath his door. He picked it up, took the chip out and slid it into his burner phone.

Turning the phone in his steady hands, he switched it on and dialed a number.

"Hello."

No introductions, no pleasantries, straight into business, just as always.

"Good to hear from you," said Russo, and Godley could hear a smile in his voice.

"That issue he has with Noor, I now have an opportunity to redress the balance."

The 'he' in question was Salim Al Douri.

"Good."

"It is a Class One opportunity."

Class One meant that Godley could architect everything from his side. There was little chance of failure in meeting target objectives.

"Very good. They will be pleased," confirmed Russo. His voice, although naturally calm, held a nuance of eagerness. Godley knew the 'they' Russo referred to meant Salim and Sabena.

"So the amount he put out, is it still ok? We have an accord?" asked Godley, a little hesitant. The message across the Al Nadir network was Sam Noor's head for thirty million dollars. Godley had the ability to deliver Sam, but he wanted to be sure he'd get the reward.

"We do," said Russo. "You deliver and he will pay what's been put out."

Godley smacked his lips, seeing the money in his mind being deposited to his Cayman Isles blank account.

"So, the usual protocol?"

"Of course," said Russo. "But be quick. Time is ticking."

"Yes, of course. I understand. I'll accelerate matters from my side."

"Good."

"Until next time," gushed Godley, still seeing the lucre piling up with his name on it.

"Yes. Until next time. Goodbye."

Godley rang off, slipped out the chip, dropped it to the floor, and smashed it under his heel.

It's always good to have contacts, he thought. Whatever side they were on. He was no different to Russo, despite the rhetoric. When all was counted, their objectives were the same. Grab as much money and power as you can before being shuffled off the mortal coil.

Chapter 72

Sam drifted back into the memory of his first encounter with Maide. He'd been working as a civil servant in the Ministry of Defense. While leading the meeting on an ultra-secret new defense technology, Sam had been eloquently vocal in his feelings about using the technology before it had been tested under extreme conditions.

Sam had reached a point where he didn't care about what others thought of him. A life of dumbing-down for ministers too thick to understand or even comprehend his advice had made him frustrated. He needed to challenge and be challenged. He was bored and desperately wanted a change of direction.

Maide had been in the same meeting. Sam recalled him in the corner, saying nothing, just watching silently. Maide had told him much later that 'he'd been extremely impressed'. Apparently, not just by Sam's stunning intelligence, but by the flicker of raw anger, a seething power inside of Sam that the system struggled to keep in check. Maide had remarked to Sam that he was 'too good to be stuck in advanced weapons and tech research. What you've got inside you, that burning energy you try to hide, could make you very powerful if it was harnessed and channeled appropriately'.

After that meeting, Maide had taken Sam to one side for a brief chat. What transpired during their initial, exploratory talk changed Sam's life forever. Within a month, Sam had been recruited to MI6. Placed on an intensive training program spanning Gibraltar, Thailand and Australia. Sam learnt everything he needed to. It only took a year.

Sam, as Maide's protégé, absorbed greedily all the new knowledge and skills with ease. Sam had been thirsty for more. This new world made his quest to learn insatiable. Sam remembered Maide when he visited the camp to see him in action, just before he was given his fully-fledged endorsement as an MI6 field operative. Pride shone in Maide's face. But Sam knew it wasn't just delight at seeing his protégé achieve, it was more the fact that Maide knew he'd made the right choice in Whitehall some fourteen months earlier. And he basked in the hubris of being so right again.

Sam recalled the fear and fury of his first assignment.

He remembered that moment, the feeling like he'd burst if he didn't tell Ellie about his new life. But he couldn't. Sworn to secrecy, he kept it all in. Sam was trained in the art of deception and Ellie never suspected him. His cover as a foreign office diplomat worked well.

Even during training, Sam gave Ellie the excuse that he was on an intensive diplomatic training course covering languages, protocols, etiquette and so forth. Ellie had been so delighted by Sam's promotion to the Foreign Office, she never thought to ask probing questions about his career. And when her new business took off, she became too busy to even notice what Sam was doing. So whipped up in her own life, she didn't see the changes that were taking place in her husband's.

They'd lived their lives like that for the past ten years. But now the façade had been shattered. His Ellie had been attacked. Her life was put at risk. Nothing would ever be the same.

# Chapter 73

Aby-od moved around the Preparation Tower. His hands floated over the crystal controls with more swiftness than a personal secretary typing the minutes from the last board meeting.

The Preparation Tower was a seven-sided structure that stood two meters in height. It was made of the same translucent crystal as the walls and was tailored to a point at the zenith. A crescent dish teetered at the top, threatening to fall to the floor at any moment. Each side of the tower pulsed with incandescent variations of color borne out of the white-light spectrum. In concert, each side broadcast a sound: a unique and intricate composition of notes.

The sound was neither upsetting nor comforting, neither loud nor soft, but resonated with a purpose like a heartbeat. And like a heartbeat, it was connected to life.

Aby-od could *feel* the power of every note. He understood the meaning behind the harmonies. His hands worked diligently, hovering over the side of the tower that was illuminated with blue light. The moment his hand moved across the panel, the crystal melted away to reveal a glittering, filigree necklace of pea-sized gems. At first glance, the filigree configuration appeared two dimensional, like an Escher drawing. However, when the viewing angle was changed a couple of degrees, a deeper third dimensional perspective could be seen. The 2D necklace became a complex cube of gems bonded together by light rays. There were seven of these cubes underneath each panel of the tower and they traveled deep into the heart of the structure.

Responding to the swift adjustments made by Aby-od, the gems throbbed with varying intensities of color and resonated with different tones. In the center of each jeweled cube was a crystal the size of a golf ball. The rock appeared more like a piece of ice. It didn't refract light and had no internal reflection.

Aby-od removed the ice crystal from the blue panel and placed it in the crescent dish.

The instant they connected; a rainbow array of light flashed rhythmically around each facet of the tower. The ice crystal in the dish pulsated in time with tower's Technicolor display.

Sounds, ever more discordant, as if written by an insane composer, rang out from the tower. Aby-od moved erratically, touching crystals and gems in a string of actions that contained no path of logic. But Aby-od's frenetic movements concealed what was really happening. The ice crystal was *telling* Aby-od what to do.

At the point it was placed into the crescent dish, the ice crystal became sentient, reading its own internal properties and inherently knowing the correct configuration of light and sound needed.

Aby-od felt vibrations running through his body as the ice crystal communicated instructions directly to his hands. While the process continued, Aby-od had no will of his own. He understood that he was being possessed by the ice crystal, but this was what was needed to happen to complete the process. Without concern, Aby-od allowed the vibrations to take him over and control him unconditionally.

Gradually, cacophonous noise formed into harmony and flashing rainbow lights concentrated into a deep, rich color. Through Aby-od, the ice crystal had sought out its predefined color and harmony.

Aby-od was undertaking a process called 'Tuning', and this was vital for the successful reconstitution of the Protector.

All seven ice crystals had to be Tuned. Gradually, each found their respective color and harmony. Each color represented an energy power that would eventually be bestowed on the Protector. Even more importantly, however, was the predefined musical harmony contained in each crystal. When all seven harmonies were brought together, they would enable the biological framework of the Protector contained in the life-force holder to be overwritten with the Protector's new physiology.

Having completed the Tuning, Aby-od placed the seven crystals, each now sparkling with their own color, into a satin-lined box. A translucent casket sat at the far side of the hall. Aby-od walked in front of it, knelt down, and raised the box of ice crystals high into air, as if he was offering up a sacrifice. Whispering ancient words, he lowered the box deep into the casket and pulled down the lid. On connection with the casket's body, the lid sparked like a firework and promptly vanished.

Aby-od rose from his knees and walked back to the Preparation Tower. Two small crystals were flashing, one black, the other white, signaling that the Preparation Tower needed to 'sleep'. Simultaneously, he touched the monochrome crystals.

The room vibrated for a second then the Preparation Tower began to descend. Aby-od watched the tower sink into the floor, knowing that, in a blink, it would be gone completely, with only a seven-sided star inlaid in gold on the floor to show its former position.

Watching the floor swallow up the tower, Aby-od thought about the role of the Protector and the many times he'd raised the Preparation Tower in the past, often in the vain hope that a balance shift on a planet could be reversed.

Aby-od prayed that, this time, his hopes were not in vain.

Chapter 74

The three men gathered together in the small committee room in Whitehall. A look of sheer horror took over each of their faces, as if some inhuman atrocity had taken place before their eyes.

In fact, it was their ears which had received the full brunt of the horror.

"Sam Noor knows and he's going to rip us apart for what we did to Ellie."

Maide delivered the news to an incredulous Quentin and stupefied Davison. They both sat back in their chairs. Maide could see they were desperately trying to process the information. And were failing.

"Maide, that's impossible," Quentin said, shaking his head.

"I know it is. But I'm telling you. Sam has pieced it together. When he arrives back, we will be his next target. Believe me, gentlemen. I speak the truth."

Maide was sweating profusely. Why didn't they understand?

"He has knowledge and that makes him a threat. And you know how we deal with threats."

Suddenly, the room erupted into monotone chatter.

Quentin spoke up. "You can't be serious. You're talking about Sam Noor. *Our* Sam Noor. He can't be neutralized. He's the best we have. You know that, Maide. You discovered him, for God's sake."

"And that's *why* I'm serious. I know what Sam is capable of. This situation must not continue. He arrives tonight. We can then take necessary action en route to his home. Do we have an agreement here?"

Maide stared at his colleagues. No one moved. In an effort to mask the reoccurring shakes that ravaged his body, Maide grabbed the decanter, poured a treble shot of Glen Fiddich and downed it in one.

The door handle suddenly started to turn. Maide signaled to Quentin and

Davison to look at the door. Both head turned to see the door handle being shaken, and then, someone on the other side banged aggressively on the door.

Maide stepped back. Concern flooded his face.

The handle rattled like inner demons were inside pressing to get out. Maide stared nervously at the door. He hadn't anticipated interruptions. A thorough sweep for bugs had been made. No one should know that they were there. An uneasy stab hit inside his stomach. Something wasn't right.

But he knew he couldn't remain silent. It could, after all, be a cleaner wanting access to the room. Then, if it was a cleaner, why didn't they just use their passkey?

The door banged. Increasing annoyance sounded with every thud. Then a voice.

"Let me in."

Maide instantly recognized the voice. Charles Godley, Secretary of Defense. What was he doing here?

Maide tried to remain silent. His finger went to his lips, indicating to Davison and Quentin to stay quiet. But Godley was forcefully persistent.

"If you don't open this door, I'll get security."

"Maide, you've got to let him in," Quentin whispered.

Maide sighed, coughed and shouted in the most authoritative voice he could muster, given the vat of whiskey he'd imbibed over the last few hours, "Who is it?"

"Charles Godley, Defense Secretary. Let me in. Now!"

Maide motioned for Quentin to let Godley into the room.

His mind raced. This was going to get tricky. He had no idea what Godley was doing outside the door. But nothing in life, especially in his life, was a coincidence.

Chapter 75

Godley had left the hotel after his discussion with Russo and headed directly for Whitehall, where he knew Maide and co. would be. Outside the door, Godley stood with two military police. Under the PM's explicit instructions, Godley was handling the situation.

"Stay here until you are called for," Godley instructed the MPs. Then he turned the handle again.

The door opened and Godley entered.

Godley, a small, squatty man, whose stature belied the power that he wielded ambled into the committee room. Piercing, rat-like eyes glared at the men assembled. They ventured not to speak.

"Didn't you hear me knocking?" Godley snapped, staring at each man. "And what the hell are you all doing here at this time of night?"

No one spoke.

"Well? Isn't anyone going to tell me what's going on here?"

Godley glared at Davison, the weakest in the group.

"Dr. Davison, please tell me why *you* are in this meeting?" Godley didn't break his eye contact with Davison. He pushed one thought onto Davison: 'say goodbye to your future'.

Davison opened his mouth. "Sir, erm-"

Maide interrupted with smooth precision. He turned, smiling at Godley. "I'm sorry, old chap. This is classified. Need to know only."

But Godley knew his ground. Maide's bullshit 'top secret' nonsense cut no ice with him. He moved towards the table. Maide realized the folder was in front of him. He reached out to remove it, but Godley's sober hand swept it up out of his reach.

Maide stood up abruptly, wavered slightly, an after effect of the Glen

Fiddich, and walked with the most amount of purpose he could muster towards Godley.

"Really, sir, this is classified. I'm sorry, but I'll have to ask you to return that folder to me." Maide's hand outstretched in Godley's direction.

Godley shook his head and didn't move. Only the pages in the folder moved as Godley flicked through the information contained within.

"Sir, I must protest. You don't have clearance to read that."

"Clearance?" shouted Godley, deciding that he'd had enough of polite procrastination. "I've got clearance at the highest level. Shall we talk? Or would you prefer to talk to the MPs waiting outside? Your choice, gentlemen."

Maide threw up his hands. Godley recognized the look on the MI6 Chief's face. He knew there was nowhere to go but truth central.

"It's a long story," Davison muttered, breaking the silence.

"We have all night," Godley stated.

"We…erm…we didn't mean to hurt her," stuttered Davison, the first to fall.

"Shut up, Davison," hissed Maide.

"Hurt who?" Godley asked, ignoring Maide.

Quentin spoke for the first time in front of Godley. "Mrs. Noor."

Godley watched as Maide cast a savage look at Quentin. It was obvious he was now unable to come to terms with the unbelievable betrayal before his eyes.

Godley knew Quentin was a lightweight when it came to keeping quiet. Always a great believer of when survival was on the table, loyalty went out the window.

Godley maintained his attention on Davison. His beady, charcoal, rat-eyes drilled into him.

"You mean Sam Noor's wife?" Godley queried

Davison swallowed. "Yes."

"How did you hurt her?"

"She was extracted. We used NMS on her." Davison pointed to Maide. "He thought she was a security threat."

"You used NMS on a defenseless woman?" Godley delivered an academy-award-winning pretense of being horrified.

"Godley, there was a reason for all this. Sam Noor breached security. He divulged his secrets. You remember Sarah Masters. We had good reason backed by surveillance to believe Ellie Noor could be another ticking time bomb. May I remind you; we are at war with Al Nadir. And war requires extreme measures. Sometimes to the detriment of others. I am not ashamed of what we did. We acted in the interests of national security."

"National security?" Godley repeated, now staring hard at Maide. "Or your security?"

"I'm not sure I follow you, sir."

"It doesn't matter. I've heard enough. Ready!"

Godley watched as the door opened and two burly MPs stepped through. They strode over and took their position behind Maide. Godley expected some remonstrations on Maide's part, but he did nothing. In his eyes, Godley could see the knowing, the awareness that his time was up. Maide rose from his chair and stumbled. Godley swiped a glance at the tumbler full of whiskey. Clearly, Maide had imbibed a lot. It was understandable he had no energy left to fight. Maide walked with the MPs and smiled.

"You find this humorous?" snapped Godley.

"Ironic," muttered Maide, and Godley got the inference. If Maide was in custody, Sam wouldn't be able to touch him.

Just before he passed through the door, Maide turned to face Godley. "How?"

"I'm sorry, old chap, but that information is classified. On a need to know basis only. I'm sure you understand."

Maide nodded silently. His face told the fact that he understood only too well, and he slipped through the door.

Turning to Davison, Godley spoke with sinister coldness.

"Time to leave, Dr. Davison. Appropriate disciplinary procedures will be taken in due course. Consider yourself on gardening leave until further notice. Your security pass, please."

Godley held out his hand. Davison removed his pass from his pocket. He rose from his chair, walked over and placed the pass in Godley's hand.

Godley caught Davison's sad scan across the room and recalled his profile. After slogging and toiling through seven years at medical school, and four more years specializing, he'd finally reached his esteemed position in MI6. He'd reached the top.

Only for it all to be dashed down in seconds. A victim of consequences.

An air of hushed dishonor surrounded Davison as he left the room.

Chapter 76

Quentin kept his eyes trained on the center of the table, not daring to look at Godley.

How would he cope? What would he do? What a fool he'd been to align himself with Maide. He should have seen the damage that would ensue.

With the MPs gone, only Godley and Quentin were left alone in the room. Neither spoke. Quentin looked away. The wait was intolerable. The silence was audible. It screamed in his ears. Godley sat and glowered ruthlessly at Quentin.

Standing it no longer, Quentin spoke. "Sir?"

But Godley's dispassionate expression made him halt his plea. Silence enveloped them again. Quentin felt claustrophobic. It was like he couldn't breathe. Bile filled in his stomach and his heart hammered hard inside his chest. The tension was visible.

Finally, Godley spoke, releasing the pressure in the room like a valve in a boiler pipe.

"What do you think Sam is going to do?"

Quentin was not ready for this. His expectation had been to receive a severe reprimand followed by imprisonment by the MPs. He stared at Godley, puzzled.

"Well? Answer, man." Godley was impatient.

Quentin's mind raced hard. Where was this going? What was Godley trying to do? Quentin's answer was measured and slow.

"I don't know. Maide believed he'd kill us."

"Did you believe that?"

"Of course not!"

"But you do think he could be a threat?"

"Perhaps. Politically speaking."

"Please accompany me. We need to discuss this more thoroughly."

Godley opened the door and beckoned for Quentin to follow him. Walking with Quentin into the lift, Godley punched the button for the basement. Quentin's paranoia kicked in. Maybe Godley had a more sinister and final punishment awaiting him.

Godley flicked the remote on his Mercedes and opened the door for Quentin.

"Where's your driver?" asked Quentin nervously.

"I prefer to drive myself tonight. Much more…appropriate."

Quentin slipped into the passenger seat. Godley drove quickly out through the security check.

"You're a sound man. A reliable man. Aren't you?" Godley shot Quentin a questioning look. But it was not a question of standing. It was a veiled command to say yes.

Quentin nodded, unable to comprehend Godley's actions.

"Sam could be a threat, but not a murderer. Right?"

Quentin was astonished. He answered impulsively.

"Of course not. Maide was completely mad to think that."

"But it's clear to me that he will be a problem in other ways."

Godley's bellicose smile made Quentin shiver. Quentin gradually started to understand Godley's direction.

"He could be. Well, I guess, he will be. He's good. He's going to find out the truth pretty damn quickly. According to Maide, he already has."

Quentin stumbled over his words, suddenly wary of Godley in a new, frightening way.

"I haven't come this far to be destroyed by him or anyone else. Appropriate remedies need to be employed." Godley kept his eyes on the road but continued with his grave decision. "It is your responsibility to neutralize the threat."

Quentin swallowed. Globules of sweat sprang up as his forehead perspired profusely. His collar tightened. So this was his path.

"Do we have an understanding, Quentin?"

Godley pulled into a side street and turned off the ignition. With belligerent menace, he revolved to glare at Quentin.

Quentin looked away. His life. His career. His status. It would all be dust if Sam was left to continue his investigations. Sam would bring them all down. He would lose everything.

At a crossroads, Quentin stared into the night. One way, he would lose everything but keep his soul. The other way would see him remain powerful, maybe even ascend to be prime minster in time, but his soul would descend to the depths of damnation.

"Well?" pressed Godley, his intolerance of the situation building.

Quentin thought again of his precious life. The money. The power. It's no decision really, he thought blackly.

"We have an understanding."

Chapter 77

Entering the apartment, Ellie sensed irregularities. Each item gave the outside impression of being right, but Ellie knew it was all wrong. She tried to disguise her anxiety from the two MI6 officers who had accompanied her. But they picked up on it instantly.

"Are you okay, madam?"

"Yes. Yes, I'm fine."

"Would you like us to stay in here until Dr. Noor arrives?"

"No. That won't be necessary. But thank you."

"Very well, madam. We shall be outside. If you need us, just call."

Ellie nodded and the officers took their place like sentries on each side of the door. It felt strange to have guards outside, but Sam had been insistent, refusing to take no for an answer.

Ellie closed the door and walked quickly to the bedroom. On the way, she passed the study and noticed her handbag was next to her briefcase. I'm sure I left it in the wardrobe, she thought. But her recollection was musty, full of images and paths with dead ends. Her memory was fragile and untrustworthy.

The telephone rang, breaking her concerted effort to remember. Ellie picked up the receiver, slightly shaken by its noise.

"Hello?"

"How are you, sweetness? How are you feeling?"

"I'm okay."

"God, Ellie, you're too precious to lose. I love you so much, Ellie. So much. I'm sorry I wasn't there for you."

"How could you be? You've got your job to do."

Ellie's reply was touched with bitterness. Sam read the implication.

"I'm sorry. For everything."

Sam's words came slowly and sadly. So loaded were they, Ellie could palpably feel his anguish and guilt.

"You've got nothing to be sorry for."

"Haven't I?"

"No. You haven't."

A pause took over their exchange of emotions. Sam coughed, breaking the heaviness.

"Look, I'll be landing in just over an hour. I'll be with you around midnight. Please, my love, go to bed. Get your rest. Don't wait up. Okay?"

"Okay. I love you."

"I love you too, sweetness."

Ellie replaced the receiver and stretched. The simple movement took her aching bones over the pain threshold. It was like she'd lived through a lifetime of mining some precious ore. Every muscle, every bone, screamed out for rest.

Scowling at her weakness, Ellie breathed in and tried to control the throbbing aches surging through her body. Standing up, she breathed rhythmically, defiantly suppressing the pain, and walked across the bedroom.

Her reflection in the full-length mirror caught her attention. The clothes she wore hung heavily around her like lead had been sewn into the hems. She had a sensation as if she was a stranger in her own familiar surroundings. Everything felt out of synch. It was like she was the weak link in a chorus line, not quite able to catch up with the choreography. Always trailing behind.

Slipping out of her clothes, Ellie stepped into the shower room. Warm, clear water washed over her. Enveloped by the sensuous tingle of hot droplets, Ellie closed her eyes. Her tired limbs relaxed.

Sam was returning.

Ellie allowed herself a fleeting smile. His voice had sounded so powerful, so demanding. Suddenly, his words, his touches, were all around her. Closing her eyes, she succumbed to the moment. No secrets. No words. Just love.

Standing there, water gushing down her body, Ellie blushed like mankind's first lady at her moment of exposure. Wrapping her nakedness in soft cotton, Ellie looked into the mirror, touching her face. Her skin felt dry, flaky even, like fragile, late autumn leaves. She smoothed it in moisturizer, but nothing seemed to hydrate the lackluster skin.

Looking at her hand covered in moisturizer, Ellie experienced detachment. Through her translucent skin, Ellie could see the intricate network of thin blue veins snaking through her fingers. She could see the ingrained lines that turned the fortunes for gypsies. She could see crisscross lines at the junctions of her knuckles. She could see her hand. It looked like her hand. Common sense said it was her hand.

But the tingling feeling like electricity running through at the base told her something different. Shivering, Ellie stared back into the mirror. There it was again, that out-of-synch feeling.

She couldn't pin point it properly, but it was as if her body was not her own. She sensed everything as unreal, like life was layered and reality was deep underneath, hidden from her view.

Her mind had been filling with images and emotions she couldn't explain since she'd awoken. Glimpses of fire, faceless people, green corridors, bright lights then utter darkness. Feelings of abject pain and calm harmony co-existed at the same time. With the images and emotions reaching saturation, Ellie's mind was heavy and confused. She knew she couldn't handle much more. Listening to the music play in the lounge, the words of Queen's song 'I want to Break Free' suddenly found new meaning.

"Either tell me or leave me," whispered Ellie instinctively, but she didn't know why.

Stepping down the stairs leading from the study to the lounge, a mental storm whipped up inside Ellie, deluging her in flashbacks, overpowering her sight completely.

❦

The room was very dim but not completely dark. In the far distance, there was a faint light. She could see a door had opened. A man stepped through and advanced quickly. Now but a few feet away, the man struck a match. She knew it was a match; she could smell the phosphor in the air. The man, cast now in light and shadow, the flame flickering in front of his face, smiled sadistically. She stared, petrified. Her eyes fixed on the little light on the end of the slither of wood. Fire was her greatest fear. Still smiling, the man dropped the match to the ground. Instead of dying out, the match ignited the floor, sending the room into a sudden sea of flames. Circling around her, the searing heat touched her skin. She screamed.

"Tell me what I need to know. Tell me who was listening. Who did you speak to? What did they tell you? What is too far gone? Why did you scream? Is Sam Noor your target? Tell me what I need to know, and I'll make it all go away. You'll feel no pain."

But she didn't respond. She only screamed as she watched the flames lick at her feet. All around her, everywhere she looked, was a curtain of angry red.

She sniffed. A sickly, sweet smell raided her senses. At first, she wasn't immediately certain what it was she smelled. She sniffed again, and then she knew. It was her. It was her skin. Burning. Agony beyond comprehension shook her body. She wanted to run but she couldn't move. Incarcerated. No escape. Desolation sounded in her screams.

She stared in horror at her legs. Fire burnt through her skin making it bubble and blister, breaking free from the muscle underneath. She bled. Through the blood, she could see grey white. Her bone peeped through. The flames were burning away the layers, the coverings that made her human.

Pain, so intense, rocked her body. Smoke and fumes soaked into her lungs, choking her. Flames ignited and her skin darkened. She retched hard and gagged as searing pain sliced like a Sabatier knife through her.

Scorching pain from the white heat was too much for her heart to stand. Harder and faster, it pumped, threatening to collapse.

She screamed for help, but no one came.

Unconsciousness beckoned and her screams grew weaker. She was losing the will to live.

Death raced upon her fast.

Ellie's surroundings suddenly surged back into focus, from dark to light. A sharp tipping from dream to reality. Uncertain, and deeply unstable, Ellie lost her footing and fell down hard on the marble step.

The shock of the fall made her cry. Dripping hot tears, she staggered back to her feet as a dull thud of muscular pain reverberated in her lower back.

Was that a memory?

Ellie, in her conscious state, tried to recall, but nothing came. The pain of having nothing in her mind hurt her more than the physical injury.

What in God's name is happening to me?

Ellie wiped away the tears, but they reformed faster than a queue at Harrods on the first day of the sales.

Pull yourself together, girl.

Her inner voice was strong. But outside, she was broken and tired. Lost in tears, Ellie didn't realize the phone was ringing. Eventually, the insistent sound rang through to her senses and she picked up the receiver.

It was Sam. He had landed.

"I love you, darling." Ellie's voice was small and sad.

Sam noticed her lifeless tone. "Are you still in pain?"

"No. I'm okay. It's just, well, oh, fuck it, Sam. I feel like shit! And I've just fallen down the stairs. I'm seeing things! Hearing things. I think I'm going mad! I'm fed up with feeling like this. Am I mad Sam? Am I?"

"My sweetness, of course you're not. I'll be with you soon. Go to bed," Sam instructed gently, and the little voice on the other end of the line acquiesced without question.

Chapter 78

Grabbing a little shuteye in the limo proved almost impossible. Although Sam had been running on only anger and adrenaline since 4 a.m., every time he closed his eyes, all he could see was Maide standing beside Ellie's body. Her broken and bruised body.

Sam hit the soft leather of his chair with a balled fist, creating a deep valley. Maide had reason to fear him. Ripping the truth from him was just the beginning. He didn't care what lengths he went to or to what depths he sank. He'd done it before in the name of his country. Now, he was going to do it all again in the name of love.

Sam arrived home. Talk was minimal. Sam held Ellie tightly for a long, long time. No words seemed appropriate. Sam just wanted to hold her in his arms, to feel her warmth.

Seeing Ellie in the flesh, after hours of conjecture, Sam knew the ordeal had left her indelibly scarred. She'd aged in the past twenty-four hours. In fact, he barely recognized the woman he'd married. The happy-go-lucky personality and the radiance he loved had been buried beneath a landslide of trauma and haunted horror.

Sam put Ellie to bed, but she wouldn't sleep until he cuddled her. In his arms, Ellie fell asleep. But sleep did not welcome Sam. His mind, still alert and razor sharp, ticked over. No rest would be forthcoming that night. Slipping gently out of Ellie's grasp, he headed for the study and his laptop.

While Ellie slept, Sam hacked into MI6 personnel files. Code breaking was a skill he excelled in. With his sci-tech background, hacking came naturally, and his capability was sublime. He cross-referenced his name with Ellie's and the screen flashed with information.

He stared at it, amazed.

It was her. His Ellie. Dissected. Scrutinized. Analyzed. In the minutest detail. Who she was, what she did, what her background was. They knew what music she liked, what clothes she bought, what food she ate, even what her sexual predilections were.

They knew *everything*.

He shook his head. He never knew. He'd never suspected. And then...

Sam remembered back to the time when he took his vows, when he'd signed his allegiance to 'protect God, queen, and country above all others'. The words came back, shattering him. His loyalty had been unreserved. Why should they have betrayed his trust? But Sam knew. In the intelligence business, information was power. They *had* to know everything.

Anger coursed through him, and his hands shook. On opening the ops reports for Sunday, he found the Al Nadir attack on Silent Waters was the only major activity. Every angle had been documented. Although the medical reports were harrowing, they offered no further information than what Sam already knew. Accessing and speed-reading each report, Sam was still no closer to understanding what had really happened to Ellie.

He sat back in his chair and stared at the report listings, and then it struck him. The files had been deleted.

His fingers skipped over the keyboard with increasing swiftness and he hacked into the central server. The deleted files wouldn't be there, but Sam hoped that by running his Sniffer program while accessing the machine code, he could ascertain that a deletion command by Maide had taken place during the day.

Sniffer worked just like a bloodhound hunting out a trail of commands from specific users to illustrate a particular process that had been undertaken. Sam knew that a lot could be said about a string of commands. Sniffer went to work. Sam waited. It would take some time.

He stood up and walked towards the bedroom.

Chapter 79

Ellie slept peacefully. The pain Sam had first seen had slipped softly away as slumber had taken her. She now once again resembled the wondrous woman he'd married. Sam took the moment to gaze at her. He knew it was a cliché, but Ellie's beauty was timeless. Even with the experiences she'd endured, that unmistakable radiance that had instantly attracted him remained unhampered.

Touching her face softly, he remembered their first horizontal rendezvous back in '94.

23 Years Earlier

Sam had lived alone in an atypical bachelor pad. It was spotless and clean. His flat's appearance was a physical representation of himself. One part was filled with the latest techno-gadgetry of the era and the other was a celebration of a richly colorful heritage. Intricately woven silk rugs graced the pinewood boards. A large dallah, a traditional Arabic coffee pot, sat on the floor, sharing space with an oscillator and a ripped-apart motherboard. An antique wooden Ottoman table with delicate, hand-carved rose petals held hi-fi separates joined in a mind-bogglingly complex configuration that suggested the owner could only be a man. A crudely beautiful peasant's water jug sat diagonally opposite the computers of the moment.

In a room that screamed a cacophonous clash of cultures, an unseen battle for dominance was ongoing. For every bit of tech, there was a traditional antiquity vying for space.

Most bizarrely, the room's unintentional interior design worked. It was emblematic of Sam: the unconventional, totally original, and away from the norm. It was his maxim, how he lived and survived in his life.

He'd been cooking kebabs in the kitchen when Ellie arrived. It was a few minutes after twelve. Sam heard the doorbell as he rested the tray on the hob. Steam rose from the elongated, meaty cigars and filled the kitchen with a heady mix of spicy smells.

Trembling slightly, Sam removed his oven gloves, placed them neatly on the hook, and ran quickly to the bedroom for one last look at himself. The reflection in the mirror looked good in a pale blue silk shirt and dark blue chinos.

But would she think so?

Nervously, he ran his hand through his short, black hair. Despite all his arrogant posturing where women were concerned, he possessed a certain innocence. It gave him uncharacteristic humility.

Sam never really understood women. He'd had plenty, sure enough, but he never really understood what was going on inside their heads.

His problem was that he couldn't read their signs, and as such, he came over either too self-deprecating or too conceited.

The blame for this lay squarely on his background. He'd had a masculine upbringing that stated that women had their place in the bedroom and kitchen and nowhere else. And the women he did meet didn't help him change the doctrines of his formative years. For Sam, women fell into two categories: scaredy-cats terrified of him or gold-diggers coming to their first date with a wedding catalogue. He'd never found a woman that he could really talk to or connect with.

Until Ellie.

From the moment she started in the office, he'd been desperate to get into her knickers. And she wasn't shy about her intentions. Unashamed and blatant, it mattered to her not one bit that Sam was her boss. But Ellie wasn't like the rest of the women he'd known. She wasn't a gold digger. Nor did she fawn around him, acting with false sincerity. When she was with him, they talked one on one at the same level. Her supreme confidence shouted, 'Despite your age, experience, and wealth, I'm as good as you!'

Ellie had an arrogance that matched his, and a fire in her belly to succeed at anything she turned her hand to. That included getting him. He could do nothing but acquiesce to such a gorgeous, powerful siren.

They had been on dates for the past few weeks. But as desperate as he was, he hadn't had the courage to move the relationship from being purely platonic. Ellie was still very young, just turned nineteen, and he was fast approaching thirty.

He was aware of their age gap. And although he wanted her, a quick peck on the lips was all he felt comfortable to give her. But Sam also knew Ellie was a very physical person. She liked to touch and hold him, and if their relationship was to have any hope, he was going to have to leap out of that comfort zone of matey cuddles and innocuous squeezes. Like the title of a Rod Stewart song, he thought, 'Tonight's the Night'.

The bell rang again. A touch of impatience sounded in the pattern of the ring. No going back now, Sam, he thought, as he breathed out a tense sigh. The bell depressed and rang continuously on the third time. In parallel, the letterbox sprung open as Sam descended the stairs.

He could see Ellie squatting down on the other side of the frosted glass.

"Sam, are you there?" screamed Ellie, peering through the opening.

Sam smiled but didn't call out. Ellie was always so very loud. Their recent dates revealed that to him. In restaurants, when she spoke, it was as if she was addressing the rest of the clientele rather than holding a private tête-à-tête with him. Ellie was 'over the top' and naturally theatrical. Her behavior constantly called 'look at me'. He loved her, but that element of her personality was at odds with his need for privacy and seclusion. It almost made him rethink their relationship. Almost.

But one glance at her animated deliveries, her eyes vivaciously bright, her loud mouth spouting the inconsequential and intellectual in equal measure, and he couldn't resist. She was so full of life, so full of everything that life should be. He couldn't help but become addicted to being part of the 'World of Ellie Vale'.

Sam reached the bottom of the stairs and opened the front door.

Ellie stood there, an ancient goddess trapped in Topshop. A pale, rose-pink, cotton and Lycra crop top skimmed her rounded, firm breasts, and a short, sexy denim skirt graced her slim but not skinny waist. A thin, black, studded, leather belt draped over one hip, suggesting a touch of rebellion.

Long, blonde hair eased down her shoulders, hiding a golden-brown tan courtesy of the sun bed at the gym where she'd been most of the morning, frantic to ensure her physique was bronzed and toned to perfection.

Sam was mesmerized. He imagined his jaw, like a character in a cartoon, dropping to the floor and his eyes popping out, heart shaped, towards Ellie. Sam caught himself before his leg started bashing the floor and the wolf-whistle scenario hit him full on.

"We having lunch here then?" Ellie's bold eyes shone as she laughed mischievously.

Sam couldn't read the signs, but he knew Ellie was a master code breaker. He was embarrassed and excited, and watching Ellie, he knew his predicament was clear. Those two emotions he was caught up in had created the pregnant pause that both now experienced.

"Oh, yes. Erm, sorry. Come in," muttered Sam, totally incoherently. He blushed, backing to one side to allow Ellie to proceed past him up the stairs.

Sam could smell a light fragrance. She smelled good. He turned to follow her.

They had been friends for a while, but this was the first time Ellie had been in Sam's flat. Her eyes were darting everywhere. She was nosey to the point of annoying. But Sam didn't mind. He was so overwhelmed to have her there, she could have played twenty questions on every item and he wouldn't have been bothered. That concession alone indicated to Sam that Ellie was much more than just an ordinary girlfriend. She was to be the love of his life, all of his life. He intended for her signature to experience a drastic metamorphosis. For, very soon, Sam would turn Ellie Vale into Ellie Noor.

He watched Ellie reach the top. She sniffed the air like an elegant pine marten, turned her head, and trotted down in the direction of the room from where the gloriously tasty smell had emanated. The kitchen was compact and hi-tech, a place where arctic-white cupboards encircled a stocky center table. Deep, dark blue, granite worktops gleamed, clutter free. Checkerboard flooring stretched out giving the illusion of greater depth. Bold, polarized color and straight, dominating lines featured everywhere.

It was unquestionably a man's kitchen, an ultramodern, totally testosterone-fueled design.

Ellie looked around at the clinically clean hob and spied the culprits wafting the spicy smells. "Oh, kee-babs! I love kee-babs."

Her hand sneaked out and grabbed the end off of one of the tasty morsels. As she popped it into her mouth, she looked up and smiled, Cheshire cat like, at Sam. He'd followed behind her, watching as she analyzed the kitchen. Leaning sideways, his shoulder resting on the doorjamb, he could detect movement in his trousers. God, he wanted her. But instead, he just corrected her pronunciation of the cuisine. He felt pathetic.

At that moment, it was as if Ellie was psychic, for she picked up on his desire instantly.

"It's got bite."

Ellie grabbed a larger piece of meat between her thumb and forefinger.

Sam watched and then moved awkwardly towards her. He could smell her perfume again. Sweet honeysuckle, magnolia, and vanilla. Good enough to eat. He was getting hotter and it had nothing to do with the kebabs.

"Yeah, I meant to warn you. I made those ones for me. I like them hot. I made you some without Tabasco. They're in the oven. I didn't know whether you liked hot things." Sam's voice mumbled off. God, what the hell was he saying? He sounded like an actor in a B movie trying to get his leg over the eye candy.

But Ellie grabbed the hook. She laughed and Sam joined in. It helped to disperse his tension.

Ellie looked at him, her eyebrows raised. Intentional or subliminal delivery, Sam could see she'd gotten her cue. Ellie couldn't let go now.

"Oh, I love hot things. I can really take the heat." She slinked closer to Sam.

He froze with nowhere to go, his back pinned to the table. Ellie advanced, padding panther-like towards him. With just a couple of feet between her and Sam, Ellie placed the kebab up to her lips, inserted its meaty head in her mouth and bit off the end. Sam was spellbound.

"Erm, you like to eat that, don't you?" Sam asked, watching her.

Like everything else about her, when she ate, the movement was exaggerated and expressive, but not crudely so. Her entire face appreciated every fragment of food. She poked the rest of the kebab in her mouth and moved in, closing the two feet to one foot and then to none.

"I prefer to eat something else if you're asking."

Sam looked down at her messy face and fingers. Pulling a tissue from his pocket, he dabbed the corner of her mouth and her fingertips.

Ellie lifted up, snatched the tissue away from his fingers, and placed it on the table behind him. Returning to face him, her eyes like deep-water pools, their power, dragged him under. The heat inside him was unbearable. Ellie glanced down, ran her fingers gently over his growing bulge, and then moved up his body, her lips brushing against his neck.

Strangely, he didn't react at first. He wanted Ellie so much, but he didn't want to put a foot wrong. She was so much more than any other girl he'd known. He was literally terrified at that moment of making a wrong move and destroying the precious friendship they had together. Fear and anticipation hurtled on a collision course through his body as he tried to focus on what to do next.

Ellie tried again. Tilting her chin upwards, she softly opened her mouth and encased his in a tender kiss. Fear and anticipation hit head on. Sparks flew up his spine, igniting something deep inside.

His arms dangling idly by his side suddenly found their vocation. Slipping around Ellie's trim waist, they pulled her very close. Sam returned Ellie's kiss, tentatively at first. And then, as his courage grew, so did his passion.

"You're really hungry, aren't you?"

He didn't answer but swept Ellie up in his arms and carried her to the bedroom. Sam laid Ellie on the bed. Then he pulled away to look at her.

Ellie smiled. They both knew that the time had arrived to take their relationship to the next level.

Back in the present, Sam lifted his fingers off her face. Sam loved her so much, that day existed as a constant in his mind, as fresh and vivid as if it were but a moment before. She was everything. She had given him everything.

He kissed her forehead. Ellie stirred but did not wake. Sam caressed her hair softly. She moved her arm out and he noticed the bruising.

He would tear them apart.

Maide was the ringleader. Of that, Sam was positive. He'd seen something on the surveillance data, and that something had caused him to react with ferocity. He had to protect Ellie from now on. He had to keep her safe. He told her he would not let her down again. She hadn't understood what he meant. But he knew.

Leaning down, he kissed her again.

Ellie moved, in half-sleep, and slurred, "You okay?"

Sam smiled and wiped the tears away. "Yes, darling."

"What are you looking at?" Ellie's eyes half-opened to look at Sam.

"Just an angel, my sweetness."

Ellie smiled, sank back into her pillow, and slipped back to sleep.

Upon returning to the study, he saw that Sniffer had scored.

On the screen was a string of commands from Maide's computer. From the grid node reference, Sam could tell Maide had been operating from his office at River House. The command strings showed his boss had been using and exporting audio files. An external storage device had been used. It was obvious he'd tried to cover his tracks. Deletion commands were everywhere.

But he'd been sloppy and clearly frantic about something. Sam looked at the export command again and balled his fist tightly. Everything now depended on getting that storage device.

Chapter 80

At River House, Sam swiped in. Security didn't bat an eye. He had top-level clearance. They'd seen Sam in the building at the oddest hours before. They knew not to enquire further.

Using his electronic skeleton key, something he'd procured as a precautionary measure against terrorists ever getting a foothold into River House, he broke silently into Maide's office.

He sat in Maide's chair and swiveled to the left and to the right. He flicked his head around the sparse, tidy office. Where would he put it? Sam pulled open the desk drawers idly as he put himself in Maide's shoes. Getting up, he checked the shredder, but the basket was empty. He tugged open the filing cabinet, but it was locked. Collecting a paper clip from Maide's desk, he picked open the cabinet. Riffling through files, Sam hunted for any object that could be a portable storage device.

Nothing turned up. Closing the bottom drawer, Sam leant against the cabinet. His eyes scanned the room. Something had to be there. He was missing something.

Sam looked intently at the desk. Pen, post-it notepad, paper-clip holder. Hardly anything. That was Maide. That was his style. Secretive. Closed. He never left anything of value in his office. He never left anything that mattered.

Sam glanced back. A flash of black with an outline of red caught his vision. He stared again. Castanets. They were the paper-clip holder. It was the only item on the desk that spoke of personality. Sam knew Maide loved Spain. He'd designed his home to match an eighteenth-century Spanish mansion.

His home.

Of course, it all made sense. Time was slipping away. Sam had to get to Maide that night.

Chapter 81

Aby-od knew that, for the Protector to be awoken, a planet had to be facing a severe risk of annihilation. He shook his head sadly. Ki wasn't even an adolescent and it was facing extinction. What had gone so wrong? Where had Kudamun gone wrong?

Staring at the gold star on the floor, Aby-od's eyes misted over. He couldn't let the High Council sever the chance for Ki to change and make amends for its waywardness. There was no other alternative. The Protector had to succeed.

The Protector, under Kudamun definition, was a hybrid being created from one part Kudamaz and one part native inhabitant. This being possessed powers to protect the planet they lived on. The hybrid being was termed the Protector's holder. They literally held the Protector's life-force inside of them until the time when the Protector would be called from Kudamun and the reconstitution process would begin.

In creating the hybrid being, it had always been the way to ensure that no trace of their Kudamaz half was apparent to the native. The Protector's life-force was always assimilated completely inside the native. More often than not, the Protector's holder would live their life nascent and absolutely unaware as to why they perpetually had the feeling there had to be more to life than what they experienced.

Such feelings of longing and eventual displacement of their own reality grew, the closer their planet moved towards the Zone of Great Risk. Just before the call, the Protector's holder would feel outside themselves, not in synch with their own body or the world around them. But until they received the call from Kudamun, a native would never know the real reason as to why they felt so disturbed and unsettled in their own body. Aby-od knew that many Protectors would live through their many lifetimes forever waiting to arrive at the full realization of their purpose.

Aby-od walked over and drew his hand across the translucent wall. A gallery of captured visuals appeared. Looking at them, Aby-od remembered when he'd first selected the Protector for Ki.

The most recent images still showed that special something that had attracted him to the Kudamaz citizen he had eventually selected. There had, of course, been physiological changes over the thousands of years that had passed, as one might expect, but the powerful determination that he'd seen, and which had impressed and moved him, was still very much present.

Chapter 82

March 24, 2017

The gates at Maide's estate were locked and surveillance cameras constantly swept, like an overeager street cleaner, for any trace of movement.

Sam sat in his AMG with his laptop and hacked into the surveillance feed. The camera views around the outside of the house popped up on his screen. The control room was strangely dark. Maide always had his team of two guys monitoring activity. But now the screens were running on their own without observation.

From the surveillance feed, Sam checked on where he could enter undetected. Although he'd visited Maide's house a few times before, it had always been with the PM or Quentin. And of course, always through the front door. He'd never had an opportunity or a need to check on camera positions before.

Sam grabbed his rucksack and moved swiftly to the position clear of cameras. It was the highest part of the wall, at least eight feet, and it was topped with glass pieces. Sam scowled. The glass was a new addition to Maide's security. He popped the trunk of the AMG and took out a pink and green picnic blanket Ellie had bought for their countryside excursions. Thank you Ellie, he thought, grateful for her quirkiness.

Back at the wall, he dove into his rucksack and pulled out a grappling hook. He tossed it over the wall. It made a light thud. Sam listened for anyone.

Nothing.

He kept the blanket double folded and draped it around his shoulders. He gripped hold of the rope, pulled it to make sure the hook was fixed and started to scale the wall. When he was half way up the wall he tossed the blanket across the glass. The blanket gave him just enough insulation from the glass to pull himself up quickly. He snatched the grappling hook, threw it down and jumped onto the grass below. He rolled into the landing, softly and safely, as a decade worth of experience had taught him, and he skirted around the house. No lights were on. Maide could be sleeping. But somehow, Sam didn't think so.

Being in the field for so long, Sam sensed occupation immediately. The house *felt* empty.

Having been at Maide's residence on many salubrious occasions he recalled the alarm controls were behind the door. It was a seven-figure code. Sam frowned as he tried to bring back in his mind the pattern he'd seen. Only a few weeks ago, Maide had mentioned that he'd changed it. Something to do with a great date in history.

Sam shook his head. Too much interference. He'd have to go business as usual and cut the wires before the alarm sounded.

Sam took a deep breath, picked the lock, and pushed the door open. The alarm countdown sounded as soon as the door opened a millimeter. Acting fast, Sam whipped off the alarm cover and exposed the wires. Despite the elaborate surveillance, it wasn't a sophisticated system. He could have cut the alarm with his eyes shut.

With the alarm disabled, Sam ran across the white marble floor with turquoise interlocking Ayyubid star patterns. Sam scowled at Maide's quiet ostentatiousness, and headed to his study.

Instinctively, he knew that was where Maide would have done whatever he had done. Like a glowing red beacon in the darkness, the flashing 17:30 on the screen called to him.

Cold, thick sweat dripped down Sam's back.

He moved over to the desk and picked up the sat phone. The jury-rigged concoction of equipment wires suggested speed. Maide had done this with little thought that anyone would ever see it. He believed he was safe. Sam's body numbed. He disconnected the sat phone and hit play on the laptop sound program.

"Payload dispatched. Silent Waters target neutralized."

The voice struck Sam harder than any physical blow could ever possibly have done.

He closed his eyes to control his rage and walked away from the study to control the visions of his beloved as they withdrew her from the apartment. Anger would not bring him the results he needed that night. Ascending the stairs, Sam knew that Maide was long gone. The row of empty bedrooms only confirmed his sixth sense.

Returning downstairs to the study, he stared at the laptop and noticed a tiny blue square by the side of it. When he'd entered the study earlier, the flashing LED on the laptop screen had snapped up his attention and nothing else had registered. He hadn't seen it. The square looked like a sweet, but on closer inspection, Sam realized it was what he'd been searching for all along.

Sam picked it up and hesitated. He wasn't a man who protracted events, but something was holding him back. Maybe it was a prescient flicker that caused him to feel such dread.

Sam looked at his hand holding the tiny device. He was trembling. He sighed deeply with resignation, gritted his teeth down, pulled the lip of the USB out, and shoved it into the laptop with a hefty thrust. Hearing metal scrape on metal, he wondered for a second whether he'd busted it.

Expectantly, he looked at the screen and waited for something to happen.

The folder opened automatically showing a media file. Sam's throat tightened as he clicked on the movie icon.

Chapter 83

6,000 Years Earlier

Selema had been the Kudamaz citizen from whom the Protector of Ki had been created. Her innocence and selflessness had driven Aby-od to choose her above other Kudamaz who volunteered for the role. At just 2,000,680 Earth years of age, still young in Kudamaz terms, Selema was eager to go through deconstitution and give up her life-force to protect a world she knew nothing about and who knew nothing about her.

Born to the House of Giznu, Selema had dedicated her young life to upholding the protocols and practices of the High Council. She had taken on the position of overseer and had worked hard to ascend to the position of lower elder. Oblivious to the politics that were rife in the High Council, Selema addressed every argument according to the antediluvian laws. She never pursued any internal agenda to better her own prospects. Aby-od termed her 'white of heart', meaning nothing could influence her decision making.

Thinking back, Aby-od was reminded of the moment of uncertainty that had grasped him, as he realized that the High Council was about to lose one of its best. In secret, he pleaded with Selema to withdraw. At the time, he knew he'd run the risk of being sentenced to death for breaking their antediluvian laws. But he couldn't conceal his feelings. He could still feel her hands in his as he reiterated the explicit dangers of the role she was planning to adopt. Selema, however, had been steadfast in her decision. Knowing the dangers, she stubbornly wanted to continue.

On the day of deconstitution, Selema had virtually glided into the Hall of Umray. In the Kudamaz language, Umray meant 'life'. Given what was about to happen, one could be forgiven for thinking that the Kudamaz had an uncanny sense of irony.

Taking her place in the center of the hall, Selema smiled calmly and waited. She knew she was relinquishing the life she had on Kudamun forever. She was surrendering her corporeal body and the pleasures she had enjoyed from such embodiment.

Aby-od watched his protégé, her face smiling, her eyes flashing with an ethereal beauty and incredible calm, and he was immersed in pride and sorrow. He had schooled Selema from a very young age, and during those formative years, it had become obvious to him that she would ascend the ranks of the High Council. At the time, he hadn't thought her ascension would be as a planetary Protector, although now, despite his earlier dissent, he realized the role was a natural one for Selema.

Selema's lover, Dumuzi, a Kudamaz nobleman and senior elder of the council, blew her a kiss. It was an honor to be selected to be a Protector, and his pride for his loved one was visible. The tears that trickled down from his solemn dark eyes emoted a further state: his clear devastation at her decision to accept the role.

Selema stared at Dumuzi, her inner strength shining through, and she smiled. Her eyes delivered the truth that he knew. "I will always love you. We are forever connected."

Another Kudamaz High Council member known as the Operator commenced the deconstitution process. He placed a small crystal, The Vessel, on a tall, ornately decorated stand to the right of Selema. He ran his hand over the wall panel and a massive crystal materialized in the hall high above his head. Slowly, he maneuvered the crystal until it was situated directly above Selema. Once in position, the crystal began to radiate stunning white light.

Aby-od recalled how Dumuzi had stood silent and watched his love being lost to him. Dumuzi had shot a hurt look at Aby-od. Although he'd been aware, Aby-od had not responded. Absorbed in the moment, his eyes had been locked on Selema, as if no one else existed. Aby-od knew Dumuzi had been grief-stricken. But realizing he had no way to reverse the situation, he returned his attention back to his beloved Selema.

Rays had surrounded her, infusing her body with light. Pulsating around and inside her, the rays grew more intense, making it impossible to distinguish her physical form. The huge crystal projected its light, and in parallel, a stream of jarring sounds rang out from its center. The sounds were the harmonic arrangement of the planet native's physiology. Their DNA was described in musical notes. The more advanced a race became, in terms of recognizing and respecting each other, the more aligned and pleasing to the ear the harmonic arrangement would be. This mix of light and sound stated deconstitution had begun.

An observer witnessing the spectacle would have likened it to a sacrifice. The powerful energy that pulsed through Selema would eventually engulf her body. Once atomized, her life-force would then be blended with the chosen Ki native's physiology.

Aby-od cast a swift look at the other elders of the High Council. Their faces were impassive to the dramatic show in front of them. Perhaps experience had made them blasé.

Aby-od was deeply disturbed by their lack of sentiment. They had the power to change the fate of every planet in their care. The creation of a planetary Protector was second only to integrating the dark and light power blocks into a planet's development. It was a critical event, but his fellow members appeared to view deconstitution with apathy and virtual disinterest. The honor the council had in the past was now lost.

Aby-od remembered the vow he'd made in that hall. Should one day he became leader, he would force their attitudes to change.

Turning back to the deconstitution, Aby-od listened as the huge crystal bellowed out a high-pitched, ghastly sound, indicating that the harmonies depicting the native physiology had been successfully aligned inside The Vessel.

The center of the hall where Selema once stood was now a brilliant, fierce sun. The sun elongated its shape, condensed its power, and narrowed to form a thin, bright flame. The flame leapt off the floor and arced over to The Vessel. This signified to Aby-od that his beautiful protégé was now nothing more than pure energy.

Absorbing the flame, The Vessel glowed, signaling it was ready for transfer, a task that Aby-od himself was selected to oversee.

Aby-od took The Vessel and shimmered to Ki. The leader of the High Council had already selected the native that would be the Protector's holder. She was a young woman, an elegant, noble princess from Sumer, the first civilization on Ki. Pregnant but one day with her first child, she had all the qualities that the Kudamaz High Council demanded.

Aby-od shimmered into her room. The princess, still in deep sleep, was unaware of his presence. Quickly, for fear that she would wake, he placed her in stasis and took out The Vessel. It glowed vibrantly in his hand.

He held The Vessel above her stomach and watched the rays descend. On contact with the embryo inside her, the energy from The Vessel went to work. Unleashing its programme, it began to redesign the DNA code, making a new strand of amino acids that would eventually hold the Protector's life-force sequence. This process did not harm the embryo. On the contrary, the baby, once born, would become a very special, very lucky person.

Nine months later, Aby-od smiled gently as he witnessed the birth from an Observation Screen on Kudamun. From the moment of the baby's first cry, the Protector commenced their journey on Ki, or, as the inhabitants had nicknamed it, Earth.

Over the centuries, Aby-od monitored the Protector's holder, always watching over like an unseen guardian. The holder's balance of kindness, compassion, power, and strength never faltered. Innocence in its many human forms never diminished. The holder remained as 'white of heart' as the day when Selema had stepped into the center of the Hall of Umray to begin her ascension for the greater cause.

Now, the holder would return to Kudamun to go through reconstitution in that same Hall of Umray, and finally take their rightful position as the Earth's Protector.

Leaving the hall, Aby-od could not begin to consider what would happen if the Protector failed. The terrifying, incredible power hidden on Earth was secret to everyone but Aby-od. Not even the High Council was aware of it. Aby-od knew that if Earth continued its dramatic balance shift, the omnipotent force would be released, and darkness would overwhelm the universe. Not even Kudamun would be saved from the universe's fate.

Chapter 84

March 24, 2017

Sam waited for the movie to run. It took an age to load. Time slowed, and thoughts infiltrated his mind. He tried to expel them. He tried to imagine it was just another mission. And he had to handle it in his usual cold, logical way.

But Sam knew he was only fooling himself. Where Ellie was concerned, logic didn't hold.

Sam watched the timeline and realized it had moved on. The movie was playing but nothing was showing. Sam peered at the blank screen and caught a faint outline, and then suddenly the scene lit up.

Sam swallowed deeply, breathed in, and looked away, cursing.

Small, firm breasts, sloping shoulders, long, slim legs and a gently rounded belly all called to him. It screamed to him an identity.

Steadily, Sam clicked on the zoom and focused in on her body. Despite the black hood covering the woman's head, Sam knew who she was. The woman in the chair was part of him. Her light balanced his dark. Her laughter drowned his sorrows. To say she defined his life, gave it meaning, and gave him a reason to survive was too flippant a statement. It was too clichéd a response.

Without her, he simply didn't exist.

She was everything and he would do anything to protect her, to keep her safe.

He breathed heavily, balled his fists, and toughened up as the scene unfurled. For all his precious piousness, the screen told him the truth.

He had *failed* to protect her.

Ellie's head hung low as the sedative she'd been given stormed through her body. Sam watched as a man came into shot. He grabbed her arm and thrust in a needle. The savagery of the gesture was obvious. Sam hated the memories it brought back. Depending upon how vicious they were planning to make the interrogation, the injection would either be a stimulant to bring her around, or a paralyzing agent. Sam didn't need to think long on this as the man withdrew another syringe and pushed it hard into the fleshy part of Ellie's arm.

They were following standard procedures for interrogating a Class A terrorist.

But this was his *own* wife.

Chapter 85

Sam stared at the screen in cold disbelief. And then everything went dark.

He moved the mouse around frantically, trying to bring the image back. But nothing. It took Sam a few seconds to realize what had happened. The light had been cut to create fear in the captive. The captive would wake disoriented, unable to move, and in complete darkness. This was the very method he'd devised to 'soften up' hostiles and get them talking in record time. Little did he know that six years later, they would be using his own interrogation style on his wife.

The screen flickered and turned a ghostly grey green. Ellie was highlighted by the infrared camera now trained on her.

On screen, Sam watched her lift her head. The drugs had made her groggy. Sam could only imagine the fear she'd be experiencing, waking up, hooded, in her underwear in complete darkness.

Looking at her through infrared, she seemed unnatural and not quite human, like he had stumbled upon some kind of weird supernatural art-house film made by a leftfield director.

Slowly, Ellie regained full consciousness. Her movements showed severe panic. She looked down, up, and then flicked her head from side to side. They had left her in just her bra and pants. She became aware of her nakedness and tried to cover herself, but her wrists had been clamped to the chair. On attempting to move, Sam heard her whimper in pain. He shook his head, still in disbelief.

A paralyzing agent? How could they?

Sam knew each movement his wife made would feel like a lathe cutting through her. She pulled at her wrists and cried out again. Sam placed his hand on the screen as the tears welled in his eyes.

He felt every second of her pain. Having gone through the same in training, he knew exactly what agony and fear she was going through. Her head would be cloudy, and heavy, like a dark, woolen blanket had enshrouded her mind. She wouldn't be able to remember anything and that would make her panic even worse.

He watched her pull again at her wrists and then scream even louder. He breathed deeply and looked away, cursing again. God, he was going to make his people suffer for this.

Why couldn't she just be still and stay calm?

But, of course, his thoughts were insane. Calm wouldn't be on her agenda. Ellie had no training, no experience. She possessed no knowledge on how to handle the situation.

Sam knew she'd be awash with supposition, with her mixed-up mind doing its best to fill in the gaps. That moment, prior to interrogation, was the most dangerous for both the captive and the captor. Well known in the business as 'the terror point', it delivered such gut-wrenching fear no human alive should feel. It was also the moment when the captive's mind could easily crash and burn thus making the interrogation meaningless.

Ellie didn't call out or try to speak. She just flicked her hooded head from side to side, upwards and downwards. Leaving her in such an exposed state was perverse and cruel. Sam knew she'd be thinking 'what's next?' The act of stripping an alleged hostile was simple interrogation psychology. Remove the ability to shield through clothes and the alleged hostile breaks down. Sam was thankful they had left her with a modicum of modesty. Many female hostiles he had interrogated over the years had not been given such a courtesy.

Sam only just refrained from punching through the laptop screen. The disbelief he had at seeing Ellie had morphed into rage. Although he'd captured and interrogated people for ten years without a blink, the practice now seemed alien to him. What they had done to his wife had made him an outsider.

Ellie had been taken and he knew nothing of it. By this action, he was no different from any other Joe in the street going on about their business, living in a prescribed condition, limited to a drip feed of knowledge that defined a reality in which they lived. It was a reality ruled by political sound bites, constant terror threats, and harsh national security practices, and sweetened by reality TV shows, online casinos, game shows, and soap operas.

MI6 had run roughshod over his loyalty and trust. And now someone had to pay.

Chapter 86

Sam knew he had done things, terrible things, shocking things. But never on a whim and never driven by insane paranoia. Everything he'd done had always been driven by a sole purpose: to keep the country safe. He had had a passionate, righteous belief that he was always doing the right thing.

He couldn't deny that innocents hadn't been hurt. He'd probably done the same to the wives of many men. But he'd swallowed his abhorrence and carried on for the sake of national security.

As Sam stared at the screen, a realization hit him that he didn't want to face. He'd had no compunction to brutally interrogate anyone as it had never been anyone that he knew, anyone who mattered to him. He had compartmentalized his life.

When he was with Ellie, he was a different person. He was all loving and kind with an addictive crazy humor that Ellie adored. At work, he was cold and ruthless, a completely different person capable of doing anything for the greater good.

But those carefully honed boundaries had broken down, crumbling into the tears that now streamed down his face.

Someone walked into view. It was a man Sam immediately recognized and knew from experience to be a rather unpleasant individual but an extremely effective interrogator. The man wasted no time in administering the third injection, which Sam knew to be sodium pentothal. The truth drug.

Ellie screwed up her face as he thrust the needle into her soft skin.

Sam snarled, visualizing the beating he intended to give the interviewer when he caught up with him. He was one of many Sam was determined to get.

The interrogator pulled away the hood, and in parallel a light came on.

Brilliant, piercing white everywhere. Instinctively, Ellie covered her eyes from the shattering light and screamed in deep pain as the paralyzing agent burned through her arm muscles like a laser.

"We know you're activated, but not in the same way as the nano-bomb. I wouldn't be standing here if you were loaded."

The interviewer's turn of questioning explained his vicious approach. He believed he genuinely had a premier league terrorist in his hands.

The interrogator kept behind her at first.

Ellie caught her breath. Sam was amazed she'd lasted this long without speaking or collapsing. He watched her catch her breath again, her chest rising and falling as she breathed in and out in long gasps. It was obvious that her body ached as it struggled to cope with the violent pain. But despite the agony, she still did not speak. Sam wasn't sure how long she could hold out under that level of interrogation. Certainly, no more than a couple of minutes, at the most.

Clearly, the interviewer thought the same as Sam. He waited a few minutes before delivering the lead question to kick off the session.

"Sam Noor's your target, isn't he?"

Sam couldn't believe what he was hearing. Did they really think that Ellie was that kind of threat? Maide must be completely insane. The Masters case must have made him snap.

"I said, Sam Noor's your target. We know all about it. No point in denying it."

But Ellie didn't deny it. Nor did she accept it. She just sat, pulled at her clamps, made a painful face, and remained mute.

The interrogator walked around to confront Ellie. Sam growled as he watched his suggestive attitude towards Ellie.

The interrogator continued to press Ellie, but her eyes didn't focus. Sam remembered when she'd looked like that before. One Christmas, she had overdone it on the booze and woken the next morning completely out of whack. Nothing registered with her. It took several black coffees before she finally connected again.

Sam could see the interrogator was at a loss to understand. Following a heavy dose of sodium pentothal, Ellie hadn't answered a single question. The interrogator had pressed harder, with no effect. Sam realized the considerable reputation the interrogator had, and his results with Ellie meant that that reputation was now on the line.

Somehow, he had to secure the results expected.

"We saw you scream. We know that was the initiation, wasn't it?"

That scream. Sam remembered his moment of revelation. He shook his head. What was being suggested was absurd. Beyond absurd. Ellie was Ellie. His Ellie. He knew everything about her. Didn't he?

Sam took a second to question himself. Did he know everything about Ellie?

His mind focused on the scream. Its reason was the one thing he didn't know.

No. No, this wasn't right. None of this was right. He looked back at the screen. Ellie being taken, tied up, and drugged was a travesty of human justice. Nothing could make him believe what they'd done was right. He could never believe Ellie was Al Nadir.

"The Sleeping Assassin technology, we know all about it."

Sam listened. Sleeping Assassin technology, what the hell was that? He'd never heard about any such technology, unless it was above his pay grade, which he seriously doubted.

It sounded more like a ruse to extract the truth from Ellie.

Chapter 87

Although Sam knew it was absurd for Ellie to be considered as an Al Nadir plant, he couldn't explain why Ellie wasn't falling apart. Anyone else by now would be fully induced, either gibbering garbage like a village idiot or continuously screaming from sheer dementia. He'd seen both responses many times. But Ellie was doing neither.

From what Sam could see, it was as if the sodium pentothal had not even hit her system.

Sam watched as her beautiful face descended into anguish as pain cut through her mercilessly. He tried to ignore the questions that were building quickly in his mind.

"Listen, darling, Guantanamo Bay is heartbeat away, and we all know how they'll treat a pretty thing like you."

The interrogator eyed Ellie's body salaciously, dropped down, stroked her legs; his face close to her stomach, and his hands moving slowly up her thighs. Watching, Sam balled his fist, confirming in his mind that he'd show no mercy to the interviewer. With the interrogator's face just inches from hers, Ellie still did not speak. Abruptly, the interviewer pulled away, smiling smugly.

"I will continue to ask you questions all day and all night. I'll be replaced with another person just like me. But we're gonna keep you in that chair until you speak. No toilet breaks. No food. No water. No sleep. You will speak to me. Sooner or later, you'll have to. So let's avoid all this unnecessary stress. Tell me what I want to know."

Ellie ignored the interrogator completely.

"Your friend, Rikard, fessed up just before he blew in Oslo. He told us everything. Keeping silent isn't going to help you."

Sam could hear the interviewer speaking calmly but pointedly. He needed answers. Sam could detect wavers in his voice as the stress and tension increased, charging up his adrenaline. Her silence was gradually infuriating him. Soon he would take drastic action. And Sam knew only too well what kind of action that would be.

Swallowing deeply, Sam hit fast-forward, every so often stopping to hear the interviewer's words. Sam was well trained in interrogation. The 'we know what you know' drill would continue for a while longer until the subject broke.

The video clip was two hours long.

He sped it forward to just before the end. Although he hadn't played everything, Sam could see that Ellie, despite what had been asked, had stayed silent throughout. The interviewer's body language told Sam the same story.

Ellie had just pulled and pulled tirelessly at her clamps and ignored all questions. In the last few moments, Sam could see his wife utterly exhausted and in terrible pain. Sam knew that every time she tried to move, the paralyzing drugs would have made her feel like her body was being cut open. The cruel drugs had been designed to ravage the body until the body itself broke down.

Sam was enraged. But as much as he hated it, he was also intrigued.

They obviously wanted to break Ellie. But why? Was it just because of the scream?

Sam watched Ellie close her eyes. Fatigue was taking her. It was natural. Her strength had been unbelievable. He just couldn't get away from how incredibly strong her will was. It was far stronger than he ever believed possible. And it was a will the interrogator was determined to break.

"Are you with-"

The interviewer never had chance to complete his question, for Ellie interrupted by screaming, "Oh! Go fuck yourself!"

Sam had to smile, despite the travesty he witnessed on screen. This was his 'take no shit' Ellie on full blast, and God, was he in awe of her.

It was clear that the interviewer's droning, debilitating voice had pushed Ellie beyond caring and her customary impulsiveness had gone into overdrive. Caution, at that moment, was not in her vocabulary. Sam knew Ellie's somewhat ill-advised words of courage that had ejected from her shaking lips had been reckless and would only rile the interviewer to initiate another level of interrogation.

He shook his head. They couldn't possibly do that. Not to an innocent woman. Not to the wife of an agent, no less, someone who'd taken an oath to die for his country. They couldn't.

Sam stared while breathing fast as Ellie's arm was yanked to the side and another needle was driven into her skin with naked brutality.

The video suddenly stopped playing.

Sam took it back frame by frame and caught a glimpse of blood in the syringe.

He froze.

Although he couldn't see any more or find any further video, he knew the next instalment of the interrogation. He was only grateful that his wife remembered nothing of it.

Chapter 88

Sam exited from the player. In the corner of the screen, an automatic download that had been installing pushed the system into restart mode. Sam's mind, still immersed in what he'd seen, didn't register the countdown to restart.

What Maide had done was reprehensible. Sam vowed he'd make him and whoever else was involved endure far worse. It was time to face facts. He was a trained killer, trained by the government to take care of their little problems, trained by the same government who had just shat all over his loyalty and trust. Now he had to make that training mean something.

Absorbed in his thoughts of revenge, Sam failed at first to notice movement outside. Then he saw a splinter of light shoot across the floor. He peered out of the study window. Two black vans sped up the driveway.

Shit! Sam recognized the uninvited visitors as Section D Special Forces. Obviously, they were on a clean-up. He had to get out with the evidence before it disappeared completely.

Suddenly, the laptop began to reboot on its own, chiming loudly its initiation tune. Sam didn't have a choice. He had to get out. With the tune ringing throughout the house, the dark figures now streaming into the hallway turned their attentions onto the study.

Cursing under his breath, Sam inched the window up and slipped out. Ducking down, Sam kept in the shadows and ran fast across the lawn.

More dark-clothed occupants climbed out of the vans and entered the house. One of them broke away and began to initiate a perimeter inspection, heading straight for Sam.

Sam looked around for cover. A gap between the hedge and the outer wall provided it. Hunkering down into the gap, Sam held his breath. Heavy padding passed him. Sam breathed out.

He watched as the team emerged from the house, carrying the laptop, timer, and satcomm, all the evidence he so desperately needed. A man who could have been the team leader made a hand signal, indicating there was nothing else. The last man out turned around, took something out of his bag, and stuck it to the wall.

Reversing quickly, the vans made their exit. As the second van moved, Sam could see that one of the doors was still open. A dark figure in the doorway made a movement with his hands and the Andalusian palace exploded. Majestic magnificence turned to flame-filled fragments in seconds.

Sam looked on in utter disbelief. It was obvious they wanted to bury everything. He suddenly doubted he would ever see Maide again.

Chapter 89

Mrs. Adams stared at the empty chair.

Some of the class turned to look at the chair as well, causing Mrs. Adams some anxiety. It didn't feel right that her classmates were just as surprised by her absence.

"Does anyone know where Zoe is today?" asked Mrs. Adams across the classroom. She scanned faces for recognition of the girl's whereabouts, but nothing was forthcoming.

"Clara?" said Mrs. Adams, fixing on a small girl with red hair cut into a bob. "Aren't you her friend?"

The girl shook her head, and another girl started sniggering behind her.

"Something funny, Susan?" said Mrs. Adams sharply, and the girl behind answered with insolence.

"Yeah, Zoe's a slut. She made out with Clara's Mike. Now they're not talking."

"Oh shut up!" yelled Clara, flushing up pink, and she turned to hit Susan on the hand as the rest of the class descended into inane giggles and whispers.

"That's enough!" shouted Mrs. Adams, glaring at Clara and Susan. "So you haven't seen Zoe Whyte at all today?"

"Nah, the bitch hasn't been around," muttered Clara, smirking at a fellow classmate, a guy with a sporty look, tall with blond hair and a stupid grin.

"I saw her at the grocery store on Friday," said the grinning boy. "She looked hot."

"More like a whore," shouted Clara, slouching back in her seat.

"Whatever. She looked good to me," added the boy.

"Right! No more talk. Read act one, and I'll be…back," said Mrs. Adams hurriedly, and a sense of unease washed through her as she headed for the door.

Inside the principal's office, Mrs. Adams stood with her face getting redder and more irate.

"I don't have a good feeling about her absence, Mr. Watson," she said. "I know it's only the morning, but you know her father is someone important in the government. I just have a really bad vibe."

She wrung her hands, forcing down the increasingly dark instincts she sensed. She'd always been a little psychic but never wanted to acknowledge it. Now the principal regarded her as almost insane.

"Mrs. Adams, you're being neurotic. Nothing has happened to Zoe. You know she enjoys making everyone panic. Not turning up for class. Hanging out with the older boys. Doing God knows what. It's what she does, the horrible little attention seeker!" Mr. Watson sneered at the teacher and regarded her with derision at falling for Zoe's tricks again.

But this time, Mrs. Adams felt that something was different. She shook her head.

"No. No, Mr. Watson. I think we ought to call her mother. Check with her."

Then Mrs. Adams realized Zoe's brother could verify his sister's whereabouts. "We can ask Peter."

Mr. Watson's eyes took on a pensive stare and his face paled.

"What is it?" asked Mrs. Adams, holding down her coursing worry.

"Mr. Coulson just came in. Peter's not in class either," said Mr. Watson, reaching for the telephone. "I think it is time to check on the Whyte household."

Mrs. Adams listened as Mr. Watson requested the call through to the Whyte's house from his secretary. He placed the call on speaker.

The line rang, and then after thirty seconds, it dropped into voicemail.

Mr. Watson cleared his throat and stated firmly, "Mr. and Mrs. Whyte, this is Principal Watson. We are concerned that both Zoe and Peter failed to turn up to school today. Please call me as a matter of urgency."

Mr. Watson switched off the speaker and glared at Mrs. Adams. She swallowed, held his eye, and prayed she was wrong about the unsettling vibration that surged through her.

Chapter 90

"Cancel the meeting. You're not up to it."

"Like hell I will. I've worked hard on this. I need this meeting. I'm not going to screw things up just because of that bloody attack."

After a night's sleep, Ellie's strength had regained rapidly, almost unnaturally. But she hadn't wanted to dwell on that fact. Unfortunately, her stubborn streak had also returned, full blast. Sam was on the wrong side of the argument.

"For God's sake, Ellie. This is madness. What meeting is worth your health? May I remind you, darling, you were the victim of a terrorist attack yesterday? You just can't go back to work after something like that. It's not ...Well, it's not normal."

Sam heard his own voice. The words. 'It's not normal'. He was right. It wasn't normal.

Ellie's sudden recovery had mystified him. He looked at his wife as she scooted around the apartment, collecting the things she needed. Inwardly, he was concerned she was hiding her real feelings; that she still wasn't well but was too proud and too stubborn to acknowledge her injuries.

Ellie spun around to stare at Sam. Her look was utter determination. She showed an inner strength he'd never seen before. For a second, he couldn't read his wife. There was no connection between them. She was cold and distant. An unexpected shiver sailed down his spine.

"This is my life, and no *fucking* Al Nadir attack is going to take it from me," she said. "This deal is vital. Not only for money but also motivation. It's going to send a message that we're playing tough, rolling with the big boys. I need this deal."

The cold and distant look held for a moment more and then was superseded by a flicker of warmth. Sam's internal anxiety passed. He walked over to the table and grabbed the car keys, hoping that would prevent Ellie from leaving.

"You can give me the keys, drive me, or I'll get a taxi. But I am going to that meeting." Ellie's hand extended out to Sam.

He was deeply unhappy about letting her go. He wanted to cosset her and never let her face leave his eyes.

"I'll drive you," stated Sam, resolutely accepting that no amount of argument was going to influence Ellie's determination.

"Good." She walked briskly through the opened door. "Now, come on. Let's go!"

Sam watched her. She was incredible. Whatever he sensed earlier, there was no denying Ellie was a fighter. But wasn't he the one who'd started the war?

Emotions caught him as he remembered. Tears rose inside his tired eyes.

Ellie flicked her head back when she sensed Sam wasn't walking with her.

"Come on, Sam," she shouted testily. "We've really got to hurry. The traffic will be murder."

Sam considered for a brief moment that the timid, dependent Ellie of last night had been a welcome change. Then he reprimanded himself for allowing such a thought. The woman who strode purposely in front of him was the real Ellie.

The Ellie he loved.

Sam dropped Ellie off at PalmerPharm headquarters in Canada Waters. With the briefest of kisses, Ellie instructed Sam to collect her at three o'clock.

"Any change and I'll call you," she said.

Sam noticed the cold and distant look had returned. He assumed it was just Ellie psyching herself up to play powerful businesswoman.

Straightening her jacket collar, Ellie questioned sternly, "How do I look?"

"Perfect. Go get 'em, tiger!"

Sam forced a smile. He didn't like Ellie being cold. It wasn't her nature.

Ellie turned around and proceeded into the tall granite and glass building. Sam did not leave immediately. He watched an assistant greet Ellie and take her into the inner sanctum of the building.

Sam, relieved that Ellie was safe for the moment, turned his attention to even more pressing business.

Chapter 91

Officer Nichols fancied a taco.

Yes, it was against his strict diet, and, of course, he wouldn't hear the last of it from Susan, his partner. But he'd had enough of green salad, quinoa and pulses. That was rabbit food, for God's sake. A man needs meat to survive, thought Nichols, as he pulled into Taco Express. He caught a glimpse of his never-decreasing stomach and sighed. Sue would never find out. A quick meal, and then he could resume his health food regime fortified by the real sustenance he was about to eat.

He parked and got out. It was only outside, walking to the restaurant, that he noticed the nose of a car parked around the back. He'd recently sat through a talk at the precinct that claimed half the drug deals took place behind restaurants and bars.

It could be Bill's car, the restaurant owner. Maybe his Chevy gave up the ghost and he finally shelled out for a new vehicle, reasoned Nichols. But somehow, his senses had already heightened. He stepped inside the restaurant and headed towards the counter.

Seeing the owner at the back, he called out, "Hey, Bill, you got a new car?"

A big guy with a surly face turned around, frowning, "No way. The rust bucket's in the garage."

"So who's parked around the back?"

Bill shrugged. "Dunno. Grace gave me a lift in. Haven't been out back yet. Didn't come in yesterday. I had some chores Grace needed getting done."

"Bill, can I go through? There's something I want to check out."

The owner made an open gesture with his arm and Nichols proceeded through the kitchen. At the back door, he opened it cautiously. The new Toyota SUV he'd spied was parked a little at the side by the ventilators. There didn't seem to be anyone in the car. He moved forward to take a closer look. And noticed blood on the headrest.

His hand dropped instinctively to his gun. He raised it and carried on gingerly, sweeping the area as he walked.

Nichols arrived at the car and looked inside it.

A man in his fifties with grey hair lay on the passenger seat. A bullet wound to his temple. The cream, leather upholstery was soaked in the man's blood.

Nichols stood for a second, aghast at the scene. The man's mouth was pulled down as if to scream in pain. In the moment of his death, the expression had fixed on his face. His grey eyes were open. Nichols stared into them and his throat constricted. In the man's eyes, a shadow of deep sadness and shock still registered. It was as if something had been unexpectedly taken from him beyond his own life.

Nichols shuddered and looked away. He needed time to process the scene.

Something terrible had happened to the man. He could almost feel the pain emanating from the car. What did his Sue say? "Vibrational energies can be detected from things." Nichols had never believed in that shit before. But the sensation of immense loss was tangible. He didn't know who the guy was, but tears were starting to well up inside him. In a bid to balance his emotional state, Nichols stepped away from the car, holstered his gun, and radioed in the body.

"Control, 10-23," said Nichols, forcing himself to stay focused.

"Location?" asked Control.

"At the back of Taco Express on 8th off Main. A man, GSW to the head, in a car. 10-52."

"Officer, 10-101?"

"That's a 10-106. Request assistance. 10-79."

"10-4. Assistance on its way. What's the license plate?"

"Young, Henry, Paul, nine, four, one, seven."

"Copy that. 10-4."

After Nichols had given the license plate, the line went dead, and he wondered if his radio was still working. Then a weird clicking sound he'd never heard before ran over the line before the line descended to silence.

"Control? Control, do you copy?" said Nichols, with a growing panic.

"10-4. Officer, remain where you are. 10-60."

Nichols heard that there was a squad in the vicinity, and they were on their way. The line started to click again, and another voice, not Control, took over.

"Officer Nichols, what can you see in the car?" asked the mysterious, deeper voice.

"Who is this? Where is Control?" asked Nichols, concerned by the intrusion on a secure channel by a person he didn't know.

"Not your concern, Officer Nichols. Answer the question. What can you see in the car? Is there anything beside the body?"

Something about the ultra-commanding tone snapped Nichols to attention.

"I'll look."

"Do not touch the car. Just tell me what you can see."

Nichols turned back and peered into the car. The man's body was large enough to take up the front seats. He was dressed in a suit. Good quality, understated, and probably designer, but not one of the flashier brands. The seat wells were empty. The middle compartment was open with keys and a sweet wrapper from a Hershey bar. Nichols strained his neck to look over into the back seat from the driver's window, as the back windows were darkened. He couldn't see anything. He walked around to the front and looked directly through the windscreen, and then through the passenger window. From all angles, he validated, from what he could see, that there was no person or object in the back seat.

Nichols was just about to turn away from the passenger window when a white card, almost hidden underneath the Hershey wrapper, caught his eye. He stared at the card and realized it was an ID. In the top right-hand corner, he could just about make out the symbol of the Department of Defense.

As he stared, his radio erupted.

"Officer Nichols, are you there. What can you see?"

"There's nothing in the car, just the body, some keys, candy wrappers and an ID card that I think shows the guy works for the DoD."

The line started to click again.

Nichols, frustrated by the lack of communication, called into the radio, "What is happening?"

"Clear the car park. ETA in two minutes. Bird arriving," spoke another voice. It was different to the one before. Nichols could hear coldness in every syllable.

"Bird?" said Nichols, confused. He knew, having served in the US Army in his early years, that bird was military slang for helicopter.

"Clear the cars, Nichols," replied the hard voice.

Then the line went dead.

Jeez, what the hell is going on?

Nichols stepped toward the diner to advise the customers to move their cars. He looked at the four customers chomping away on their food, engrossed in their own worlds.

"Excuse me, ladies and gentlemen," yelled Nichols, displaying a confidence his badge gave him but one he didn't really feel.

Heads whipped up on Nichols' announcement.

"We have a situation. May I ask for you to park your cars behind each other in a line directly in front of the diner?"

"Right now?" said a woman, looking flustered.

"Right now!" repeated Nichols, and he eyed each of the customers to indicate that he meant business.

The customers stood up, muttering about it 'being a darn nuisance'.

Bill came out from behind the kitchen counter.

"What's going on?" he said to Nichols.

"Can't say. I was just told that the car park needs to be clear within two minutes."

Behind him, engines fired up. Nichols watched the customers meet his request as cars moved into a caterpillar formation in front of the restaurant. The customers returned back to inside to finish their rudely interrupted meals.

Then, suddenly, the air was filled with thundering noise.

Nichols bent down to look out of the window. A helicopter descended into the center of the car park. At the same time, a flurry of black Dodge SUVs screeched to a stop surrounding the chopper.

The woman who was annoyed at Nichols' demand stood at the entrance of the diner and turned, bewildered, as the helicopter landed.

"Come inside please, madam," called Nichols, as he made for the door.

Out of the helicopter, ducking to avoid the rotor wash, alighted a massive, dark-skinned man, flanked by four others who'd exited from the SUVs. Nichols could see they were government. Their suits. Their posture. He knew this wasn't any ordinary homicide.

Swallowing to steady his nerves, he approached with an outstretched hand.

"Officer Nichols?"

The man ignored Nichols' hand and flashed a badge quickly at him. Nichols could only just make out the words CIA and Greene, before the badge was replaced inside his jacket.

"We're taking over. Show me the body and then leave."

Nichols was stunned by the aggressive attitude of the man known as Greene. But he knew not to respond negatively.

The guy had power and he had a pension.

And the last thing Nichols wanted to do was mix those things up.

Chapter 92

Sam drove to River House. Intuition told him Maide wouldn't be there. But maybe he could pick up some breadcrumbs to lead him to the truth.

When questioned on Maide's whereabouts, the acting head of MI6, Nathan Cartwright, advised firmly that Maide was 'unavailable'. Cartwright did not proffer any further explanation but implied the information Sam searched for was on a 'need to know basis', and right now, Sam did not need to know. Sam ground his teeth and gripped the doorframe in Cartwright's office. He knew he was being stonewalled. Cartwright's expression was unbreakable. Sam realized he wasn't going to get through. Silence was all he could expect.

Knowing when to stop, he didn't press Maide's replacement any further. After last night's explosion, Maide's removal was expected. Had Maide been working alone? Or had Quentin Ludlow been involved? Sam thought back to Quentin and Maide's tight relationship. Oh, yes. He'd know. Sam was going to make him talk, whatever the cost.

But did anyone else know of his involvement? Quentin couldn't go the same way as Maide. A foreign secretary suddenly vanishing would cause too many questions. He could be forced to resign, but that would undoubtedly fuel media frenzy and, of course, more questions. No, Sam thought, he would have covered all his bases. He's a survivalist, the smug little shit!

At the foreign office, Quentin's Parliamentary Private Secretary (PPS) was courteous but closed. Sam was aware that his questions were being skillfully avoided.

"You know, you can tell me where Quentin is. I've got security clearance. Is he with PM at the house? Where? Come on. This isn't a game. I need to know."

Sam's tone showed growing annoyance, but the PPS was blind to his aggravation.

Feeling that nothing short of full-scale, no-holds-barred, Sam-style interrogation would make the PPS talk, Sam turned to leave. Only then did he notice the meeting agenda on the desk of the PPS.

The agenda displayed the date: March 24. With surreptitious swiftness, Sam read the information upside down. It was a technique he had been trained in. Sam issued his thanks to the unsuspecting PPS and left.

Dangerously overtaking at every opportunity, Sam maneuvered Ellie's Porsche through West London to the meeting's location. His top-level security clearance gained him 'no questions' access, and he parked in the underground garage away from the CCD cameras. Remembering the times on the agenda, Sam knew the meeting would soon be closing and Quentin would appear. From memory, he recalled that, for these clandestine briefings, Quentin always drove himself in his own Jaguar.

Sam could see the Jag parked a little farther away. He slipped out, sat on the tarmac on the passenger side of the Porsche, facing away from the Jag, and waited. He was good at waiting. In his business, gathering intelligence was a waiting game.

Chapter 93

Quentin was a creature of habit. After the meetings, he didn't hang around chatting with the others. He preferred to get away quickly.

Yes, Sam just had to wait.

Fifteen minutes passed. Sam got lucky. Quentin emerged from the lift and hurried towards his Jag. Alone

Sam skirted around the outside, out of Quentin's field of view. Softly, swiftly, silently, he moved up behind Quentin. Trained in stealth combat, Sam was upon him before Quentin had time to process what was happening.

Suddenly, Quentin felt the crook of Sam's arm tightly on his windpipe. Gasping and struggling, he clawed at Sam's tightening arm.

"I want answers. Not dead ends."

Quentin heard Sam's voice, laden with anger and revenge. He thought back to Maide's words of fear and realized that Maide may have been far saner than he'd ever believed.

"I don't know," Quentin spluttered, issuing an ineffectual and pathetic kick at Sam's shin.

But for a split second, overcome by personal anger, Sam lost his grip. Seizing the opportunity, Quentin pushed his elbow back into Sam's ribcage. But he wasn't a trained fighter. He was way off target. Growling, Sam grabbed Quentin viciously and slammed his face against the side of the Jag.

"I want fucking answers. Why did they take my wife?"

Sam's hot breath on Quentin's skin made him feel queasy. He was now a thorough believer of everything Maide had said the night before. Sam was most definitely a threat to be neutralized.

"Why?" hissed Sam, like an adder before the strike.

"I…d-don't…" stammered Quentin, trying to shake his head.

Sam wrenched Quentin around to face him. Raising his fist, he drove it hard into the terrified foreign secretary's face.

Quentin fell backwards towards the floor, pleading for Sam's mercy. But Sam, driven by images of Ellie's broken face and her haunted, soulless eyes, was relentless and unforgiving. Pulling Quentin up by the scruff for the second time, he smashed him against the car's bonnet.

"You fucking liar. What do I have to do to make you talk?"

Under the full force of the impact, Quentin heard his teeth crack. Pain shot through him. His mouth filled with blood.

"Talk, you bastard!"

Quentin's silence fueled Sam's anger. Enraged, Sam threw a punch that sent Quentin hurtling across the bonnet of his Jag. Hitting the ground, Quentin lost consciousness.

Chapter 94

This was the make or break meeting.

Ellie knew it, but she didn't want her business target in front of her to know it too. She smiled and took a sip of her wine but kept Gerald Clearwater, CEO of PalmerPharm, firmly in her sights. Her eye caught his as he glanced up from flicking through the presentation folder. The meeting was the final stage. The hard negotiations had already been fought and won with the legions of directors working for Clearwater. However, Ellie and PalmerPharm's directors understood that if she failed to impress Clearwater during that meeting, the deal was off.

Ellie moved a little forward and pushed a reaction of surprise, and then looked down with more than a little demure sensitivity. As her eye descended, she caught Clearwater's chauvinistic smirk. It seemed he enjoyed making Ellie uncomfortable. Ellie straightened her posture, pushed back her shoulders and took in Clearwater, who'd slipped back into the pages of the presentation again. Typical CEO. Five grand suit. Good tan despite coming out of winter. Manicured fingernails. Overbearing and ego-driven. Weighing up whether I'd sleep with him to close the deal.

Some chance.

"What do you think?" said Ellie, her tone ringing with an element of, perhaps, too much confidence. It may have been presumptuous, but Ellie knew she had one of the hottest products on the market. Block chain capability married with unprecedented cybersecurity using the latest artificial intelligence algorithms had her Cloud Nine's virtual warehousing application pitched alongside the best tech warehousing companies in the world. And her upside, she didn't carry the heavy overheads they had, nor did she have investors crowing for their monthly reports and quarterly returns. In the tough tech world, she had the unbelievable: independence.

Clearwater's silence, Ellie reasoned, was just an intimidating trait to undermine her. She dug into the green curry, played out the lack of words between them with grace, and drank more of the Châteauneuf-du-Pape.

Finally, after what seemed like hours of uneasy quiet, Clearwater shut the presentation folder and placed it on the table beside his fork. He glanced back at Ellie with the merest smile of amusement on his face. Ellie concluded that he definitely had a *thing* for wanting to generate awkwardness.

"Ellie, I'm satisfied with the proposal. I think we can work together."

Clearwater's brown eyes stared straight into Ellie's. She could still see a flicker of amusement. He placed his hand out in front of her. She shrugged, making him see she was expecting it, and slipped her hand into his, held it tight and shook it hard.

"Thank you, Gerald. I won't let you down."

"You'd better not, otherwise…"

"Yes?"

Clearwater flashed his eyes darkly. "Ellie, let's not go there."

Ellie held down a smile, and changed the subject.

"Are you off anywhere for Easter?"

Suddenly, Clearwater changed from being a dominant, big shot CEO to a guy who couldn't shut up about his travels. I've hit on sweet spot for him, thought Ellie.

"I'm a bit of a budding Indiana Jones on the quiet. Extremely fascinated by ancient temples, sites, and relics. Don't you find them fascinating?"

"Oh, yes. Incredibly. All those things they brought out of the pyramids. What's not to be amazed by? Yes, tell me more. You said you'd visited a Sumerian temple. That must be old. Where was it?"

Ellie feigned interest but she was extremely bored by Clearwater's loquacious ramblings about early civilizations, and she wanted his more uncomfortable stance back. At least she was having a little fun playing his game.

When the talk got to a six-thousand-year-old ziggurat in Ur in the Middle East (Ellie didn't hear the actual location as she'd zoned out), she issued a polite excuse and headed to the restroom.

Inside, she hit speed dial and waited for Sam to answer. Unexpectedly, she got his voice mail.

"Hi, darling. You won't believe it. I've got the deal! Just having lunch with Clearwater now. God, the old bugger's boring. Yapping on about bloody ancient temples. If this deal wasn't in millions, I'd have walked. Anyway, I need a pickup around 3 p.m. from Sanuk. It's a Thai restaurant around the corner from PalmerPharm. Love you. Bye."

Ellie returned to the restaurant and clocked Clearwater. She took a deep breath, smiled and strode forward.

For my business, she thought. But as Clearwater launched into another convoluted tale of his adventures, Ellie seriously wondered whether she'd last until 3 p.m.

Chapter 95

Morgan Greene, deputy director of the CIA strode over to the Toyota SUV parked behind the Taco Express diner. He recognized Dr. Ross Whyte immediately from the sizable security file he knew only too well. Before starting on Project David, the secret quantum weapons program, Whyte and his family had been thoroughly checked out. Despite a lifetime in defense, the president had to be sure he had selected the right man to head up the program. Whyte's face had been stuck on Greene's desk for a quite a while as his team made sure the president got his wishes.

Greene took one look at Whyte and then hit a contact on his phone.

"Check on Project David," said Greene to the recipient of the call. "I've just found Dr. Whyte dead at the back of Taco Express on 8th off Main."

"The safe is on a time lock. Only POTUS can override it. I'll inform him immediately," said the deadpan voice at the other end, and the caller rang off, leaving Greene to face Whyte again.

"Time of death, Franks?" asked Greene, pushing a calm he feared wouldn't last as his forensics team crouched down and leant inside the car.

Franks, a slender woman in her late forties, in blue forensic overalls and with platinum blonde hair swept sensibly but so tightly into a bun it pulled at her face, looked back over her shoulder at Greene.

"From the lividity, cold, stiff rigor and dried out optics, I'd say over twenty-four hours. No decomp, so I doubt it's more than two days. I'll know better when I get poking around." Franks was from England and her clipped Home Counties accent hit the deputy director.

Greene scowled. "Nothing more concrete than that?"

"Well, unless you want me to slice him up and start examining his organs here and now, that's the best I can offer," snapped Franks.

"Cause of death? Definitely GSW?" said Greene with fierce authority, not caring to entertain Franks' Brit-baked sarcasm.

"Absolutely. Bullet's lodged in. From the casing, it's a 9mm. And this is definitely the scene of the crime. He was killed here. Blood spatter on the head rest confirms the shooter would have come from the driver's side. The angle of the shot indicates the victim may have had his head down, looking at something. I'm sure there was someone else in the passenger seat with him when he was shot."

Franks stared at Whyte's body and shivered.

"Cold?" snapped Greene, eyeing Franks. He had no time for emotional crap.

"No. Of course not. It's just…" Franks shook her head. To Greene, it looked like she really didn't know what she was trying to say.

"Out with it, Franks. Something on your mind?"

"It's his eyes. He looks like he's seen something horrific."

Greene smirked. "Franks, what the hell is wrong with you? That's just the shock of death. Victims carry it. You've seen it before, haven't you?"

"Yes, I have. But…his look is different. It's absolute shock. A dark, terrible pain. Can't you feel it, sir?" Franks stared over her shoulder at Greene, her smoky, sienna-brown eyes softly grabbing at his.

"All I can feel is my dinner coming up if I listen to any more of your emotional bull."

Franks looked down, embarrassed that she'd said something so stupid in front of her superior. Greene clocked her flush up. Maybe the pretty missy had something, he thought.

"You got a theory, Franks?"

"Did the victim have a family?" she said.

"Yeah, he did."

"Are they safe?" asked Franks, as she patted down Whyte for a phone.

Greene didn't answer but issued his usual deep harrumph.

Franks felt a bump against Whyte's jacket and stuck her hand inside. The phone was dark. She pressed the home button and got the lock screen. Franks stared at the victim's thumb, and then she leant over, and placed the phone underneath his thumb. The screen recognized the imprint and came on. The battery was low but still had some juice.

"Sir, I've got the victim's phone."

Greene reached in to snatch it. He clicked on the telephone icon and scrolled through the call log. Whyte had received no calls for the last two days.

Surely his wife would have called him?

"Strange. The guy hasn't had any calls," said Greene, and flicked into Skype, WhatsApp and Facebook Messenger. But there was no activity at all.

Franks pulled herself out of the car and stood up in front of Greene.

"No calls anywhere?" she said, looking surprised. "The guy's been gone over twenty-four hours, and no one missed him?"

Greene stared at the Whyte's body and wondered. After the Al Nadir mole, Sam Noor's knifing stunt and DG Downer's reprimand that kicked his promotion back years, could his life possibly get any worse?

Then his phone buzzed, and suddenly he knew it could get worse. Much, much worse.

Chapter 96

Petrol. It assaulted his senses. Quentin opened his eyes. Recollection stirred. He was tied to a table leg. His ankles were also bound together. He was naked, save for his boxers. And he stank of petrol.

Fear rose in him. The stench was overpowering. It could only mean someone was going to turn him into Guy Fawkes. Sam approached, flicking on his lighter. Quentin's stomach made an involuntary flip back like an insane chimpanzee, and Quentin wretched on the ground.

"Hello, Quentin. Nice of you to join me."

Sam's wicked sarcasm forced Quentin's head up. Always preened and perfectly dressed, Quentin now looked like a wreck, a shaking, pathetic ball of despair. A glob of sick dripping down from his thin mouth only emphasized the mess Sam had made of the foreign secretary in a matter of minutes.

"My dear boy, what kind of fashion is this? I'd fire your tailor if I were you," said Sam, choosing the words with relish.

At the mention of fire, Quentin's eyes expanded. "Sam, you've got to see. You can't get away with this."

"What? You mean the way you got away with attacking my wife?"

"We didn't attack her. We're not criminals."

Sam grunted his reply. "You're not? Okay. Let's analyze objectively what makes a criminal. How about falsifying a terrorist account by creating a bogus Al Nadir intercept and orchestrating a vicious, almost fatal, attack on a defenseless woman? Wouldn't you say that makes a criminal?"

"No. No, we had to follow protocol. National security, Sam. Remember!"

"Don't give me all the 'Queen and Country' crap. Your actions speak louder."

"You've got to understand we had no choice."

"Of course, you had a choice."

"I had to. There was no other way. You've got to see that," pleaded Quentin desperately.

Ignoring the pathetic pleas, Sam went up close to Quentin, who was visibly shaking. He took out his fire lighter, pushed the button, and struck up the flame.

"This is how I see it." Sam moved the flame away. "You can live." He moved the flame inwards towards Quentin. "Or you can die."

"What do you want?" screamed Quentin, petrified.

"What I've always wanted. Answers."

Sam flicked on and off the fire lighter in an erratic, crazy way. His expression told Quentin that he had nothing to lose.

Quentin, however, had everything. "I really don't know."

"Arh arh!" Sam made the noise of a buzzer on a game show. "Wrong answer." The lighter snapped on. Sam moved the flame very close to Quentin's right leg.

Quentin's eyes followed the flame, his body shaking. Sam wouldn't do it. Sam really wouldn't do it. But as the flames neared his naked skin, Quentin knew Sam would. Panic gripped him. Fear knotted hard in his stomach. Sam was really going to kill him. Maide had been right. He'd been right all along. Coldness from the concrete he sat on seeped through his body and mingled with the ice in his heart.

Sam's hand lingered even closer to his skin.

"I'm sure this isn't the way you wanted to die," said Sam. "But we can't have everything. You've had a good life. Say goodbye to it."

Sam moved the flame quickly towards Quentin.

"I'll tell you!" screamed Quentin, visualizing himself as a human torch.

A flick and the flame was gone. Sam crouched in front of Quentin. "From the beginning."

"Know this, Sam, we did what we had to do."

"What you had to do?"

"When we saw the surveillance, we had no choice. We had to act."

"What did you see?"

Quentin shook his head, remembering the image of Ellie's frozen scream.

"She spoke to someone. That someone was giving her orders."

Sam stared at Quentin, examining him. "Someone? That's impossible! How do you know?"

Quentin realized Sam wouldn't understand. He just told him straight.

"Sam, she spoke to an empty kitchen. She said 'I'm listening. What do you want?' and finally, 'What is too far gone?' And then Ellie went totally berserk, screaming like a mad woman. We couldn't find out why."

"The surveillance captured her saying this?"

"Yes."

Sam shook his head. "From the surveillance, did you find out who she spoke to? What made her scream?"

"Nothing. We found nothing."

"You're lying," Sam moved back in with the fire lighter on full flame.

Quentin's eyes widened. "Believe me. We tried everything. But she never spoke."

"Everything?" Sam asked darkly.

Quentin looked away, ashamed. How could he tell Sam what they'd done to his wife?

"Everything?" repeated Sam, closing in on Quentin, the lighter appearing back in his hand.

He was damned. Damned if he spoke and damned if he didn't. Whatever way he looked at it, Quentin knew that today was the day he was going to die. At least if he spoke, he might be able to cleanse himself. And just maybe, his soul might be redeemed.

Sam stood up, shivering with anger and confusion. Ellie's scream. The sound that had awoken him, unveiled his secret and almost destroyed their life together. She'd never explained it. The spider story was just that. A story. He hadn't dwelled on it. He hadn't wanted to dwell on it. Then he'd left for Langley and everything went to hell.

What Sam had seen on Maide's laptop was only the beginning.

Uncharted territory lay before him.

Chapter 97

Six billion Earth years ago saw the genesis of Earth, a great event that was carefully overseen by the elders of Kudamun. In keeping with the antediluvian laws of the universe, the elders had deposited the dark and light crystal power blocks. Using their dimensional lapse field technology, they placed the powerful but fragile blocks half a degree out of Earth's reality. Such positioning provided protection from the blocks being smashed to dust by the noxious and volatile world evolving around them.

After positioning the power blocks at two central points on Earth, the elders had waited for the programme embedded in the blocks to follow its ancient instructions.

Aby-od mused for a moment, contemplating the actions of his elders. For as long as he could remember, the Kudamaz elders had been responsible for delivering the dark and light powers, the seeds of good and evil, to every new planet in their care. He had watched species after species engage in the debate: What *is* the true origin of good and evil? Is it nature or nurture?

If only they knew that the core of their debate hinged upon two small, unassuming crystals woven into their planet at a time when good and evil didn't exist.

Over time, the positive and negative energies trapped inside the crystals diffused out, breaking through the dimensional lapse field just as they had been programmed to do. Free to roam, the energies rooted themselves into the quantum fabric and grew. Darting through a new world, each of the energies left a trail: a sense of good or evil. These complex energy trails, or lanes of dark and light, infiltrated the base elements of life. Elemental formations making up the very building blocks to life itself connected with the energy lanes. On contact with the energies, these elemental formations vibrated. The frequency of vibration reflected the degree of positive and negative connected energy prevalent in that elemental formation. Through this behavior, each elemental formation would have a mix of light and dark energies.

As these elemental formations coalesced to form strings, particles, atoms, and finally the molecules making up every living thing, the light and dark frequencies aligned to balance all life on the planet.

On Earth, the effect of the power blocks was no different. The embedded energies fanned out from the two power crystals to encapsulate the entire world. All plants, minerals, and animals were attuned to the effect of the vibrations. Everything on Earth was connected. Humans, through their consciousness, were hardwired to connect directly with the dark and light energies. Human thought, the conduit for sending and receiving energies, fueled the positive and negative energies through emotions, feelings, and eventually actions, thus formulating reality in relation to the universe around them.

This shielded symbiotic relationship of man and crystal grew. Thousands of years of civilizations rose and fell. Periods of great darkness followed periods of great revelation and enlightenment, and still humans had no real understanding of how one small kindness or one moment of bitterness could change the path of the world.

Aby-od paused again to consider the effectiveness of their actions. Did the dark and light crystals serve the purpose for which they were originally designed? To deliver a balance of light and dark throughout a planet's life. Or did they only assist in creating a constant imbalance? With planets' inhabitants continuously veering towards the dark side, tempted by the fortunes that the evil afforded.

Why was there even a need for good *and* evil? Aby-od, despite his knowledge of how the universe works, had, at times in his long life, pondered deeply on this question. But unlike so many of the ignorant inhabitants who also asked the question, he knew the answer only too well.

Irrespective of where they originate from, the components that form the internal make-up of any species, such as drive, ambition, imagination, motivation, courage, and initiative, all require a percentage of the dark crystal's energy to work. If a species was imbued with one hundred percent light energy, they couldn't possibly function. They would not have any drive to do anything and would soon cease to want to live.

Conversely, if a species was one hundred percent imbued with dark energy, they would be too evil to engage in anything. Paranoia and psychosis would absorb them, and they would fall into a cycle of power, greed, and corruption. Their path would lead to eventual self-destruction.

The Kudamaz elders realized that for there to be light, there had to be dark. Each of the energies sought to define and validate the existence of the other. Life on the universal plane could not survive if these energies existed in isolation.

Of course, the Kudamaz had heard of 'other places' where only good or only evil prevailed. But these places were completely out of Kudamaz jurisdiction. Under the antediluvian laws, they were strictly forbidden. Only the Ancient Ones had the authority and the right to access, and no one in Kudamun would ever question their judgment. For, by that very action, they would question the word of God. It was a path Aby-od knew never to go down.

The Kudamaz's main responsibility after a planet had been created was to nurture life, encourage intelligence and civilization, and most of all *maintain* the equilibrium between the light and dark energies. A deviation of two percent on either side was permissible. Anything greater and the Kudamaz were required to intervene and deploy measures to redress the deviation, known as balance shift. From perceived natural disasters to the emergence of ideas and innovations that helped redefine a planet's future, all were strategies created by the Kudamaz to redress a balance shift and bring equilibrium to a planet.

In exceptional circumstances, when their methods failed to bring the balance shift back to equilibrium, the High Council sanctioned the awakening of a planet's Protector.

Such cases were, however, very infrequent. To warrant the involvement of a planet's Protector, a balance shift of over five percent would need to have happened, indicating that the planet was entering the Zone of Great Risk and therefore no further Kudamaz measures would have any effect on the shift.

Awakening a Protector was the very last action the Kudamaz elders could take before agreeing to dispatch a planet to oblivion. Earth was now experiencing a balance shift of seven percent towards the dark energy.

Aby-od moved to the Observation Room. On the translucent, shimmering wall, lights pulsed with different colors. Aby-od touched the lights rapidly in a convoluted sequence. Behind him, Earth appeared. The manifestation was transparent. Aby-od could see the geography of the world: the rich green of the continents and the brilliant blues of the oceans.

Aby-od's hand rested on the violet light in the wall. Immediately, the apparition of Earth showed a mass of dark and light energy lanes layered and stretching over the continents across the world. The two pulsating crystals were visible in the center of the planet. A floating line, the 'equilibrium', materialized and mapped across in front of the Earth. Aby-od could see the dark crystal dipped below the equilibrium line.

Numbers flashed up in front of the equilibrium, showing the actual level of balance shift to the dark as each second passed on Earth. Aby-od watched the balance shift increase. He knew that each number reflected another act of evil, cruelty, corruption, greed, and suffering.

Looking at the numbers leaping exponentially, Aby-od became incredibly doubtful as to whether the Protector, for all the astounding powers given at the time of reconstitution, could realign the balance shift and halt the intransigent evil energy that was gradually enveloping the Earth.

Chapter 98

"Sodium pentothal wasn't working. We tried NMS," admitted Quentin finally, cowering against the table leg.

The words hit Sam like bullets, ripping into him. Sam felt his heart split open and bleed. It was as he'd feared, although he prayed he'd been wrong. The moment he saw blood in the syringe, he knew.

Kicking Quentin's thigh hard, Sam hissed, "You bastard. You fucking tortured her. You knew she was my wife and you still did it."

"We didn't mean to. We were just caught up in the moment. We needed answers. Maide needed them. But it didn't work. Sam, she didn't use the back door. She didn't return to reality."

Sam absorbed what Quentin was telling him. If she didn't return to reality, NMS should have killed her. At least, that was what he understood of the process. But maybe the process affected some people differently. NMS was still in its early stages despite being one hundred percent adopted by the security services. The truth was they still didn't know what side effects NMS could generate.

For a second, Sam remembered Ellie's cold, distant aura that morning. His failure to connect with his wife, if only for a moment, had hurt him. Maybe she had been damaged by the NMS.

Sam took in a breath, calculating carefully his next words.

"If she didn't use the back door…" started Sam, confused.

"Why isn't she dead?" finished Quentin. "We thought she was."

That did it. Sam couldn't hold back. He tried to control his rage but no signals of sense got through. Flicking on the fire lighter, he moved in fast.

"But Sam, you…You know she's not dead! We didn't…God, Sam. No. You can't!"

Quentin's stuttering pleas were cut short as Sam brought the naked flame up against Quentin's right calf. The tip of the flame contacted with his bare skin and Quentin screamed.

"For God's sake. No!"

The flames licked hungrily at his leg. Instantly, the heat made his skin redden then brown.

Sam remained immobile. Quentin's screams of pain didn't penetrate the wall of revenge he'd built up. In stoic duty to his love, Sam fixed the flame on Quentin's fat calf.

White terror flew through Quentin. The agony caused by the tiny flame was unbelievable. His skin blistered and bubbled like pork fat. Quentin screamed. His bladder emptied.

"Now you know the terror she went through!" shouted Sam sadistically, finally breaking free of the anger he'd kept pent up for the past twenty-four hours.

Ellie's greatest fear had been fire. Sam knew that, by enduring NMS, she would have imagined herself being burned alive. What she must have gone through. He shuddered, and then he narrowed his dark eyes at Quentin.

"Burn, you bastard. Burn. Feel her pain!"

"Sam, please. For God's sake. Please. Stop," whimpered Quentin, shaking. Sam could see he was slipping, despite frantically trying to remain conscious.

He flicked off the lighter. The skin around the impact point bubbled contentedly like melting toffee in a pot.

Quentin howled, "Please, help me. You can't leave me in pain like this!"

"And what do you think Ellie was in when she went through NMS? You evil bastard. Her greatest fear was fire. You and that fucking paranoid partner of yours put her through a living hell. How could you do that? How could you even contemplate it? I should kill you now and put an end to all this."

Sam kicked Quentin hard in the stomach, winding him. Pain on top of pain. Sam was out to make Quentin suffer.

Quentin wheezed in and breathed out.

Still, Sam ignored Quentin's agony. His mind was only on Ellie and her broken body on the stretcher.

Quentin recognized it was no less than he deserved. His stomach, taken over again by the crazed chimpanzee, flipped over and over and his bile rose. The pain ceased to register as trauma set in. His vision blurred. He couldn't focus on Sam. His body shivered. He knew his temperature had taken a nosedive.

"Please Sam! You know they'll catch you. You'll never be free if you do it."

"Yeah! And how many people know where you are?"

Quentin understood the implication. And he didn't like it.

"And how many people know where I am?"

In shock, staring at his burning leg, Quentin didn't answer. Instead, he moaned in pain.

"So, you see," said Sam. "I can pretty much do anything I fucking like with you. And no one will know."

Breathing hard, sweating, with eyes trained on his blistering, browned skin, Quentin attempted to explain the reasons for Ellie's extraction.

Chapter 99

The man who Greene had spoken to was Grayson Filip, the president's newly appointed Chief Scientific Officer (CSO). The previous CSO had walked off the reservation citing stress and a need for a change. The president had dissuaded from his science tech team making efforts to find him, and Filip had been appointed just hours after his predecessor's resignation letter had been discovered.

Filip was a California man through and through and wasn't au fait with the political machinations of DC. His brother, a top energy lobbyist pushed his name forward. The opportunity came at the right time. His tenure at CalTech was coming to an end, and new pastures beckoned. His marriage with Sarah had also come to an abrupt close, thanks to her need to be pally with his best friend. Filip shook his head, thinking back and realizing sadly that his life had become a cliché.

He was on the run from failure, hitting a mid-life crisis, in a new town without much of a clue as to the political maelstrom he was about to fall into.

Filip picked up the phone. The president's closest aide and chief of staff, Nate Van De Maart, answered swiftly.

"Dr. Whyte's been killed. Project David may have been compromised. POTUS needs to come back to Blacksburg and disable the time lock on the safe."

Filip waited for Nate to respond. He listened to the chief of staff inhale sharply.

"Right! I'll get Marine One on standby. POTUS is in a conference with his security team and the British PM with his security counterparts. The UN Peace Summit is the only item on the agenda. Secretary Cowl is in there with him. But this development, he needs to know."

"Look, let's think on the positive side. Everything may be ok," said Filip, determined to keep cheery.

Nate retorted with a dark undertone, "Whyte is dead. Project David is under threat. Show me the positive side in all that. I'll call you with an ETA when we're airborne. Get everyone ready." Nate rang off with abrupt efficiency.

Filip replaced the receiver and looked out from in his office through the clear windows that showed the quantum lab area and the president's private safe beyond.

At that moment, Filip wished he had the x-ray eyes Superman possessed to see what was or wasn't in the safe. But, like everyone else, he just had to wait it out until the president arrived.

If the quantum bomb wasn't there, Filip knew everyone would feel the full brunt of Treeborne's fury.

He only hoped he'd still be standing afterwards.

Chapter 100

"She was taken because we needed to know what she knew. What she said. Her words implied she was wired up, talking to someone, and her mad screaming. We couldn't understand it. What we don't understand scares us. You know that Sam. Always look for anomalies. Her behavior was an anomaly. Maide couldn't be sure she wasn't a threat. He needed to know for certain she wasn't a hostile."

"Quentin, she's my wife. What threat could she possibly be?"

Fueled by pain and his no-win situation, Quentin shouted, "You fucking fool! What did you expect? You're responsible for national security. You know things no one else in the country knows. We had to make sure, even after ten years of marriage, that your wife wasn't a plant by Al Nadir or any other organization wanting to bring us down. I don't think I need remind you of the Masters incident. I was only following orders, just like you've been all of your life. It wasn't personal."

"It fucking was," sneered Sam, clearly repulsed by the information he was hearing.

"You, above all, should know that what we did was for national security and the protection of Queen and Country," gasped Quentin, shaking as the pain ravaged his central nervous system.

His self-righteous reasoning enraged Sam. Turning events on their head and giving national security as the reason, Quentin had unexpectedly gained the moral high ground.

"Protection from who? My wife! Jesus Christ, Quentin. Surely you must see that you went too far."

"I was only following orders. For God, Queen and Country above all others. Remember your oath, Sam. It means our safety is in your hands. On no account could that ever be compromised."

Sam hated the revalidation of what he'd felt back in the apartment earlier, when he'd hacked into the personnel files.

"Please, Sam. I've told you what you wanted to know. My leg is killing me. Could you get me to a hospital or a doctor? I really don't think I'm going to last much longer."

"Shut up, you wet fuck. It's only a flesh wound. God, you wouldn't last a second in the field."

"I never said I could. You're a better man than me. Please, Sam."

"Oh, for God's sake!"

Sam grabbed a wet cloth he'd had on standby. Quentin's skin had blistered in small pustules and was bleeding. But the area of the burn was small compared to the huge agony it had generated.

Contrary to his belief, Quentin wasn't soaked in petrol. Only the floor had been doused. But Quentin had believed he was going to be turned into the Olympic flame. Mind games. Sam had a special gift for them.

Slapping on an antiseptic pad, Sam looked up at Quentin's sweating face. It showed release.

His moment of torture had passed. Sam, however, felt that his hadn't even started.

Chapter 101

Something dreadful was about to start.

Greene wasn't big on premonition. But then, he didn't need to be. Finding the head of a secret government weapons program shot dead was never going to be a good omen.

When his phone buzzed, he answered it. As he listened, he realized Franks had been right.

"Neither one has been seen in school? What about the mom? Has she answered any of your calls?"

Greene waited for Simon Broughton, Divisional Head of the FBI, to confirm any sightings with his on-the-ground team.

"No. Nothing. No sign of Peter or Zoe. Last sighting of the kids was with their mother at the grocery store on Friday afternoon. Patsy doesn't work," said Broughton.

"What about their house? Has anybody been there?" asked Greene, exasperated. Did he really have to do everyone's goddamn job?

"Yeah, of course! I've got a team at the Whyte's house now," said Broughton, taking umbrage at Greene's blatant dig. "You got your tablet close by?"

"Right here," answered Greene, clicking on the app to launch the body cam viewer in live stream mode. He selected Broughton's team from the list, and put Broughton on loud speaker. "Okay. I've got the feed coming in now."

Greene watched the first agent walk up to Whyte's impressive colonial-styled house on Prince Fork Road in the exclusive Virginia Tech area. Immediately, Greene noticed the front door. It was plain molded wood, unpainted, and it definitely didn't match the more ornate exterior of the house. The agent noticed breakaway wood pieces in the door jambs. Someone had tried to cover up the fact the front door had been busted open. So hard, it seemed, that the door surround had deep, splintered grooves.

"The door's not the original," said the agent on screen to his partner's camera. The agent rang the doorbell and waited. "No answer. Proceeding inside with force."

The agent kicked in the door, entered the hallway, and panned with his gun, looking all around to give those viewing a clear impression.

Greene could see that the floor had been cleaned.

"Check for wood or glass on the floor," muttered Greene, staring at his tablet.

"Copy that," said the agent, and he bent down, searching.

"Nah, nothing…" started the agent, getting out his torch and shining it on the floor. Something glinted in the space in the corner before the first step of the stairs. "Hold on." The agent crouched down. With a gloved hand, he picked up a fragment of glass and held it up against the camera.

"Glass found, sir."

Greene nodded. "Check all rooms and then send forensics in and strip the place. I want to know where that family is!"

"Copy that, sir," said the agent.

Greene watched as the agent then entered the large lounge dining area. On screen, nothing looked unusual or out of place. The agent walked into the brightly lit kitchen. Everything was gleaming and spotless.

Greene didn't like it. No one keeps their place looking that good.

"Check the trash," requested Greene on a hunch.

Experience showed him that clues to people's whereabouts were often hidden within the remains of a trash bin. The agent took off the top of the swing bin to get better access to what was inside. He leant over and Greene could see MacDonald's boxes and fries bags.

"Check the boxes," commanded Greene to the agent in Ross' kitchen. The agent dove his gloved hands into the trash bin and pulled out one of the Big Mac boxes. He opened it. Inside, as Greene had expected, a completely uneaten burger with an uneaten portion of chips.

"Bag and tag that trash as evidence."

"Copy that. But evidence of what, sir?" asked the agent, slow to catch on.

"No one started their meals. The family could have just arrived from getting take out and been snatched. See any receipt in there with the boxes?"

The agent poked around in the rubbish, and then shook his head.

"We need to get these back to the lab to go through it properly. Difficult to do here, sir."

The agent took a photo of the trash with the boxes in situ, and then grabbed the bag out of the bin and tagged it as evidence. Another agent stepped up and removed the evidence, allowing the agent time to continue inspecting the house.

"Heading upstairs, sir."

Greene stared as the agent swept with his gun and arrived at the top of the stairs onto the wide landing. He turned to the left and entered the first bedroom. Pink and black décor showed on screen. The ceiling was black with sparkling stars and the duvet cover on the black shiny metal-framed bed looked like it had been ripped and torn from the inside. Greene could see it was just an effect of the crazy print design of the cover, and not something that had been done intentionally. Within the slashings embedded into the material were shining diamantes and glass rubies that pooled like blood. Greene shook his head. Kids' tastes today. He'd never understand.

The agent stepped over to the large, built-in wardrobe. One of the sliding, mirror doors was ajar. Inside were the clothes of a bang-on-trend teenager.

"Looking for tech, devices and phones," said the agent, moving in front of a desk situated by the window.

Greene noticed the desk was immaculate, not left in the untidy mess he would have expected from a young girl's room.

The agent pulled open a drawer at the side of the desk.

"Found the laptop."

The agent took some snaps of the laptop in the drawer and then flicked open an evidence bag and shoved the laptop inside it. He sealed it and placed it into the waiting hands of an evidence team member behind him.

Other drawers were pulled out and Greene could see books and files. All college stuff. But no phone.

The agent turned and yanked out the bedside drawer. Within it quietly sat Zoe's iPhone. The agent snapped a photo and then removed it. He pressed on the home button, but the phone was dead. He pressed it on, but the red battery indicator showed on screen.

"No charge in it, sir."

"Get it back to the lab. Run tests," said Greene sharply, annoyed that the phone couldn't give him any immediate clues.

A teenager's phone being switched off did not bode well.

Greene continued to observe the agent's inspection of each room, knowing that the result would be the same as Zoe's.

Switched off tech everywhere.

Rooms in pristine order.

The agent bagged and tagged all devices as he found them. Greene watched as the agent searched the rest of the house, the attic and the basement. But he found nothing more to note.

Everything was immaculate.

Everything appeared right.

Except it wasn't.

Greene recognized a cover-up. Whatever had happened to Ross' family, evidence of the event had been removed with meticulous precision.

A show home created to mask the truth.

It was either done by the kidnappers or by Ross himself. Greene tended to veer towards the latter.

He imagined how it may have gone down.

Ross arrived home, saw the door smashed in and scenes of a struggle within the house. In the kitchen on the table, unopened Big Macs boxes and fries packets waiting to be dished out. Perhaps Ross had found crockery or glass on the floor or a phone on the worktop. Maybe even signs of blood.

But why didn't he call the police?

Greene realized they'd made their play before he had an opportunity to call.

"The place is spotless. I could do with Whyte's cleaner," said Broughton, demonstrating his typical insensitivity that had gotten him into trouble before.

"Yeah. Too spotless. Someone's done the place over on purpose," responded Greene.

"Kidnappers?"

"No. Ross. They must have called him before he had a chance to log the crime with the police."

"Didn't Ross' phone show no calls since he'd left the facility?" said Broughton

"Yeah. I know," smirked Greene, thinking fast. "But the call logs are only one way to check the calls."

"Ah. The chip," said Broughton, getting Greene's line of thought.

"Exactly. The chip," echoed Greene.

He was suddenly hopeful that his tech guys would locate the family before their time ran out.

Chapter 102

What had exposure to NMS done to her?

It was a question that Sam demanded an answer to. Having used NMS on terrorists only gave Sam a more confused backstory. He would have been better off knowing nothing. But, as it stood, Sam couldn't get away from the fact that NMS was a killer drug. He'd seen it kill. Many times.

Stupid, pig-headed, and, although he hated to admit it, brave captives had gone to their deaths to keep their secrets safe. He had looked into their eyes and seen naked fear. It was a fear so great, so overpowering, and generated by God-knows-what horror, it had consumed them totally and forced their hearts to beat faster than humanly possible. He had witnessed mortality chase them on every scream, and he knew it would eventually catch them by way of a sudden cardiac arrest precipitated by arrhythmia. Of course, revealing their secrets immediately catapulted them from their nightmare state back to reality.

That was what confused Sam. There were only two choices with NMS: divulge or death. He'd never heard of any other option.

"I want you to tell me what really happened with Ellie. None of this bullshit about her dying. Tell me the truth."

Quentin, still shaking, stared at Sam.

"Sam, it's not bullshit. She suffered a sudden cardiac arrest."

"No. No, you're..." Sam couldn't finish his sentence.

"Sam, I know you find it hard to understand. But I'm telling you the truth. I know she died because I was there."

His head spun. He felt the ground slip from under him. With massive stamina, he steadied himself and turned back to Quentin.

"You're lying. I left her just now. She's not a corpse."

"I saw her die, Sam."

Quentin looked at Sam for a reaction, but Sam was motionless, just listening, evaluating.

"Impossible!" spat Sam. But his voice now was shaking.

"Davison tried to revive her. But she was gone."

Sam glared back at Quentin, his eyes burning coals. Quentin cowered back, anticipating a strike, but Sam just stayed where he was, glaring with evil intent.

"But she's alive. You know that," rushed Quentin in defense.

Sam's eyes narrowed. "I don't understand."

"Sam, surely you have felt there is something about her."

Sam listened, remembering her cold, isolated manner. But he shook his head, disagreeing with Quentin.

"I couldn't put my finger on it," Quentin continued. "Neither could Maide. That was why he ordered her extraction. But she is different. Think about it, Sam. Why she didn't reveal anything during NMS? She didn't even give her own name. Her tolerance was incredible. Every indication showed she'd been conditioned and was hiding something from us."

Sam thought back to what he'd seen on the laptop. The incredible resilience his wife had shown against the paralyzing agent and truth drugs had made him proud but also extremely uncomfortable.

Quentin now acknowledged what he had suppressed.

"What're you saying? She's a spy?"

Sam couldn't bring himself to believe that, not after all the time they'd spent together.

"I don't know what she is," replied Quentin. "But something is wrong with her."

Chapter 103

Inside the lab at DARPA's Blacksburg facility, Greene sat beside a tall, young tech guy who looked a little like a praying mantis. Stretched body, small head, spindly arms. Altogether weird, thought Greene. Plus the guy's name, Dabs, didn't counter Greene's impression of strangeness about the man. Still, as long as he could hack the chip and reveal what happened to Ross' family, Greene didn't care if he ran around in a bright pink sarong and called himself Daphne.

Dabs took out the SIM chip from the iPhone and plugged it into a piece of tech. As smart nerds tend to do, Dabs began working at speed and explain what he was doing.

"So I've plugged the chip into the in-circuit emulator's pod. The ICE is going to go into the circuitry and I'm interrogating the chip. In a minute, we'll be able to see if there have been any silent calls on the memory of the chip."

"You can pull off times and dates, can't you?" asked Greene, staring with cold intent at Dabs.

The tech guy grinned in Greene's rippling face of intimidation. "Of course. That's easy."

Greene raised an eyebrow at his bold attitude, and grumbled, "So tell me then."

Dabs scanned down the data packet he'd pulled from the chip.

"Definitely a silent call made Saturday, March 22, 10.10.15. See that line," said Dabs, pointing to the screen. "A silent call means it came in on a different protocol comms setting. Otherwise it would have shown up in the call log. The call came in on some other network. Most likely, the caller was Al Nadir. I've seen this data ID before."

Greene knew it would be those bastards again.

"Ross left here on Friday around 1900," said Greene, "and it's a short drive to his house. Can you triangulate the signal to where it may have come from?"

"Of course. That's what I do," said Dabs, sounding too smug for his young years.

Greene harrumphed at Dab's cocksureness. But he needed him to succeed. "Well get on with it then!"

Dabs swung back from the tech bench to his bank of monitors. He typed swiftly and brought up the list of repeaters in the vicinity of 8th Street off Main near to Taco Express. Greene watched as Dabs entered in the time and date as to when the call was received and waited on activity logs to hit the screen. He got three pings from three repeaters at the exact time frame of 10:10:15.

"Running analysis on the signature ID of the silent call."

Dabs waited for a few seconds.

Greene drummed his fingers with impatience

"Easy, pops. It'll come in minute."

Greene sneered. The arrogant little…

"It was a data call. Maybe a vidcall. I'm tracing back signals with the same signature ID in the immediate vicinity. Ok. This call was pinging around the repeaters like a hornet in a jar. But a pattern's emerging."

"Can you find them?" said Greene roughly, pulling Dabs back to face him.

"Yes. I think so. I'm running a Cartesian algo on the signals. It analyses signal strength and determines distance from the source. I can only give you an approximate area."

"Better than nothing," snarled Greene. "Let's have it."

"Ok. From the analysis, I'd say the family is around this area."

Dabs took a felt tipped pen and drew a circle encompassing a wide radius of at least four blocks.

"Industrial Park Road," said Greene. "Check on cameras in that area. Then run analysis on Al Nadir, Al Douri, or anyone even loosely connected owning anything in that area."

"Running it," said Dabs, flicking into the CIA's AI system.

"Yep. One of the biochem labs 'Molecular Moldings', majority shareholding five years ago with Marisal Li Dou, a French cosmetics heiress on the paperwork. But, in fact, she's not. It's Salim Al Douri."

"Jeez. How on earth did the company not know who they were dealing with? Even I can see it's a shitty anagram." Greene was astonished by companies who cared more about equity going into their coffers than where the actual equity was coming from.

"Maybe because you're looking for it," suggested Dabs.

"Yeah, well, that's it," said Greene, gearing up with his team to raid the premises of Molecular Moldings. "I just hope to God we're not too late."

Chapter 104

Sam shook his head and tried to establish a foothold back to what he knew about Ellie. This was his wife they were talking about. He wasn't having it.

"No. No, you're wrong. Ellie's just really strong and very stubborn. There's nothing strange or different about her. And she doesn't take any shit, which is all I'm getting from you."

"If you think I'm giving you crap, that's fine. But I know I saw her die."

Sam flinched but didn't speak.

"And then, a few hours later," Quentin continued. "I saw her alive. If that's normal in your book, then your intelligence really is on a different level to mine."

"I don't understand," said Sam. "What's more, I don't want to understand. Ellie's normal. That's it."

Quentin shook his head. "Whatever you say, Sam. Believe what you want to believe. It's clearly not for me to tell you how to think."

"No. It isn't. But I'll tell you what I think. You didn't like Ellie knowing about me. So you took her and interrogated her, but something went wrong, and you were left with a problem. What I don't understand is, why the ME9? NMS would have given her amnesia. It would have hidden your tracks."

As Sam spoke, he remembered her body on the stretcher. He remembered the bruises and the sadness in her eyes. The man before him was the reason she'd ended up in that state. He reached out and grabbed Quentin by the throat.

"So why the fuck was the ME9 sanctioned?"

Quentin tried to swallow, but the pressure of Sam's grip made him choke. "Sam, I don't know what you mean. What's an ME9?"

"Don't give me that. It's a false flag attack. You know it. I can see it in your eyes. You remember what happened. Why did you do it? Why did your thugs attack her after all she'd been through? What kind of fucking sadist does that?"

Sam's hand was tightening. His eyes were burning bloodshot with tight black dots trained on Quentin.

"I'm sorry. It was all Maide's idea. After her 'life after death' stunt, he couldn't depend on her getting amnesia. He wanted her emotional memory to be totally overwritten. It was necessary to create a cloud of confusion. The false flag attack was designed to deliver a memory more overpowering than the interrogation. We never, at any time, planned to kill her. You've got to understand that."

But Sam didn't understand anything. Everything he understood, everything he knew, it all meant nothing. With frosty disdain, he glared at Quentin.

"You really think you rule, don't you? I run around doing your dirty work while you sit back like kings."

"Sam, you know it's not like that."

"It seems, in this grand world of intelligence…" Sam turned and slapped Quentin's face hard as he pronounced each word. "I." Slap. "Know." Slap. "Nothing!" Slap.

Blood slithered down the side of Quentin's mouth. He gritted his teeth. "Enough!" he spluttered. "Don't touch me again!"

"Your days of telling people what to do are over. The PM's going to hear of your sordid little home goal."

"And what are you going to say about this assault on me?"

Sam stared coldly.

"Unfortunately, Sam, you can't implicate me without implicating yourself. I have national security as my defense. What's yours?"

"Shut up!"

A sick, twisted smile etched across Quentin's face. After all the games, the torture, it was Quentin, who still could stand victorious. "So, all this has been pointless. You can't expose me. You'll only expose your own act of vengeance."

"This wasn't pointless. I did it to teach you a lesson, to let you know what it's like to really suffer like Ellie suffered." Sam pushed his face up against Quentin. "And to let you know. If you mess with me, or if you ever, ever touch Ellie again, it won't be just the floor that's soaked in petrol."

Sam's psychotic glare was enough for Quentin to know that he wasn't bluffing.

"Now, I've had enough of your pathetic face." Sam took out his knife and cut free the plastic binds tying Quentin's hands and feet.

"You know in your heart we were acting in the country's best interests. I'm pleased you now understand," mumbled Quentin, still maintaining his moral stance.

On hearing Quentin's pious reasoning, which implied even he was in some way complicit in their despicable actions, a rage surged up, burning through Sam. Slowly, as Quentin raised himself shakily from the floor, Sam smashed his hardened fist into his stomach. Quentin fell back to the ground, wheezing.

Struggling back to his feet, Quentin looked startled at Sam, his eyes asking why. Sam answered swiftly by punching Quentin brutally in the face. Quentin dropped to the floor, unconscious.

Standing over his body, Sam replied icily, "I never said I understood."

"Are you OK?" questioned Ellie, noticing as she got in the car that her husband was distracted.

"I'm fine. I just had to…grill an old colleague," replied Sam, smiling furtively into the wing mirror as he pulled away from the curb.

Chapter 105

President Jonathan Treeborne sat at the top of the table in the Situation Room. Surrounding him was his human war chest: Director General of the CIA Ted Downer, Foreign Secretary Dick Cowl, Defense Secretary Frank Weitz, and Dave Reiner, Chairman to the Joint Chiefs. In front of the president, bisecting the table width-ways, was a silvery curved screen that connected to the ceiling. A guy behind Reiner on one of the periphery seats pointed a remote-control device and the screen sparkled silvery white.

Within the time it took for the accompanied group to settle into the chairs and get into a comfortable position, the silvery element disintegrated. It then showed an incredible, 'virtually real' holographic presence, through the HoloLink system, of British Prime Minister Ashton, Defense Secretary Charles Godley and MI6 and MI5 Chiefs, Nathan Cartwright and Dudley Gibbs respectively. Treeborne noticed Cabinet Secretary Martyn Redfern just on the edge of the shot seated next to Godley.

"Ok, folks. We haven't got time for much chitchat. It's all about the summit. Is everything nailed down, Prime Minister?"

Treeborne was aware that this was a formal meeting and he couldn't spin into his usual banter, dropping protocol and generally pissing off the British PM. But that didn't stop him from adopting an intimidating stance with those holographically present.

Ashton pushed his back straighter in his chair. Treeborne watched the PM play down the nerve he'd just touched.

"Of course, Mr. President. The security assessment report from my intelligence chiefs is sound and confirms no threats or any intimation to attack the summit."

"What about that new cell? Is it gonna cause us any concern?" said

Treeborne, staring hard at Gibbs and Cartwright, who both appeared alarmed but tried to quell their anxiety. They both looked back to the prime minister. Treeborne caught the flicking of their eyes and noted their discomfort about the 'new cell' being talked about so quickly and openly.

"Well, Mr. President," started Ashton with some hesitation. "The exact location is still under analysis. However, we have a fix on their area and have instituted our nano-mote visual and auditory surveillance and AI systems, as well as obviously monitoring chatter. Nothing significant by GCHQ has been raised. Full security and armed protection will be provided throughout the summit. There will be more fire power surrounding the QEII than anywhere else in the UK. It will be a totally encased bubble. Nothing will get in."

Ashton daggered at Treeborne and the president read the response. *This is my playground and I make the rules.*

Treeborne raised an eyebrow to Ashton's confident stance.

"Mighty pleased to hear that, Prime Minister. Ted, you got anything to add?"

Ted moved forward. "Can you share with us that intelligence report?" he said. "Just to put any doubts to bed."

"Why do you have doubts?" spat Cartwright piping up.

"Well, Cartwright, there's a lot riding on that summit. No matter how slim the risk, we've got to see that all risks have been contained or eliminated completely. There's no room for error on this one. We can't afford any more screw ups."

"What do you mean?" interrupted Ashton with force.

His mouth turned down and his expression had turned glacial.

Treeborne waved away the comment his security chief had made.

"No, no. Don't worry. I think DG Downer here is still a bit sore about Dr. Noor's little episode. But we're all good here. Aren't we, Ted?"

Treeborne tilted his head downward and looked pointedly at Ted. The security chief nodded with reluctance.

"And I can hear you guys are all good there too", said Treeborne. "But, Prime Minister, it would be helpful to see that report in the interests of bi-lateral intelligence sharing, of course. I know you all want the summit to go without incident, and as we've still got those three Al Nadir top lieutenants here, if you need any more intel, perhaps we can help. I mean, that's what friends are for, aren't they?" Treeborne smiled at Ashton, and tipped his hands out, palms facing upwards to show benevolence and solidarity.

Ashton issued a customary smirk and swung a look to his entourage. Treeborne recognized it as Ashton's 'back me up guys' glance to gain their support.

"I'll get the report over to you, Mr. President," said Ashton, after he received two solitary nods from his security chiefs.

"Great. And we'll continue to wring out Al Nadir's guys here and deliver to you any actionable intelligence as we extract it that could affect the summit."

"Oh, and how is Resolution 8091, Mr. President?" enquired Ashton.

Treeborne shuffled. He wasn't too happy about talking about 8091 just yet, even in front of top security cleared officials.

"Yeah. Yeah, coming along nicely. Just bubbling and almost to the boil. Secretary Cowl is going to showcase it at the summit, aren't you Dick?"

A big-boned, sly-faced guy to the right of the president nodded and murmured, "Sure thing, Mr. President."

Treeborne returned to face Ashton, looking smug. "It's the main tabled item for ratification."

Ashton's eyebrow rose. "Erm, don't you mean for discussion and then ratification if approved?"

"Of course. Yeah. That's what I mean," mumbled the president. But his face didn't convey his conviction. He was all out to steamroller Resolution 8091 through the UN, and he didn't give a damn about reservations and discussions.

Treeborne was about to finish the live HoloLink when a call on the Situation Room's phone burst through his words of closure.

"Mr. President, apologises for the interruption, but you'll appreciate the graveness of the situation. Project David may have been compromised."

Treeborne listened to Nate's trembling voice coming out of the speaker.

"Fuck!" responded the president.

Then he got angrier as he realized the Brits were still in live HoloLink mode and could hear everything.

"Gentlemen, I have a matter that requires my immediate attendance."

The president indicated for the HoloLink to be shut off and then glowered at each of his staff in the room.

"Heading for another goddamn clusterfuck, aren't we, folks!"

No one in the room said a word.

Treeborne stood up and pushed his chair back. His fury was building with every ticking second. By the time he was standing, he was yelling.

"Get me on Marine One. Now! I gotta get me to fuckin' Blacksburg and sort this fuckin' mess out!"

Chapter 106

Treeborne hurled his bulk out of Marine One having moaned and fumed throughout the short journey down from DC. He walked with such considerable speed, given his wide girth, that his security detail could barely keep up.

Grayson Filip waited with nervous anticipation in a huddle with other DARPA senior officials at the end of the path from the helipad.

Treeborne strode forward like his legs were jet propelled. In front of Filip, he lasered him mercilessly, and growled, "What the fuck's happened?"

Filip gulped and Treeborne observed his new CSO's Adam's apple bob up and down as he struggled to keep calm.

"Mr. President, sir," Filip fawned, "we cannot be completely sure as to what has happened. As you know, sir, the safe is on a time lock only you can override."

"Yeah, I know. That's why I'm here. Idiot!"

Treeborne pushed past the mortified CSO and carried on into the facility. Filip found his legs and scampered along, trying to keep at the president's side like some kind of faithful but dopey Labrador.

The entourage of officials and the security detail in a tight diamond formation around the president kept him shielded. Even at such a secure facility as the one they were entering, Treeborne knew Al Nadir could (and had) infiltrated virtually anywhere with complete impunity. None of them could afford to lower their guard.

Inside the facility, the security breathed a little easier.

Treeborne noticed. "Not dead yet, fellas." Then he added ominously, "But someone may be if that safe doesn't have my bomb in it."

Eyes behind the president flickered with anxiety, but Treeborne didn't turn around to see the impact of his casual delivery.

Filip maneuvered himself in front of the party and stood beside the high-security safe.

"So, this is it. Right. Let's see," said Treeborne, as he arrived at the safe.

"Mr. President, sir, it is your retina scan and hand print that needs to be used to override the time lock," said Filip, trying to sound authoritative.

"You're gonna get a medal for stating the fuckin' obvious, kid!" snarled Treeborne, glaring at Filip, who visibly paled under the president's attack.

Treeborne shoved his palm on the reader and stuck in his face towards the retina scan plate. The two scans processed simultaneously, and a whirring sound came from within the safe. A soft hiss as the hydraulics pulled away and a loud click indicated to all assembled that the time-lock had been disabled and the safe was now open.

Treeborne swung the door out and dove in. He brought out a small box, square, metal, with a depth of several centimeters. He placed it on the side counter. Filip moved in, pushing various lab equipment aside to make room for the box, and stepped hurriedly back to allow the president full access to the lab bench.

"Ok. Moment of truth, folks." growled the president.

Everyone appeared to move closer.

Treeborne opened the box and stared.

A grey lump and a gold pen.

Treeborne picked up the gold pen and brought it over the grey lump.

Nothing happened.

No light shining like a second sun.

No twinkling, incandescence of a million trapped stars.

Treeborne's hand begun to shake as he snatched the grey lump of plasticine. He pulled at it, remembering the compound's auto-shaping properties. The lump of plasticine stretched. Treeborne released the pressure, waiting for the material to ping back into shape.

It didn't.

The grey lump remained elongated. Gravity took hold and it bent.

Treeborne turned around to his entourage of scientists, officials and security officers. His face was a red mass of anger. In his hands, the pen and the plasticine, now drooping down, touched the back of Treeborne's fingers. He suddenly started tearing at the plasticine with manic rage. Bits of the grey lump flew in all directions, hitting the surrounded group on the face, and for Filip, unfortunately, in his eye.

"Where… the… fuck is my bomb?"

Treeborne's scream bellowed out of him and slammed into the entourage like a hurricane.

No one made a single movement.

Time headed off on vacation.

Treeborne's tirade captured their very existence in a form of verbal stasis.

"Mr. President…" DG Ted Downer eventually broke the spell.

Treeborne, breathing hard, stared with vehemence at his CIA Chief.

"I think, sir, it may be with Al Nadir."

The group issued a collective swallow and looked at the bravery or stupidity of Downer. Within the shocked moment, Filip took the opportunity to sneak his hand up to pull the plasticine piece from his eye lash. Others brushed the plasticine pieces from their jackets and white coats.

The president breathed harder, his nostrils flared out, and his mouth slipped into a scowl of utter hatred. A single thought pelted around inside him. *Al Nadir has my bomb.* The speed of the thought increased velocity inside Treeborne's mind. It screamed at him. Louder and louder.

Until he could feel something within him burst.

And he heard a voice.

"Impending doom will take over the Earth. This will be your time to take your stand against this relentless evil. You will stand defiant against their darkness. And you will win. You will rise to reign over all."

He looked at those around him. Their faces demonstrated their weakness and their cowardice.

But he was the chosen one.

He would be strong. He would be dominant.

Treeborne understood what needed to be done. He would follow his god to the end.

And at not one step would he falter.

Chapter 107

Greene didn't believe they'd be in time. Al Nadir was all about total annihilation. No witnesses. No survivors.

His Dodge SUV turned in through slightly rusted metal gates and drew up by a large grey slab of concrete with a few small oblong windows. Two double doors were encased in a wire cage with a keypad for entry.

Greene got out of the car. He peered around. The place looked deserted. Behind him, wheels span fast as another SUV arrived. His SWAT team.

Greene touched his earpiece. "Alpha, hold until I give you the word."

"Copy that."

Glancing over his shoulder, he saw his agents step out of the car, their Glocks up against their chests as they joined Greene.

He racked his gun and held it close then moved around to the front of the building. The car park was empty. Greene looked at the security camera above the entrance. He noticed that the red light wasn't on. He checked the other cameras. None of them were on either.

The whole place was like a ghost town.

Something wasn't right.

"See anyone?" asked Greene to his team.

"Negative. No activity."

"Standby, Alpha, and go!" said Greene, as he headed towards the building.

"Copy that. Alpha are a go."

Greene ran to the front of the grey slab, his gun pointing outward. With a swinging glance, in his periphery, he saw Alpha Team streaming out of the SUV and running towards the back of the building for a north side breach.

He scanned across the flat roofs for signs of shooters, glints of sights, or sudden movements. Anything that revealed the hostile's position. Intel said

Molecular Moldings was operational.

So where were all their employees?

The sign above the door caught Greene's attention.

Something was off about it. But he couldn't place what.

His agents bunched around the entrance while Alpha took the back.

"Alpha, do you see a sign over the back door? Black lettering on a white mount?"

"Yes. There it is," confirmed the voice in his ear.

Greene moved closer to the sign and noticed the M looked a little lopsided, like it hadn't been aligned properly.

"Breaching the door now."

Greene suddenly knew what Al Nadir had done.

"Don't touch the door!" screamed Greene to everyone.

Then an enormous explosion deafened him.

"Alpha team, do you copy? Alpha?"

Greene sped around to the back of the building with his agents. He shut his eyes momentarily to center himself before his sight descended upon the charred and burnt remains of two of his five-man Alpha team.

"Get a medic team. Stat!" yelled Greene, glaring with hatred at the remnants of the sign.

He recognized their tactics. It was the same bombing technique they'd used with the Piccadilly tube bombing four years ago. Nano-explosives integrated into the adhesive that stuck the posters to carriage walls in the underground trains. The Molecular Molding signs were just stuck on. That was why Greene felt something was odd. They didn't look professional. And that's why the M was lopsided. They'd rigged pressure sensors or range sensors to the doors. Coming close to them triggered the detonation in the nano-explosive underneath the sign.

Greene shook with anger. He knew the sign at the front was also rigged to blow.

"Don't touch the door. The sign above is rigged to blow. Get the explosives team now."

One of his team confirmed the instructions. Greene knew they'd have to undertake a controlled explosion as there were no wires, just sophisticated nano-tech and advanced chemical compounds.

He proceeded through into the blasted back entrance. He swung a look at his agents. In their eyes was fear but determination. They'd just seen their colleagues blasted into pieces.

Greene vowed no more would die.

With that thought, he pushed ahead of his team, taking command and making sure he was the first to encounter whatever was in the building.

He panned his gun as he entered each room. Walking through the labs and clean rooms, Greene stared, taking in the equipment. There must have been some fancy sci-tech wizardry going on here, thought Greene.

But now the place was dark and silent.

The strange oblong, slim windows only allowed in minimal light, and most of the journey through the building was bathed in shadows, making progress edgy and staccato.

Greene arrived at a room different to the rest.

It must have been someone's office when the place had been in business. Now it had been decked out to look like a tacky lounge. Greene made his way into the room, flanked by two agents just a step behind him, and gasped. Other agents inhaled sharply.

A woman in her mid-thirties with blonde hair and a full, curvy body lay on the floor in her own blood. A gunshot wound to her temple. Alongside of her, a girl in her mid-teens, beautiful with a lithe figure, joined the woman with an identical gunshot to her temple. Blood had congealed down her face and her long, blonde hair, now splayed on the floor, was streaked with crimson. The top she wore had been ripped down the front. Greene couldn't see any panties on the girl.

He shook his head as bile rose with him.

Resting on the girl's leg, where he'd fallen, was a young boy of eight or nine. The gunshot had tunneled straight through his head. The bullet had blasted out the other side, leaving a large hole of mangled skull, blood and brain matter.

Greene looked away, disgusted.

Only Al Nadir could be this depraved during a kidnapping.

Killing was never enough for them.

They always had to go that extra mile to destroy completely, body and soul.

Without checking IDs, Greene knew it was Whyte's family.

"They were dead the moment they were taken," said Greene to his agents, searching the bodies. "Whyte was just being played."

"Sir, the explosions team are detonating the front sign," Greene heard in his ear.

"Copy that. Secure the area."

A dull boom resonated through the building.

"Controlled explosion contained."

Behind him, footsteps came quickly. Greene's forensic team ran in, taking photos and samples, doing their clever crime scene stuff. But Greene recognized the perpetrators of these heinous crimes had already flown days ago.

Greene heard a gulp behind him and turned.

Franks, his British pathologist had arrived and took in the scene. Her eyes fell with sorrow onto Zoe. Her lips thinned into a hardened line.

"Someone had better get those bastards soon!"

Greene remembered the two Al Nadir senior lieutenants he still had incarcerated in Langley.

Right now, he wanted nothing more than to get Lupez and Stein-Muller, and slowly take away their lives.

With a shudder, Greene realized the vengeance that stormed through him was no different to the rage that had overcome Sam Noor.

Staring at their broken, abused bodies, Greene wondered how he would have reacted if it had been his loved one.

Chapter 108

It started out a beautiful spring day in Washington DC. The cherry blossom had taken over Pennsylvania Avenue in a gorgeous mass of pale pink and white, and the sky was dotted with light, fluffy, white-cotton-wool clouds in a sky of brilliant blue. It could have been just darn perfect.

But it wasn't.

It was the worst day in Treeborne's life.

His precious quantum bomb, which he knew had been delivered by god to do his bidding, had been stolen by those who threatened to destroy him.

Treeborne stared out of Marine One as it descended onto the lawns behind the White House. He had to take measures. He had to act fast. He had to show to others his strength to dominate and destroy Al Nadir.

But first, what he needed to do more was to feel the tablet within his trembling hands, to allow the energies within it to penetrate into his pores and marinate his mind.

He needed to feel again his powers. Lately, he'd not touched the tablet so much. The strange sandstone tablet had been a gift from his god, giving him his trinity of abilities. Persuasion. Manipulation. Trust. Of course, these abilities were always front and center, now an integral part his being, and he knew he could flip anyone and get them to believe him totally. And trust him implicitly.

Treeborne walked quickly. Van De Maart, his chief of staff, advised that he should slow down. Stupid idiot. Scared he'd have a heart-attack. Didn't want a president's death on his resume. Treeborne ignored him and strode faster.

Doors flew open as he approached, and people moved out of the way when they clocked his seething disposition.

Inside his private lounge, he turned.

"Give me a few minutes alone. I need to get things clear. Right!"

The president's entourage stepped back and nodded uniformly to his instruction.

He banged the door shut and locked it. He drew the drapes closed. Then he grabbed the memory stick from his pocket (it always remained with him) and stuck it underneath the console table beneath his portrait. A key pad emerged and Treeborne punched in the code. The painting above him sunk back into the wall and a shelf rose up inside. The ancient inscribed sandstone tablet sat there where he'd left it a few days before.

Treeborne reached in and picked it up. He slipped it into the pocket of his jacket and restored the room back to normal. But he kept the door locked.

Sitting on his sofa, Treeborne withdrew the tablet again and held it close to him. The deep vibrations started to flood him in waves, imbuing him with absolute confidence.

He left the tablet in his lap while he opened his laptop and called Number 10.

Ashton came on the line after his PPS, Cumberford, answered the call.

"Hello, Mr. President. How-"

"No time for chit chat, Rich. Got a problem. My quantum bomb's been stolen by that motherfucker Al Douri. I need your boy Noor on it with a few of my own. That okay?"

Treeborne stared hard at Ashton, who instantly looked flabbergasted by the fact that the US president was telling him who to put on an intelligence mission. Treeborne dropped a hand down to rub the sandstone tablet. In his mind, he said the mantra that had worked for him a million times. *Trust me. Trust every word I say is true. Fix the belief. Don't let it leave you.*

"Erm, well, this isn't really the way things are done," muttered Ashton, shocked. His voice was hesitant. "Maybe we could, erm, look at a joint operation? MI6 and CIA together, perhaps?"

Treeborne scowled. He'd wanted Sam Noor to take the heat. He'd been furious about his dumb stunt with Rasheed. But having read his file, Treeborne recognized the guy had talent. Sam Noor was probably the best man available to get his bomb back.

And Treeborne wanted only the best.

"Yeah. Right. Joint-op. That could work, Richie."

Ashton winced at the name and Treeborne smirked.

"But I *really* need Noor on this. He fucked up my chances to get Al Douri when he knifed Rasheed. I could easily bring him back here to be charged for that. Of course, that wouldn't look too good for you now, would it?"

Treeborne watched as the British prime minister listened. His face was getting tighter and his stare darker.

"But I don't want any animosity with my friends," continued Treeborne. "We've got that special relationship to consider, haven't we? So I thought you guys can win me back in your good books with a bit of cooperation. I've seen Noor's file. He's the perfect guy to go in. Otherwise, Richie, I gotta handle this a different way."

"A different way?" repeated Ashton, eyeing the president suspiciously.

"Yes. I'm gonna nuke those fuckers!"

"Oh good Lord, Jonathan, you can't do that! You'll start a war!"

"They started it six years ago. I'm just gonna end it!"

Ashton blanched, shaking his head. "Okay, Jonathan. You can have Sam Noor. Our agencies can work together on a joint-op. Just don't go pressing any buttons. I'm rather enjoying this life."

Laughing, Treeborne said, "Me too, Richie. But I ain't putting up with Al Nadir's shit for much longer. Somebody gotta take a stand. You understand?"

Ashton nodded. "Of course. But that isn't the way."

Treeborne smiled. "See you, buddy."

He switched off the face of the traumatized British PM.

It may not be your way, Richie-boy, but it certainly is mine.

Back in London, Ashton stared at the screen that had displayed the US president.

What had he just agreed to?

Why the hell had he just allowed Treeborne to walk all over him?

For the few minutes he was speaking, it was as if his mind was in a fog. He couldn't get out the words he really wanted to say. They seemed to be caught somewhere inside him, and all he could find to articulate himself were the words Treeborne wanted.

Glaring hard at the screen, Ashton shook his head.

His thoughts were only broken by his PPS.

"Prime Minister, you're required now in the Cabinet Room."

Ashton stood up, his body in Downing Street, but his mind still caught in the moment where Treeborne had blinded his brain.

Chapter 109

Back in the office at Langley, the aftermath of what had happened that morning still hung over Greene like a dark cloud. Greene wasn't a rookie. He'd seen enough things to have a hardened constitution, but Whyte's family touched him. Maybe it wasn't their deaths so much as the potential lives that could be lost now the quantum bomb was in Al Nadir's wicked hands.

Greene wasn't into all that psychic mumbo-jumbo but he couldn't stop himself feeling a deeper sense of dread.

He prayed it wasn't a prescient wave, a flicker from a future disaster he didn't even want to consider.

His phone buzzed, flipping his mind back to practical matters. It was DG Downer.

"Yes, sir," answered Greene roughly.

"POTUS has instructed he wants Dr. Sam Noor on the Project David retrieval mission. Code name Operation Wren."

Greene waited for Downer to finish but struggled to suppress his utter surprise.

"That's not normal protocol, sir!"

"I don't give a goddamn fuck about protocol. It's the US president making the demand. Do you really think I'm going to question him? You know the president saw Project David as his chance to take down Al Nadir. Anyway, he said he's going to launch a nuclear strike if we don't get Noor."

Greene breathed in. Anger coursed inside him.

"Nobody wants that. So get this done. Call Cartwright and get Noor on Operation Wren."

"But sir, psychologically Sam Noor may not be the best option. His wife's just been attacked by Al Nadir."

"Hell, Greene, even more of a reason for him to be on this job. Gives him a chance to stick it to them."

Downer's voice was adamant. Greene wasn't going to win this battle.

"But, sir, Noor could be unstable."

Downer tutted heavily, dismissing Greene's overt concerns.

"He looked stable enough to me when he left Langley. Raging, yeah, but no wonder after his wife's attack. He certainly seemed okay enough to tear some Al Nadir fuckers apart. That's what the president wants, a man who's fearless, and savage enough to get the job done."

Greene didn't like it. The blood-lust he'd seen in Sam had a way of breaking into missions and busting them wide open. From what he could see, Noor was a liability and should be nowhere but by his wife's side.

"Sir, in my opinion he's a liability."

Greene stated the facts, but Downer wanted to hear none of it.

"I don't give a fuck about your opinion. No one asked for it. And no one wants it. But POTUS wants Noor. Get it sorted, Greene, and don't be a dick about it!"

Downer didn't waste any niceties on his deputy. Greene got it hard. He swallowed, viciously annoyed, but knew being subservient to the commander in chief's demands was his one and only option.

"Yes sir," said Greene through tightly gritted teeth.

"Good man. No point rocking the boat. Not when your future is so bright."

Downer rang off and Greene slammed down the phone. He dropped his head into his hands.

That feeling of dread, it had now gotten a whole lot worse.

Chapter 110

Greene flicked open his HoloVid screen and called River House. Nathan Cartwright, MI6's new chief, popped up in front of Greene. He'd caught Cartwright walking around his office. Greene could see a plush, white sofa, a SmartTable still showing intel suspended in the air above it, and, to Cartwright's left, the edge of a glass desk. The windows behind showed a murky Monday afternoon in London by the Thames.

"Hi, Cartwright. You and I have to talk."

In River House, Nathan Cartwright noticed the light on his HoloVid screen flashing. He depressed the button and Morgan Greene appeared in full splendor at his desk in Langley. Behind him were photos of Greene with past presidents, generals and notable individuals. Medals and awards littered the shelves denoting his near on thirty years of distinguished national service. Cartwright swept a glance around his own office and recognized he'd dialed the pomp and circumstance of his life down to one photo, taken outside Buckingham Palace on the day he'd been awarded an OBE for services to the crown from the Queen.

It was enough.

Before Cartwright allowed his mind to start meandering, Greene spoke.

"Project David has been stolen by Al Nadir. Dr. Whyte's family was taken as inducement for Whyte to steal the quantum bomb. After he'd stolen it for Al Nadir, they killed him and his entire family. The president himself has demanded Dr. Sam Noor takes the lead on this. Operation Wren."

Cartwright stared, hardly catching a breath. The news was devastating. He'd read the reports on Project David. Built by DARPA's brilliant quantum geniuses, it was touted to have a blast capability far greater than any other ordnance on the planet. Although small in size, if applied correctly, the quantum compound bomb could take out entire countries.

According to the 'Eyes Only' briefing, the compound was 250 cubic centimeters and needed the pen device to activate it. The compound could be shaved, a process similar to cutting thin slivers of parmesan with a very sharp knife. But, in the compound's case, the pen was used to slice through the block providing the right proportion of quantum explosive for the blast size required. Complex quantum mathematics were needed to be worked on prior to any shaving activity. Cartwright bitterly recalled Sabena's Cambridge doctorate and background as a quantum physicist. Al Nadir didn't just have the bomb; they had the expertise to use it.

"Cartwright, did you hear anything I just said?"

Greene glared, his black, pin prick eyes piercing into Cartwright's with fiery impatience.

"Yes. Yes, I did. Sam Noor. Is that really what the president wants?"

"Cartwright, man. I just said that." Cartwright didn't have time to answer as Greene continued to bluster on. "Treeborne is pissed at Noor for what he did to Rasheed. He wants him to do something to redeem himself. Seems he did a bit of digging and liked what he found about Noor. Thinks he's the right guy for the job. Otherwise, he wants to extradite Noor and charge him, and he's gonna send in nukes to take out Al Douri in Zagros."

"He's what?"

"Jeez, guy. You gotta get yourself a hearing aid. POTUS wants Noor to go in. If not, he wants the cuffs on him, and he's gonna make Al Douri drink a nuke cocktail. That clear enough? Fuck!"

"I got it the first time!" snapped Cartwright, glaring at Greene.

"So what's wrong with you?"

"Greene, this is blackmail."

"It ain't. It's politics. You in with Noor or not?"

Cartwright swallowed. "This isn't the way things are done."

"It is now."

Greene stared back. Cartwright thought that, despite the request, he seemed calm. Greene was just following orders, of course. Just passing it down the line.

Silence drifted between them.

Greene looked on. His face dripped recalcitrance. No other position would he accept other than the one he'd just proposed. Cartwright knew it. There was no way around it.

He nodded to Greene, who responded.

"Okay. Now we're talking."

"It's just…Well, I'm thinking about that bomb in those maniacs' hands. Will Sam Noor be enough? Shouldn't we send in a joint task-force?"

Greene moved forward, taking a dominant stance. The image of his shelves behind him was now obscured completely by his massive bulk.

"POTUS wants it to be a joint op. Your guy and mine. Keep it real low key. A tactical in-out. Richard Lydell's been in the region for the last few months. He mingles with the locals in Baba Heydar. Speaks Farsi. Great on the ground man. He's been monitoring activity. We've got a complete log via his SmartLens. Sending it now."

Cartwright watched as the file almost instantaneously appeared on his screen courtesy of the secure comms uplink to the CIA's satellite.

"Got it," said Cartwright, immediately opening the file. He scanned it for rapid intel. "No image data on Lydell." Cartwright realized as he said it that Lydell must be a black on black guy, or a BoB.

"No. That's right. Lydell's a BoB. Slip text cipher meet. 2:2 config is the only way he'll accept this. Can't allow him to be on any database, however encrypted. The risk to Lydell and his on-going ops are too great. That's why this has to be low key. Noor goes in guns blazing and Al Nadir will get spooked and may detonate that fucking bomb. They need to get their hands on it and cause the least amount of attention possible."

Cartwright nodded with sage authority. But he didn't like the way things were happening. He couldn't quite comprehend that the president himself had dictated the operational spec for the mission. He wasn't sure how Ashton would react. But he knew he wouldn't welcome the news with open arms. Someone else, even if it was the president of the USA, telling Six how to run their missions was the ultimate insult. He couldn't see Ashton taking it any other way.

"So, Cartwright, can I leave it in your capable hands to get Noor on the case? You've now got the mission specs. Anything else, you just call."

"Greene, one more thing," said Cartwright, stopping the CIA deputy from flicking off his HoloVid screen.

"Yeah?" grumbled Greene, his eagle eye taking in Cartwright.

Cartwright knew he was being analyzed. He smiled briefly, remembering something his partner had said, 'No one reads books anymore. They're all too busy reading each other!'

"POTUS isn't going to be interfering with every future mission spec, is he?"

Greene shook his head, and then looked down, a little flustered as he answered.

"No. No, this one's personal with the Rasheed stuff, and the fact it was his bomb. It's a one off. I'm sure."

Cartwright flicked off the screen having said his terse goodbye to Greene.

He dived into the intel file and couldn't believe what he was seeing. A requisition resource request to use another agency outside of the US appeared and Cartwright scrolled down to see the scrawly handwritten signature of the president.

Cartwright had never, in his thirty odd years with the Firm, seen anything like it.

He picked up the phone and dialed out.

The Cabinet secretary, Sir Martyn Redfern, came on the line.

"Redfern, I need an urgent national security council meeting today."

"New developments, sir?" said Redfern, purposely digging in his clipped, cold tone.

Cartwright glared again at the mission specs for Operation Wren.

"Yeah. New developments. You could say that. Get the usual suspects in this meeting, Redfern. And Redfern, it *has* to happen today!"

A tone of affirmation greeted Cartwright following his request to the uptight Cabinet secretary.

Chapter 111

Ashton entered the room and stared with vicious coldness at his national security council team: Nathan Cartwright, Quentin Ludlow, Charles Godley, Dudley Gibbs, Head of MI5, Paul Weaver, Home Secretary, and Amos Ridley, Head of Special Forces.

The look he gave them was one he'd kept isolated from his electorate. It would never have graced the television screens.

"What's the present position?" snapped Ashton as he sat down.

"Prime Minister, our intel shows a plane under the ownership of Molecular Moldings flew out of Montgomery at Virginia Tech direct to Dubai. Call tail signs changed from the one registered for the flight. Another flight out to Tehran suggests they're heading for the Baba Heydar base in the Zagros Mountains. It's known for high-tech developments and state of the art labs. The CIA, Interpol and Mossad agree with us. They think that's where the quantum bomb is," said Nathan Cartwright, giving Ashton the complete run down.

"Right. Well it's obvious we're going to be the fucking target of this quantum bomb. What the hell are we going to do about it?" Ashton's voice, usually slightly effeminate to show his edge of vulnerability to the UK people, was now granite hard. "So what's the worst case? What are we talking about?"

"Latest test results show the compound has incredible blast capability. Imagine Hiroshima times a million. That's what we're talking about. Experts estimate that Britain could be taken out completely with just a five-centimeter cube of the stuff." Cartwright's voice was grave.

"Jesus Christ!" hissed Ashton, turning ghost white. "And those bastards really have that stuff?"

"Intel is at maximum. I've agreed with Greene that our next course of action is to reacquire the compound. We cannot afford to wait. We must act immediately."

The PM nodded in agreement. Al Nadir had not just upped the ante on weapons of mass destruction. They'd rewritten the entire scale.

Cartwright kept his eyes from the PM, and Ashton noticed. "Something else you want to say?"

"Yes, Prime Minister. The president wants Sam Noor to take back the compound."

Ashton feigned surprise. He knew Treeborne would work the channels through from Greene to Cartwright.

"Sam Noor? Why?"

"That fiasco back at Langley with Rasheed, the president's taken it personally. He wants payback for it. He's read Noor's file and thinks he's the right guy for the job."

Ashton pretended to look astounded. Then it hit him. That feeling he'd had during his conversation with Treeborne. A type of helplessness. He couldn't say no to him.

Suddenly, Ashton felt ashamed he'd allowed such a situation to happen. The president of the USA telling him who he wanted on his own intelligence missions, it was unthinkable. Ashton's face flushed up red with anger at the president's activity. He breathed in, and tried to center his fury.

"And you, you're happy to go along with this…suggestion?"

Cartwright shuffled in his seat. Ashton realized he wasn't happy, but there was a political precedence taking place. In Cartwright's face, Ashton could see it. Being at odds with the CIA wasn't a good place for the UK to find themselves. But being at odds with the US president was even worse.

"There's too many missions on-going where we need their support. If they get pissed at us, and POTUS is annoyed as well, all this could turn very personal and nasty. It's not right, but I don't see we have much of an option. Also, sir…"

Ashton listened and glared. "Yes?"

"The president is livid. He wants to strike Al Nadir's bases. He will if Noor isn't put on the mission."

"And Sam Noor's chances of getting the bomb? What are they?" said Ashton, ignoring the blatant inference of blackmail that Treeborne had already used on him.

"He's good, sir. One of our best. If not the best. He'd be my choice without the encouragement from our US cousins," said Cartwright, looking around the table for further corroboration of Sam's abilities.

"I agree. Sam Noor," said Godley, slithering into the conversation and fixing Ashton with a confident eye. "He knows Al Nadir's MO better than any other agent. He's been in and out of their bases faster than a vicar in a brothel. He's your man."

Ashton searched around the table and was greeted with a slow round of nodding heads.

"CIA's already in the Zagros region. I've agreed with Greene to make it a joint op. That way we'll get to the target quicker," stated Cartwright.

"Gentlemen, agreed," said Ashton. "We've got a Peace Summit in London in less than eighteen hours, and I'll be damned if I let those Al Nadir fuckers get anywhere near with that bomb!" Ashton's voice, thrusting, brutal and urgent, no longer reflected the tight, public school tone honed to perfection to deliver his smooth media soundbites.

"So does anyone know where Noor is?" piped up Ridley, looking around the table.

"Taking some time off to be with his wife. Remember, she was the one caught in the Silent Waters attack over the weekend." Quentin's words sounded hollow. He'd buried his conscience deep within his lost soul.

"Ah, yes! I heard something. Blocked from the media, as I remember rightly." Ashton recalled the efficiency of MI6's info-blanket where the media was concerned. "Is she okay now?"

"She is. Rapid recovery, I gather," answered Quentin.

"Prime Minister, we need Sam Noor. At this moment, his wife doesn't." Godley's statement captured the thoughts of everyone around the table.

"Godley, that's a trifle hard. Look what that poor girl went through," muttered Ridley, an uncharacteristic compassionate streak breaking through his words.

Ashton stared at him as if he was soft in the head.

Cartwright picked up on the stare and spoke. "It's vital for our national security. Al Nadir's new weapon must be rendered useless immediately. Sam Noor can achieve that swiftly. His wife is not a priority."

"I'd like to see you say that to his face," said Quentin, subconsciously touching his face.

"He's required. It's his job."

"Do what is necessary." The PM's tone was brisk and abrupt. He didn't want to get involved. He just wanted the job done.

"Yes, sir," said Cartwright. Then he spoke on a secure line to his assistant. "Recall Sam Noor. Active immediately."

Chapter 112

In their apartment, Sam's phone rang. Ellie watched as he swiped it open and flicked a switch on the side to scramble the line.

It's his work, she thought. An icy chill touched the back of her neck.

Instructions lasted less than a minute. Sam listened, gave his brusque response, and snapped it shut. Ellie saw he really didn't want to go but the call was an explicit order. And from his face, it was serious. Deadly serious. Once again, like so many times before when she'd said goodbye so quickly, she realized he had no choice.

Ellie was beyond distraught. She hadn't expected him to be recalled so soon. She wanted more time with him. They'd had barely a day together.

Sam stared at her. In his eyes, his message. He just wanted to comfort her.

They held each other tight. The world was but a whisper away. They were together. Nothing else mattered.

Their love was pre-eminent. Unsurpassed.

He kissed Ellie's lips and smoothed back her short, blonde hair.

"I love you, Ellie Noor."

Sam nuzzled her neck.

She pulled away, staring at him. Everything was happening so fast again. She took in his loving features: his deep, dark-chocolate eyes that constantly devoured her and his tall, muscular body that radiated warmth and transported her to planes of total ecstasy.

The pressure built inside her. No words could be spoken. She smiled bravely. Sam wrapped his arms around her, and the pressure flowed out unrestricted.

Ellie thought the tears would never stop.

"Promise me one thing," said Ellie breathlessly. "Just one thing."

Sam waited for Ellie to continue, but she seemed overwrought with emotion. Bending down to kiss her, Ellie burst free to issue her final command.

"Don't die!"

Sam smiled and continued his kiss, strong and passionate, enshrouding Ellie in his love for a few more snatched moments.

Chapter 113

A car collected Sam soon after Ellie delivered her loving command. Sam was forbidden to tell Ellie anything about his new mission. All Ellie knew was that she was saying goodbye to her husband. She did not know when or if she would ever see him again.

Sam wasn't a soldier in the true sense of the word. But watching him disappear in the car they'd sent; Ellie remembered all the stories her aunt had told her about World War II and the way she'd felt watching her own husband leave. The terrible crushing pain in her heart. The sobbing tears that threatened to choke her. The twisted nausea in her stomach. All these symptoms that her aunt had described, Ellie now suffered as she watched her own soldier go off to win his war.

Before the car vanished completely through the gates, Ellie let out a loud, "I love you!"

The car was too far away for Sam to hear, but as she turned from the window, she thought she heard Sam's husky voice whispering, "I love you, sweetness."

Chapter 114

Sam walked into the room. Ashton greeted him warmly, slapping him on the back and hugging him. Eyeing the PM's overt body language, Sam knew that they needed him, badly.

"So what's happening?" Sam took his place at the table and awaited the briefing.

Bringing up the visuals, Cartwright started to point out the target on the satellite reconnaissance data, and then swiftly, without emotion, he outlined Al Nadir's new weapons capability.

At the end of his report, Cartwright stared at Sam. Shifting in his seat, Sam felt uneasy. He thought he was well clued up on weapons technology. God knows, for the greater part of his life he'd been at the cutting edge of most of the classified projects. But the weapon Cartwright had briefed him on was way beyond anyone's current capability.

The weapon was a compound that required knowledge of engineering at the quantum level. Sam severely doubted that Al Nadir, despite their momentous wealth, had that kind of expertise. At that moment, a perfectly formed dog turd would have been easier to swallow than what he was hearing from Cartwright.

But then Sam remembered the message delivered on the phone had confirmed the 'coursework' was 'grade A material' and 'teacher' was 'satisfied by this assessment'. It was MI6 code-speak for the 'intelligence being from a highly credible and validated source'. However, the origin of the intel had yet to be revealed. Sam decided to quicken the information flow in his direction.

"Where is all this coming from?"

No one answered.

Sam, never good at subtlety when tasked with having to believe incongruent information, spoke out directly and somewhat rashly to the men assembled around the table.

"Well, I need to know. I am the one who's going to be risking my neck."

Ashton looked awkwardly at Cartwright, muttering, "Can we?"

Cartwright shrugged. "He's got clearance."

"Got clearance for what?" Stuck in a sudden crossfire between his superiors Sam searched their faces for the truth.

"Dr. Noor, the quantum compound is owned by the US Department of Defense. It was part of a top-secret military experiment to harness quantum power for defense applications."

"You're telling me this compound belongs to the States?"

"It did, before it was stolen today from a secret military lab near Blacksburg."

"How come this is the first I've ever heard of it?"

"You didn't need to know. Above your pay grade." Quentin's retort was smooth and biting. Sam stared hard at him, not blinking for a full five seconds. Gritting his teeth hard, Sam gave Quentin a look fierce enough to cause the British foreign secretary to shudder inwardly.

"Well, now you know," Ashton clipped. He'd noticed the look. His swift response was designed to dampen Quentin's innate ability to antagonize Sam.

"So, if it belongs to the US, why isn't the CIA crawling all over Al Nadir's back? Why has it landed on our doorstep? Yanks a bit below par on the intelligence front?"

Smirking, Sam got up, walked over to the drinks tray and poured himself a brandy. He knew he was crapping on meeting etiquette, but he didn't care. Ashton had annoyed him by implying he needed clearance, and Quentin…Well, Quentin, the idiot, always pissed him off. As far as he was concerned, they could give him his marching orders right there and then, and that would be just fine by him. He'd had enough of them. They played politics while guys like him cleaned up their mess. Let them go on a mission. Let them face the bullets for a change. They'd all soon change their bloody tunes.

Ashton looked over to where Sam was leaning against the cabinet like he was in a bar.

"The summit's in London. Latest intel has confirmed it's the target for the quantum bomb."

It was all he needed to say. Deep wrinkles creased like craters around his eyes declared the rest.

They were going to hit London.

Suddenly, Sam felt like a fool. The quantum bomb was serious. His job was serious. He had to pull himself together.

"I'd say that was a good enough reason for this to land on our doorstep," snapped Cartwright, disgusted by Sam's cavalier behavior.

"Yes, sir."

Sam slipped back into his seat.

"Live ground intel shows the quantum compound's been moved to their labs in the Zagros Mountains on the Iraq/Iran border here." Cartwright pointed to the live sat surveillance on screen. "You'll be co-oping with the CIA on this one. We got these pictures from their ground man. It's a quick in-out. We don't want Al Nadir to know you've been there. Entry codes change daily. You'll have to pick them up from Rich Lydell, your CIA co-op, when you arrive. The lab's on the far side. That's your target." Cartwright pointed to a dark, rectangular mass on the screen. "Remember, no dramatics. Even if Al Douri himself is there. Your task is to get out with the quantum compound. That's all. You'll be good to go in an hour. Any questions?"

"I want to go in alone. The CIA will go in heavy-handed and screw things up. Or they'll have another agenda and I'll only know when it's too late. The way they do business, I'm better working alone. At least then I know I'll get the compound and won't have to manage fucking politics and field ops at the same time."

"No, Sam. Not this time. After your circus act at Langley over the weekend, you're not laying down any demands. I would have expected you'd want to gain back ground with our American cousins. Now, if you have no more questions-"

"Yes, one more. Any ID on Lydell?" asked Sam tersely.

Cartwright skimmed down the briefing documents. "Sorry, no. He's a BoB. Slip text cipher ID only. You okay with that? Two by two configuration as usual."

"Not happy with the blind date, but I don't have a choice, do I?" snapped Sam. He'd worked 'blind dates' before with the CIA and Mossad, and although they'd always gone to plan, he always had a sense of unease. He was always unsure of where the true loyalties lay.

"No, you don't. Speed of operations requires it to be this way. Question time's over," answered Cartwright roughly, getting up to leave.

Sam stared at Cartwright, his heart pumping hard, his brain assimilating fast. He looked at the terrified faces around the table. And then he remembered Ellie and her terrified face. These people, or rather their establishment, had been complicit in her abduction, mistreatment, and eventual staged attack. They had hurt her without cause or reason. Why the hell should he do anything to help them? Why shouldn't he just take Ellie's approach and tell them all to go fuck themselves? He looked back at their faces, their pleading, pathetic, and desperate faces, and recognized the dependence they placed on him. They needed him so badly. He knew it the second he walked in the room. But he didn't want to acknowledge it. The backslapping and warm greetings from an otherwise cold collection of men only signaled their absolute desperation.

"This is for real."

Somewhere inside him, Sam repeated the line to himself. From the moment he heard the words 'quantum weapon', disbelief had taken over.

The PM nodded sadly, his voice faltering slightly on answering. "This is real, as real as it gets, Sam. You know what could happen if Al Nadir attack with the compound. They'll rewrite history, their way. We can't let that happen. You can't let that happen. We're all depending on you. Not just us in this room, but everyone. The whole of UK. This nation is looking to you to keep safe our sovereignty and protect our future."

The PM's patriotic speech may once have touched Sam. But, after Ellie's incident, he was unaffected by the pomp and glory. He seriously wondered how long he could do a job he had little conviction in.

"So, no pressure then," replied Sam, his irony falling on unhearing ears. No one was in the mood for a joke, however dark.

"Medical's prepped and ready for you. You can pick up your op-tech from strategic support at the same time." Cartwright finished his briefing with his usual curt efficiency.

Standing up, the PM walked over to Sam and put his hand out. Sam shook it. Despite his effeminate posturing for the cameras, Ashton's handshake was very hard and firm. Sam looked deep into Ashton's hazel eyes, searching for any indication of another agenda. He saw only trust and admiration.

With the meeting concluded, Quentin left the room quickly, his usual modus operandi. Godley followed. Ashton lingered, discussing something private with Cartwright.

Sam stood up to leave, and then a thought struck him. It could be the only way.

"Prime Minister, may I suggest something?"

Chapter 115

The door closed too quickly.

Godley tried to listen, but he got swept out with Gibbs who unexpectedly wanted to question him on matters pertaining to anti-terrorist sweep squads, special armed police working with the army and hitting on areas where intelligence had shown growing levels of potentially anti-establishment activities.

The last glance Godley had before the door was shut was of Sam speaking hurriedly to Ashton. Sam's face was earnest, and the PM's was absorbed, listening to what the agent had to say.

Godley struggled to block out Gibbs' incessant chatter in the seconds before the door closed.

"Prime Minister, may I suggest something?"

"Of course, Sam. What is it?"

"The summit, I think you should…"

Sam was discussing the summit. And he was giving the PM instructions. But what? Godley stared at Sam, watching his mouth moving, but he heard no more words.

You should do *what*? What was Sam suggesting?

Frustrated, watching Gibbs, Godley wanted to push him aside and re-enter the Cabinet Room. He could use some pretense; he'd forgotten something, or he had to tell the PM something. Or something…

But he was still walking further away from the room with Gibbs in tow bleating on about home security. As if Godley cared. Al Nadir was going to take the UK tomorrow. They would make a better go of it than the present clowns in charge.

"So what do you think, Minister? Could we find some funds to support this programme?"

"Erm, yes. I'm sure we can do something. Send me in a paper outlining your business case and I'll review it with my team," said Godley, not knowing what the hell Gibbs was talking about. He looked over the man's massive shoulder. The door opened and Sam emerged and walked the other way. A few seconds later, the PM came out and headed in the same direction.

Were they meeting up to talk again?

"I'm pleased we had this opportunity to catch up, Minister," muttered Gibbs, and then strode away.

Godley turned back to try and see where Ashton and Sam had gone but the corridor was empty.

He cursed the bumbling Gibbs and his crap timing at choosing that moment to corner him.

He had to find out what Sam had said, and whether it made any difference to where the summit would eventually be held.

Chapter 116

After a restless night of terrible, mixed-up dreams showing vivid scenes of Sam in danger, Ellie woke to the sound of her mobile.

"Hello?" she answered.

"Hello, sweetness," returned the deep, husky tone, filling Ellie with instant happiness. "The business is expected to be quick. I'll see you on Wednesday." Sam's words were careful and measured, showing little emotion.

"Oh, love. That's wonderful. See you soon."

Ellie waited on the reply, but Sam had gone. In the field, this meagre emotional ration was all Sam could afford.

She threw down her mobile and leaned back on the bed, wishing dearly that she'd never found out what Sam really did. She cursed the day she'd seen him with that gun. Ellie still couldn't remember what had made her scream. So much about the weekend was still unchartered territory. What was real and what was fantasy?

Those worlds converged when Ellie had discovered Sam's true purpose. But God, she would have given everything she owned to be oblivious again. To be deceived. If those seconds could just be wiped off time. If only she could revert back to her blissful ignorance, content to know just the scraps of information that formed Sam's cover. The pain of knowing all yet knowing nothing crucified her.

Tortuous emotions played constantly in her mind. Maybe he'd go on one of his missions and never return? Ellie couldn't bear to think that. If she did, the reason she lived—the power that drove her to rise every morning—would cease to mean anything.

Continuing to live would only contribute to a lie. Without Sam, she was an empty soul, a void of nothingness. Despite her success, her individualism, if Sam died, she couldn't survive alone. Time heals all wounds, people say, but Ellie knew that proverb would never ring true for her. They were too connected to be apart.

Sam had often joked about Ellie being the love of his life throughout all his past lives. Ellie, however, was more reserved in this jovial conclusion. It was the one thing she couldn't joke about. For deep inside her, she knew it to be true.

From the first moment she met him, she knew they had lived and loved before.

Surging passions amplified as her past lives with Sam flashed forward through her mind, and Ellie was more certain of her immediate and unconditional love for Sam, than she was of her own existence.

Ellie had more than enough courage to close her current journey. It wouldn't cause any hurt. She had no family to grieve her passing. Her aunt had died when she was in her late teens, and she never knew her mother or her father. Sam was the sum of her total family.

If she lost him.

It would be the only choice.

Ellie's morbid thoughts sucked her in, and the room around her visibly darkened as her eyes filled with tears. A choking claustrophobia crept upon her, making her oxygen drop and her nose block. She couldn't breathe. Panicking, Ellie inhaled and exhaled faster, but it was as if she were caught in a vacuum; there was no air to breathe. She clasped at her throat and tried to stand. Her strength failed her, and she dropped heavily to the floor. Juddering vibrations shot through her body, suddenly shifting whatever had caused her respiratory impedance. Sitting on the floor, Ellie breathed deeply and heavily. *What the fuck is happening to me?*

She dried her tears and shook her head sullenly. *I've got to get a bloody grip, or else I might as well take the pills now and stop prolonging this pain.*

Ellie stared around her, still breathing in the air that had albeit vanished a few seconds before. She glimpsed her briefcase. *I've got to get my life back on track. Sam wouldn't want to see me like this. I've got to live my life again.*

Disbanding morbid thoughts, Ellie rang her office to get the latest news. Ellie listened to her secretary rambling on. New contracts, new opportunities, who's going out with who, what the latest was on the virtual warehousing systems' industry grapevine, and she got the urge that she wanted to be there. Work gave her stability, an assurance of sanity in her totally insane world.

Without a second to retract, or think logically on what she was really doing, Ellie grabbed her bag with impulsive enthusiasm and vacated the apartment.

With the whole day ahead of her, Ellie headed west to Winchester. Her heart was no longer heavy. Sam had confirmed that whatever he was doing would be over by Wednesday. She would see him then. Ellie beamed in the mirror. That thought raced continuously through her mind, matching the speed of her car as it hurtled down the motorway. *I'm going to see him on Wednesday.*

The road was clear of any hold-ups. Ellie took it as a sign that life was becoming clear again, free from obstacles and hidden trauma.

If only she could convince Sam to resign from his job, everything would be just perfect. She'd sensed from their last discussion, before he left, that time was ticking fast and he didn't intend to continue to take the risks his job commanded. He wanted to be back with her. After her attack, his attitude to the job was one of jaded indifference. Ellie noticed his unquenched desire to remain and protect her. In her heart, she felt that Sam was soon to return, and all would be well again.

Chapter 117

With the special pen, that wasn't a pen, in her hand, Sabena concentrated on the grey sparkly block. She'd reviewed the quantum mathematics. She knew the detailed instructions housed in complex equations and understood what she needed to do. Clothed in a white all-over jumpsuit, mask and cap, Salim entered the stainless steel, glass and glistening white quantum lab. He rolled up behind Sabena who was clothed in the same outfit. He touched her back, and she turned, smiling through her mask.

"How's it going?" asked Salim, indicating to the block that was positioned within what looked like a deep aluminum sink. The sink however, had positioning sensor prongs within it, which held the block and fed back data into the computer.

"Almost finished," said Sabena, wielding the strange pen.

Then she pulled over a steel, shiny rig with a binocular viewer integrated into an optical microscope. Sabena looked through the viewer. The highly magnified image of the quantum compound block flickered up onto the plasma TV screen alongside Sabena's workstation. On the screen, the compound blew up into a lattice frame. But, as Sabena stared, she couldn't place ever having seen anything that resembled what she now saw in front of her. The structure appeared to fluctuate, not quite keeping within the normal geometric boundaries, and light, instead of carbon, was the element that held the form together. Sabena was truly awestruck.

Salim, watching the screen, touched her elbow.

"It's light based. Extraordinary," said Salim with equal amazement.

"A non-carbon structure. Believe me, Salim, Treeborne, DARPA, Area 51, whoever…none of them created this compound. This has to be from-"

"Somewhere else," completed Salim, staring at the screen and then down at the block.

"Wherever it came from, it's ours now," said Sabena, smirking.

Salim nodded, smiling, and watched as Sabena took the pen and started to turn one of the two dials around its circumference. A light emitted from the top of the pen. Sabena twisted the other dial and the light became stronger and brighter. As Sabena brought the pen closer to the compound, a light within the block erupted, making the sparkly surface shine. On screen, the light lattice glowed like a small sun. Around the brilliant illumination, the structure oscillated.

Sabena revolved the first dial gradually to the other side. The light from the pen became darker with more of an orange hue, and the internal light reduced its intensity. Sabena twisted the second dial to a groove point on the pen, and orange light slimmed to a fine needle. Sabena stared into the viewer. She brought up a reading of the block from the data collected by the sensor prongs onto a small monitor and punched in some numbers on a keyboard. She adjusted the calculation and moved the pen over to the block. Following the guideline quantum calculations and the numbers feeding back from the sensors, Sabena positioned the pen's thin needle of light and brought it down across the block, effectively shaving a miniscule amount from the edge of the compound. On screen, the orange, thin energy beam sliced through the light lattice. As the beam passed through, the light lattice sparked and seemed to spit out particles of photons.

Salim watched, transfixed, as Sabena repeated the process known as 'quantum shaving'. She continued until, on the other side of the block, in the sensor embedded sink, the wafers of the quantum compound started to grow. From the instructions she'd taken from Treeborne's computer, estimated blast capacities were provided according to the total geographic area for countries across the world. Sabena didn't have the UK calculation. That hadn't been part of the package, as Treeborne hadn't had annihilation plans on the UK. But she could calculate it using the existing figures.

Sabena plugged in the number of 248,532 square kilometers, representing the total area of UK and calculated the exact amount of quantum shaving and the final size that the new block needed to be. It equated to 4.95 cubic centimeters.

Sabena observed the second compound grow.

The size of it reminded her of something. As she stared, suddenly it hit her.

She grinned.

Sabena knew exactly how she was going to disguise the quantum compound bomb.

Chapter 118

Ellie pulled into the drive and turned off the engine in front of her rambling Victorian house. Ivy climbed the walls like a sneaky red-blooded siren stalking another's husband. A gunmetal slate roof, only fixed a few months before, gave the house an aura solidness. The house was tinged with an almost fairy-tale feeling with two massive white pillars, a giant's seaside rock, and well-pointed red brick that gave the walls a gingerbread quality. Ellie could be forgiven for believing she'd stepped into a Brothers Grimm story. Wide-eyed sash windows enticed sun into every room, and the house had a light and airy feel. It was a bright, happy house. Ellie had sensed it from the moment she'd walked in with the estate agents.

It had been one of the two things Sam had bought her after he'd scored big time on the lottery. The other had been her cappuccino-toned Porsche Carrera. Of course, that was where he told her he'd gotten the money. But now, she wasn't so sure. In his job, he could have snatched it from any unsuspecting individual skirting a dark path that happened to cross with her husband. Thinking back over the past ten years, so much of what Sam said he'd done could be questioned. His life outside of her arms had been nothing but words, a script he'd devised to keep her ignorant of the truth. And he'd played his role well. With certain bitterness, she thought back to the moment of revelation and shook her head. To keep her safe, that's why he'd created a smokescreen across the truth. But he should never have lied to her.

Pulling her handbag roughly from the car, the strap got caught on the gear change lever and ripped. Ellie got annoyed and suddenly irritable. She thought about Sam and how much she loved him. Did he really love her as much? Would she have lied to him if situations had been reversed? And then she realized she had. That stuff about screaming because of the spider, that had been a full-on lie. She had no idea why she screamed, but it certainly wasn't down to some roaming arachnid. A feeling washed over her. Betrayal. But this time it wasn't the result of her lying husband. It was refusal by her brain to give up its secrets of that morning. Somewhere in the shadows of her cerebrum, the truth lay. But how to get to it? Maybe all I need is peace and quiet and then the truth will reveal itself, thought Ellie.

Forcing herself to be calm, Ellie got out of the car and stared at her house. Had it only been Friday when she was last there? It seemed like years, not days, ago.

So much had happened.

Stepping into her lounge, Ellie smiled. Although their apartment on the Thames was stunning and sophisticated, Ellie really loved her house. It was old but full of character. Over the years, she'd spent innumerable hours on her own. Her house had become her companion and had kept her happy when Sam had been away. She adored every little crack and imperfection that her home possessed.

Walking into the conservatory, she looked out onto the velvet lawn. Two beautiful wrens fed from her bird table. The forced calm condition Ellie had put herself in had worked. Standing in the conservatory, sunlight streaming in, Ellie felt inexplicably happy. It was all going to be okay. So what if she couldn't recall one morning? So what if she'd married Chelsea's equivalent to Jason Bourne? They'd work it out. Sam would soon be home and then she was going to put her new plan into action. Leave the job or leave her. Emotional blackmail, yes. Of course it was. But Ellie could see no other way to resolve the situation. She'd only spent a few days knowing the truth, but pain burned inside her. She couldn't shake the feeling that he'd never come back. It gave her physical pain. She could not continue another day let alone another ten years. She'd surely die of heartache. That was why Sam had kept it all from her for so long. It wasn't betrayal at all. He'd been protecting her. He knew that emotionally she just couldn't take it.

And then, of course, there'd been her attack. His work had brought the terrorists directly to her. She knew he couldn't forgive himself for that. It would make her ultimatum easier to deliver. Although, strangely, as Ellie thought about it, the attack was harder to remember. It came in snippets of hazy recall like in a dream. Did it really happen? How could she be sure? Absently, she rubbed her arm and winced, touching the bruises. No, it hadn't been a dream. That pain was all too real.

Ellie's eyes closed as tiredness swept over her. With her eyes shut, her senses heightened, and she was suddenly aware of a beeping in her bag. Her voicemail had a message.

"Hi, Ellie. Verity here. Can you ring me sometime? Maybe we can go out for a drink and catch up on all the gossip."

Verity Harrington, an old friend from Ellie's college days. They had kept in touch over the years. Verity had, like Ellie, devoted herself to her career. She ran a select but successful PR company. But unlike Ellie, love had not traveled down her path. Single and forever searching, Verity used any occasion to go out on the prowl.

Ellie smiled, picking up the phone. "Hi, Reetie. Been let out on good behavior?" Ellie had called her Reetie ever since they meet. Verity somehow seemed too prim a name for her bubbly character.

"Yeah, something like that. Listen, do you want to do something this afternoon?"

"What do you fancy?"

"A bit of retail therapy and then a boozy dinner?"

"Sounds great. Just what I need."

"You okay? You sound a bit, well, knackered!"

"Long story."

"I've got big ears. Tell me the lowdown."

"When I said it was long, I meant it. Over dinner, okay?"

"Okay. It's not Sam, is it? He's not turning into a wife basher or a cross-dresser?"

"God, no!"

"Pity. I could do with a real juicy one!"

"Not at my expense."

"Aww. Come on, Ellie. What's the news? By the time dinner comes, we'll be talking about anything and everything. It's A to Z time when we're together. You know that. Tell me now."

"No. Later. Where shall I see you?"

"I'll come around and pick you up. Three o'clock okay?"

"Okay. See you."

Ellie rang off. Telling Reetie that Sam was a spy was not on the cards, although she would have loved to say something just to see the look on her friend's face.

Chapter 119

Sabena left the Zagros base with Pedro soon after she'd shaved the quantum bomb. In the plane, heading back to the UK, Sabena received an encrypted text from Godley. He'd started the process to deliver Sam Noor. Sabena smiled cruelly, and then she scrolled down, and the smile stuck like a cold mask to her face.

He also wasn't sure now about QEII being the target.

Sabena shut her eyes and tried to quell her fear.

"Fuck!" she found herself saying underneath her breath. She thought quietly but Russo looked up from his tablet.

"Everything okay?"

"Yes. No. Well…I'm not sure."

"What do you mean?" said Russo.

"QEII. The target."

"Yes?"

"It may not be."

Russo's eyes narrowed. "You told Salim it was. You've cut the bomb to that spec."

"I know. But Godley's just said he's not sure about it. Something about Sam fucking Noor saying something to the PM."

"Can't Godley just ask Ashton?" said Russo, surprised by Westminster's cloak and dagger attitude.

"It's not as simple as that. Everyone's wary of everyone else in Westminster village. He'll know Godley was eavesdropping. That guy, Ashton, he's too damn smart. I don't want anything to reveal Godley's position. He's invaluable to us where he is."

"Just capture Noor. That's what Godley's sorting for us, isn't he?"

Sabena nodded. "But it may not be enough time for us to know the venue of the summit. He may not…" Sabena hesitated. "No. He *definitely* won't break. He's trained to take it. If it gets too much, he'll just die. He won't give anything away."

"He will if we have leverage."

Russo handed Sabena the tablet that he'd been tapping on whilst she was speaking.

Sabena took it and smiled, getting Russo's inference immediately.

"Brilliant, babes. Just brilliant."

Chapter 120

Ellie sat in her lounge and flicked through the TV channels while she waited for Reetie to arrive. She landed on Sky News. It showed yet more Al Nadir attacks in North America and the Far East.

Ellie shuddered as she realized Sam could be a part of any mission to bring down Al Nadir across the world. He could be in amongst the bombs, the bullets, and God knows what else. Still, she couldn't get over knowing what he did. She hated it. She hated knowing. Watching the news now only made her feel nauseous, and her stomach flipped constantly with tension.

In the past, she'd actually read up a great deal on Al Nadir. She'd been intrigued about the organization and the people behind it. They played totally against type. They hadn't fitted into the standard terrorist model of religious fundamentalist, bearded nutter. Al Nadir made sure they were caught on camera, and each time they appeared, they'd be suave, sophisticated, and often good-looking, and of course, incredibly brilliant and utterly ruthless. Their unique positioning brought a new era to the fame game. The celebrity terrorist. Magazines sold copies by having Al Nadir on their front covers. Ellie could see it was almost as if the editors were saying to readers, 'If you're fit, it's okay to be a murderer!'

She remembered an article she'd read about how Al Nadir started. Their network sprung up in the Middle East, but soon they spread like cancer throughout the world. The author had described them 'twisting their poisonous tentacles insidiously through countries and cultures, and like a corporate raider, ruthlessly taking over smaller factions and regimes to create a powerful conglomerate'. For some reason, that description always made Ellie think of a python squeezing the life out of its prey.

'On takeover,' so the author described, 'Al Nadir's regional executives rooted out deadwood, streamlined, and improved efficiencies'. A nice term for killing everyone not required, thought Ellie. All the stories showed that whatever regime they took over, their one defining goal remained: to destabilize governments through international terror for their own financial gain.

On the emergence of Al Nadir, Ellie recalled so many strikes, so many summits, and so, so much war. She'd watched live on television as the bombs blackened the skies, depleted uranium floating in the hot, acrid air and filling the lungs of the guilty and innocent. Ellie imagined families, eating and maybe watching TV, in an instant reduced to strewn body parts. Each time, Al Nadir broadcast from a point of strength. Their fluid, coordinated, and pervasive operations remained ahead of the game despite the bloodshed. As the purest souls streamed to heaven, evil grew and hell started to reign on Earth.

Although the celebrity status of Al Nadir was mainstream and regarded by many as 'thumbing a nose' to the ever-powerful, all-watching establishment, Ellie knew that a dark future signaled for a world who could accept terrorists as 'cool'.

No one denied that Al Nadir was evil, but there seemed to be a sort of moral acceptance that they had taught the government a lesson they needed to learn. And of course, Al Nadir had put the US back in their place after they'd played the role of policing the world for so long.

Perhaps what made Al Nadir's success so unusual, and therefore the target of such media attention, was the fact their victorious lead could be traced back to just one man: Salim Al Douri. The son of an oil and shipping magnet, most of his formative years had been spent at Eton, Cambridge, and finally, Harvard. A self-confessed genius, Salim was snapped up by the CIA and trained to be the best.

After a while, remembered Ellie, Salim realized they were losing more battles than they won. And it was obvious Salim didn't like losing. So he turned.

One of their own turning was bad news indeed for the intelligence agency. His background could have made him the ultimate adversary. He could have been hunted and a bounty put on his life. But Salim had been clever. He'd contrived an image of a rich boy sucked into a crazy party world. Ellie read that Al Nadir actually started as 'naked alien prayer parties' where rich boys and party girls could live it up in a drug fueled palace of hedonistic excess.

The CIA and other agencies ignored him.

Then, Salim dropped off the world. Became a hermit and overnight, gave up all the material pleasures and the life of excess he'd taken to the brink.

Volumes had been dedicated to Salim's supposed 'early years' and copious publications detailed how the CIA had got it 'all so very wrong'.

CIA psych analysis attributed his behavior to having a breakdown and labelled him a 'harmless' religious irritant. It was a term that had been repeated and recited with zealous conviction by every hack that had ever reported an Al Nadir story, much to the chagrin of the intelligence agencies.

By reverting to the simple life free of electronic communication, Salim became invisible. Off the grid.

Forgotten.

The Agency's attention turned to other dictators that were deemed a 'very real threat to global peace'. So engrossed were they in their own vendetta wars that they neglected to notice what was really going on. As one journalist stated, 'It's like one giant sleight of hand'. The security services looked one way, tracking activities of known terrorist groups while, on the other hand, Salim quickly and quietly initiated Al Nadir's global machinations and critical maneuvers.

By the time they realized the trick being played, it was already too late. Sudden bombings, so massive and so economically undermining, shook the world violently out of its complacency.

Salim Al Douri, the 'harmless religious irritant', was back.

The state-of-play picture that epitomized his leadership position had been reproduced a million times and was iconic, like Monroe on the air duct or Warhol's self-portrait. Ellie recalled the first time she'd seen it. Despite the glamorous surroundings, it had made her squirm. The picture showed Salim Al Douri, old peasant clothes now discarded, descending from his Gulfstream jet, the midday sun somewhere shining strong as he smiled, waved, and looked fabulous in a sharp designer suit and shades. The conceit was clear. Salim was back in business. And he was sending a broadcast to the world. This was their wake-up call.

Agencies around the globe certainly got the message.

With the financial might of a large Western country behind him, and loyal subjects in their millions willing to die for him, Salim knew he held the global joystick. His organization, Al Nadir, covered the entire world. No country had avoided their stranglehold.

Al Nadir's incredible wealth enabled them to fast-track on leading weapons technologies. With top nuclear scientists either bought or kidnapped, Al Nadir had nuclear capabilities in a matter of years.

Ellie had read about how governments across the world had assigned their best people to bring down Al Nadir. After operations, some reporters got wind of Al Nadir operatives getting captured and interrogated. Snippets of information would filter through. But the impact on Al Nadir's global operation was like someone picking a stalk in a sea of wheat. The overall formation remained the same.

These interruptions were just a trivial inconvenience to Al Nadir, like a fly landing in one's chardonnay, unpleasant but not deeply affecting. Pundits put the intelligence services' ineffectual performance down to Salim's excellence in second-guessing their moves first. Trained in counterterrorism, Salim knew just how to fool the world's best and keep them running in ever-increasing circles of incompetence.

Ellie now knew Sam must have been involved in these operations, and he'd never spoken a word. She remembered reading accounts of British agents who had been captured by Al Nadir, and the things that had been done to them. Ellie shuddered. It was all so horrible, and now, with Sam amongst it all, not to mention her attack, it was so very close to her. Right on her door step, in fact. She could no longer read about Al Nadir from afar, from the comfort of her lounge or in her office. They were part of her life. They had affected her life.

And she hated them for it.

Numbly, Ellie watched the horrors flow on screen. How could one man be responsible for such utter wickedness?

Chapter 121

Reetie picked Ellie up, but to her surprise, it wasn't her friend's car but a large taxi that pulled into the drive.

"Where's your car?" Ellie asked, climbing into the back seat.

"I drivez every bloody where. On my time off, I'll get someone else to do zat for me. Meet Jeffrey. He'z zour driver for the rezt of our fun-filled day!" Reetie flung her arm out in the driver's direction, smiled, and slipped down in the seat.

"Hi," Ellie answered with a coy smile. It was obvious that Reetie had been hitting the shots a little too early. "Are you okay?"

"Courz I am." Reetie struggled to sit back up again.

Ellie stared at her, concerned. "You don't look it. Are you going to be all right to go to town?"

"Courz I am. I'm always all right. Good ole Reetie. Always alright!"

"What happened?" asked Ellie, convinced that Reetie had been dumped.

"Nothing."

"Who was he?"

"A fucking shithead tosser that I had the misfortune to meet!"

"And you loved him?"

"Yes!"

Suddenly, Reetie was crying wet, hot tears into Ellie's shoulder.

"He's not worth crying over, Reetie. The right guy will come along sooner or later."

"You always say that. But when? I've been waiting ten fucking years for Mr. Right. In that time, I've met Mr. 'Maybe but the FA Cup's on at the moment so I've got to dump you before you get too serious', Mr. 'I'd much rather shag your brother', Mr. 'How much did you say you earned?' and, of course, not forgetting Mr. 'Where shall we put the nipple clamps tonight?' In all that lot, do you see a Mr. Right?"

"Maybe you're not looking in the right places."

"Well, we can't all walk into a job and meet the man of our dreams simultaneously, you know. Some of us have to work at finding love."

"Excuse me, ladies. Where did you want to go?" The driver looked a little put out by the intimate discussion and wanted to get on with driving, not listening.

"A bar," slurred Reetie.

"The Hotel du Vin, please," Ellie suggested, hoping to tuck Reetie into a little corner and sober her up.

"I'm fed up, Ellie. Your life is so perfect. Got the man, got the money, got the life."

"Well, you've got the money and the life. I'm sure you'll find the man."

"But you've got to admit you have got it all, your perfect little world."

If only you knew, thought Ellie.

"It may seem like that, but believe me when I say my life is anything but perfect."

"But Sam's so gorgeous. What does it feel to fuck a bloke like that knowing he's still going to be around in the morning?"

Ellie blushed. The driver coughed. Both were embarrassed by Reetie's blatant diatribe.

"Reetie, I think you've said enough."

"Tell me what it feels like."

"Reetie!"

"Tell me, Ellie. Because, you know what? I don't know. I don't what it really feels like to be loved, to be wanted, to be more than just a meal ticket for some pretty boy."

"It's not that bad, is it?"

Reetie didn't respond. She looked down at her shoes and then dried her tears. Ellie grabbed her hand to comfort her friend, who smiled wanly.

The driver pulled up outside Hotel du Vin. He leaned over and gave Ellie a card with a mobile phone number.

"Call this number when you're ready to leave."

"Thank you. I will." Ellie pocketed the card.

"Have we arrived?" asked Reetie.

"Yes. Come on. Let's get you sorted."

The rest of the afternoon and much of the evening, the conversation was one sided. Reetie poured her heart out to Ellie, telling of the acute injustice that was her life and how, after so many letdowns, she deserved a stab at 'real love'.

By the end of the evening, Ellie was exhausted. After her own emotionally draining experiences, the last thing she needed was another bleeding soul to heal. Had she known Reetie's true intentions, she would have declined the invitation for a girl's night out.

Ellie rang the number and Jeffrey answered, saying he would pick them up. Ellie bundled Reetie into the back and slid in with her. Arriving at Reetie's home, she grabbed hold of Ellie's arm.

"Come in for a drink."

"Reet, you've had enough."

"Now you don't even want me."

"That's not true. But you're pissed, sweetie. You need your bed."

"I do." Reetie got out of the car. "But I think here's fine." And she promptly fell down onto the shingle driveway.

"Oh shit!" Ellie struggled out to help her friend. Then she turned to the driver. "Listen, I think this is going to be a long night. Can I call you to collect me later?"

"No problem," said Jeffrey.

After much histrionics, Ellie eventually got Reetie to bed. She picked up the phone and dialed Jeffrey's number, but she got an engaged tone. She waited a few minutes and tried again, but the line was still engaged.

Oh, sod it, thought Ellie. That's typical! I'm tired and need to go home, and I can't get the driver. She tried again, but still the same response. He must be speaking to someone.

Annoyed, Ellie looked up a taxi firm on Google on her phone and clicked on the call button. An operator came instantly on the line. Ellie gave her location and was told the car would be around immediately. Ellie was rather surprised. She expected at least half an hour to wait.

The taxi arrived promptly. Ellie left a note for Reetie and departed.

Sliding in the back, she gave the driver her home address.

He nodded and started the engine. It hadn't been Ellie's intention to imbibe massive quantities. She had never been a heavy drinker. But the companion drinking had taken its toll on her mixed-up mind and she struggled to stay awake. The car maneuvered through various roads and Ellie's lids dropped.

The driver looked in the rear mirror at Ellie and smiled.

Chapter 122

The plane touched down in Tehran. Sam grabbed his equipment and raced down the stepped toward a tall, blond man in a grey business suit. The man put his hand out. Sam didn't respond courteously. He kept his hands by his side and said, po-faced, "These techniques have brought a newly refreshed opportunity to plan and perfect our strategy."

On finishing, Sam stared hard at Lydell.

"However, strategies that join together define our initiative and make a zoned investment easy to factor gains making significant monetary returns."

Lydell answered fluently, without hesitation.

Sam smiled, relieved. The slip text cipher used in a two by two configuration spoke clearly the name of the person who stood in front of him. Although to anyone listening, it just sounded like a couple of bankers talking money.

The pass code both agents had memorized and used worked on a simple but ingenious use and placement of words. Sam's announcement, when broken down, spelled TBNOPPS.

The pass code was constructed to ensure that the first letter of every second word was relevant. To decode the mix of letters, it was necessary to slip back one letter, making the T=S, B=A, N=M, and so forth, eventually spelling out a name: SAM NOOR.

Lydell's announcement used the same configuration:

SJDI MZEFMM.

RICH LYDELL.

Now reassured that the man in front of him was really Richard Lydell, Sam stretched out his hand. Lydell took it warmly, his smile open, his body language free and welcoming.

Sam paused briefly as he strode across the tarmac to the waiting helicopter, flipped open his mobile, and speed dialed Ellie's number.

Sudden shyness sneaked up on him, and he looked away from Lydell as he waited to speak to Ellie, but all he got was her bubbly voicemail. He whispered private words, assuring her once again of his anticipated return by Wednesday evening. Leaving with a fleeting "I love you, sweetness," Sam closed the intimate connection and turned back to address Lydell. "So, what's the picture? Have you recced the area? What's the latest intel? Do we know the exact location of the compound?" Lowering his head and stepping into the helicopter, Sam grilled Lydell at speed.

Lydell followed behind, replying dutifully to Sam's questions. "We've thermal sat recon images. Analysis shows Salim's installed at the Zagros base in Baba Heydar. We've intercepted their comms and we know he's handling the compound personally. The entrance is guarded four by four config on either side of the complex, maybe similar numbers inside. The perimeter fence is electrified, but the ground team have already accessed an area at the side, hopping the current over the breach, to keep the pulse unbroken as usual. The plan is to hit with C4 and knock out the stragglers with CS gas. We think that the safe holding the compound is in Salim's own personal lab. We've procured Salim's private pin, but of course, he could have changed it since yesterday. We'll just have to hope he hasn't."

Sam was deeply disturbed. To the untrained ear, everything sounded plausible. But to Sam, it wasn't good enough. The thermal sat recon images were not as sharp as he'd hoped. And the mission seemed to be a 'play by numbers' approach. He wasn't going to stand for the shambles that his mission was turning into.

"Lydell, this is fucking crap! We'll just have to hope he hasn't?" What's that supposed to mean? Do we have the correct pin or not? And do we know the compound's even in Salim's lab. What have you been doing? I thought you'd recced the area. You don't even know the exact location of the compound. And these photos and data tell me nothing."

Sam threw the papers on the floor in disgust. Shuffling in his seat, Lydell stared uncomfortably at Sam. Sam watched him, thinking he was embarrassed at the reprimand.

Frustrated and angry, Sam turned away and glanced out of the window.

Lydell saw his chance. With speed and precision, he thrust the hypodermic that he'd slipped from the inner lining of his jacket into Sam's neck. Sam's back convulsed and his head fell to one side. In seconds, he'd slumped into his seat. Lydell grabbed the remaining photos out of Sam's limp hand.

"You won't be needing these where you're going."

Chapter 123

Ellie awoke with a start. Her head felt musty from the drink. She looked at her wrist for her watch but then remembered that since the attack she hadn't been able to find it. Out of the window, buildings and trees raced by, but she failed to recognize the area. It was dark and the car was moving very fast. She could see lights of other cars coming towards them. They were on a motorway. Her house was nowhere near a motorway,

Panic shot through her.

Actions consumed thoughts. Ellie reached into her bag and clasped hold of the tiny gun that nestled in the corner, its home for the past four days since she had placed it there. Releasing the safety catch softly, just like Sam had shown her, she drew it slowly out of her bag.

The driver, who'd watched with satisfaction as Ellie drifted off to sleep, suddenly noticed her movement in the back. Without a word, he thumped his palm hard on the hazard button. Bright white light from flashing headlamps of the vehicle behind lit up the taxi.

Shielding her eyes from the blinding light, Ellie turned to look as a van accelerated. Terrified, Ellie knew she had to act fast. Lurching forward, she thrust the gun into the driver's head.

"What's happening?" Ellie screamed; her gun trained on the driver. "Where are we?"

The driver didn't answer. He jammed his foot down hard on the foot brake and pulled up the handbrake. The car skidded across the lanes and spun around furiously.

The centrifugal force threw Ellie onto the driver and then to the side. The gun slipped out of her hand. Hearing the gun fall, the driver whipped around, his eyes glaring wildly, and lunged out towards Ellie's throat. His intention was to silence her, not to kill her. Closing his fingers on her neck, he pressed viciously hard on her windpipe. Ellie clawed at his thick hands, but even her nails digging into him didn't make him lose his grip on her.

Then it all came back to her: the dream, the nightmare that had her wake shaking and disoriented so many times was now happening for real. Ellie could feel her airways instantly crush. She gasped for air, but life was draining out of her. Her fallen gun was in front of her, on the car's floor.

The car slowed, coming out of its spin, and Ellie concentrated, stretching out her fingers. She was so tantalizingly close to the gun, but not close enough.

With energies dissipating rapidly, all signs acknowledged her forthcoming fate. Motor functions failed to respond, and numbness flooded her body. Her vision clouded, and her ears rushed. Pressure and pain built inside her. Ellie knew it could mean one thing.

She was dying.

Just like in the dream. But it wasn't going to end like this. She was determined it wasn't going to end like this.

Drawing together what shred of strength remained in her, Ellie thrust her hand towards the gun, just as he tightened. Burning rushed through her and a volcano erupted in her chest. Ignoring the searing pain, Ellie strained forward, and her fingers closed lovingly around its cold metal.

Holding the gun gave her strength, if only psychologically. With just pure adrenaline and a primal need to stay alive stopping her from taking that flat spin into nothingness, she pulled the gun up to face her assailant, and without a thought, she fired point-blank into him.

His grip relaxed as the bullet hit his brain, spraying blood over her. She touched the blood slipping down her cheek and shuddered, staring at what she'd done.

A surreal mix of fascination and horror gripped her as she observed what humans are made of. Somehow, in the movies, they made gunshot murders seem glossy, almost clinical. If someone was shot in the head, it was a neat, exact wound, with the rest of the face still intact. The reality was gruesomely converse.

It had all happened in a micro-blink. Ellie positioned the gun and fired. The sight was a little towards the driver's left eye. On impact, the bullet had tunneled straight through his eye, into his brain, and beyond.

A gaping hole, oozing a mixed-up mess of glutinous eye gunk, blood, and brain, now splayed out before her. Her heart thundered inside her. Her senses were alert. She had to get out. The car was in the middle of a motorway. Other cars were bound to hit it.

But she couldn't move. She had killed a man. Oh God. She, Ellie Noor, had killed another person.

Overwhelmed by the act she had committed; her frozen body refused all movement. Petrified and fascinated, she just couldn't tear her eyes away from the dead driver.

Ellie felt wind on her face and a sudden heat in her chest.

The instant before her eyes closed, Ellie saw dark figures reach in.

Chapter 124

Frank Weitz wasn't a timid man. Nor was he a yes man. He had his own mind and his own opinions. And he knew that the compound was bad news from the very outset.

Standing and watching its performance, he'd been terrified. It was unlike any weapon he'd ever seen. It was more like the wrath of God. It shattered the air! What kind of power does that? How could it possibly do that? The only redeeming thing about the compound was that, at the time, it had been in the hands of the US and not Al Nadir.

Only now it wasn't.

That power, that awful shrieking, air-shattering power, was now in those maniacs' hands.

Just thinking about it made him want to puke.

A plan had been instigated. The best people had been chosen.

A good plan that had now gone very, very bad.

DG Downer had rung him with the news.

It seemed everything surrounding the compound was tainted with darkness. He'd felt it standing out there, hearing the Earth scream, as if the explosion caused the Earth real physical pain. It was not of this world, that stuff, whatever they'd said about long-term experimentations. A power like that shouldn't ever have existed.

They shouldn't have had it at all.

And now, despite that great plan, they still didn't.

Weitz didn't know how the hell he was going to tell the president that Noor and Lydell hadn't succeeded.

"Something you wanna say, Frank? You've been flicking your pen on and off all through this meeting, but you've hardly said a word. Spit it out, boy. I don't like people procrastinating around me." The president fixed his eye on Frank Weitz and waited.

Weitz had entered into a general security update meeting with the chairman to the joint chiefs and the vice president in the hope that, at some point during the meeting, he'd be able to pluck up enough courage to inform the president. He had to tell him the news that both Sam and Lydell had gone AWOL and the quantum compound still remained in Al Douri's hands.

So far, all he'd plucked up was greater nerves and a rather sore thumb.

Of course, all that was about to change. The president had asked him outright. He couldn't obfuscate delivering the message. He just hoped it wouldn't be a case of shooting the messenger.

"Erm, Mr. President, there's been a new development."

"That boy Noor got my bomb back yet?" Treeborne's eyes squeezed to two little blackened peas.

"No. Erm…"

Weitz lost his courage, his words drifting into the orbs of granite that pierced his soul, the eyes of a man who understood power and used it to intimidate and brutalize.

"So? What's this new fucking development?"

"We no longer know where Noor or Lydell are."

Weitz waited, ill at ease, as the president received his words.

With a roar of unrestrained anger, the president exploded. His face was lined with utter contempt for Weitz and his so-called elite security agencies that had now failed him so incredibly.

"How the fuck's this happened? I thought those boys were good."

The president glowered at Weitz, his blood rising.

"Mr. President, I'm sorry."

Treeborne closed his eyes. His fury had reached its apex. He could feel the blood drumming in his ears. His heart raced as his mind contemplated his truly awesome power was still in his enemy's hands.

The president's fat face turned aubergine as he stared with dark eyes, his mouth taut and ingrained with lines of mounting aggression.

"Has a second recovery team been deployed?"

"Yes, sir. But we are still trying to re-establish contact with Noor and Lydell. They're either dead or being held hostage in the Zagros Mountains near Baba Heydar. As far as we know, the compound's still in Salim's hands. We're working on a tactical strike with our contacts in the region."

The president sat down heavily in his chair. He cradled his forehead in his hands.

He knew one thing with absolute certainty. Under the instruction of his god.

The moment was coming.

Chapter 125

Cold wall rushed towards his face. In the same moment, his head was yanked back as if it were a beer top, and stiff, huge hands gripped his jaw, pulling his mouth open. In the mêlée of big hands, Sam saw something flash silver and felt metal ice in his mouth. Clamps fixed tightly and pulled. The crown came away, with an adjacent tooth.

A sharp, hot knife ripped through Sam's nerves. Heavy hands still held him. Sam could feel blood slip down his throat. The wall visited him again with a vicious velocity and blackness took him.

Sam had awoken to shaking pain. The blood in his mouth told him he'd been betrayed. The leak was at the highest level. The thought blasted around in Sam's head, as hard rubber piping tore into his naked back. Sam knew they would continue like this all night, their methods getting progressively worse.

Sam couldn't recall how many lashes they'd already dealt, but the pain on coming around had been excruciating. But then Sam had focused, taking himself to an inner place deep, deep inside. All operatives were trained in the art of meditation, trained to handle pain by controlling the activity levels of the insula in the brain. Sam knew that to survive, he had to regress into himself. He literally closed down his system—not speaking, not looking, and hardly breathing. And arrived at place where pain failed to register.

"Who are you?" The voice of his aggressor was monotone, monosyllabic, and quite young. Sam, fixed to the wall in a star formation by leather straps around his ankles and wrists, his face flush against the concrete, could not see anyone behind. Another of his own techniques to shake the captive's sanity, to keep in their blind spot, the area where basic instinct suggested there was someone, even though they could not be seen.

Then the lashes stopped. Sam was aware of talking.

"I'll deal with him." Sam recognized the sharp, cold voice: Salim Al Douri, leader of Al Nadir.

"Sam Noor!" Salim slid up against the wall, his face almost touching Sam's.

Salim's voice ejected Sam abruptly from his peaceful place. His senses registering and in parallel, unexpurgated pain hit him full blast. The intensity of his injuries took his breath away, made his eyes water, and then anger overpowered him as he realized Salim had actually called him by name.

"If you knew who I was, why has this fucker been beating the crap out of me?"

"Gave him something to do. Kept him from being under my feet. By the way, that fucker is my son."

Sam stared at Salim. Soulful, black eyes and chiseled, handsome features, one could easily forget the inhuman monster that lurked beneath the model looks.

"Like father, like son, eh?"

"Well, you know how much I love the nuclear family!"

Salim laughed at his own nefarious innuendo. Sam shook his head, eyes glaring with coldness and frustration. He doubted the young man beating him was really Salim's son. Just a line to deliver his pathetic joke.

"But I apologize…" Salim picked up a stun baton from a nearby table. "For such an eminent official such as yourself. You should have been treated correctly and not by an apprentice but by…"

Salim failed to finish the sentence vocally. Instead, he pulled Sam's pants down, thrust the stun baton deep between his tight buttocks, and pushed in hard with vicious determination. Sam breathed in sharply as burning, bruising pain pressed through him. His eyes screwed tightly shut like shriveled peas as Salim forced the baton inward, ripping through natural resistance. Then he shot point-blank.

Volts leapt through Sam, sending every nerve on fire. Blood rose in his mouth, his teeth chattered, and his eyeballs seared, threatening to explode.

Watching the reaction, Salim nodded, smiled, and then increased the voltage as he shoved the baton farther in and fired. Sam screamed, unable to keep it in. Something inside him ruptured and tore. Hot blood flowed down the inside of his leg.

"I hope my delivery is meeting your expectations."

"I'm certainly feeling the point of your argument," slurred Sam.

"You know I can exceed expectation. I suggest you tell me now where the summit is being held. I've been monitoring activity. I can see it's changed from London, but I haven't got much patience to decipher all your Intel. Or much time. That's why I'm going straight to the source. Tell me the location."

"It's New York," slurred Sam as paralysis started to grip his facial muscles.

"Now you can do better than that."

Salim moved in close. Sam steeled himself for another blast, but none came. Sam could feel Salim's breath on his face.

"You will do better than that." Salim's lips flicked seductively against Sam's skin. Sam recoiled, disgusted at Salim's debased behavior.

"I promise you, sweetness." Salim lifted his hand and stroked Sam's face. "You will do better than that." He pressed his lips hard against Sam's cheek. Sighing gently, Salim yanked out the bloody stun baton, turned, and left Sam to contemplate his words.

Their tone, their rhythm, chilled Sam. He prayed to God that his thoughts were wrong.

Chapter 126

Quentin looked out of the window. Nothing but blue skies stretching to the horizon. The blue looked like it had been poured straight from a painting in a kindergarten. Unreal. Snatched from a distant wonderland.

Quentin turned back to the papers in his lap. He hadn't really prepared for the summit. He'd had other things on his mind.

He tried at that moment to concentrate, but his interest barely covered the end of the line he was attempting to read. His mind had wandered back to Sam Noor. Shame, like a veil, drew across his face. And then his leg twinged. An eye for an eye, my dear boy.

Quentin, tried again to focus, but Sam's face kept drifting in. He sipped his whiskey and smiled slyly. To secure his future, he had sacrificed Sam's.

Godley's words to him in the car had demanded no other interpretation. "It is your responsibility to neutralize the threat."

Such a passionless, detached way of saying you wanted someone dead. But that was what he had done. Killed Sam Noor. Maybe not with his own hands. But certainly, by his own hands.

Godley had passed him in a corridor at Whitehall. His hand was suddenly full, and his ears echoed with the words, "Close this chapter."

Quentin paused and looked at his hand. A perfectly folded Post-it note with a small, flat storage chip was tucked inside. Quentin read the information.

A computer file location and a mobile phone number.

Quentin didn't know, and furthermore, he didn't want to know, how Godley had arranged what he had arranged.

Acting swiftly, which as a politician he was unaccustomed to do, he located the file and saved it to the chip. The file had an innocuous text1.txt title.

Intrigue plagued him. He sat down at his desk, slotted the storage device into his laptop, and watched the information flash up on screen.

It looked like a stream of some kind of advanced software code. Just rows of numbers and letters. It didn't mean anything to him. But he knew that it would mean something to someone. Godley wouldn't have provided it otherwise.

He closed the file, pocketed the device in his coat, and then stared again at the Post-it note. The mobile number taunted him. He knew he had to call it.

Sudden indecision, like a man trying to overtake on a motorway, swept through him. What do I say? He stared at the note. The numbers burned through his eyes, and his stomach flipped. He remembered the last time he'd felt such fear: his confrontation with Sam.

"Close this chapter," rang in his head.

Without further thought, he picked up his own mobile and left his office. Outside in the street, he dialed.

"You have it?" asked the voice before Quentin could say hello.

"Yes." Quentin, totally amazed the person knew why he was calling. Quentin was not au fait with ways of the intelligence community. The number he'd dialed, patched directly into a complex network of cloaked satellite communications, which filtered down to mobile number in another country. The mobile number had been assigned for only one task: Quentin calling it.

"Clapham Common. One hour. Sit on the third bench from the entrance. Fix the device inside the center of a Times newspaper. Read for five minutes. Then leave it behind on the bench."

The voice rang off before Quentin had a chance to verify any of the information. Filled with trepidation, Quentin proceeded to follow the instructions he'd been given.

He wasn't spy material. He was a politician, and although Machiavellian tactics he could muster, true espionage had so far been anathema to him.

At Clapham Common, Quentin found the bench, sat down, and read for five minutes. He'd sealed the device with sticky tape and stuck it on the middle page.

As the fifth minute was about to finish, Quentin carefully folded the paper, rose from the bench, and left. A second man approached, sat on the bench, and nonchalantly picked up the paper to read it. Then after a few minutes, he left and dumped the paper in a waste-paper bin next to the seat.

The device was now tucked inside the lining of the man's coat.

Quentin didn't look back. In his mind, he could see Al Nadir operatives analyzing his every move. Walking away, a woman brushed up against him, and he felt a package deposit in his pocket. His heart raced as he prayed it wasn't a bomb.

Safe inside a cab heading back to Westminster, he dug into his pocket and drew out the package. A wad of fifty-pound notes several inches in thickness nestled in his hand. His blood money.

Before he'd departed for the summit, Godley had sneaked his head around the door in his office. "Sam's captured. Lydell's gone to ground!"

Godley's eyes sparkled gleefully as he stared with admiration at Quentin's appalling achievement. But his face remained grave and sullen. A show for the onlookers.

On hearing the news, Quentin raced down the corridor to the bathroom, his body wracked with guilt and self-hatred. He knew what he'd become: a killer. No other word could describe him. He cursed his weakness, his failure to be recalcitrant in the face of Godley's evil dominance.

Closing the door on the cubicle, Quentin vomited freely into the toilet. He prayed the foul release was an evacuation of the wickedness that had possessed him. That he could return afresh. A virtuous human being again.

But as he left the cubicle and washed, he could still smell the putrid stench of death. It was embedded in his clothes, his shoes. It was in him. He could never wipe clean his facinorous actions. He was destined to be assaulted by the vile odor until the day he died.

Abruptly, Quentin returned to his own surrounding, as the plane shuddered to a halt. He looked down at his papers. Little droplets of water had appeared on the documents. Quentin touched his forehead and realized he'd been sweating.

If I am to get through the rest of my life, I have to forget that Sam Noor ever existed.

Quentin collected his papers and made his way out of the aircraft.

His colleagues were babbling busily. Always the aloof one, he kept his distance. The UK's UN ambassador caught up with him. "Dreadful news about Dr. Noor's kidnapping. You just wouldn't think a diplomat would be a target, would you?" muttered the ambassador as Quentin stared ahead. "Hope he comes out of it okay."

"Yes, so do I. But these are difficult times. It just goes to show all of us officials have to be extra vigilant," answered Quentin coldly.

"Yes. Yes, quite. Excuse me, Quentin. I have to catch up with the US ambassador. See you later."

The ambassador shot off, leaving Quentin alone to consider the gravity of his selfish actions.

Chapter 127

The president shook with fear and anger. The compound had been their last chance against Al Nadir, a chance that had been taken away from him.

And now the plan to get it back had crumbled.

He could feel the heat rising in his body. The rage was igniting him. It seared under his skin, behind his eyes, and down his throat. Only the cold, cleansing waters of revenge would douse the flame. But what would he do now? What did his god want him to do now?

"Operation Wren can still be achieved," said Treeborne, but he was a little distanced from his own tongue. His mouth was just an instrument. He felt all at once calm. His demeanor turned thoughtful, calculating.

The president's wrath had abated.

"If we dropped a nuclear device on the Zagros base."

Treeborne's words were direct and emotionless. He did not flinch as he drove home his solution to the crisis that faced them.

Listening, Weitz's abhorrence was naked. Vice President Hutchinson and the generals could not believe what they were hearing. At that moment, all the brass in the room went into a state of shock. Weitz took the stand and spoke for all. "Mr. President, sir, a nuclear hit on the base would chain-react the compound. You know, sir, what the compound is capable of. You'll knock out Africa, India, Russia, the Middle East, maybe even China and Japan. We're talking complete devastation of the entire eastern side of the world. Billions will die. The world would never recover or forgive. Surely you cannot countenance such an attack?"

Ignoring his defense secretary's pleas, the president placed his hands together.

"In God I trust. I will do whatever I have to if it rids the world of this evil.

Call an emergency session of the Senate. There are decisions to be made."

The president ushered his men out quickly. Stunned silence gripped the group as they walked out in single file. Thoughts of the oncoming cataclysm filled their hearts and tore at their souls.

Chapter 128

Ellie came around slowly. She opened her eyes cautiously and took in her surroundings. The confined space, an expanse of grey, riveted metal and the gentle rocking motion all suggested a van. Ellie scanned the inhabitants. Two men, dressed in dark clothes. One of them tapped away on a laptop while the other flicked switches on equipment that looked like a graphic equalizer. The men were at the top of the van; Ellie was at the bottom, close to the door.

Her wrists were tightly bound. So tight that plastic ties had cut into her skin, making her wrists bleed. Ellie winced on seeing it. Looking down, she was thankful her legs were still free. Ellie moved carefully. The men had not noticed that Ellie had woken. Both were too engrossed in their respective activities. Ellie felt a sudden jarring movement, and she moved forward automatically. The van was braking, maybe to turn a corner. But no, the van's movement was halting. It was stopping. Realizing the van was at traffic lights, Ellie decided to make her move.

She stared hard at the door's handle, analyzing its operation. She knew that her time frame was in milliseconds. She had to open the door correctly. She'd only have one chance.

Ellie drew on her inner strength. Although groggy, she concentrated. *It is down. The handle's action is down.* Her confidence grew. Springing up, she pushed the handle down hard. The door swung outwards. Ellie breathed in as she felt the fresh air on her face. But the sensation was only fleeting. Aware of men jumping up behind her, Ellie hurled her body through the door as the van started to move.

She hit the ground, rolled, and pushed her palms against the road to get up. Upright, she ran, her heart thumping, her feet pelting hard on the tarmac. Racing away. Adrenaline fired through her. Ellie heard shouts from behind.

Shots were fired at her. Not daring to look behind, Ellie increased her pace. She knew her captors were following fast. She had to keep going.

Her chest burned. Frantic and scared, she ran even faster. Her heart hammered hard. She wanted to rest, to slow down, but she couldn't. She could only run.

In desperation, Ellie ran down the nondescript road away from the carriageway where the van had been heading. She reached a roundabout and carried on. Roads flashed by, and Ellie tried to discern her location, but it was so dark. Nothing registered. She couldn't recognize anything. She knew she had to find out where she was, but right now, she couldn't stop.

Lights below her indicated she was on high ground. Little sparkles illuminating a certain sanctuary. Ellie sped towards her starlight town.

Blindly, she raced across a junction, but the sound of an engine made her look up. The van accelerated fast, bearing down on her. Struggling against the pain wracking her body, Ellie increased her pace. Stealing a look behind her, she was stunned to see the van had vanished.

Ellie stopped for a second, to catch her breath and check on the direction of the town. Spinning round, getting her bearings, Ellie checked the quickest way to reach the sanctuary of the town below, and she stumbled down the hill.

Ellie threaded through the mass of briar and heather that festooned the hill. She persisted in pushing them away with her hands tied, but the briars still snagged and ripped into her clothes and skin. Bravely, she ignored the cuts. Her focus was the town. It was gradually getting closer. Scrambling down the remainder of the hill, Ellie could see the red roof tiles. *Refuge.* Ellie ran hard.

The houses were in view. Twinkling streetlights were getting brighter. *I'm gonna make it.* Ellie took the corner, running into the urban estate.

Then the van appeared directly in front of her. The van's speed was just too much for Ellie. Her body, exhausted from the drugs and the nonstop marathon, couldn't take any more. Her heart sank as she turned and ran away from the van, for she was also running away from the town, her twinkling sanctuary. Ellie scrambled back down the rest of the hill where there were more estates and more hiding places.

Footsteps were closing behind her. Panic stricken; Ellie jumped over the mound that connected the rest of the hill. She braced herself for more briar and brambles, but instead, she landed on a small, grassy area before the brambles took hold.

Hitting the grass, Ellie felt pain, then sudden heat in her shoulder. Her vision misted, and she vaulted head first onto the grass.

"Got the bitch!" shouted one of her captors as he pulled Ellie up from the grass.

Her resilience to the drug had grown, and unlike before, she didn't slip into unconsciousness. Only her strength and coordination were weakened.

Even in her disoriented state, Ellie lashed out, skillfully kneeing Thug No. 1 hard in the testicles. Pain shot through him, and he instantly crumpled. As he let go of Ellie, Thug No. 2 grabbed her from behind, securing her in a bone-crushing arm lock with savage enthusiasm. He tugged Ellie's head back. She caught her own reflection in his ebony eyes, a glimpse of fear beneath the courage she tried to so valiantly show.

Thug No. 2 tightened his grip. "You okay?" He watched his partner collect his breath after Ellie's strike.

Thug No. 1 puffed out, nodded, and then smirked angrily as he turned to face Ellie. Suddenly, blood rose in her mouth. His fist work was so fast Ellie didn't register it until it had happened.

"You know what I like about my job?" Thug No. 1 smiled, as his eyes ran up and down the length of Ellie's body. "The perks."

Chapter 129

The screen in the Observation Room in Kudamun sparked alive with scenes of Treeborne's decision to nuke Al Nadir.

Aswa-da, the observer of the activity in the Situation Room smirked and nodded to himself. Ever since ten year old Treeborne had found his hidden artefact, every moment following had been leading up to this point. With his finger literally on the nuclear trigger, Treeborne was taking Earth down the path of total destruction.

Aswa-da reached into his robe and pulled out a small crystal device. He pressed a button on the top of the device and a set of numbers appeared, floating in the air. The numbers ascended rapidly in value. Aswa-da hit the button again and a line popped up showing two crystals in a diamond formation, one dark and the other light. Both bobbed up and down against the Equilibrium or Balance Line. But the dark crystal dropped lower beyond the line. Much lower. Towards the Zone of Great Risk.

And now it would begin, thought Aswa-da, proud of what he had engineered.

He flicked his hand and on the Observation Screen real time images of Ellie and Sam Noor came up. Their predicaments overlapped on the screen.

He smiled.

Everything was as it should be.

Now his plan was completely unstoppable.

And his smile, like starburst from a firework, faded.

Chapter 130

Sam was alone.

"I promise you, sweetness, you will do better than that."

Salim's words burned like a rodeo brand in his mind. Sweetness. It was his word, her word. *Their word.* It belonged to them. It was precious. It was secret.

A movement flickered in his peripheral vision. Sam strained to look behind him. But still the position he was in made it impossible. After his "session" with Salim, he'd been taken off the wall and steel cuffs had been fixed on his wrists. They were held together by a rod that had been manually welded. His reputation for escape was well acknowledged in MI6. And it seemed Salim was taking no chances.

He was taken to another room where a meat hook dangled high from the ceiling, close to the wall. Three guards had heaved him up onto the hook and left him there. Now he hung, aching and bleeding, cold and in the dark.

I've got to get out.

Salim's words were no coincidence. Sam knew he'd been betrayed. His life had been sold. And with that kind of information, Salim would be planning something big. Sam turned over theories in his mind, each time coming back to the same horrifying conclusion. His exposure placed Ellie in immediate danger, and he could do nothing to warn her.

Activity at the entrance homed in on his attention. He could hear two voices: Salim's and another person's. Sharp, pronounced footsteps sounded on the stone floor. Sam tried to twist around but still couldn't see.

Struggling, Sam felt a sharp prick of a needle in his thigh. Another drug. Sam fought to keep it together in his mind, but the drug was not one he'd been given a resistance to in the medical prep he'd had before he left. More proof that Al Nadir had access to "eyes-only information." They knew what drugs to use.

Quickly, the drug took hold. The ceiling spun down and landed on the floor, and suddenly Sam was in a Ferris wheel of ceiling and floor, turning and turning and turning.

A guard released Sam from the hook. Hanging like a piece of meat, the blood had drained from arms. He was numb from the hands down, and stinging cramp kicked in as his feet touched the ground.

Closing his eyes for a second, Sam tried to concentrate. Pushing himself up against the wall, Sam steadied himself, and then he charged at the guard, landing an upper cut to his chin. But the effectiveness of the drugs pumped into his system had knocked severely his ability and his aim was way off. The guard lashed out at Sam, throwing him sideways. Dizzy, disoriented, and heavily nauseous, Sam lost his coordination and slammed against the wall.

Sam's failed target winded him with a sharp blow to the stomach, and then he pulled him up against the wall. A second brute approached and grabbed Sam's muscular neck, forcing it upwards, smoothly pinning Sam to the wall. His hand pressed harder with every passing second.

Sam thought of Rasheed. How quickly the tables had turned.

Without the restraints—the steel cuffs and the drugs—Sam could have killed the man before him with one lethal blow.

"Get that déjà vu feeling?"

In that moment, Sam knew nothing was a coincidence. Everything was being staged for Salim's enjoyment.

"What do you mean?"

"Sam, you don't mean to tell me you've forgotten your little 'misdemeanor' at Langley?"

Jesus Christ, how much of his life did this monster know? "Can't say as I remember."

"For a man whose record states 'an incredible recall ability,' you certainly don't remember the things that count."

Sam didn't answer. The hackles on the back of his neck sprung up and his body run cold. In his last psych eval with the chief psychologist, she had made the same comment, and had written the same in his personal file. Who the hell had sold him?

"So Sam, let us find a way to stimulate your memory."

Without indication from Salim, the room was plunged into darkness and Sam was aware a low hum, like a PA system, had been activated and someone had left the mic on.

"Oh yeah, baby. Oh, come on, sweetness!"

It took Sam a couple of seconds to register what he was listening to. The blasting voice coming through the high-definition, surround-sound system was detached, disembodied. Although it was his voice, in that moment, in the darkness, it had no human connection. Unable to block out the deafening sound, Sam endured the intimate broadcast. Every syllable floated in the air like nineteenth-century London smog making him choke. Creeping uneasiness for Ellie's safety surfaced again as the words penetrated like hot needles in his mind.

"I love you, Sam. God, I love you so much."

In the darkness, something grabbed at his throat so tightly he could not breathe. He closed his eyes and listened.

"Come on, Sam. Fuck me, sweetness. Fuck me hard!"

The voice, whorish and perverse, a backstreet slut, made him retch. It wasn't his wife; it was some kind of temptress putting on a show to torment him. But the gripping tightness in his throat and the disgusted bile rising in his stomach revealed otherwise.

With the same immediacy of the lights dropping, the room illuminated with light. Salim stood in front of him, eyebrows raised, eyes laughing, relishing in the fact he knew something that Sam didn't. He was way ahead of the game.

"Feel like talking?"

Sam remained silent. *Damn you, Maide. Look at what your reckless surveillance has caused now.*

Salim circled, tutting and shaking his head. "I thought you would have capitulated by now."

Sam glared boldly at him. His resistance unrelenting, in Sam's eyes he told Salim he would never break, whatever they did to him. He would die before revealing anything. Sam knew the Summit was closer than ever. Time was not a commodity Salim had.

"Oh, well. I guess we'd better get going." Salim delivered the words with an air of eventuality. Like Sam knew what was happening.

The second man moved his hand away from Sam's throat. Salim pushed Sam in front of him. Sam entered a corridor with dark-grey walls lined with flickering fluorescent lights. Snatching a glimpse as he was herded along, Sam could see lab technicians working in a clean room environment. His mission seemed a world away. His thoughts were only on Ellie. After what he'd just heard, she absorbed his thoughts completely.

Chapter 131

Thug No. 1 took a stubby steel rod from his pocket. He flicked it towards the ground, and the rod grew longer. He swiped it through the air, as if he were a musketeer and it was a sword. Thug No. 2 let go of Ellie, throwing her towards Thug No. 1. The steel rod connected with her stomach, and instantly Ellie doubled. Searing pain shot through her. Agony so fierce she thought her abdomen had shot out of her back. She dropped to the floor, winded and wheezing.

Thug No. 1 bent down, grabbed her by the scruff of her neck, and growled in her ear, "This is what happens to naughty girls."

Ellie snarled and spat in his face. The force of the retort smashed her to floor, blood dripping from the gash on her face.

"No, no, no. Didn't your parents tell you to respect your elders?" He indicated to Thug No. 2 to pull Ellie up. Thug No. 2 duly responded, digging his fingers into her shoulder as he yanked her up from the ground.

A mobile phone sounded in the night air. Thug No. 1 slipped his hand into his jacket to retrieve it.

The effect of the drug had worn off. She had to do something to get out of the grasp of the thugs. Once away, she could run, and she could run fast. But she had to get free.

Speaking on the phone, Thug No. 1 had moved a little away from Ellie. Thug No. 2 still held her by the shoulders, but his grip had loosened slightly when the phone rang and his attention momentarily shifted to the identity of the caller. Ellie knew she had to make her move. Her heeled shoe came down hard on Thug No. 2's foot while her elbow shot out, hitting his stomach. Not expecting such a reaction, Thug No. 2 released his grip and Ellie broke away, running swiftly down the hill.

Thug No. 1 realized what was happening and lunged towards Ellie like a premiership goalie. His arms grabbed at her legs, and she fell to the ground.

On the ground, he moved his heavy body on top of her. "Someone's got to teach you some manners. You really are a naughty little girl."

He moved his hand up, touching Ellie's cheek. Ellie recoiled, her face expressing utter distaste. "And you know what we do with naughty little girls?" He slapped Ellie hard, and pressed his coarse, hard lips on her soft neck.

Ellie struggled, but his strength was raw and primal.

Unable to break free, Ellie closed her eyes. She knew what was going to happen. It was something that every woman, whatever creed or color, feared, and prayed would never happen to her. In the press, the word was mentioned in abundance. Association with such horrors had become commonplace. And yet now, she could barely summon the strength to think of the word.

Rough hands pawed her body. Buttons on her blouse snapped open. All the while her eyes remained closed, she felt that she could cope. That the experience was not really happening. That she was somewhere else. That this was happening to someone else.

"Hold her," Thug No. 1 commanded to Thug No. 2 as he ripped at Ellie's trousers. "And get her fucking eyes open. I want her to see this."

Ellie's blue eyes stared courageously at her assailant. A look of cold, hard determination. Although her position was unwieldy and escape was impossible, Ellie was not going to give them the satisfaction of seeing her afraid. She would rather die than let her terror surface in front of their eyes.

"Good-looking bird," muttered Thug No. 2, looking down her body.

"You first then me. Right?" Thug No. 1 nodded, smiling.

Ellie's hands remained tied above her head and fixed cruelly by the boot of Thug No. 2. He sneered. His aerial view showed him everything.

Mauling Ellie's breasts, Thug No. 1 became more excited. With one hand, he unzipped his jeans and pushed them down. "Gonna enjoy this, babe!"

He moved his heavy body up upon her, his foul-smelling breath invading her senses. He pushed his face up against Ellie's and licked her face. Then he pulled back, his knees pressing hard against the side of her neck.

"Open your mouth, bitch, and suck! And I'll take your fucking eye out if you don't do it good."

To emphasize his statement, Thug No. 1 flicked open his knife and brought it close to Ellie's left eye. Ellie could feel the cold steel against her eyebrow.

Fighting back nausea, Ellie obeyed.

"Good girl. Good girl." Then he smiled like a sick child who torments an animal for pleasure. "You're gonna enjoy this, Marcel! She's got talent."

Marcel nodded as he watched Ellie. "Yeah! Well, get a fucking move on and I may get my turn."

Thug No. 1 pulled Ellie's face from him. "Enough." His heavy weight, like a refrigerator, pressed down on her body. Ellie felt the knife against her hip. She closed her eyes and prayed.

Thug No. 1 slipped the knife underneath Ellie's panties and sliced them open with the blade. The cotton fabric gave way. Ellie's instinct was to cover her nakedness, but with Thug No. 2 pinning her arms, she couldn't.

Thug No. 1 moved to Ellie's breast and bit her nipple with savage pleasure.

Ellie's head swung to one side as she mentally tried to convince her mind that this wasn't happening. She tried to zone out, to go somewhere else, but as he licked her face again. She shuddered, and her mind broke down.

His hand grabbed violently between her legs, and he thrust his fingers in, probing quickly upward inside her. Ellie gasped. She tried to believe it wasn't happening. She tried to be brave, to fight back the tears, but the pressure was too great. The mix of pain, humiliation, and terror overwhelmed her. A reluctant, solitary tear welled up at the side of her eye and trickled down her bruised and bleeding face.

On seeing her tears, Thug No. 2 screamed out, "The bitch is breaking!"

"Don't cry, beautiful," remarked Thug No. 1, his devilish expression more manic as he pursued his act of debasement. "I won't hurt you. Much!" He laughed hard as he positioned himself for entry.

"What…the fuck…are you doing?"

A cruel foreign voice rang out in the darkness. Thug No. 1 looked up, begrudging the interruption at the worst possible moment. Ellie turned to look as a tall, dark-haired woman strode forward with an automatic, her face displaying absolute disgust at the men's actions.

"Oh! We were just playing. You know…"

Thug No. 1 never had time to finish. The woman interjected with streaming abuse. "You are fucking crazy. Do you know what Al Douri would do if he saw you? He'd kill you. He was explicit in his instructions. She was not to be harmed in any way. Look at her. She's a mess. Anyone can see she's damaged. Now I have to clean her up, make her look presentable for the broadcast. God, you fucking amateurs. Get out of my way!"

Sabena had received advice about the "kidnapping not quite going to plan" and decided to act on the situation personally. So much was riding on

Ellie's unharmed capture that, at that moment, playing guardian angel was the only response. But that was the one and only reason she'd halted Ellie's rape. At any other time, she would have let her thugs continue and would have enjoyed the entertainment.

Ellie stared at Sabena. Her face seemed familiar. Hadn't she been in those terrorist celebrity photos spread throughout those insipid gossip magazines that Reetie read? Ellie tried to recall what they'd said about her but couldn't. Her mind was still crushed after what had just happened.

Ellie didn't know she was in the company of terrorist royalty. Sabena Sanantoni, second in command in Al Nadir. A woman who, despite her feminine appearance, had meted out torture and death without compunction or concern; hundreds of thousands of innocent people had died by her hand alone. She had proven her worth to Al Nadir countless times. And she never hid the fact she was a mercenary. No cause. No reason. Just money.

Sabena bent down and picked up Ellie's trousers from where Thug No. 1 had thrown them in his moment of debauched ecstasy. She knelt down and pulled the trousers up over Ellie's legs. Pulling the trousers up, she took a minute to admire Ellie's body. Her gaze flicked from breasts to crotch. Sabena held back her insatiable instinct to touch Ellie. She forced self-restraint, but her lips moistened as she imagined getting Ellie alone. Woman to woman. Her tongue darted out to lick the moisture from her lips away. She trembled as she fastened Ellie's trousers around her svelte waist.

Ellie stared with terrified fascination at Sabena's aberrant behavior. Sabena worked up towards Ellie's upper body. With unexpected tenderness, she cupped Ellie's breast in her hand. She could feel Ellie's heart racing. Her skin was so soft, so supple. Sabena's eyes dilated. Her want was unashamedly obvious. She placed Ellie's breasts back inside her bra and buttoned up her blouse.

Thug No. 2 pulled Ellie to her feet.

Sabena caught hold of Ellie's chin. She turned her face back and forth, assessing the damage. Given the time, Sabena was unsure whether make-up would be able to hide the deep cuts and bruises.

"You're both fucking pathetic!" Sabena shouted irritably, dragging Ellie back with her. She seated Ellie on the back of the van and brought some make-up from her bag. Hurriedly, Sabena set about applying heavy foundation cream and blusher to hide the evidence of Ellie's ordeal.

Ellie realized that she had been saved from her captors' advances for a reason. A very important reason. The name Al Douri had been mentioned.

Al Nadir. Her captors must be Al Nadir. If Al Douri, himself wanted her, it had to be because of Sam. This is what he'd been afraid of. This is why he'd kept his life secret. She understood it all now. But much too late. She thought back to what would've happened if the woman hadn't intervened. She doubted she would have survived.

Awash with gratitude, Ellie muttered quietly, "Thank you," her usually loud voice relegated to small and deeply traumatized. Sabena whirled around, smiling, her dark eyes as menacing as they were stunning.

"Don't thank me too soon, babe."

Chapter 132

Jonathan D Treeborne, president of the United States of America, sat alone in his office. He was a diminutive man who, in other circumstances would have amounted to very little. Treeborne entered politics after graduating from Georgetown. He rose rapidly through the political ranks. Without the prefix of *President*, he would have been just another American Joe. But as luck would have it, Treeborne *was* the president.

Luck, however, had nothing to do with his astronomical political ascension. He believed his position was a calling. His success was a sign from the heavens that he'd been chosen to deliver God's will on Earth.

Treeborne's staff had left, shocked, numbed, and mute, after he'd delivered his inhumane intentions. But Treeborne was unperturbed by their reticent, weak attitude. He was driven and totally remorseless in his obsession to destroy Al Nadir. Over the years, he had seen millions die through their actions. Al Nadir had decimated his country and destroyed so many major cities with their constant, unforgiving attacks.

Now he was the peacemaker. He was the *only* one who had the power to stand against the evil that plagued the world.

His plan had been to use the formidable military power available to the US to drive Al Nadir to surrender. But that had been years ago, and no surrender was forthcoming back then. And it wasn't forthcoming now.

In desperation, the strikes Treeborne sanctioned across the world got more reckless and unrestrained. Innocent lives were suddenly not seen as innocent, if they were unfortunate enough to share their town with an Al Nadir base. They were, in Treeborne's words, "accepted casualties in the war against Al Nadir."

But his latest decision would send more than the B52s that had generated such sheer horror during earlier wars at the start of the millennium. It would send a message that countries, whole continents, were now expendable. He knew there'd be retaliation. He was prepared for it. He would do anything to uphold his mission. To be the savior of the world his god told him he was destined to be.

Chapter 133

The man ahead of Salim opened the door to a dark room. Sam was led inside. A chair was placed in front of a screen that took over the entire wall. Sam swallowed hard. The horrible uneasiness manifested again and grew in intensity in his stomach.

Straps were brought across his chest and around his legs, binding him to the chair. He didn't fight. He was oblivious. He could only stare with deep sorrow at the screen.

Salim walked over like a game-show host, a camp smile on his face. He pivoted on the spot and pointed his remote control at the giant screen.

The screen leapt to life, at first, a fuzzy static view and then the image sharpened as a woman appeared. Sam instantly recognized the snarling, rasping voice of Al Nadir's top assassin and Salim's No. 2: Sabena Sanantoni. He remembered his last encounter with her in Dubai, when his old pal Ricky didn't make it, and her vicious massacre of the Kinley clan. Where she went, death always followed.

"Good morning, Salim," Sabena purred convivially as she smiled slyly.

Salim turned to face the screen; his camp game-show persona still intact. "And good morning to you, my dear Sabena. I hope all I well with you, and your very important guest."

Sam whipped his head round. All that uneasiness had a reason. He just knew. Growling underneath his breath, he snarled, "You fucking bastard."

Instantly, Salim's hand smashed across Sam's face. And then he smiled, obscenely pleased to see his actions were so quickly achieving the desired effect. "Let's not keep our guest waiting." Salim clasped his hands together and rubbed them, urgent to get on with proceedings.

The camera panned left from Sabena, settled, and focused in tightly on a woman bound to a chair. The camera zoomed into her face, and Sam's heart broke.

It was Ellie.

Someone had made a poor attempt to cover up her injuries with make-up.

The camera moved out slightly; Sam stared at her clothes. She loved Escada. He remembered when he'd bought them for her at La Guardia Airport. Now his sentiments of love were ripped and torn.

The camera zoomed in again on her petrified face. He stared at her and tried to read her expression. Showing deep shame and hurt, her eyes echoed damage Sam barely wanted to contemplate.

He stared at her ripped clothes, then back into her tragic eyes, and his throat constricted. He choked. He'd seen that face before, on female agents, prisoners of war who'd suffered systematic rape and torture at the hands of the enemy. But never, in his darkest nightmares, did he expect to see the same expression on his own wife. Standing it no more, Sam let forth a roar of absolute rage and made to grab Salim. Had he not been tightly secured, he would, at that moment, have literally torn Salim apart.

Salim laughed, sidestepping Sam's pitiful attempt. He was happier than ever. Sam's reaction was textbook. He knew it wouldn't take long.

From where Ellie was, she witnessed Sam's attempt on her giant screen. Staring at her beloved husband, bruised, bleeding, and exhausted, bound to a chair, his body showing evidence of extreme torture, a shocking conclusion hit Ellie: neither was going to make it out alive.

Facing this truth gave her strength. A resolute bravery. Pushing her chin up, her face challenging and insolent, she glared at Sam, willing him to be strong. Sam stared out at her, and Ellie concentrated. I love you, darling. Please, be strong.

But before Ellie had the chance to see if Sam had received her telepathic whisper, Salim stood in front of the camera, blocking Ellie's view.

"Well, this is all very nice, and we could watch these love birds all day, but the clock is ticking and we really do need to proceed with today's business. Sabena, get on with it." Salim flicked his hands up like a conductor commencing an overture.

Sabena nodded to one of thugs waiting in the corner, out of shot. He walked forward into the camera line, grabbed Ellie's blouse, and pulled down, ripping clean the right sleeve. Ellie was petrified. I know worse is to come.

Sam watched the thug's actions, his bile rising again. Sabena nodded again, and the thug retreated to the corner. Turning around, she signaled another person out of shot. A tall, gaunt, young man walked in wheeling a trolley. The camera zoomed in on the trolley's top level. Observing the contents, a fierce knotting pain hit the pit of his stomach.

Smiling to camera, Sabena lowered her hand and picked up a scalpel from the medical trolley. Transfixed by the little shiny piece of metal, Sam's eyes did not move from the screen.

"Now Sam, I asked you a question before and you ignored me. I hope this time your etiquette has been restored."

Salim looked at Sam. Given the situation before him, he expected instant surrender. But Sam remained silent. Anger fired through him as Sam's constant silence tipped his fragile balance. With murderous aggression, he hissed, "Make no mistake, Sam. We'll fuck her body and then fuck her mind. She'll *pray* to die."

Sam closed his eyes as he heard the words. He knew from experience they weren't just idle threats said in the heat of the moment. Salim was a man good to his word; he would carry out everything he'd said to the very last detail.

What faced him now was what had haunted him all his life. It was why he'd kept his real job secret. Frustration coursed through him. He was impotent. Ellie was there, wherever there was, awaiting untold atrocities. And he was helpless to save her.

Telling Salim where the summit was would not save Ellie. It would only quicken the last escape they could expect: death.

Salim's temper hit. Spinning around to the screen with vitriolic rage, he screamed, "Get on with it!"

Chapter 134

On Salim's command, Sabena approached Ellie with the scalpel. Ellie watched, naked terror rising in her face. *And to think I thanked that bitch,* she thought.

"The summit's location. Tell me," hissed Salim, as Sabena advanced on Ellie.

Sam looked at Ellie. Their eyes locked, their lives brought together by the wonders of a low Earth-orbiting satellite thousands of miles above them.

Ellie shook her head, indicating to Sam to remain mute. Both knew Salim would target the summit. Thousands of lives would be lost. Sam couldn't let that happen. And strangely, although she was not an agent sworn to protect, neither could Ellie. Their lives were over but other lives could be saved. At that moment, both were united in a common destiny to protect.

"Tell me the location of the fucking summit!" screamed Salim, losing it completely.

In answer, Ellie shouted back, "Don't tell the bastard!" Her amazing strength was still very much intact, despite what she had endured that morning.

Ellie's eyes blazed fiercely. Her stunning, selflessness and sublime courage took Sam's breath away. *God, Ellie, I love you.*

Sam's obstinate silence charged Salim. With fury pounding through his blood, he yelled insanely, "Do it!"

Sabena drove the scalpel into Ellie's bare shoulder, brutally digging in at an angle to go deeper and faster. Ellie screamed hysterically. Nausea washed through her as she watched the blade carve in, unfolding her skin to reveal the subcutaneous tissue and bloody muscle beneath.

Sabena, enraptured by the intolerable pain she was inflicting, purred with desire. Erratically, she drew the knife down Ellie's forearm, slicing her like a blowtorch through butter. Blood sprayed out in thick bursts, turning her cream blouse dark crimson. Sabena severed vein after vein on her incisive journey. With rivers of blood flowing and her vision darkening, Ellie's agony-filled, frenzied screams lessened as unconsciousness beckoned.

Sam looked away. His body shook from the extreme trauma of what he saw emblazoned across the super-sized screen. Sickened and devastated, he pitched forward, vomiting on the floor. Her pain, he could feel. Physically feel.

Malta. It was only a word. All he had to say was that one word to end Ellie's pain.

He opened his mouth. Salim watched, waiting expectantly. But it wasn't that easy. It wasn't just a word. Once revealed, Salim would know he'd broken. He would use Ellie as leverage, constantly torturing her to make Sam reveal more MI6 secrets. Agents in the field and their whole intelligence network would be immediately compromised. Salim would gain complete control. Although Sam didn't know everything at MI6, he knew enough to enable Salim to decapitate the command centers and put thousands of agents and assets at risk. Millions around the world could die as a result.

Sam looked back at the screen. Ellie's eyes, bloodshot and frightened, stared bravely back at him. She shook her head, signaling for Sam to remain silent.

"Talk, you fucker, or we'll rip her apart."

Salim's madness overpowered him, and he smashed his fist into Sam's face, venting his sheer frustration at Sam's continual lack of surrender. The force of the impact sent Sam reeling. Landing on the stone floor, he hit his head hard against the surface. And again, he heard his wife's crazed screams. God, what were they doing?

On screen, Sabena had stuck the scalpel firmly in his wife's thigh, and with euphoric joy, she was drawing the knife down. Drenched in her life's liquid and submerged in a waterfall of scarlet-black blood, her death-white, pain-soaked face stared defiantly and bravely. She shook her head again. Her selflessness was unbelievable. Sam never believed his wife could ever be that strong.

Sabena smiled at the camera, enjoying every sadistic minute.

"Wanna talk, Sam?" She laughed, flashing her beautiful eyes at the camera. "Or shall we start slicing up Ellie's really interesting bits?" To ram home her inclination, Sabena brought the scalpel up between Ellie's legs.

Sam snapped. He couldn't bear it any longer. Fuck MI6. Fuck the government. Fuck the summit. Fuck it all.

He looked at Ellie's face. It was mess of agony and abject suffering. She couldn't endure anymore. This wasn't her life. It was his. It wasn't her fault. It was his. He'd failed her. It was all his fault.

Sabena moved the scalpel in towards Ellie's crotch. Suddenly, he could see Ellie's face going berserk. Looking at the blade and its intended destination, she couldn't take it anymore. Fear entered another level and her once brave expression instantly drained.

For God's sake, Sam, tell them. Don't put me through this. Ellie breathed hard, staring scared at the camera, pleading to Sam with her eyes to talk. To tell it all.

But she remained silent. Something inside of her prevented her from talking. Her mouth couldn't connect with her mind. Although terrified, an inner voice reassured her. It calmed her. If her life was to end, she would go to her death knowing that many lives had been saved. That was enough to give her peace and find a place beyond the pain.

"Stop!" shouted Sam, shaking.

Sabena froze, her scalpel poised but a few centimeters from Ellie's crotch.

"Talk," replied Sabena with cold determination, but she kept her hand still deep between Ellie's legs, unmoving, until she heard what Sam was going to say.

"It's Malta!" screamed Sam. "Please, for God's sake, don't do that. I'll tell you anything you want to know."

Sam stared frantically, waiting, willing Sabena to move the blade. Sabena knew his gaze was fixed on her. She loved the attention. She turned, her evil face filling the screen.

"Good boy! Malta corroborates with our present intel. But with all the chatter you put out there, it was impossible to know we were right. Now we do."

Slowly, she pulled the knife away. Sam breathed out. He'd broken, but Ellie was still alive.

"I'm pleased you stopped me when you did. It would have been a hell of a waste. I've got plans for your little Ellie."

To illustrate her intentions, Sabena yanked Ellie's face upwards and kissed her full on the lips, her tongue pushing hard, invading Ellie's mouth.

Sam watched grimly. He knew Sabena's predilections towards the fairer sex. Witnessing her performance and knowing what treatment Ellie could expect, his insufferable anger exploded. But all he could do was yell at the screen, an action that made both Salim and Sabena highly amused.

He could do nothing. He had been his wife's protector and now he was paralyzed. Sam was helpless, powerless, and pathetic.

Salim laughed loudly and slapped the back of Sam's chair. The great Dr. Sam Noor had finally broken. Good old Ellie. Salim knew that one would work.

"Get her cleaned up, Sabena. I'll enjoy relaxing with Sam later and watching one of your sensational floorshows."

Horrified, Sam whipped his head up to Salim. Sabena's *floorshows* were notorious. And they were not the type to command a standing ovation.

Sabena smiled excitedly. Stroking Ellie's hair, she remembered her gorgeous body that she had, so reluctantly, covered earlier that morning. Sabena would have relished the opportunity to explore such a creature, but she was aware they had a mission. Time was against them. Ellie was going nowhere, and the floorshow would be ready for her return. She would make sure Ellie took the starring role.

Sabena turned back to Salim, her face stern and calculating.

"We've got the summit's location. Now we need to show the UN what strategies Al Nadir have for world peace!"

Salim nodded enthusiastically. "It's a summit to surmount!" Salim laughed at his own pathetic joke.

Then Salim flicked off the screen. Sam looked on as Ellie dissolved into static again. In Cambridgeshire, Sabena did the same and Sam vanished from Ellie's life.

"Patch her up. Make her ready for me," instructed Sabena to her medic, leaving the room at speed.

Isolated, desolate, and alone, Sam sat on the cold, stone floor in his cell, his mind replaying the devastating images he'd seen. His wife's petrified, hysterical screams resounded constantly in his ears.

Sam had never been a religious man. In his line of work, people were bought, and life was cheap. It was difficult to believe in a God that allowed such a world of utter evil to proliferate. Sitting down, knowing escape was absolutely impossible and fully aware that their torment was far from over, he found himself praying to God for a miracle, one of such enormous goodness that would save them from the evil and unrelenting onslaught of Salim Al Douri.

TO BE CONTINUED …

END OF BOOK THINGS

The Resonance
Part Three * Book Three

Chapter 1
26 March, 2017

Ellie clutched to life like a stray, starving cat clutches to a chicken bone. Her time to go wasn't yet. She wasn't letting go of the life she held so precious. After her torture, reality swam in and out. One minute she was in the broadcast room. The next, she lay in a shiny, sterile medical lab.

People encircled. Her clothes were removed. Injections were given. Valium to calm her frenzy and morphine to douse her pain. Someone gave her water. Someone else wrapped her naked, shaking and hysterical frame in a medical gown.

Ellie moved her head and watched helplessly as a young man injected her. She was too weak to struggle, too immersed in pain she never believed she would ever feel. She didn't care what any of them did.

"I'm a doctor. It's an anesthetic," said the man, who smiled in half-hearted way.

The others left him to deal with Ellie on his own.

Suddenly, Ellie was aware of his behavior. Despite her pain, she couldn't help being struck by the situation. It was surreal and ironic. Here was a doctor who administered a local anesthetic to treat wounds that his paymasters had so enjoyed inflicting. It was a masquerade of a real hospital, and she was being tended to by a caring and compassionate doctor.

Ellie felt awkward. The young doctor was gentle. He was totally out of place in the hellhole around her. Ellie knew he could sense her awkwardness and chose to remain silent. She stared at him, incredulous at how a professional could provide their life-saving skills to an organization hell bent on making people suffer.

The doctor avoided the woman's stare. He knew what she was thinking. She knew that he didn't belong and that what he did was wrong, like when his brother forced him to superglue back on the wings of butterflies only for them to be ripped off again. Only now, he patched up injuries, not to save himself from being beaten but to feed his heroin craving.

He'd been a good doctor. Had it not been for the one case of malpractice, he'd still have been on the right path. But the girl had died. His colleagues had given evidence, claiming they had seen him 'chase' just before prepping for theatre. It wasn't true. But it was all they needed. Dealers came out of the woodwork. His respectable façade, like an onionskin, peeled away, revealing his shadowy other life. And he was struck off.

Unable to practice, but with an addiction leading him further into debt, he'd been desperate. When Al Nadir approached him, they were like a godsend.

Now, he knew they were the devil incarnate.

He'd seen what atrocities they were capable of. Thinking back, he shuddered. No human should have to endure or witness such barbarism. He was fully aware that his role was to provide just enough medical care to keep his patients alive so Al Nadir could continue their torture and prolong their suffering.

He looked at the woman and knew her story was no different. After he'd finished sewing her leg, he turned to look at her. The woman's hypnotic stare held him. It hooked him, like his soul had been adrift and it reeled him in.

"Let me go," she whispered. The woman gazed into his pale eyes as he leant over. Her eyes burned into him. "Please. Let me go."

The doctor caught her frantic stare. His emotions rose as he realized the captured creature before him had no hope of surviving.

"Please," she implored, her face desperate and terrified. He knew he was her last hope.

The doctor held onto her clamps, staring into her eyes. Her pain was tangible. He paused. He could let her go. He doubted that, with her injuries, she'd get far. That wasn't his concern.

His hand rested on her wrists. He was indecisive and deeply confused.

The doctor heard her. He could sense her reaching into him, trying to connect with his good side. The part that had made him become a doctor. She pleaded persistently for release. Her persistence penetrated. Trance-like, he started to unclamp the woman from the trolley, first her left leg and then her right. Then, he proceeded to unlock her wrists. The woman's whispered, breathless 'thank you' had barely left her lips when the doctor recognized what he was doing. He clocked the back of a guard in the doorway, and started to sweat. Looking down at the empty clamp in his hands he realized the enormous risk he was taking.

He knew Al Nadir were inhuman sadists, and if they'd discovered he'd helped one of their captives escape he could expect the same treatment the woman had received. He locked the clamp back around the woman's ankle.

As the lock sprung back into place, the woman gasped. The doctor wasn't facing the woman, but her sense of sheer horror was palpable for him. Her engulfing desolation seeped into him as he returned the clamp wrists.

"For Christ's sake. No. Don't do this. You know you could let me go."

But the doctor knew he couldn't. After years of narcotics abuse, he was malleable, vulnerable and weak. He'd killed his conscience to survive. He buried it the moment he mainlined his first wage from Al Nadir.

"Please, help me. You know they're going to kill me. You can't want to see that happen. You're a good person. I feel it. You're not like them. You're not evil. You know you want to help me. Please, for God's sake, help me. Please, let me go. I won't say anything. Just let me go."

The doctor listened to the woman's hysterical pleas.

"They're planning a floorshow with me in it. I don't know what it means, but I know it's not good."

The doctor shuddered instinctively on hearing the word floorshow.

"Oh dear God, no." he muttered, and the woman's eyes widened at his exclamation.

"They're going to kill me aren't they?" whispered the woman

The doctor stopped clamping and stared back at the woman waiting on his answer. Kill her. If only that's all they were going to do. Before he could stop them, scenes of the last floorshow that he had been a guest at stumbled into his mind, and bile rose in his throat and he wanted to physically vomit.

The woman eyed his reaction with terror.

"Oh God! You *do* know what it is, don't you?"

The doctor shook his head, too frightened to face the woman for fear his emotions would leak telling her the whole story what she'd be enduring.

Silently, he continued to secure the clamps, fastening them to the sides of the trolley in turn.

The woman continued her incessant pleading, focusing on the 'floorshow' to force him to change his mind. He couldn't. Lest he become the central attraction of a future show.

Her eyes followed him as he secured the last clamp. He felt her silent anger. She accused him, blamed him for the eventual fate he knew she'd soon meet. She said he wasn't evil. That was true. But he was lost…very, very lost.

Ashamed, the doctor couldn't meet her eyes. But he did not have to. He could feel their intensity burning into his heart. Her attempts fruitless, the woman turned to him, her face full of contempt and disgust.

"How do you live with yourself?"

Finally, the doctor revolved to face her, his eyes wretched, his face sallow and lined with the years of misery he had seen.

Slowly, he replied, "I don't."

The silhouette of the doctor's retreating back defined for Ellie a total lack of hope. Falling back into softness of the pillow, a lump like a pomegranate welled up in her throat. Harsh fabrics would have been less painful. But the soft cotton brought back home. Along with the feeling, memories flooded. Waking up with Sam, playing mischievously, leisurely making love on a Saturday morning, walking along the Thames, watching the ducks, going on seaside drives and country treks, sipping wine, eating curries, watching TV, having rows about who had the remote control.

All these normal, natural, simple things were now lost. Her days with her Sam were over.

Lying there, waiting the return of Sabena and her constant, cruel intentions, Ellie knew she had taken so much for granted. Alone, out of the mean, remorseless eyes of her captors, Ellie cried.

Her tears came in powerful throes. Sobbing deeply, she set free the pain in her heart. Closing her eyes, Sam was there, smiling, holding her, caressing her hair, kissing her.

Ellie's tears flowed.

"I love you," she whispered. "See you on the other side, my darling."

READY TO CONTINUE THE RIDE?

Dear reader,

Sam has taken savage revenge against Al Nadir operative Rasheed, but subsequently, he discovers the real, terrifying facts behind Ellie's attack. But getting to the truth has taken Sam over the edge and his actions lead to horrific consequences. Duplicity runs rampant through Whitehall. Sam has been captured on the Iraq/Iran border. Thousands of miles away, in the UK, Ellie has also been snatched.

Both are now at the mercy of Al Nadir.

Are you ready for the next instalment?

The Peace Summit is hours away. Sam has broken revealing its location. Al Nadir are gearing up to use the quantum bomb.

Can Lord Aby-od, Leader of the inter-dimensional realm of Kudamun find the Protector of Earth in time, and restore the Balance?

Or will President Treeborne's god-complex take over with lethal results.

And what really does Lord Aswa-da, the dark opponent of Aby-od have up his sleeve?

The Resonance will take you further than you've gone before. The first two books only scratched the surface. Get ready to be fully submerged in an adrenaline-pumping experience that will blast everything wide open.

Strap yourself in, hold on tight for a ride you'll never forget.

Continue with the adventure
Download The Resonance here!
https://geni.us/HUxW

GET OPERATION SNOWDROP FOR FREE

You may have heard about Operation Snowdrop in this thriller series. Now is your chance to get the inside track on what really happened. Get exclusive access to Operation Snowdrop and get the truth behind the mission that crossed the line.

If you want to get insider intelligence on Sam and Ellie next adventures, early bird discounts on all future releases in *The Trusted Thriller* series, access to competitions or instant access to me, Michelle Medhat, then subscribe by hitting the link below and we can continue this journey together.

Operation Snowdrop Feedback

"OMG! Talk about edge of your seat, grab you by the ba… The author kept the book moving at a good pace with plenty of twists and an ending that will make you question the world around you!"

"Snowdrop is a fiercely paced book. Characters are dynamic, & powerful. A great spy thriller good versus evil gets blurred. Looking forward to next book."

"Kept me guessing and enthralled right up to the end. Looking forward to reading the next book"

"A very well written, suspenseful book. The description of the agents emotions and conflicts was very well done."

"I loved the constant adrenaline rush in this book. Looking forward to the next book."

"So similar to the situation in the world today that it's hard to read. Well developed"

"This book is exactly why I read new authors as often as possible. The intrigue and characters are heart-stopping. 5 stars +"

GET ACCESS TO OPERATION SNOWDROP
https://dl.bookfunnel.com/nz69zq8lp2

ENJOY THIS BOOK?
YOU CAN MAKE A DIFFERENCE

You have probably heard this before, but for an author, reviews really do make a difference. It takes no time at all to type in a few words, a sentence at the most, but it means the world to an author.

Honest reviews help others to find out about books they wouldn't have heard of before.

If you have enjoyed this book, I would be very grateful if you could leave a review on the book's Amazon page.

You can jump straight to the review page by hitting the link below.

LEAVE A REVIEW HERE
https://geni.us/AfPzq52

Learn more about Michelle Medhat

www.forever-connected.com
michelle@forever-connected.com

THE TRUSTED THRILLER SERIES

This Thriller Series is an edge-of-your-seat, ruthless, non-stop ride packed with gripping spy action, provocative sci-fi suspense, sex, political intrigue and such amazing sci-tech it would leave Bond's Q salivating! If you're searching for something that's nail-biting to the very end - you've found it in this extraordinary Thriller Series.

If you've read this book first, and haven't discovered the rest of the series yet, you need to read these books. Don't miss out, get them now and get the full story!

The Trusted (Book One – Part One)

A split-second action can change the future… forever!

MI6 field operative Dr Sam Noor is up against it.

His oldest friend is in danger, his colleagues are untrustworthy, and his wife feels betrayed.

For so long he's balanced idyllic home and lethal career, but that lie has been uncovered, and his carefully separated worlds fiercely collide.

Distraught and conflicted, Noor concentrates on his latest mission and discovers the terrifying truth behind attacks on agents around the globe. With time running out, Noor has to take down the super-terrorists with powerful connections before they unleash their next-gen weapon on an unsuspecting world.

But Noor has no way of knowing forces beyond his understanding are manipulating reality around him and the stakes are higher than he could ever have believed.

Suspicious of everything he trusted, with politics biting at his heels and traitors changing the game, can Noor protect millions from a bloody end?

The Dominant (Book Two – Part Two)

Everything changes when the lies are revealed.

MI6 field operative Dr Sam Noor gets to the truth in any way possible.

Whilst overseas in the CIA, interrogating terrorists, he's unaware that his wife Ellie faces similar treatment from his own employer. MI6 want answers and they think Ellie has them

She hasn't.

Everything falls apart and shocking decisions are taken, putting Ellie in the line of fire. Devastated by events, Noor's revenge ripples from the Oval Office through the CIA and MI6.

Disgraced, Noor returns to the UK only to discover he's been played. With no other option, he goes rogue and abducts the one who holds the truth.

As Noor learns what really happened, his sense of duty is corrupted.

Caught up in the political crossfire, forced to bury the treachery, Noor must stop the super-terrorists from releasing the world's most powerful weapon, but other forces beyond his comprehension are directing the way fate will flow.

With little time on his side, Noor must make a choice – speak or stay silent. And what he decides could change the future of the world.

The Resonance (Book Three – Part Three)

The world is spinning out of control. Who will save humanity?

Ellie Noor's hope hangs by a thread.

Tortured to within an inch of her life by sadistic terrorists, she now awaits a horrific fate.

Thousands of miles away, Sam has broken to save his wife, and brutal super-terrorists, Al Nadir have done the unthinkable. Salim Al Douri and Sabena Sanantoni are now at the top of their game. An unstoppable force, holding the global leaders by their throats.

As the world awakens to the shocking truth, in London, British Prime Minister, Richard Ashton attempts to find his own balance between fear and anger. But his pain pushes him into further into darkness, vowing ruthless retribution for everything Al Nadir has done.

US President Jonathan Treeborne presents the final solution to rid the planet of Al Nadir forever. PM Ashton falls into line, trusting Treeborne, unaware of a growing insanity taking over the President.

On the cusp of World War III, darker forces gather to fuel the conflict across the globe to satisfy their own evil ends.

Mankind is on the brink of extinction. Only one person has the power to reverse all out destruction.

But can they bring light back to a shattered world knowing they'll lose everything in return?

The Refracted (Book Four – Part Four)

A global, unstoppable peace movement. A new energy takes the world by storm. Religious leaders get proof of God's existence.

Leading on all these headlines is charismatic British Prime Minister Richard Ashton. Uniting nations and religions, and, bringing clean, carbon-free energy, Ashton is a man who appears unable to do anything wrong.

But all is not what it seems.

A tidal wave of disruption is building, and mayhem unlike anything witnessed before will be left in its wake.

Ashton's fighting for world peace, but what personal sacrifices will he make to achieve it?

A young boy, Xiao Chang, lays unconscious in a London hospital bed with an unknown illness. His mother Lei believes he's possessed by dark forces. But can she convince her fashion-celebrity husband Chen of this? He has demons of his own from a painful past he's hidden from his family.

In the inter-dimensional world of Kudamun, change is everywhere, and a once ordered and bureaucratic society is in a disarray.

A new era of enlightenment beckons for Earth, but a shadow of uncertainty hangs over all.

Will Ashton's drive for goodness herald a new destiny for mankind? Walking a path that can never be altered?

Or will something darker take over completely?

The Sum (Book Five – Part Five)

The world is in harmony, and humanity's light shines bright. But is there more at play than what can be seen. And what will be the Protector's role now that Earth has shown it has no use for the age-old superbeing.

The sadistic global terrorist collective, Al Nadir is gone. World leaders have joined together in Freedom Earth. Religious heads have put aside their differences. The Balance is in equilibrium. Cheap energy is available for everyone.

This should be a time of peace. But The Protector isn't so sure.

There is a feeling of something dangerous bubbling beneath the smooth surface. Struggling to shake those instincts, The Protector remains suspicious of British Prime Minister Ashton. His sly smirk and wandering eyes undermine his perfect, family-man façade. But how can The Protector denounce the most popular man in the world?

As pressures grow and lies build, one thing is for certain, when, in the end, the truth is revealed, it's going to be cataclysmic!

A WORD FROM THE AUTHOR

It would appear, if you're reading this, you took the leap!

I hope you're loving where you landed.

The Dominant is part two – book two of a thriller series that has become part of me. The characters are reflections of people I've met and known, and the storyline has been borne out of extraordinary experiences I've had around the world, throughout my career in Science, Technology and Innovation.

I am aware that many people reading my books will immediately find them addictive; others may question why I have brought sci-fi elements into a high-octane spy story. Oil and water, the two don't mix. I disagree (well I would, wouldn't I!). To stay innovative in this world, you need to mix things up a little.

Cause disruption.

Challenge the status quo.

Energies and vibrations, the nature of reality, good and evil and omnipotent beings watching over us – just a sample of elements I have in my spy sci-fi fusion books. And of course always against a backdrop of a fast-moving spy story that reveals the political machinations of those in power.

I know my books won't be to everyone's taste.

But then, if we were all the same, it would be a pretty boring place.

And I'm sure you'd prefer to see a world of color and diversity.

Being different is the heart of being human.

So, enjoy being extraordinary!

Michelle Medhat

Find out more
www.forever-connected.com/thedominant
michelle@forever-connected.com

Twitter @theconnected1 Facebook @michellemedhat

<u>The Playlists of *The Trusted Thriller Series*</u>

The Trusted
Everlasting – Take That
Secrets – One Republic
Have I Told You Lately that I Love You – Rod Stewart
Rock You Like a Hurricane – Scorpions
Khalina Lewahdina (Let's stay alone together) – Amr Diab
E.T. – Katy Perry
Solsbury Hill – Peter Gabriel
Angel with a Shotgun – The Cab
Only Love can Hurt Like This – Paloma Faith
Who Wants to Live Forever – Queen
Rule the World – Take That
Fighting Suspicions – Rebecca Ferguson
The Architect – Paloma Faith
Rewrite the Stars – Zac Efron & Zendaya
The Last of the Secret Agents – Nancy Sinatra
New Divide – Linkin Park
Army of Two – Olly Murs
Demons – Imagine Dragons
Shine a Light – Bryan Adams
Don't Stop Believin' – Journey
What Part of my Body Hurts the Most – Rob Fowler & Sharon Sexton
Please Don't Leave Me – P!nk
Set Fire to the Rain – Adele
Guilty – Paloma Faith
Almeno Stavolta (At Least this Time…) – Nek
Candlelight – Jack Savoretti
I Belong to you – Caro Emerald
Try – P!nk
Redemption – The Strange Familiar
Nothing Breaks Like a Heart – Mark Ronson (Feat. Miley Cyrus)
Many Shades of Black – Adele & The Raconteurs
See Who I am – Within Temptation

The Dominant
Secrets – P!nk
La Tortura (The Torture)– Shakira
L'Altra Dimensione (The Other Dimension)   Måneskin
Amor Eterno (Eternal Love) – Fonseca
My Immortal – Evanescence
Revenge – P!nk with Eminem
Killer Queen - Queen
So Am I – Ava Max
Any Way You Want It – Journey
Me – Taylor Swift & Brendon Urie
Lucy in the Sky with Diamonds – The Beatles
Some Guys Have All the Luck – Rod Stewart
Perfetto (Perfect)– Gianna Nannini
Half the World Away – Aurora
Raise Hell – Brandi Carlisle
The Pretender – Foo Fighters
Too Good to Lose - Rebecca Ferguson
Maybe – Lewis Capaldi
Something's Gotta Give – One Republic
Torna a Casa (Come Back Home) – Måneskin
I Want to Break Free – Queen
Amo Soltanto Te (I Only Love You)– Andrea Bocelli & Ed Sheeran
Love at First Sight – Kylie
Whiskey Tango – Jack Savoretti
Wonder – Naughty Boy with Emeli Sandé
Retribution – Jeff Scott Soto
Ayami Beek (My Days With You) - Elissa
Wasted – Jack Savoretti
Light My Fire – The Doors
We Share the Same Sun – Stereophonics
Surrender – Paloma Faith
What Have You Done – Within Temptation
Out of the Frying Pan and Into the Fire – Meatloaf
Rockstar (Salim's Theme) – Nickelback
Radioactive – Imagine Dragons
Back for Good – Take That
Danger Zone – Kenny Loggins

What Doesn't Kill You (Stronger) – Kelly Clarkson
Sweet But Psycho – Ava Max
Welcome to The Jungle – Guns and Roses

The Resonance
Strong - Mark Kingswood
Hiding – Florence + The Machine
The Sound of Sunshine – Michael Franti & Spearhead
All of My Heart - ABC
Toxic – Britney Spears
Burn it to the Ground - Nickelback
On Top of the World – Imagine Dragons
The Scientist - Coldplay
Blood on My Hands – Jack Savoretti
Music's Too Sad Without You – Kylie Minogue & Jack Savoretti
Suspicious Minds – Elvis Presley
Girls Just Wanna Have Fun – Cyndi Lauper
Traitor - Daughtry
Torn – Natalie Imbruglia
Dear Mr. President – P!nk
The Prayer – Celine Dion & Andrea Bocelli
The Winner Takes It All - ABBA
Guilty – Paloma Faith
Strip Me – Natasha Bedingfield
Won't Get Fooled Again – The Who
Changing – Paloma Faith
Drops of Jupiter – Train
Liar – Camila Cabello
Bring Me To Life – Evanescence
Venus – Bananarama
WW3 – Paloma Faith
Find U Again – Mark Ronson (feat. Camila Cabello)
Get Lucky – Daft Punk (feat. Pharrell Williams & Nile Rodgers)
Dancing in the Dark – Bruce Springsteen
Rescue Me – One Republic
Superheroes – The Script
Get Outta My Way – Kylie Minogue
Set Fire to the Rain – Adele

Who's Crying Now – Journey
Pain is So Close to Pleasure – Queen
Dark Night of the Soul – Van Morrison
Maybe Tomorrow – The Stereophonics
One Last Kiss – Kylie Minogue
Any Other Way – Jack Savoretti
Truth Hurts – Bullet for My Valentine
Stuck in the Middle with You – Stealers Wheel
Firework – Katy Perry
Red Light Spells Danger – Billy Ocean
Breaking Your Own Heart – Kelly Clarkson
Everything is Broken – Bob Dylan
Simples Corazones (Simple Hearts) – Fonseca
Greatest Mistake – Jack Savoretti
When Love Takes Over – David Guetta (feat. Kelly Rowland)
Shine – Emeli Sandè
I Saved the World Today – Eurythmics
Cold – James Blunt
Hold Me Close – David Essex
We Are Bound – Jack Savoretti
The Power of Love – Huey Lewis & The News

The Refracted

Do You want the Truth or Something Beautiful – Paloma Faith
Holding Out For a Hero – Bonnie Tyler
From Outta Nowhere – Jeff Lynne's ELO
Love and Understanding – Cher
Love is Fire – Freya
Strange Energy – World Collision
Titanium – David Guetta feat. Sira
You and Me as One – Jack Savoretti
Here to Love – Lenny Kravitz
Just You and I – Tom Walker
Bang Bang Bang – Christina Perri
Feel like Makin Love to You – Bad Company
Love too Much – Keane
Human – The Killers
One World – Billy Ocean

Power Over Me – Dermot
Always on my Mind – Jack Savoretti
Fades Away – Avicii Feat. Noonie Bao
One More Try – Jessie J
Games Without Frontiers – Peter Gabriel
Money Money Money – ABBA
The World We Live In – The Killers
Temptation – Heaven 17
Trapped – Bruce Springsteen
The Fighter – Keith Urban (Carrie Underwood)
Shallow – Lady Gaga & Bradley Cooper
Forever Yours – Avicii
You Are Not Alone – Emeli Sande
The Man who sold the World – Lulu
Amazed – Lonestar
Believer – Imagine Dragons
Shut Up and Dance – Walk the Moon
Fighter – Christina Aguilera
Roar – Katy Perry
Bruises – Lewis Capaldi
Dreams – The Cranberries
Survivor – Destiny's Child
Everybody Loves Me – One Republic
Bad Influence – Pink
Oh I do like to be beside the seaside
Before You Go – Lewis Capaldi
Aprendiz (Apprentice of the Heart) – Antonio José
In Another Life – The Darkness
If There's Any Justice – Lemar
It's a Mystery – Toyah

The Sum
Pour Some Sugar on Me – Def Leppard
Just Give Me a Reason – P!nk
Liquid Lunch – Caro Emerald
I Will Survive – Gloria Gaynor
Never Ever – All Saints
Tell Me When It's Over – Sheryl Crow (Feat. Chris Stapleton)

Stand My Ground – Within Temptation
Supermassive Black Hole – Muse
Strangelove – Depeche Mode
Beam Me Up – P!nk
Glitter & Gold – Rebecca Ferguson
Deep Waters – Jack Savoretti
Nothing Without Love – Nate Ruess
Someone That You're With – Nickelback
Don't Stop Me Now – Queen
I Say a Little Prayer – Aretha Franklin
Nothing Has Been Proved – Dusty Springfield
The Architect – Paloma Faith
One Vision – Queen
Cherry Bomb (Hello World) – The Runaways
Bonfire Heart – James Blunt
…Baby One More Time – Britney Spears
Leave Me Lonely – Ariana Grande (feat. MacY Gray)
We Are The Champions – Queen
Hold Me In Your Hands – Pixie Lott
Glad All Over – The Dave Clark Five
One Day Like This – Elbow
Dangerous – Within Temptation (feat. Howard Jones)
Under Attack – ABBA
Greatest Mistake – Jack Savoretti
Someone New – Hozier
Hot Stuff – Donna Summer
Without You – John Newman & Nina Nesbitt
Use Somebody – Kings of Leon
Family Affair – Mary J Blige
Sex-o-Matic Venus Freak – MacY Gray
Bad Romance – Lady Gaga
You Don't Own Me – Grace
Save Me – Queen
Don't Go Breaking My Heart – Elton John & Kiki Dee
Leave While I'm Not Looking – Paloma Faith
Believe – Cher
It's Getting Better – Mama Cass
React – The Pussycat Dolls

Everybody Wants To Rule the World – Tears For Fears
Need You Tonight – Inxs
Don't Speak – No Doubt
I Try – MacY Gray
Impossible – James Arthur
This is the Place – Tom Grennan
Read All About It Pt. III – Emeli Sandé
Warrior – Paloma Faith
Tainted Love – Soft Cell
Superwoman – Rebecca Ferguson
I Wish I Was James Bond – Scouting For Girls
Let Me Go – Gary Barlow
So What! – P!nk
Greatest Day – Take That
The Truth – James Blunt
The Hammer's Coming Down – Nickelback
I Will – Brandi Carlile
Lose You To Love Me – Selena Gomez
All You Need is Love – The Beatles

ACKNOWLEDGEMENTS

The name that has made this book a reality is Sam Medhat, my husband. He is my inspiration, and without him this book, and the series that follows, would never have been created. He is the one who listens to every word written. He is the one who endures my frustrations when I have writer's block. He is the one who is constantly woken up by my unsuccessful attempts at creeping into bed in the wee small hours, after I've become lost in my writing world.

Without Sam, no writing would have happened.

Whilst writing this series, I lost my brother, father and mother. None of them lived to see this in print, however their love is embodied within the words, and I hope, somewhere, they can see the result of the faith they had in me to achieve.

I would like to thank my fabulous editor, Ceri Savage, who has been with me on this journey, and who has been incredible in her support and advice.

Michelle Medhat

Printed in Great Britain
by Amazon

12315373R00233